To Trap a Soul

Duskwalker Beginnings

Book One

Opal Reyne

Cover art: Sam Griffin
Editor/proofreader: Messenger's Memos

Author's note on language

I'm from AUSTRALIA.

My English is not the same as American English.
I love my American English spoken readers to bits. You're cute, you all make me giggle, and I just wanna give you a big ol' hug. However, there are many of you who don't seem to realise that your English was born from British English, which is what I use (although a bastardised version since Australians like to take all language and strangle it until it's a ruined carcass of slang, missing letters, and randomly added o's).

We don't seem to like the letter z.

We write colour instead of color. Recognise instead of recognize. Travelling instead of traveling. Skilful instead of skillfull. Mum instead of mom. Smelt is a past participle of smell. We omit the full-stop in Mr. Name, so it's Mr Name. Aussies cradle the word cunt like it's a sweet little puppy, rather than an insult to be launched at your face.

Anyway, happy reading.

Trigger Warning
Major spoiler below

Please only read further if you have triggers, otherwise you will seriously spoil the book for yourself.

Firstly, I will list what triggers **AREN'T** in the book so you can stop reading in order not to spoil it: No rape, non-con, purposeful harm done to the FMC by the MMC, torture, suicide/self-harm, ow/om drama, abortion, mental/emotional abuse, incest, or drug/alcohol abuse.

Please consider stopping here if your trigger has been detailed above as the rest are spoilers.

This duet (2 books) contains a wide range of triggers. Most of these have been detailed in the Duskwalker Brides series, but we see them from Lindiwe and Weldir's perspectives.

Trigger warnings relating to book one:

There is A LOT of pregnancy. There are also scenes of childbirth, some post-natal depression, and child rearing. These are all of our lovable Duskwalkers.

There is death, grieving over death, and child loss. Nathair dies. We know this from the main series, but the scenes revolving around this may be upsetting for many. He IS alive, just within Weldir's realm, but that doesn't make it any less heartbreaking at the time for Lindiwe. There is also the fight and issues revolving around this between Lindiwe and Merikh, as detailed in the main series.

There are depictions of depression and mental health. Loneliness. Loss of identity.

There is loss of religion, due to Lindiwe giving up her human life to another god. She is also betrayed by people of her original faith.

Weldir is a god that eats souls, and Nathair is a serpent. There are vorarephobia triggers due to this.

Ophidiophobia trigger due to being bitten by a venomous snake.

Animal death, due to our Duskwalkers eating them and Lindiwe hunting them. Mention of domestic animal death in passing.

I'm going to put this here even though I don't really want to, but... the dreaded miscommunication trope. This series will be riddled with it, but understand that almost all of their problems can't be fixed with a simple conversation. There are deeply rooted issues, and much learning has to happen before any healing can be done. This is a **slow burn.** Sex happens, but it's going to be a while, and it fixes nothing.

As always, my books have gore.

To all the MonsterFuckers out there who love a shadowy
daddy,

this book is for you.

We've come so far together – now let's go back to the
beginning. Where you didn't pretend that you've never wanted
to be railed by a skull-headed monster, and opened those book
pages. I gift you a new dark entity.
Don't stare into the void for too long...
He will stare back.

I would like to give a big shoutout to the wonderful **sensitivity readers** who helped to make this book a safe place for those I am trying to positively represent. As you all know, representation is a big part of what I want to do, but I want to do so in a way that isn't harmful.

Thank you to Diamond, Erin, Nicole, and Anica for your contribution towards BIPOC sensitivity.

I would also like to give a special thank you to Crystal for your contribution towards BIPOC and overall sensitivity.

I appreciate all the time and effort you put into helping me with this book. You will forever have a place in my heart.

PROLOGUE

A time unknown, but one of suffering

Along the edges of a magically made canyon clung a black mist that was so thin and stretched out it was inconceivable to the human eye. It shimmered, as if black glittering dust had been thrown into the air and had frozen in time as it fell.

It had no smell, no taste, and it didn't even cause one's skin to ripple with goosebumps. To most, perhaps all, it was nothing.

Yet deep within it, an inconceivable being lingered throughout all the mist that spanned thousands of kilometres. Limitedly powerful, and so utterly powerless all the same. A watchful demi-god who prowled constantly like a mindless beast at the end of a rigid tether.

A tether he constantly pulled at, to then not only be yanked back into that mist, but through it and back to his own realm. Like an unintelligent creature, he tried and tried again, seeking a different result that would never come to fruition.

A truly pointless endeavour. One which he'd long given up on and willingly receded to the shadows where he belonged.

With that hope gone, the fingers of his tattered and tethered soul clawed at itself.

Make it stop, his expansive mind screamed into his metaphysical self.

It came out as nothing but a whimpering echo which reverberated all throughout his large and complicatedly vast being. A sound of his mental anguish, which called back to him cruelly. He was alone, and it was so quiet that only he should have been able to hear it.

A tidal wave of wailing cries warbled louder back through the endless, sightless darkness in response. Hundreds of beings listening, and they were never ceasing. They screamed, clawing at him to the point of insanity.

His consciousness, his phantom nothingness... his impalpable, incomprehensible, discarnate essence coalesced tighter to its centre – like one might when they lay on their side in the foetal position. It drew in so tight there was the impression of tension, of pressure, of the sinew of his soul balling up, but nothing more.

No pain. No pleasure. Absolutely no relief.

As he floated in complete and utter darkness, which was made up entirely of himself, his realm shuddered along with him. The rumble of it shook his empty home, as if there were foundations he'd never been able to touch – to reach. More wailing cries reached the lonely place he tried to hide, this time higher pitched due to surprise or fear from his metaphysical self shifting.

Those fingers clawed deeper while he stared into himself, and yet into nothing at all. There was nothing there, as there never had been. Just shadows and darkness that went on seemingly forever. Like a horizon that never stopped moving further out of reach.

He released a false breath, and it gave him nothing, not even mental relief. *Please... make it stop.*

He'd been pleading for this for however long, despite knowing there was no one to hear him. There was no one listening to him. No one to save him. He'd been abandoned in this place.

Cast out, alone.

Well, not entirely alone, not anymore.

He missed the long stretch of the foreverness where he'd been in his solitude. Odd, considering the yawning loneliness that had been slowly eating at him throughout all of it.

Now those that were with him tortured him until he knew his mind was twisting into a pitiful, wounded creature. If he could lick at the back of his wrist like it was an injured paw, he may have started doing that long ago to pacify himself.

He tried to push them back – those mind-bending cruel twists. Tried to shelter himself, with no materials to safeguard him from screams like the wind slicing through trees. With all his might, he used every bit of willpower to keep himself *sane.*

A sharp cry pierced his thoughts. Somehow, in the endless choir, it was louder than the rest.

More heartbreaking. More distressing.

More panic inducing.

I can't take it...

Parts of his essence and self were left behind as he materialised from the layer of his mind he'd been hiding in and teleported to the area of his stomach.

He wished he could do this on Earth – transport himself where the whim to explore took him.

But going there was pointless, and the fact that the world was out of reach was more depressing than he could take. He'd rather not dangle it in front of his eyes, especially as his intangible hands couldn't touch it.

So, he remained there. Especially as the noises of horror and terror would pervade his mind and ears no matter how far he tried to run from himself, from his own realm.

His consciousness and soul could only freely move within himself, stretching back and forth within his realm and the pockets that connected to it, like his mind chamber he'd been hiding in futilely. In his gut, his main realm, he found the loudest voice, that of a confused woman, and slammed a tendril of essence across her lips. She felt it, but he perceived nothing, and her eyes widened in awareness and fright as tears welled in them.

She couldn't see him; his mana was so weak and depleted that he had no visible body to offer.

She fought him, reaching out to the nothingness and through his very body, only for her eyes to roll back and her head to fall to the side. Once asleep, the physical reflection of her, which was nothing more than a spectral body, dimmed until it was almost as white as the flaming soul floating within her chest.

His bodiless ethereal form drifted backwards from her, but in her silence, there was no relief. The agony of his thoughts continued. There were so many voices, so many screams, so many who were afraid.

All of them created a sea of warbling groans and wails.

Too many to quieten. As a horde, they were too much for him.

Weldir wished he could make them all stop without withering away what little power he had obtained by consuming them. He wished he could help them feel at ease within his lonely, dark realm, but he could offer them nothing more than shadows. Shadows he sometimes didn't have the strength to see through either.

They didn't feel foreboding to him. To Weldir, they were comforting, but to a human...

Darkness only incited confused fear as they sightlessly fumbled through it, bumping into each other, only to weep in each other's arms.

Tenebris, the realm that lay within his stomach, which he'd had since the moment he was born, was darkness. It was nothingness, just like him. There was no joy here, no beauty, and not a speck of light unless he provided it. He had no spark to give. He was the Warden of Darkness through and through, and what would it be used for anyway? To see further into the shroud?

Any light he made was solely for himself, for wanting to see something other than... *this*.

But there was nothing to see.

Even his own body had a spectral shroud to it, black as the very night sky; glossy and almost reflective. He knew he *could* have a physical form that looked solid, but there was just not enough of him.

Not with the mist he laid on Earth, consuming all of him to the brink of near death.

He placed his hands over his face, feeling for resistance where his horns may be, and gripped them with mental anguish.

Behind him, a man yelled out. Weldir silently roared in answer as he slapped a black sandy tendril of magic across the deceased spirit's mouth. All the colour from his body, from his light skin to his blue shirt, faded.

Like the woman from before, he, too, turned into a white essence as he fell asleep. The flaming soul inside his spectral chest glowed brightly.

Make it stop... please. His bodiless form drew tighter once more, like a ball, as his tired mind and exhausting power weighed heavier on him. *Why, Mother? Why give me this task?*

How could she forsake him for so many years, locked away inside a box, only to give him freedom with a task that tormented him? He missed his box. His prism.

His fucking prison!

He longed to have the only sounds be her shallow, weak breaths and slow heartbeat lulling him. He no longer wanted to witness the fear and sorrow from those he consumed as they realised over and over again that they were dead. Nor did he want to understand and relive their final moments and their lasting regrets alongside them. And he had no need to be privy to their confusion as to why their gods had forsaken them, or their discovery that their assumptions about there being no afterlife were wrong.

He was a terrible being of death. He was incapable of providing them guidance or comfort or a second life. Just limbo.

There were too many souls here now for him to silence without it enervating him beyond his capabilities, not unless he wanted his limited mist to fade on Earth.

I should let it fade... What use was it for him to collect souls when he'd stopped... *consuming* them? He brought them here, but he was too afraid to add their echoing wails to the others already here. Just beyond his stomach, in another chamber of his consciousness, hundreds of souls remained collected but uneaten, waiting for him.

For Weldir.

For him to cleanse them, fix them, and add them to his slow-growing collection of human souls.

Once more, he shuddered, and the world around them all rippled in response, like a minor earthquake. Patient violence once more restrained, Weldir held back the desire to destroy each soul with sharp teeth and claws.

Just as he considered it, his bodiless spirit felt a tingle.

Weldir drew back and let himself fall through the crystal waters of his layered self to go back to the chamber of his mind. Although he was further from his stomach, the wails of scared souls could still be heard as if they did so right in his non-existent ear.

He ignored them as best as he could as he opened up his viewing eye – a disc that let him see onto Earth. The magic was murky, proving just how little power he currently had. It was enough for him to see along the border of his mist – a black cloud that floated on the edge of a narrow Demon-made crevasse. His mana was too overtaxed to shroud the land below, so the most he could do was circle the cliff edge of the gap in the earth that would continue to grow wider little by little each day, forcing his reach wide as well.

So far, the lengthy canyon only struck through the middle of this large land mass – the name of it he didn't know. Soon enough, it would grow to be a formidable size. He worried it would consume all the world if it wasn't stopped.

But that wasn't why he was here. The disturbance he felt wasn't due to the rare Demons that continued to come through a portal situated in the middle of the canyon's base. His interest was on... *humans.* And he knew only two types of humans came to the edge of the Veil.

Those dumb enough to stare into the abyss in curiosity, and those cruel enough to think of other stupider means.

It's another sacrifice, Weldir thought, as he watched five men drag a woman to the edge of a deathly cliff-fall.

The men wore leather armour, and Weldir didn't understand enough about humans to know if they were truly soldiers of some great land, or just people who had bought their garments for self-protection. They appeared dirty, each in different stages of beard growth, and the quality of their clothing differed.

The woman they dragged through his mist was tall, and her lithe legs stumbled over themselves in tiredness. The skirts of her pale-yellow dress were caked in dirt, while leaves and twigs were tangled in her long locks of wavy blonde hair framing bright-blue eyes. The bruises, scrapes, and gauntness of dehydration were noticeable on her fair skin and cracked lips.

She looked so worn from her adventure that she didn't even put up a fight. Bleak, tired eyes suggested perhaps she'd already accepted her fate.

I could save her.

Unfortunately, the men appeared spooked from a twig

snapping nearby and shuffled towards the edge of the cliff. Then they carelessly tossed her poor body forward. Her skirts caught and flapped in the wind as she fell a kilometre to her death. She was too winded and afraid to scream, and the sounds of the men's frantic chanting overshadowed any other noise from her.

They usually prayed to whatever cruel deity would even ask of this *before* they launched their offering off the edge. But they were quick to run, as if they knew lingering meant certain death.

Weldir tsked. *Not enough time.*

But the impact did mean her soul was untainted by the decay of Demons who would come to eventually eat her corpse.

When he moved his mist to collect it, he brought it straight to his side, and it gave him a little more strength than usual when he opened his mouth and chose to consume it. All the others waiting for him... they were too rotten for him to want to try.

What a waste of cherished life.

He found this behaviour, this insanity of sacrificing innocent women to the canyon, vulgar and brutish. It also only strengthened the very monsters they were trying to rid themselves of, making their situation worse.

Perhaps next time, then.

Maybe the conversation would also go better than the last time he tried to speak to a sacrifice. One who had been stabbed and left at the edge to die of her wound.

Before long, he groaned when a new scream was added to the crescendo already singing for him. Her voice was even more ear-piercing than the others.

Fresher. More pained.

More startled.

Once more, the claws of his essence ripped into himself...

ONE

April 24th, 1683

Between her feet, potato and carrot skins fell into a shallow wooden bucket. Two sets of hands belonging to two different people skilfully worked their blades, both ensuring they didn't cut into the meat of their paler palms.

Comfortable silence had long fallen between them as they watched the afternoon sun descend towards the horizon. Minimal dust glittered through the beams of golden sunlight shining into their neat and tidy home, letting the afternoon feel tranquil. It would be many hours before night truly began to fall, and the mesmerising hues of dusk still had yet to paint the sky.

There was little reason to fear, especially as the house she sat in was well secure and warm. It was simple in nature, although rather generous in size for a farmhouse. Its wooden walls and tall ceilings had been built by her grandfather, and so far, it had stood the test of time with very few leaks and flooding.

Then again, he'd been an intuitive, hardworking man.

She sat in the kitchen, staring out the window, with the dining table next to her and a counter right before her. The kitchen hearth was deeper into the nook, ensuring it was safely away from anything flammable. She was unable to see beyond a hallway that had a sharp right angle to it that lead further into the house, especially with someone in the way.

Her companion, who was much older than her, groaned as she stretched her neck to the side. She halted her peeling of carrots to alleviate a crick or an ache before tugging on the rigid muscles of her nape. *I knew she pulled something earlier when she was outside.*

Her lips thinned in annoyance as a concerned, albeit annoyed, glare slitted her eyes. She eyed the woman's deep-navy woollen peasant gown and how the skirt of it was caked in dirt from where she'd leaned on her knees. Even her white apron, which should be pristine, had specks of dirt and grime on it.

Sweat had collected on the other's forehead and beaded against her brown skin right along her dark-brunette hairline. Although the day was luckily warm, it wasn't hot enough to incite such a reaction in the woman – especially as they'd been sitting next to the window together for quite some time. A cool breeze fluttered in past the open wooden blinds, but a droplet trickled down her temple, revealing the light fever that continued to ail her.

She never listens to me. Why does she continue to go outside when she knows she mustn't?

Instead of staying inside and resting like she was supposed to, she insisted on helping.

"Don't give me that look, Lindi," her mother bit playfully, albeit sternly.

A set of vibrant brown eyes slipped to Lindi's, and they squinted back, returning her glare and catching her off-guard. Lindi's back immediately went ramrod straight. She darted her gaze away with a coy expression, fixing it upon the wooden slatted ceiling above her.

"I have no idea what you're talking about," Lindi muttered sheepishly, yet she couldn't contain the curl of humour that pestered her lips.

The woman's thick brows descended, and her full, mauve lips pulled inwards disapprovingly. Although it was an expression that indicated she was quickly getting on her mother's nerves, her rounded facial features were too gentle to make her appear truly angry.

"You listen here, Lindiwe Bernadi. If I wish to pick my own carrots for supper, then so be it."

Her mother then proceeded to pick up discarded carrot and potato peels from the bucket with the threat that they might be thrown or dumped onto her hair. In retaliation, Lindi pointed the tip of her knife at her – although a safe distance away.

"Try it. I dare you."

I just cleaned my hair! She better not dirty it.

"Oh!" Her mother gasped as she dropped the peels so her hand could flitter to her chest in false and overdramatic shock. "You would threaten your own dear mother?!"

Already, it was obvious they were both trying their hardest to hold back giggles.

Before Lindi could respond, a pair of large, warm hands smacked between hers and her mother's shoulder blades. A deep voice filled with mirth interjected, "What are you two bickering about now?"

A quiet shriek left both of them, Lindi's heart nearly in her throat. The man carelessly laughed at their distress, and even when he had to duck, his laughter and touch persisted as his shoulder was accosted in retaliation.

"You rotten scoundrel!" Her mother screamed, one of her feet slipping to the side as she reached forward in her seat to keep smacking him. "You almost stopped my heart."

His amber eyes fell to Lindi with a plea, just as the bangs of his loose, spiralling brown curls fell across his strong brow. "Why does your mother always hit me?"

His bronze skin was slicked with sweat from being outside in the sun all day working. His white tunic and brown slacks were caked in grime as they always were, but at least he'd changed his boots before coming inside.

With chiselled features, a roguish smile, and a cleanly shaven face, his age only made him more handsome. The peppering of grey in his hair merely enhanced his good looks. His clothing also hid a very strong and muscular body – the result of someone who had worked the land all his life. It was leaner than it should be, as most commoners who worked the land were, but his strength was enough to lift one of them onto his shoulder and mischievously run off with them.

Lindi's features dropped into a cold, emotionless mask. "You're lucky I didn't accidentally stab you with my peeling knife. Sneaking up on a woman with a blade in her hand is just asking for a bad scar."

His lips drew downwards as his eyes dipped to it in her hand, then to the knife her mother had accidentally dropped from being startled, and finally to the bucket of discarded peels between them. A large smile pulled at his full lips before the corners of his eyelids crinkled in humour once more.

"Now that would have been bad. I should pick my moments better, no?" Then he shoved forward and kissed the side of Lindi's temple before repeating the action on the top of her mother's long, springy coils. "How are my two favourite women on this fine afternoon?"

"We're the only women you talk to, so calling us your favourites is a bit underwhelming," Lindi retorted.

Wrinkled laugh lines deepened on his face at Lindi's playfulness. "Fine then. How about... my two beautiful women? My most cherished flowers? The lights of my life? My..."

Lindi's features screwed up in disgust as he peppered them with compliments, which only humoured him further.

"Better if you'd stop dirtying my dresses," her mother stated when she looked down at his dirt-encrusted, calloused hands. She tsked as she dipped the bottom corner of her plain-white apron into the wash bucket between them and began carefully, and lovingly, cleaning his hands. She tsked once more as she inspected his fingers. "You always hurt yourself, Nico. I wish you'd be more careful."

Her mother stood with a harrumph to no doubt obtain some medicinal poultice or other, her navy skirts swaying as she walked down the short hallway. Nico looked at Lindi, only to roll his eyes.

"What's a few bumps and scrapes to a hardworking man?" He elbowed Lindi in the side gently. "She always acts as if I've lost an arm."

"You and I both know she frets about you, Pa," she stated, before her gaze slipped to her mother, who was high up on her tiptoes, reaching into the hallway cabinet. "And I worry about you both."

"Did she go into the garden again?" he asked, his usually carefree features hinting at concern. He silently read the answer written on her face, and his wide jaw clenched as he straightened from his leaned position at her side and turned. "Allira, what did the doctor say about any strenuous activity?"

His voice was stern, and his tone conveyed that he refused to be ignored. He placed his hands on his narrow hips and widened his muscular legs to show he meant business.

Which never worked with her mother.

"It was a handful of carrots and herbs!" Allira squealed, turning her face to the side with her plush lips curled back in annoyance. She threw up her lithe arms. "I'm not going to break if I go outside for a few minutes and help pick out our vegetables for supper." Then, with a brown bottle of liquid in her fist, she pointed between them. "You two need to stop worrying so much. I was only unwell for a little while, and the doctor did say I should make a full recovery by the month's end, so long as I'm not put under any stress."

With humour warming her chest, Lindi went to work peeling the last of the potatoes and carrots while her parents, Nico and Allira, playfully bickered about each other's wellbeing. He scolded her for tending to their private little garden out the back as she tenderly cleaned the wound he obtained from working on their farm out the front.

"Gosh, you both pester me too much." Allira pouted. "If anything, you two stress me out the most."

Lindi gave a snort of disbelief as she used her own apron to wipe any dirt from their knives. "You stress yourself out. Don't blame us."

Lindi stood so she could begin the next steps of preparing their supper, pulling the discard bucket closer to the kitchen counter so it was readily available for more waste. Before night fell, she'd take it out for the animals to get a good, healthy feed.

"Ow!" Nico grunted, then hissed while trying to pull his hand away, only for Allira to yank it back.

"Oh, quit your whining. It doesn't sting that bad." She continued to dab a poultice-soaked cloth on his palm. Then her lips pulled flat before she quietly muttered, "How are the fortifications coming along?"

A heaviness weighed on them at the question, and suddenly the air felt stilted and cold. Lindi froze midway through chopping into a stalk of celery, while her father's free hand clenched into a fist at his side. It released, just as he lowered his head to inspect the way her mother continued to care for him and the tiny wound that truly didn't need tending to.

It was nothing but a scrape, but her mother loved her father dearly and enjoyed pampering him.

"They are coming along as fast as I can get them to," Nico muttered in a grave tone, just as the breeze from the window blew his short hair around his ears. "It's hard to tend to the farm and build the fortifications at the same time on my own."

Somehow, the tension in the room thickened. A chill crept up her spine, and Lindi leaned across the kitchen bench and pulled the glass window closed. However, she did so not because of the cold but due to fear – like it being open was inviting evil into their home.

"Oh, don't look so concerned, girls," Nico said with a strained smile and an uplifted tone that didn't sound too confident. "We don't know if the rumours are actually true. It could just be people mistaking packs of dingos."

"That's not what I heard," Allira muttered. "They say it truly is a monstrous plague. An act of God."

Her father rolled his eyes with a scoff. "You women and your gossip. You're all scaring the wits out of each other. There's only one devil in the world, and we are devout people living by God's light. You know how people like to stretch the truth."

"Then why are you building fortifications?" Lindi stated quietly as she finally resumed cutting the vegetables that lay before her. She was quick to finish with the celery before finally chopping some carrots.

"Because I think it's a good idea regardless. It will keep out dingos, lizards, and even kangaroos, which will be better for the farm."

That was an excellent point. The wildlife was abundant, and it loved picking through their crops. Or predators trampled the fields, searching for the rodents that did eat what was growing. Then there were the chickens and pigs they needed to defend.

However, Lindi couldn't shake this niggling doubt in the back of her mind.

"Then what about Rivenspire?" she asked even quieter. "They've started building a wall, and it's been said people have gone... *missing* from other towns towards the southwest.

Apparently the native people have been fleeing."

"We have no idea what's been happening. There are bad people in the world, and all we have to do is keep each other safe," her father stated confidently.

Then, after capturing his wife with one arm and dragging her down the hall and back to the kitchen, he pulled Lindi into a tight cuddle to smother them, as always, with affection. She didn't even mind the masculine, musky odour of a hardworking man covered in a layer of sweat, when she easily melted into her father's loving hold as he brushed his rough jaw against her cheek.

But the town wouldn't erect a wooden wall around itself over a rumour. Lindi refused to believe they would be so paranoid, nor would they waste valuable resources, money, and effort to build it without a good reason. *It just doesn't make sense.*

She wished her father would get more information regarding it, but he refused to leave their little farming village to travel to Rivenspire. Nico preferred to only travel the half-day's walk to the large town when he had a horse-drawn carriage filled with food to sell.

Her village, although kilometres of land, only held a few farming steads that supplied all the food to Rivenspire. But her people preferred to keep to themselves, and information was limited.

As if her father could sense the tension in her body, or even perhaps because she didn't return his embrace, he pulled back to look at her. His thick brows drew together before lifting up his wrinkled forehead.

"Nothing will come to harm you while I'm around. Whatever these creatures are, whether true or false, I'm sure they are nothing to worry about. We've been defending our home from predators for years. What difference does it make now?"

Lindi flattened her lips, still unconvinced, but she chose to let it go. Her father released them both so he could pull a wooden mug out from under the counter. He shoved it into the bucket of clean water they had available and guzzled it down like a man who hadn't had a drop in days.

He's going back outside to work. Before the sun went down and he could no longer safely see.

The conversation about the fortifications likely lit a fire under his arse to work even harder.

Allira came to her side. Lindi slapped her hands away as she tried to assist, wishing she'd go sit down and rest, but her mother just did it back until she caved.

Fine. It's only supper. And she was nearby to make sure her mother didn't faint again.

"I heard Clyde's boy was at our doorstep with a bundle of flowers in his hand this morning," her father stated casually, breaking off a piece of fresh bread Lindi had baked earlier.

Lindi's cheeks heated so quickly she feared her long hair would catch fire. "MA!" she squealed, turning to her with a sense of betrayal. "You promised you wouldn't tell him!"

Her mother bumped her hip against her own. "I don't understand why you just won't go on a picnic with him. He's a nice boy."

"Because I grew up with him," she snapped back, the idea of kissing her lifelong friend making her want to hurl. "And he's two years younger than me. I want to marry someone older."

"Like Joshua?"

She scrunched her nose. "Not him, either."

"Well, you need to pick someone, my dear," Nico said as he patted her shoulder before heading to the door to exit their home. "You are two and twenty in a few days."

"Oh? Am I?" Lindi asked in a snarky tone. "I had no idea. Thanks, Pa."

His lips curled with humour. "What I'm saying is: find someone."

"Who?" Lindi barked as she chopped into the cabbage before her, continuing to prep the stew she and her mother had planned with a little more aggression than she intended. "Because there's only Marcus – Clyde's son – and Joshua who are around my age, and you won't let me go to the town with you to meet anyone else."

A small silence fell upon them and all that could be heard was Lindi's blade smacking against the chopping board, her mild huffs of annoyance, and her thoughts raging within her mind.

Do they think I want to be alone, cooped up in this house with them? Chop. Chop. She cringed when she nearly nicked her thumb with the blade. *I'm sure they want me to make haste and marry someone who will be happy to maintain the farm with Pa, but I don't want to just pick anyone.* Chop.

She wanted someone special. Someone who would make her heart flutter. Both Marcus and Joshua left her feeling cold, as if ice was growing in her heart and between her thighs. They were each handsome in their own way, and she thought they'd be wonderful husbands, she just... didn't see herself being with either of them.

Marcus was like a younger brother to her, and Joshua was a bit of a shy man, which was why he was six years her senior and still unwed. Although she didn't mind that in Joshua, she just wasn't attracted to him – but she'd never been able to figure out why.

I know I'm getting older and that I'm running out of time, but what else am I to do? Sitting here isn't going to get me married...

"About the town..." Nico said at the doorway, cutting into Lindi's thoughts.

Her head perked up at his strange tone, and she turned to him with her brows furrowing.

It was her mother who answered, which was likely the reason the next words were even being uttered. "We've decided that the next time your father goes to Rivenspire, you are to accompany him."

Her lips parted in disbelief, then a small smile slowly curled them. "What? Really?"

"There are a few families I have developed good relationships with when trading," Nico stated as he leaned against the doorway and folded his arms. "Your mother made me realise you're right. You'll never find someone here, and I know a couple of strapping young lads who would be suitable husbands. I'll organise some meetings."

The squeal that left Lindi was loud and piercing to her own ears as she ran for her father and threw herself into his embrace. He easily caught her, chuckling as he did, then squeezed her so tightly he lifted her to the tips of her toes.

"Thank you!" She hugged his neck tighter as she properly settled her weight onto her feet. "I would appreciate that so much."

"You're welcome," he said, releasing her just enough to place a hand on the side of her face. "Any man would be lucky to have you, Lindiwe. You're smart, hardworking, and beautiful."

Her cheeks warmed once more. "You're only saying that because I have your features."

His gaze softened, which made his amber eyes seem to glow. "I think you look like your mother." Then, like he was incapable of being serious, or perhaps because he found the conversation of her being wed uncomfortable in his own way, he said, "Unfortunately for you, I doubt you'll find anyone as handsome as me. Your mother was a lucky woman."

"You're the lucky one!" her mother exclaimed as she gripped the skirts of her dress and lifted them while turning to them with outrage. "I turned down your proposal three times."

"Ah, but you still said yes." Unable to keep his hands off her, like always, he stepped deeper within the house and put his arms around Allira's waist. "And I'm thankful for it every day. You were a gem back then, and you still are to this very day."

Lindi held back her gagging sounds as he started on a tangent of compliments while kissing all over her face, ensuring her mother went into a fit of giggles.

A smile lifted into her features. She really did love that about her parents. They'd been together since the year before she'd been born, and they still loved each other just as deeply as they did when they were young.

Her mother had been a girl from the town, whereas her father had been a farming boy who'd instantly grown smitten with this beautiful woman he saw. Of course, his playful, flirtatious charm easily won her over, even after he'd embarrassed himself by blurting out "Will you marry me?" as his very first greeting to her.

Lindi was pretty confident that the reality of her future love life wouldn't be so sickly sweet, but she'd like even just half of what they had. And, like them, she desired a daughter who looked like a blend of both her and whoever she married.

She eyed her father's dark-brown, ringlet curls, his sharp chin, and his tall frame, knowing she'd inherited all those same features from him. Lindi had her mother's nose, lips, high brows and cheekbones, as well as her deep-brown eyes – although there were flickers of her father's amber in her irises.

Her brown skin was lighter than her mother's but deeper than her father's bronze, and she towered over her mother's five feet and three inches by four inches, whereas her father stood barely over Lindi.

She had no idea where she got her breasts from, as her mother wasn't busty, but she had her same hourglass figure. She also had her father's broad shoulders.

They both fought over who they believed she looked more like, and neither could settle that argument.

She was perfectly made up of their love and affection.

And she had both their playful temperaments to go with it.

Her smile deepened as she transferred all the vegetables she'd cut up for their stew and swiped her blade across her cutting board. Each one plopped into the boiling pot of pre-prepared seasoned water, the steam smelling of spices and herbs that had already been added.

Ever since Lindi could remember, her home had been filled with adoration, laughter, banter, and acceptance. The smell of delicious food and wonderful incense wafted out the windows as they all sang, danced, and playfully chased each other. Giggles and laughter could be heard all across their farm as they pranked and lightly bullied each other, gossiped about their small village, and worked hard to make sure their farm was in perfect operation.

The only thing that ever ruined their days was the weather that made it difficult to sow their seeds or harvest their crops in time, which impacted their yields.

But even then, the rain thankfully and graciously soaked the land while they frolicked in it.

TWO

April 24th, 1683

A loud bang, like an open door slamming against the wall during a terrible thunderstorm, shocked the entire house.

With a sharp gasp, Lindi sat up, her eyes flying open. Darkness greeted her, the night late and the moon hidden behind the wooden slats covering her windows. The silence that should have shrouded the heaviness of night was replaced with scuffling and loud, thumping boots.

Rather than Lindi thinking of the sudden bang as nothing but an accident and peacefully going back to sleep, her heart stuttered and then squeezed.

Someone is in the house.

She twisted, reached onto her bedside table, and fumbled for her tinder box so she could light her candle. She bit back her squeal at another bang, this time deeper within her family home, just as she struck her flint against her fire steel. A gust of wind coming from underneath the crack of her door made the spark against the tinder roll away.

She immediately gave up at the masculine yell bursting down the hallway and hopped out of bed to open the wooden blinds.

Squinting her eyes against the oppressive shadows, Lindi used what little residual light managed to glow from the moon beyond her window. At the bitter-cold nip of autumn's air through her thin white nightgown, the frills around her neck offering no warmth, she hurried to retrieve her winter jacket and donned it with haste. Her toes knocked against her slippers, and just as she sightlessly put them on, her simple bedroom was illuminated by orange light coming through the cracks around her door.

The light should have been welcoming, but it was too bright to be a lit candle or lantern.

A scream pierced the momentary quiet – her mother's – just as Lindi's door was thrown open. This time, Lindi screamed when a man she'd never seen before shoved his way into her room, bearing a crude torch, the rag on it reeking of flammable resin. It made his shaven, lightly tanned features gleam with determination. The metal buckles strapping his leather armour to his torso, and the hilt of his short sword sheathed at his waist, glinted in that orange light.

His bushy, pale-blonde brows narrowed on her the moment he saw her.

She took in no other details of him when he dived forward to capture her with his large right hand. Instead, another scream locked in her throat as she spun around, hiked up her floor-length nightgown, and crawled across her frameless bed. Her sheets twisted around her left ankle when she stood on solid ground, but her stumbling managed to save her from the strange, aggressive man when he dived for her a second time.

"Leave me alone!" she shouted, ducking under his meaty arms to get behind him and closer to the door. "Take what you want!"

It's not like they had anything truly of value! Sure, her father may have a few coins, but they were simple farmers. The nicest things they owned were perhaps one evening outfit each, and some worthless but sentimental trinkets. The only things of value they owned were their food and their farming tools, which this man didn't need to pillage the inside of their home to steal.

Managing to get away from him, her body slammed against the opposing wall when she ran from her room. She headed down the hallway, fleeing towards her parents' room and the exit beyond – since both were in the same direction. She didn't know where all the light was coming from, but she hoped it was her mother and father with their brass candle stands.

When she turned the corner, one of her brown slippers almost came off her feet as she ran face-first into a living wall of muscle. She grunted in surprise, just as a set of hands grabbed her biceps and stopped her from falling onto her arse.

She barely had the chance to take in his tanned, beard-covered face before a grin filled his hard features and he crouched. Shrieking and kicking her legs, Lindi bashed on his firm back when he threw her over his shoulder and carted her down the hallway.

Her heart sprinted so hard she could feel it in her gut pressing against his hard shoulder, which shoved into her painfully, making her legs tingle with oncoming numbness. Her lungs were so seized with fear she was close to choking on her laboured breaths.

"Let me go!" she shouted, reaching back to yank on his long black ponytail. No amount of pulling, punching, or kicking stopped the ugly brute.

"Papa!" she yelled, her voice twisting into a high pitch when she was carried past the threshold of their bedroom door. Her eyes widened with horror when saw her parents held at knife point by a third man wielding another torch.

"Lindiwe!" he called, reaching for her as he bolted forward, only to trip back when the armoured man stabbed his blade towards him.

"Stay back!" He cut his dagger sideways through the air. "I'm fuckin' warnin' ya."

Her mother's cries and yells could be heard, but Lindi couldn't decipher anything more than her name being called.

God, please save me! Lindi's mind prayed as she pushed up on the man's back to alleviate the ache her gut from being carted around like a sack.

Just as they reached the small living area of her home, the first man she encountered lit up the space further when he cut past them. He opened the front door, and her struggles grew fiercer.

She reached back to sink her nails into the neck of the man carrying her, wishing they were deep enough to kill.

"What do you want?" she asked, frantically peering into the night when the cool air of outside prickled her skin. It was crisp and harsh with the autumn season steadily approaching its midway point, and her jacket and thin nightgown offered little warmth. "Where are you taking me?"

Other than the dewy mud squelching beneath his big boots, her sharp breaths, and the crackle of fire, there were no other sounds. She was given no answer as she was taken further away from her home. Right before they reached the fence line that separated their yard from their crops, Lindi slipped down his body and was placed on her feet.

Without a second thought, she took a single step to the side to sprint away before her wrist was grabbed. Wide-eyed and gasping for air against the terror lining her bloodstream, she slapped at him and fought as he tied her wrists together.

Her sounds of protest went quiet when she knew that no one, other than her parents, would be able to hear her. Their farm, although nestled up against another family's farm, was too far for the sound to carry. Other than the sounds of her scuffling to free herself, and the grind of his leather armour, all was quiet. A bat squeaked above, and a horse that didn't belong to them let out a loud white plume of hot breath when it snorted, but there was little else.

She was alone. She was helpless, and no one was going to save her.

It was then that tears filled her eyes and quickly spilled over. She was too afraid to do little more than tremble in case they turned violent. Currently they were just binding her wrists. She hated that she could hardly see what the man doing it looked like with the waning moon barely peaking past the treetops. The other man with the torch had stepped around the three waiting horses and appeared to be checking their gear.

Their packs were full of some of their crops, like they'd already gone through their farm.

"W-why are you doing this?" she whispered this time, her eyes searching for an escape, a weapon, just a way to avoid this.

He paused when she winced due to him yanking the rope in two different directions, the coarseness of it abrading her soft skin. His pink lips disappeared behind his full beard, as if he thinned them in thought, before they revealed themselves once more.

"Nothing personal, lass," he grated. "We won't harm you

along the way, that's all you need to know."

That didn't make her feel better whatsoever!

A sickening pool spread in her gut and her knees shook. She didn't think she'd ever been so frightened in all her life. Not even finding her mother's unconscious body halfway up the hill as she returned from the town's well in the middle of summer could best this, and that had been a hard day for both her and her father.

Tied up with nothing else but her nightgown, jacket, and brown slippers on, she felt... defenceless. How was she supposed to fight against two armed men? The one holding the torch seemed to have crazed eyes, the colour of them a piercing, cruel blue.

Her gaze kept slipping to the front door of her home, and she desperately wished her father would come out to save her. Her heart nearly leapt with hope when it opened, only for it to clench tightly when the last man exited through the doorway.

Okay, so three armed men, two of which wore leather armour.

"Should we burn it?" he asked, lifting the flames of his light source towards the hay roofing above their porch.

"Don't be a cunt, Mathews," the one who bound her wrists spat out. "Leave them be. They've got enough problems to worry about."

He eyed Lindi, meaning *her*, before he shook his head and turned away.

"Oh, shut your facehole, Gregory," he tossed back as he sauntered down the pathway. "Ya don't get ta play righteous when yer out 'ere stealing women."

The heat in Lindi's chest, neck, and face sapped away at their words.

They've done this before. Oh god, she was what they were after all along!

Her breaths turned rapid when they stopped paying her any notice, her eyes darting one way and then the other... before she bolted. Gregory must have thought she was completely surrendering since he turned his stupid back on her.

I refuse to be taken! She sprinted with her bound wrists pressed against her chest, pressing down on her ample breasts so she could run freely.

A high-pitched, banshee shriek flung out of her as she was

tackled to the ground by the man who had checked on the horse packs.

"Let me go!" She kicked, she screamed, and when he placed his forearm anywhere near her face, she bit him so hard she tasted copper.

Then, her long, dark hair was grabbed so he could yank her to her feet. She came face to face with the man, and his cold eyes promised pain.

"Ya fuckin' bitch!" Just as he raised his hand to hit her, the slap of Gregory's palm against his forearm echoed through the night.

"Don't, Sal," he warned, towering over the smaller man.

"She bit me!" Sal barked.

Although he said nothing, the grind of leather under his meaty hand and the darkening look on Gregory's face said everything it needed to: he didn't care. Lindi shouldn't have been so relieved that he was acting as her saviour, considering he was also her captor.

"Please! Just leave me alone," she begged when she was thrown over Sal's shoulder, then he hoisted her onto the backend of a horse.

Her ankles were tied, as if they wanted to make sure she wouldn't slip off and have the freedom to run away should she attempt it again.

All three ignored her and carried on in heavy silence.

It made her father's roar all the louder when he came running between their crops of barley with a sickle in his hand. He was coming from the direction of the storage shed, as if he'd slipped out the window in order to sneak off and grab some kind of weapon.

"Papa!" she cried out.

The horse spooked and shied to the side, and she wiggled to get down from it to go to him. One of the other horses knocked into hers, causing it to spin in a circle, its hooves clattering erratically, and she barely caught the men drawing their swords to ward Nico back.

Her blood ran cold.

"Stop! Go inside!" she yelled as the horse turned and turned, but she was forced to close her eyes right before the saddlebag of the third horse whacked her in the face.

By the time she opened them again, she was facing away from the farm, and everything had gone quiet.

Too quiet.

Not even a cricket dared to chirp in the heavy night.

"What's happening?" she asked, gasping for air against her worry, her anxiety of this night.

She didn't like the silence that greeted her. Where was the sound of a kerfuffle? A fight? An argument? There were no more roars from her father or grunts from these brutes. Not even the clang of his sickle against a metal sword.

No sounds of... life.

As much as she appreciated her father trying to rescue her, he was one man facing off against three armed and possibly deadly men. She wanted to be saved. She wanted it more than anything, but Nico needed to think about her mother. Without Lindi, Allira would need him more than ever, especially with her heart so weak. She couldn't farm by herself; she was feeble and frail while she was getting better.

So long as these men didn't kill Lindi – with Gregory's desire to keep her unharmed, she dearly hoped that was the case – perhaps they could be reunited. She could hope and pray for that day to keep her moving forward without them.

She craned her head to the side when the horse she was on finally came back around, and her heart nearly came up her throat.

Throwing her body around until she managed to buck herself off the creature, she screamed, "NO! No no no!"

It spooked to the side once more. She was almost trampled, but Lindi didn't care.

Not when her tears spilled to the dirt as she watched her father sink to his knees with a sword through his gut. Crimson seeped into his white sleep shirt and spread fast when it was pulled from him. As he cupped his wound, the assailant booted his chest so he would collapse to the ground on his side with a heart-wrenching thump.

"What the fuck, Sal?!" Gregory roared, grabbing the man by the scruff of his armour.

Sal, with his sword still bloodied, shoved back at him. "Piss off! He swung first."

"There's three of us! We could have subdued him. There was no need to kill the man!"

Sal raised a shoulder. "Who cares?" Then he shoved his sword into its scabbard and turned for Lindi. "We have the girl. That's what we came 'ere for, ain't it?"

He lifted Lindi on the back of the horse with the help of the third man, who had never spoken. Shocked, and unable to do anything else but cry as she tried to absorb that her father lay dying not even a few metres from her, Lindi was pliable.

She did nothing but weep as she was placed there, wishing more than ever that Nico had just stayed inside. That he hadn't come out to save her. What about her mother? What was she supposed to do now? Lindi was being taken, and Allira's husband wasn't going to be there to help her through it.

You silly, courageous man, she thought with anguish, licking at the tears that wet her lips and forced her to drink her own sadness. *What about Ma? How could you abandon her like that?*

She couldn't believe her father hadn't stopped to consider the worst possible outcome: his death. What a foolish man! He'd thought with his heart and not his head... when he should have *known* there was nothing he could have done.

What is going to happen to me? she thought with a sob. What about Lindi and her future?

She wanted to know that. She wanted to know why they had targeted her, when she barely left her home – even to go wandering through the village. How did they even know about her?

The men argued about Nico's death, Gregory apparently against the unscrupulous killing, whereas Sal appeared to be vibrating with glee over it. The two men's views didn't seem to align, and the third man, Mathews, remained ever silent on the topic.

She was cold, she was frightened, and her heart was breaking in her chest. The last thing she saw of her home that night was her mother running out to her father's corpse to collapse next to it, shake it for life, then abandon it to chase after Lindi.

Lindi knew Allira's wails would forever haunt her for the rest of her – perhaps fleeting – life. And the sight of her chasing after them as they kicked up speed would live in her nightmares and the depths of her sorrow forever.

Why me?

THREE

April 26th, 1683

Lindi had heard the rumours – then again, who hadn't?

The rumours about disgusting monsters that hid in the darkness of night. Creatures with strange, void-like flesh that often glistened like starry skies, or like inky water. Evil spirits that looked nothing like humans or animals, but often a horrifying mesh of both.

Apparently they smelt of rot, decay, and infected blood. Their very breath was said to be putrid as they fought with big, sharp fangs.

Such things couldn't exist.

They were merely make-believe to ensure little boys and girls came home before bedtime. To make sure they were good and ate all their vegetables, did all their chores, and went to bed on time so they could hide under the covers and protect themselves under the sheets.

They had to make sure they tucked up their feet to protect them from clawed hands grabbing them from under the bed.

Some people called them devils, as if they came from the very depths of hell as a vengeance for all the sinful wrongdoings of humankind. The followers of the church clung to them as a way to turn people to their faith, convincing them to follow the teachings of the Lord for protection. And, of course, people at their most vulnerable clutched their new rosaries in fear and prayed for forgiveness. They were to kneel before their

Almighty God, repent, and promise a life of their holy morals.

Lindi had never needed such convincing; the Heavenly Father had always been on her side... until now.

She'd believed, just as her mother and father had – and their parents before them. The idea of true devils escaping the fiery pits of hell to take them from the land of the living had never been a fear, but the threat of greeting them in the afterlife had always kept them firmly on their path of faith.

She'd never met one, neither had any of the people she'd known, nor had anyone they'd encountered. Yet the rumour persisted, and no one knew of its truth or its origin.

Not once in all this time travelling since she'd been taken had any sort of monster jumped out from the bushes. The rumours had been nothing but lies, especially as it was believed that the scent of fear brought the creatures upon their victims with a vengeance.

And Lindi had been afraid this entire venture.

No, the rumours were just foolish little bedtime horror stories to invoke obedience.

How can not doing anything be so exhausting? she thought languidly.

Her long, tangled, and leaf-strewn brown hair swayed back and forth as it dangled from the top of her head. With her nose squished against short, coarse, sandy-coloured hair, and the smell of dusty horse pervading her nostrils, her barely alert eyes flickered. Her arms ached from being bound behind her back on and off for days, the trio of armed men only giving her short breaks of freedom.

Enough to sleep, answer the call of nature, and eat before binding them again.

Even though they'd stopped binding her ankles, she knew she wasn't fast enough to get away, and she had no idea where she was. Nor did she know where they were taking her.

All she knew was that the nights were cooler, the days hotter, and the land was patchy and barren in parts. For a while now, it seemed they'd been crossing a desert that was dotted with twiggy shrubs she couldn't name.

They hadn't even been attacked by any large predators, although she saw an abundance of animals like kangaroos, reptiles, and even sheep. She swore she even saw a goat, although she wasn't quite sure, but she'd definitely seen plenty of hares.

She knew all about hares, and how they were introduced to the land at the beginning of the century following the settlement of western men. Those cute little things were an absolute menace to her farm, and the foxes introduced to hunt them also rooted through their crops and chickens.

Yet, she tried to count them as they travelled.

All Lindi had to entertain herself as they carted her through forests, meadows, flat plains, and mountains was her environment.

The men ignored her presence as if she mattered naught. They refused to answer her questions, and they didn't respond to her snide remarks, callous insults, or her begging. To be ignored so completely and utterly, as if her voice was inaudible, was maddening.

At least they haven't touched me. It was a solace amidst the terror of all this. Although Sal, the fucking prick, eyed her a little too fondly, her presence was so ignored it was like she didn't truly exist to them.

She was cargo. That was all.

What for? She still didn't know, and that unanswered question terrified her.

And worse still, the only thing they *had* said was, "I'm sorry." Gregory apparently had a conscience. His dark, bushy facial hair covered most of his tan features, but his brown eyes often appeared forlorn and distant.

He was the only one who appeared to wear some kind of black religious robes and lacked armour, unlike the other two.

Mathews, the silent one, never said anything from what she gathered – even when he'd cornered Lindi in her room, he never said anything. He was the tallest and the strongest of all three of them, and if he didn't look devoid of emotion, he appeared thoughtful. His cleanly shaved, light features showed everything and yet there seemed to be nothing to reveal, even when she peered into his green eyes.

Sal often sat back on his cream stallion with an air of boredom, as if he searched the horizon for more bloodshed. His long brown ponytail swayed tauntingly against his back, and she wanted nothing more than to wrap it around his thin neck and strangle him with it.

The lingering pain of her father's death, and his hand in it, continued to burn in her chest. She feared so deeply for her mother that bile constantly threatened to rise in her throat – and it was all Sal's fault. Gregory wouldn't have murdered him, and she had a feeling neither would have Mathews.

Just Sal, and his stupid, scarred-up face. He was actually a rather ugly, ratty-looking man whose entire body was covered in scars – some old, some fresh. He was battle-hardened and mean, despite his thinner, shorter frame. She figured he found fault with his appearance, and he compensated with callousness rather than the appealing confidence he should have worn.

People often dictated their own attractiveness by having a shitty personality, and he had a shovelful of dung in his heart and thick skull.

I miss my home, Lindi thought with a sniffle.

She missed her parents, her life, her friends, and even her chores. She'd never complained about doing hard work, so she even missed the burn of aching muscles from good, hearty exertion.

It's my birthday today.

There would be no birthday celebration for her, and it made her heart bleed even more than before. Gosh, she felt so pitiful that just remembering that made her tears renew. She'd been crying on and off for the past two days, wishing for time to go back so she could do... something, *anything* to change what had happened.

So many fears. So much inner turmoil she couldn't bear.

She sucked in hard through her nose to remove the disgusting drip, only to cough and hack at the taste of powdery dust. The chop of hooves over rocky desert continued to kick up fine orange dirt into her abused senses.

Then, before long, a strangeness took Lindi's focus.

After so long of seeing nothing but barren, dry desert all day, rocks abundant and boring, true greenery began to shift into view. It started sparsely, as if the flora had been growing outward, but there was evidence of new trees sprouting through the earth. The further they went, the bigger they seemed to be, until one or two appeared to have reached proper maturity.

Some were strange, as she'd never seen these kinds of trees or plants before, their branches reaching far with bristly leaves. Some smelt rich and fragrant when their leaves or needles brushed over her head, so much so they filled her lungs with pleasantness.

Everyone knew that Austrális was a rather dry country the further they travelled into the middle of the continent, so to see such vibrance was shocking. Lindi had lived on the outskirts of their more tropical forests and towering mountains that sat between her plains and the sea.

She'd always wanted to go further east to see the closest ocean, but she'd never considered going towards the centre.

Her brows drew together when wet, muddy grass crunched and squelched beneath the hooves of the horses they rode.

This doesn't make any sense. She couldn't help lifting her head to further peer around. *How did all this come to be?*

It was like an abundant oasis had grown in the middle of the dry, dusty countryside. The stagnant air even seemed to cool, especially as the early autumn heat that had been bearing down on her faded under the shade. Any perspiration lining her forehead and neck became refreshing, and she found it easier to breathe.

Insects clicked and buzzed around her head, and she wrinkled her nose side to side at the perfume of flowers sprinkling their pollen into the air. The area was rich with life.

She looked back at Mathews, whose horse she was being carted on, just as he lifted a branch to avoid its swipe. He didn't appear phased by what he saw, and neither did the others – especially as none commented on it in surprise.

Have they... been here before? This definitely felt planned and usual for them, whereas she couldn't stop her head from turning one way or the other.

The horses skittered to the side occasionally, their ears stiff and pointed forward with flaring nostrils. The further they ventured through the thickening brush, the more skittish they became, often neighing and whinnying as they tossed their heads. Although obviously very anxious, even the horses seemed well adjusted to the environment.

"Keep your wits about you," Gregory muttered quietly when true shade passed over them, and his hands tightened on his reins. "We're in *their* territory now."

"It's fine," Sal muttered with an air of indifference, flapping his hand from side to side dismissively. "We'll hear 'em before we see 'em."

In answer, Mathews grunted with a head nod before looking over his shoulder. He and her connected eyes, then he lifted a single finger and pressed it against his lips. With no idea as to why he was telling her to shush, she shied away from his gaze to stare down at the horse's hooves.

Who are they talking about? She hated admitting that she didn't know all too much about the area. She eyed the lushness around her once more. *We have to be close to the centre of the continent by now.*

Just where were they taking her? There should be nothing and no one here except perhaps the native people, but even they were few and far between. She doubted she was being carted to one of their villages, as these men would likely sell her for coin, if anything.

It wasn't uncommon for women to be taken for such reasons, forced to marry men other women didn't wish to wed. Or worse.

Lindi shuddered at the thought.

Within minutes of being in the shade, as if the forest was only a thin band, they broke the tree line. There was an uncomfortable scent in the air, but Lindi couldn't place it.

It was sickly sweet, but so very light it was more like an afterthought on the back of her palette. It came and went due to the light wind, the smells of the forest behind them mostly overshadowing it.

It didn't matter either way.

In that moment, Lindi didn't think anything could have distracted her from the shocking scene when they halted their horses and turned.

A gigantic hole, like a rip in the earth with a cavernous fall off the edge of a cliff side, opened up before them.

"A crevasse?" she whispered, gawking at it as the men rounded to the side to trot next to it.

No, a crevasse was much smaller than this.

She could *just* make out the other side, as if it was on the border of what the human eye could see in the distance, and that was only in front of her. To her left and right, it was nothing but a shadowy, gaping hole forever.

They eventually stilled their mounts and the angle they finally brought her to allowed her to see deeper inside it. There was nothing down there except the occasional tree and shrub, although further to her right, she could see a dense forest.

The other side of the canyon was nothing but barren desert, as if the forest only existed on *this* side of it.

"I didn't think something like this existed in Austrális," Lindi stated.

Ignoring her like usual, their saddles groaned and creaked as they dismounted, their boots thumping against the hard dirt of the rocky canyon edge. Two of the horses shook their necks at the release of pressure on their backs, causing their manes to flick and sway.

"We've started calling it the Veil," Gregory stated as he stroked his sandy-coloured horse's neck.

Her lips parted in surprise that he'd answered her.

"The Veil? I've never heard of a such a place." Her lips pursed as she peered into it, only for her vision to wobble at the sheer, deadly drop. "Why would you call it that?"

"The mist," he answered, scrutinising her face for a moment before quickly averting his gaze. "It's faded today, but the more we come here, the thicker it seems to get."

"It's grown again," Sal said with a strange depth to his tone, and Lindi looked over to find his usual smug expression was deeply concerned and narrowed on the horizon. "I swear somethin' unholy is at play 'ere. No forest should grow this fast."

At his foreboding words, goosebumps trailed up her arms, and the prickling spread over her when Mathews stepped closer and pulled her from the back of his horse.

"The mist shrouds terrors, like a layer of foreboding quiet that hides hostility," Mathews stated, revealing a deep, body-chilling voice for the first time, which was made ever colder by his words. "It's a cloak of lies, obscuring the beautiful growing forest to hide the nightmares that linger within it. A veil."

Lindi didn't know why she smiled, but it was weak, false, and shaky as her lips quivered, and her nose tingled with the threat of tears.

"Y-you're scaring me."

All three looked at her, and she realised then that the only part of her that wasn't surrounded was her back – yet the forest behind her felt oppressive all of a sudden. Their silence at her statement twisted her insides, and finally her eyes watered.

"What are you going to do to me?"

She eyed the deadly fall, wishing she could see how tall it truly was before nausea clutched her stomach and forced her to turn away. She feared...

No. She shook her head, dismissing the thought that came to her. *They wouldn't.* It would be cruel to bring her here... just to toss her over the edge.

There needed to be a deeper meaning to them taking her and spending days bringing her here, other than to do something so barbaric.

"The Almighty Father is angry with us," Gregory muttered as he came closer. It wasn't the first time she saw it under his dark robes, as he often held it at night while they rested, but the cross at his waist was more noticeable in the daylight when it peeked out as he moved around.

Her stomach dropped, her new fear rebounding as quickly as she squashed it, and a cold chill crept up her spine.

Mathews knelt before her with rope in his hands, and before she could step back in protest when he reached for an ankle, Sal pulled his knife from his weapons belt.

"Don't, missy," Sal bit with gritted teeth. "Don't make us chase ya. We want away from 'ere as quickly as possible." Then he gestured to the gap of sunlight pouring into the canyon. "The light is fadin', and it'll only grow more dangerous traversin' back through it with every hour."

"Please." Lindi took a step back, her bare foot ducking out of Mathews' grasp, while the other shoe-covered foot was held firm. She turned her beseeching gaze to Gregory, the only person she'd seen any kindness from, hoping for his benevolence once more. "Whatever you're planning, please don't do it. Life is sacred – that's what his teachings show us."

"We have no other option," Gregory muttered, watching as Mathews threaded the rope around her ankles. "We have to stop them, and we'll try anything and everything before it's too late. You haven't seen them, so you don't know what they're like, but we do. If we don't appease him soon, we fear we'll be overrun. This must end when we can still hunt them. Before they start forming packs and decimating villages. Before they get... *bigger.*"

"A-are you talking about those rumours?" she asked with a sob. Lindi's knees buckled as tremors assaulted her joints. "I thought they were..."

"Stories?" Sal bit. "Yeah, us too – until we saw one."

Then he pointed to the horrible scars marring his face, the ones she'd never been able to make any sense out of. The side of his cheek was missing, his nostril and upper lip split in half. How he'd managed to retain both his eyes was a miracle, considering all the puncture wounds created in oval shapes.

Now that she looked deeper into them, she realised they were pointed fang marks, as if a small creature had pinned him down and bitten his face multiple times. The rest of his body was covered in claw marks, especially upon his biceps and upper chest.

"We've seen and killed many since then," Mathews stated, his leather armour creaking as he stood.

"Why me?" Lindi asked, covering her face to hide her anguish from them, her fear, her very tears. The way her chest twisted so nastily, she wanted nothing more than to expel her heart, so it didn't hurt like this or feel so betrayed.

"Why else?" Sal stated coldly, before carelessly pushing her so she'd stumble backwards, her ankle bindings having just enough slack to let her shuffle towards the edge of the canyon. "Pretty maiden sacrificed to a God. It's well known in history, no?"

Peeking behind her, the blood rushed to her ears when Lindi noticed the ledge below the one she was on now, and the steep incline of rocks meeting them. When the heel of her shoe dipped over the edge, Lindi jerked forward with a shriek. Her ankles caught in the rope, and she fell to her knees, only to be yanked up once more by Sal.

"But why *me*?!" Lindi yelled when she was turned and hauled a safe distance away from the edge. She didn't dare hope that meant they were changing their minds.

"You were alone," Gregory answered, remaining a safe distance back as Sal and Mathews blocked any chance for her to attempt a feeble escape. "Your village was small, your parents simple farmers and easy to overpower. Sorry about your father, by the way. That... shouldn't have happened. He shouldn't have needed to die."

He cut Sal another fierce glare over it, who merely rolled his eyes in return.

"You're unwed, young enough and isolated enough to remain pure, and so devoted to our God that you wouldn't violate his teachings."

Seriously? A virgin fucking sacrifice?

That was old and barbaric! She'd heard tales of such things, but that was from ancient times, and ancient lands and people. Those sorts of things didn't happen anymore, and yet... apparently here she was, about to be one.

She was even wearing a damn white gown, all dressed and ready.

Her cries became more distressed, and she fisted the back of her nightgown, wishing with all her might that her arms were free so she could fight back. She feigned a step to the right, causing them to heave that way, then she attempted tiny shuffles to the left.

She made it about two half-steps before she was caught again.

Heart racing, with her breaths sawing in and out of her rapidly heaving chest, Lindi couldn't believe the very deity that told her to save herself until marriage would be the reason she'd die.

And there would be no one here to save her. They were thousands of kilometres from any kind of civilisation, in the middle of the continent. Hundreds of thousands of people lived near the coasts or just below the mountainsides, but not here.

She should have known something was wrong with the world, that things were changing, when she saw the lightest snowflakes in her village for the first time last year. It'd never happened before, snow a strange and foreign sight in Austrális, to the point that they melted before they even touched the ground. Gosh, the winter that year had been harsh, but she never thought there was a deeper meaning to it.

She never thought it would be the first sign of this day.

"You're making a mistake!" she screamed, twisting hard enough from Mathews' hold that she fell towards Sal with her face pointing down.

A shocked and pained gasp ripped from her when something cold, hard, and sharp lodged in her gut. With Sal holding her shoulder to keep her upright, she looked down with widened eyes to find his dagger lodged hilt deep above her navel. Hot crimson liquid spread across her abdomen and quickly cooled against the wind.

He ripped the blade from her, and Lindi instantly sagged to her knees as her arms pulled against her bindings in an attempt to cup her wound to no avail. Gregory began some kind of loud, boisterous chant, but she couldn't make it out against the ringing in her ears and the black spots in her vision.

Unable to stem the flow of her blood, she collapsed to her side with the edge metres from her. The pain was immense, her fear even more painful, and her heart racing with adrenaline worsened the throbbing.

She couldn't believe this had happened... that this was truly the end.

The shock that clutched her bones had her frozen on the ground momentarily, and she only snapped out of it when they finally stepped away to leave. To discard her here as she bled out.

To callously leave her in her final moments of death.

I thought they were going to throw me off the cliff.

She didn't know what was worse: the fast fall or this slow and lonely death.

FOUR

April 26th, 1683

With her sight growing murky, Lindi wriggled uselessly towards the edge of the cliff. Terror suffused every inch of her body as she kicked and heaved weakly in her bonds.

Please, God! Please save me, she pleaded, looking down at her feet – or rather, beyond them.

Her dry bottom lip trembled at the *thing* that skittered just within the border of the shade. Red eyes, so bright and petrifying, never left her. They looked *hungry,* enhanced by the white froth that bubbled at the corners of its maw, and the way it licked at its muzzle. Sharp, glinting claws tore at the ground as it paced, braving the sunlight by a millimetre before yelping and backing up.

"They're real," she whispered hoarsely, dehydration and blood loss having parched her aching throat. "I can't believe they're real."

And as each minute passed, those pointed shadows created by treetops were reaching towards her like a set of fingers. They were bringing the creature closer, and she was so terrified of it she had started worming her way towards the ledge of rock.

I'd rather fall. The idea of being eaten alive was horrifying – she couldn't imagine how painful it would be.

Her consciousness was slipping again, but it wasn't fast enough.

She could barely smell over the coppery scent of caked blood in her nose, but the creature had a pungent aroma to it. Its features were utterly inhuman, but it also didn't truly look animalistic. It was a monster, something that appeared part dog, part bird, part... who fucking knew? It was indecipherable.

It had bird-like legs, with wings low down near its hips. Its torso and front legs were thick and feline, yet its face was dog-like and boorish. It just looked twisted and screwed up in all the worst possible ways, while its flesh truly didn't look like skin. No, it was glossy, like it was being held together by some tainted force, like void magic, and she worried it'd consume her with just a mere touch.

She also feared it'd turn her into one. She didn't want to become a devil – was that what the men meant when they said the creatures were growing in number? Were they turning humans into whatever unholy thing this was?

She didn't want to be eaten by one, in any way, shape, or form.

What did I do wrong? she asked with a shiver of delirium rolling down her back. *I'm a devout woman. I've never violated your teachings.*

Lindi was a good person, hardworking and faithful.

For the entire time she bled, drifting in and out of consciousness, betrayal obliterated her.

Each squirm sent agony through her midsection, as if she was tearing her wound further. Yet she continued to live, as if Sal, the bastard, missed anything vital. She'd even stopped bleeding, despite the worrisome puddle of it congealing against the stone she was smearing it against. Why couldn't he have hit a vital organ or an artery?

Why did she have to be experiencing this long death?

As much as she wanted to cling onto life, it was futile. There was nothing she could do to save herself, and she'd rather get it over with than suffer to her final heartbeat.

Her eyes were so swollen and puffy from crying that her renewed tears stung so badly she hissed out a breath through clenched teeth. Each new droplet felt like razors to her eyes. Then she let out a broken cry when she twisted a certain way, and her entire abdomen protested against the pain.

She stopped, only to breathe and shudder as she fought her

bindings, wishing they'd snap. She'd been hoping for that for what had to be an hour, wanting to flee – to go down fighting rather than this pathetically sad end.

All the while, the strange creature snarled, hissed, and growled beyond her feet. Except... when she looked down once more after resting, another had joined it – the setting sun was bringing more to pace within the growing shadows.

They bumped torsos and then dived for each other as a fight broke out.

Lindi whimpered, wriggled once more, and the light smell of rot abraded her senses like she reached some kind of threshold. She finally inched her way close enough to the edge of the cliff to peer over it. Vertigo struck her at the long fall, but it soon passed as she peered at the boulders and rocks below.

It looked like the side of the wall had broken off bit by bit and landed at the bottom.

It goes on forever.

Although she could just make out the other side of the Veil's canyon, being closer to its edge really did prove just how daunting it was. She couldn't see where it ended from left to right, only what was right ahead.

Rocks cracked off and rolled down the side of the wall under her weight. Seeing them do so only brought on a chilling wave of fear, which, oddly enough, made the creatures beyond her feet grow more agitated. One even whined, as if her fear made it hunger so badly it ripped a noise from it.

"So... they've brought another sacrifice, have they?" a voice mused, so quiet and distant that she barely believed she heard anything at all.

Twisting to her side to look around, Lindi darted her head around, but nobody was there. Instead, she once more connected gazes with one of the monsters and her eyes crinkled in anguish.

They were getting closer, and she tucked her feet up in worry that they'd soon be able to claw at the bottom of her soles. Sweat slicked her brow after being in the heat of the sun for so long, unable to escape it, and yet she was so relieved by its hot presence.

"It seems you've found yourself in quite the bind," the voice stated, a touch louder than before and yet still as quiet as a

reverberating echo.

Was that meant to be a joke? If so, it was horribly inappropriate as she clenched and unclenched her bound hands. Her brows drew together as she looked around again. *Am I... hallucinating?*

Her shoulders lifted self-consciously as she asked, "Who... is anyone there?"

She didn't expect a response.

"Yes, human."

Her lips parted on a gasp, and her eyes darted around to find the source of that oddly deep and sultry voice. Not even its quietness could hide the way it slid across her subconscious in a mesmerising stroke. It sounded... *inhuman.* Otherworldly. Perhaps even heavenly.

Lindi found her body easing against the rocky ledge. "God?"

"I doubt I'm one of the many gods you seek." That didn't sound too promising. *"But yes, little one, I am indeed a god."*

"S-show yourself," she demanded, wishing her voice held the power of a yell, rather than a hoarse rasp.

She didn't want to speak to some faceless entity.

"I am unable to do that, but know that I am right before you, standing just beyond the cliff."

She slid her face against the stone and peered beyond the drop off. There was nothing and nobody there. At least she was unable to see anyone – not even an outline that could give a hint of a presence.

"Who are you?" she asked, wishing tears didn't bubble in her eyes. She thought she'd be all out of liquid by now, but they just seemed to keep coming, no matter how much she tried to stem them.

Lindi was exhausted, but she'd been through emotional turmoil over the past two days. She was facing her imminent death, and she very much wanted to live. She wanted to die old, happy, and with loved ones around her.

Not here. Not like this. Not because of men who stole her in the middle of the night and ripped apart her life.

"I am Weldir, semidei Custos Tenebris. Or, to a human, Weldir, Warden of the Darkness."

At least he didn't say he was the devil. She didn't know if speaking with this *Weldir* would be considered blasphemous, though. She clung to the idea of speaking with him because it was better than focusing on her impending demise.

She always thought there was only one almighty being. To be speaking to another... one she'd never even heard of – it was shocking. Almost mind-altering.

"Why are you here?" she whispered.

Was he answering her pleas for a saviour?

"The Daekura crawl ever closer," he said, devoid of any emotion. *"We do not have much time."*

Her brows drew together. "Daekura?"

"It's what we, in another realm, call them. I believe it would translate to 'dark beings' in your language, but your kind will one day formulate your own name for them."

He was speaking of the creatures at her feet, and their disgusting sounds continued to unnerve her. At least his voice was soothing, and she wondered if he was using some kind of magic to calm her. If so, she was utterly thankful for it.

"W-what are they?"

"We don't have the time to talk about such things. The sun will run out and then there will be nothing I can do to change your fate."

She nodded as she brought her knees up to lie in a ball, wincing at the pain the position brought. The light, cooling wind was causing chills to break out across her feverish skin, and she was tired of fighting them.

"I come to offer you a choice. Die here or become my mate."

Even though her gaze was languid, she narrowed her eyes. She'd never heard of such a term before. "Your mate? Like a buddy?"

A strange hum came from him, like a sound one might make if they were thinking heavily. *"I don't know what you humans would call it. A life partner? A companion? Someone with whom you create offspring."*

"A wife?" Lindi scoffed a deadened laugh and muttered, "Suddenly I'm a sacrificial bride." Not just an offering.

"Human, we do not have time for your jokes."

"Who are you to tell me I can't laugh when I'm the one dying?" she grumbled.

"I am offering you the chance to live."

Her eyelids slid closed against the drowsiness, and her body lost all its fight. She allowed herself a moment to rest before she continued in her journey off the edge.

"You're asking me to marry someone I've never seen, a god I have never heard of. I don't know who you are or even what you are. You could be the devil asking for my soul for all I know."

"I don't know who this 'devil' is, but your soul is what I would require, yes."

"Then no." Her answer was firm. "I'd rather die faithfully than trade my soul to an unknown god who won't even show himself."

A tsk reached her ears. *"You sound just like the others. Do you not seek revenge for what has happened to you?"* Her eyes peeked open to narrow in his assumed direction, and she received a chuckle. *"Ah. That has caught your attention."*

Okay, so maybe having the chance to go off and harm those men for payback *did* sound enticing. "My answer is still no. I would rather go to heaven."

"Whoever your 'God' is, he has abandoned you. And, if you die, you will go to my realm, Tenebris, whether you want to or not. There will be no heaven for you."

"What?" she rasped, her eyes cracking open even further. "What do you mean, I won't go to heaven?"

"I am a god of death, and you currently lie within my mist. It is how I felt your presence here on the border of this canyon. If you die, I will take your soul to my afterworld."

"Don't you mean the afterlife, then?"

"There is no life in death, merely another world in which souls linger. Those that I have consumed."

"It's not fair," Lindi sobbed out, her shoulders shuddering. She brought her knees tighter to her chest, hating how that made the coarse rope around her ankles scratch at her flesh. "I did nothing to deserve this."

"Whether that is true or not, there are no other options."

"This is so cruel!"

Her faith was being tested, and she could feel herself... *breaking.* She felt abandoned in her hour of need, betrayed that it was the reason she was here to suffer. A woman, a virgin, a fucking sacrifice for someone who apparently wasn't listening or didn't care to.

But there was another here, offering her salvation, and she wanted to take it so badly. She didn't want to die. The fact that all the rules and restrictions she'd followed closely her entire life meant *nothing* was terrifying. She wouldn't be able to go to Eden, she wouldn't meet her maker. She couldn't even confront him for abandoning her on the edge of the... the Veil, as those men called it.

If she wasn't lying in this faceless being's mist, would she have been allowed to? *I don't want to go to the afterworld. I don't want to die.*

A light wind brushed around her, and it blew a mingle of pleasant scents from the forest, and the light tangle of a pungent odour, all through her. She wanted away from the warm dirt, the light, the fear that clutched her gut like a horrible sickness.

She wanted to remove the leaves and twigs from her hair, have a bath, and feel safe and secure once more.

She wanted to go home.

She wanted to die peacefully, and quickly, and go to the heaven she'd always imagined in her old-age death. Instead, she was in this long, lulling limbo where she was conscious enough to have a raspy conversation as she felt her life slowly sapping away. Only to lie here like a grand noble's meal to two terrible beasts like a pig on a platter – all she was missing was the apple in her mouth.

"Are you a bad god?" Lindi asked through her tears, tucking her face away from the setting sun – despite the temporary salvation it offered.

"I have never taken a life, nor have I ever resorted to trickery. All I do is ferry the souls who are already dead and protect thresholds. I am neither good nor bad, for I am nothing but a carer for the deceased."

"Then why do you need a wife?! Why would you want to bond yourself to a human?"

"I need servants, and I wish to breed them through you."

The honesty in his statement shocked her. Her eyes widened and her jaw dropped.

"Excuse me? You want to use me as a... as a baby maker?"

"Yes. I have no other means to do so. I will also need you to collect souls for me and act as my physical form in this world, as I am intangible to it. You would have many tasks."

The laugh that broke from her was spiteful. "And yet I'm still tied up. It's not that I don't have any other choice – you're just refusing to provide me with any other. If you really were a benevolent being, you would have saved me by now." She shrugged a single shoulder. "Why should I help you when you won't even free me?"

"My power is limited outside of my own realm. It is why I'm unable to reveal myself to you. I cannot even touch you, or those Daekura, in order to save you. All I can do is witness."

"How can your power be so limited you can't even save me?"

That sounded like a useless god to her.

"I gain power from each soul I eat, but I also waste it in cleansing them, among other tasks. I have, in fact, rather enervated abilities in comparison to other deities of my realm. I need servants who can obtain souls beyond my reach and ferry them to me. I need a mate for that. Someone who, hopefully, will empower me, as I empower them."

"And all I get out of it is living?" Lindi snorted a laugh once more. "I'd rather not. You sound like a pervert. Why not just take my soul by force if you need a woman so badly?"

Why is he giving me a choice? Lindi didn't understand why this conversation was even happening. Didn't most gods do what they wanted without care for humans and their free will?

"Although I very much could take your soul by force, I'd rather obtain my servants consensually. I have no desire to take what is not freely given, and I would like a trusted bond with my female. I am offering you power through me. To live forever, deathless. The ability to go back and take revenge for yourself."

"I'm not that petty." She actually was – she was just being stubborn.

However, the idea was becoming more enticing by the second, and he didn't seem *too* bad. At least he wasn't forcing her, and he seemed to be truthful – from what she could gather. And to live forever while having power did sound pretty generous.

She just couldn't shake this nagging uncertainty. *Perhaps if I was allowed to look upon him, I wouldn't feel so unsure.* What if he was ugly or monstrous? Lindi grimaced at the image of having sex with some unknown face that could even be more horrendous to look upon than the creatures still frothing at her feet.

"What about protecting others who will be brought to this cliff?"

Her lips tightened into a hard line. "How many women have been brought here before me?"

"Those that brought you here? I didn't see them, so I am unsure. They're all different, although they chant the same words, pleading for the cleanse to cease. It is not a cleanse but a plague of Daekura – and nothing they do will end it." Then, when Lindi didn't say anything but rather glared at his nothingness, he sighed. *"Dozens. I am unsure how many. Most are thrown from the cliff before I can speak with them. Only a handful are discarded on the edge here like you to bleed out or be eaten as an offering, abandoning you so they may run before the Daekura come."*

Her hands bunched behind her back as her annoyance deepened. Why did her heart *ache* for all those women more than it did for herself? Was it because she'd experienced their pain, their fear, their helplessness?

This horribleness needed to end.

I could go back and see my mother. Perhaps Weldir would let Lindi help her on their farm, so she wasn't alone, especially as Allira wouldn't be able to maintain it on her own. *Gosh. I'm so worried about her. Please be okay.*

"Make your choice."

"I don't know!" Lindi yelled, her chest heaving with anxious breaths.

Her heart was beating so hard in worry that it was causing her wound to throb unbearably, and she was being forced to make an unbelievable decision on the cusp of death. Her mind was foggy, her thoughts disjointed and lazy. She wasn't in the right state to make such a decision!

"Then so be it. I will try with another–"

"W-wait!" She wriggled, as if that would help her face him

when she had no idea where he was, and then fell towards her front. Her nose peeked over the edge of the Veil's canyon, and she suddenly wished she could shuffle away from it. "Please wait. Please don't go."

His sensual voice had been oddly comforting, and it had been nice to know she wasn't alone as she lay there.

"I told you – I am a witness. It is all I can do for you sacrifices until you die."

A droplet fell from her eye to run down her cheek, onto her nose, and down below. "So, you'll stay?"

His voice held such a gentleness when he said, *"I will remain with you until the end."*

She didn't know if she was just trying to hear kindness in him that didn't exist, or if he really was, but she needed that more than anything. She needed someone to care right now that she was in pain and scared, and who wouldn't abandon her just because she didn't give them what they wanted.

Why was it his choosing to stay that convinced her the most?

"What would it entail? What kind of power would I have? What restrictions? I-I can't make a decision without more understanding."

"Unfortunately, it doesn't appear you have any time left."

A cold blade of fear cut down her spine, and she gasped as she looked down. Right there, just beyond her foot with less than a palm's worth of space between her and them, stood both the dark creatures. They were pushing each other as they snapped their jaws at her, ready and waiting.

Her skin crawled in disgust, and Lindi screamed when one braved shoving their hand through the sun to try to grab one of her ankles. They missed when she rolled onto her side to get away from it.

"Okay! Okay! I will give you my soul. I will give you my life."

"I have your vow on that? That you will become my female, and you understand what is expected of you?"

"Yes!" she squealed, thankful the creatures didn't brave ducking their hands through the sun a second time – especially as one was now writhing on the ground in pain.

Its finger bones were showing, as if its very void-like flesh had melted from being in the light for less than two seconds.

"Then our deal has been struck."

As if to punctuate that, Lindi stopped squirming, and a strange orange flame was pulled from her chest. She gasped, despite the lack of pain or even feeling.

It was then, and only then, that she saw any part of him.

His hand, tipped with long nails or perhaps claws, reflected the light of the flame as if he were made of clear glass. It glistened and flickered like a reflection, and the same happened to his body when he brought the flame closer to a leanly muscular chest.

Lindi gawked at him, at what it revealed, while also offering very little.

Then she watched as he seemed to lift her flaming soul to what must be his mouth. He parted his full lips, revealing long canine fangs, and slid her soul inside. She could still see it, although it lit up half his face in the process and became murky. She couldn't tell by just the bottom of his face being lit up if he was handsome or not, but at least he was humanoid.

That was a relief!

Her soul dimmed as it moved to the back of his throat and then down it. The moment it hit his sternum, it and he disappeared.

She thought they may have been staring at each other, although she could no longer see him now that the reflection of flames was gone. She hated that she couldn't see him anymore.

Then... she waited.

And waited.

And nothing happened.

She kind of expected to feel cold, but she felt no different whatsoever. She still felt alive, despite continuing to bleed out. She was still dying, from what she could tell. She was still weak and powerless, unable to free herself.

She was still lying there, helpless.

When the silence went on for too long, and a gust of wind rolled a leaf against her cheek, she yelled, "Well... what are you waiting for?! Please, save me!"

"I told you, I cannot. I'm merely a witness in this world. I don't have the power to aid you."

The heat bled from her face. "What the fuck do you mean you can't?! I thought you would save me."

"I don't know anything about this bond, as I've never done it before. All I know is that we are connected."

Her jaw dropped, and her gaze dipped down to beyond her feet. She whimpered and wormed herself away from the frenzied creatures until her head nearly dangled off the edge of the cliff. Her long hair swayed and ruffled in the wind, as if a gust was tearing through the canyon and pushing the hanging locks with strength.

Oh shit.

She was still in the same damn predicament, and Lindi still had the same decision to make.

To fall or be eaten alive...

FIVE

A time unknown, but a day of bonding

It's finally... peaceful, Weldir thought, and his mist spread out from his body, as if with relief.

He could feel his very essence spreading out as tension bled from it, and he basked in the quiet that had him growing dazed and groggy.

How long he'd been awaiting the silence was far, *far* too long. His darkness felt empty, but not lonely. It was tranquil, and what it should have always been.

Restful.

For him, and for the souls he'd collected.

And it was all due to the female who slumbered amidst his shadows. Even she looked peaceful as she lay curled up in a ball, her knees to her chest, her hands tucked up near her full breasts, while her white, bloodied gown floated around her.

He drifted closer and hovered next to her in the nothingness – like they were metres below the ocean's surface. Neither breathed, and yet her chest continued a pleasant rhythm as if life still coursed through her.

It did not.

What lay before him was a white spectral form. This female, whatever her name was, was dead.

Yet when he opened his hand and called her soul to appear in it, what should have been a colourless white was a mixture of red and orange. He'd eaten it, but there was the evidence of life still present in it by its mesmerising colour.

I have never eaten the soul of someone living before.

He'd felt its startling heat; it was an odd sensation he'd never experienced before. Hot and cold were not things he'd ever been able to perceive – and still couldn't. Once he'd consumed it, the *heat* that came from it faded as if he'd grown used to it.

He missed it already, but would always remember the sensation when it had moved through him.

The souls of the dead felt like... *nothing*. Like body temperature, their warmth or coolness was inconceivable to him.

But, unlike theirs, hers brightened up the centre of his conscious realm, and it was comforting, the light staggering. He'd become fascinated by it in the time he'd waited for her to reach his side. Or rather, her spectral self to reach him.

Although he'd swallowed it, he could move her soul around his realm and its many offshoots – which he couldn't do freely with other souls. Like it was a part of him, it was free of the confines of Tenebris, his stomach.

Rather than placing it in that lonely, saddening place, he placed this female's soul elsewhere. Somewhere he would always be able to see it if he so chose.

She brightened up nothingness, and it was like his realm finally had a centre he could find.

He stroked his transparent thumb up its abdomen, between its breasts, before rubbing under its jaw while being careful of his claw.

The soul remained asleep, much like its owner, as he took in the hues of its life. How the orange and red swirled like lava before its citrine flames flickered all over its body. He ran the tips of his claws through the wisps of its long, curling hair, and he wondered if the pressure pulling on his face was a smile or some other expression.

He released her flame, and it hovered beside him, seeming to halo its owner. He flew closer to her through the lightness of his large, emptier self – his entire realm a part of him, as well as separate at the same time. He brought his face barely a hand's width from hers and peered at her features.

She's rather pretty.

He was thankful a pretty female had given him her soul,

although he didn't know what justified as beautiful to him. He'd yet to see a human female he deemed otherwise, but he was rather fond of a few of her features in particular.

The medium brown in her skin reminded him of his people – the Elvish. Although its base was much redder than the Elvish grey undertone he was used to, he liked this facet about her – the familiarity of it. It was a shame she lacked their pointed ears, a trait he also wore upon the sides of his head – from what he gathered of himself. No, instead hers were small and round.

He liked the brunette of her long hair, and the way its tips moved within his larger essence, floating as if in water. The loose curls were glossy and held just a hint of auburn when he brought the light of her flaming soul closer to shed further illumination.

Her nails were long and pink, her fingers nimble and delicate. Her feet were small and proportionate. Her legs were long, lithe, but there was a strength in them he could make out in her muscled calves and soft-appearing thighs.

Since she was his female, he'd gone diving beneath her dress to see what lay beneath it, finding she had a round and perky backside, wide hips, and a flat abdomen. He hadn't seen much else, as her gown was tighter around her breasts, although he'd seen their generous mounds from below.

Since her arms weren't visible through the long sleeves, he'd taken to inspecting her face. He'd done so a few times, waiting for her to open her eyes and once more reveal those deep, mesmerising pools of molten brown with flecks of honeyed amber. Although, when she'd been in the sun, he had seen peeks of a lighter yellow in them.

He liked her eyes the most.

They'd hinted at many emotions when she'd spoken to him, not all of which he was accustomed to, and he was curious about them. Then again, he was curious about humans in general.

Now that he had one to spend all his curiosity on, he was excited to do so.

Solidifying what he could of his physical self – which was very little – he used a tendril to poke her cheek, trying to stir her into waking. Her rounded nose scrunched before she drew her hands up and buried her face against them in disapproval. For a moment, her full, pouting lips disappeared as she thinned them in annoyance before they pushed forward and loosened.

She fell back asleep.

He pinched her cheek with his tendril and pulled it until he revealed even teeth.

Her long, dark eyelashes flung open, uncovering those molten pools of mixing browns, and she gasped.

Only to *fucking* scream.

Weldir shot back in surprise.

"That is wildly unpleasant," he snapped, his mist collecting against his transparent, intangible self in irritation. "I demand that you stop that noise immediately."

He'd had enough of screaming to last him eons.

Her scream ended when she slapped both her hands over her mouth, and her eyes widened beyond what he thought should be possible. She stared directly at him, only to squint and lean forward on a singular hand.

Since she floated in nothingness, he let her weight settle on an invisible platform so she could feel the normality of solidness below her. It was only enough to support the side of her backside and legs, and he gave her an additional one where she placed her palm. She didn't seem to notice the change in her weight's pressure.

Seeing she was looking upon him, rather intently, he raised his arms to the side. Pressure pulled on where his face was, but he was unsure of the expression, as he couldn't feel its intricate details.

He thought it may be a grin of some kind.

Although he'd had many souls look upon him, it had never been a pleasant conversation. They were spectral echoes of their past selves, their personalities alive enough to react to their current predicaments but not remember them. They spent every day resetting and forgetting, just to re-experience their terrifying first moment of realising they were dead – every day... forever.

He'd given up on befriending them when they'd only forgotten him and screamed upon him introducing himself.

This felt different.

This female was his mate, and her soul was alive. She should remember her life and the way it ended properly. He already liked that her gaze appeared curious rather than frightful, and like she was really... *seeing* him.

"What am I looking at?" she stated, instantly stealing the pleasantness he felt.

It deflated him enough that his mist spread out and lost the layer it'd created against her. Although he could control his mist, it required he spend much mana to do so. He felt as though he'd wasted it by her reaction.

The pressure in his face deepened, but with no true face to pull on, he merely felt it as a stroke across his consciousness.

Her lips pursed as her eyes trailed down in a zigzag pattern. "Where's the rest of you?"

Weldir knew what he must look like to her then. He could see himself perfectly, but also saw where his flesh was darker in some spots. Like inky stripes that moved across the body of his soul, they were the parts of him he perceived the most pressure. The rest just felt light, rather than dense. Outward, rather than surrounding a body. Everywhere, except for those spots.

His mist was thick, like it was supposed to surround his body like flesh, but he was too weak, broken, and ill-formed to do so.

That which was physical was like oil moving across water, and the rest of him would appear as nothing more than a puff of black mist. That oil moved across him constantly, and sometimes dispersed to reappear elsewhere, but it never covered the entirety of the surface.

He could control *where* his physical manifestation collected to, congealing where he needed it to, but he preferred to let it move over him like oil on water freely. Except just now – for her.

He chose to do it again. Not reveal himself, but his vexation.

Weldir grunted and drew his mist tighter so he could fold his arms to show his annoyance – an action he'd never had to do before. But he knew it was human nature to move in reaction to one's emotions.

He was hoping to experiment with this now that he had someone to talk to. To act like an interactive being rather than a floating consciousness.

What else had he seen of humans? Not much. What else did they do in reaction to irritation?

Ah yes. He tapped the fingers of his right hand against his biceps. "I had hoped you would see all of me," he stated thoughtfully.

And with the power he currently held, barely a tenth of his humanoid form would be visible to her. This was also what his souls saw of him.

Weldir had been hoping, as his mate, that she would truly see who and what he was. He could see the borders of his intangible physical form – although it was rather transparent even to himself – which was actually his soul.

To say he was disappointed was an understatement, but he was also aware it was entirely not her fault. Just the unfortunate state in which he found himself.

Had always found himself.

It brought on a deeper concern, and he gestured his hand out to her. He knew she didn't see it by the fact that her eyes never tracked to it. So, standing where he was with a few metres separating them, he removed his arm from his body as if the limb didn't need to be connected – which it did not. Weldir could remove and change his form as much as he pleased.

He'd chosen his form to emulate the Elvish people, his people, but also the demonic side of him that was his reason for being. Pointed ears, hair long enough to tangle around them and the horns over his head. An Elvish face and body – long, lithe limbs – with his fingers tipped with claws to mark the similarities he had to Daekura.

When he attempted to hold her wrist with *all* of him, it went right through her. Only when the oily streaks of his physical form brushed over her wrist did she gasp and yank her hand away. She frowned, as if she saw nothing.

I can only touch her with my physical self. Which he had very little of, and it would grow thinner with his dwindling power. The rest of him was made up of the cloud of his essence, his malformation. She couldn't even seem to perceive it when he made it halo her entire body, and that, too, upset him.

"You look like bits of chalk and smoke," the female stated.

Weldir tilted his head at that.

I don't know what chalk is. He always thought he looked like oil and mist, even if his physical manifestation wasn't glistening.

It was how he defined himself, but he'd always wondered what a different perspective would be like.

Then again, he'd never seen his own reflection, so it was difficult to ascertain any true identity.

He just hoped his face was well formed and handsome.

He was something, but not. Here, in this realm, he was everything, but outside of it he was non-existent except for his voice. He was a being made of two things at all times, everything and nothing, somewhere and nowhere, intangible but physical in soul, and those things constantly collided to be conflicting and confusing.

He'd always been that way, even when he'd been born.

"This is the afterworld?" she asked, looking up, then down, and then scanning her gaze around the never-ending horizon in every direction. Her full brown lips, with just a hint of pale pink more prominent on the lower one, pursed thoughtfully. "It's remarkably empty."

"Indeed it is," he answered, unbothered by her words when they were merely truth. "Although this is not the true afterworld. We are merely standing within my consciousness."

Her eyes darted back to him through the corner of her lids suspiciously before her features scrunched up.

"Gosh, I don't even know what that means!" She brought her knees up to her chest, crossed one foot over the other, and covered her face. "I can't believe I said yes to you. Why did I do that?"

"You cannot take it back," he stated firmly.

"I figured, but I feel like pressuring me to make that kind of decision under duress was unfair."

Weldir allowed a sigh to fill his voice. "There was no other way."

How dare she insinuate otherwise when he already stated the truth?

"I knooow," she whined as she dragged her hands down, revealing the way her face had furrowed into a scowl. "I'm just being honest. Or should I hold my tongue, oh vengeful god?"

A humming chuckle flittered from him at her snarkiness. *At least she doesn't appear afraid.*

"No, there is no need. Be as truthful as you like. I will not care either way."

Then Weldir's essence drew closer on its own so that his mist wasn't so spread out, and it stuck to him as he crossed his legs. He brought his consciousness to its most relaxed state and sat across from her.

"What is truly expected of me?" she asked, her wary gaze never softening.

"We already spoke of this," he answered. "You are to create servants for me. Offspring that can do my bidding."

She picked at the groove of skin on the side of her thumbnail while chewing the inside of her cheek. He didn't understand why her features fell and appeared almost crestfallen. "Okay... what else?"

Pressure pulled across his form at her question as thought rolled through him. "You are to collect the souls of humans that have been eaten by the Daekura, but have not attached themselves to their attackers, and bring them to my mist at the border of the place I found you. Since you appear to be similar to me now, I have an inclination that you will be able to see spirits far better than the average human. You will bring those untainted souls to me for consumption."

The rich hue of her face turned ashen. "Are you telling me ghosts are real?"

He chuckled at that. "*Ghosts* are what the men have been calling them, but I doubt they are what you humans would consider normal. They are dead souls trapped in a state of limbo due to being eaten. Since they have been touched by the Daekura, they do not pass on properly and are trapped on Earth. I have taken to calling them that title, as I'm sure others have. It is part of my requirement for being in this world that I give them a place to dwell peacefully."

Not that he'd been able to give them that.

No one, not even his mother, the goddess the Gilded Maiden, had foreseen just how difficult and energy depleting cleansing souls would be. What was supposed to empower him left him in the same state repeatedly, or worse. Tired, weak, and powerless.

He wanted to change that. He wanted to do better as a deity, and as a keeper of souls.

The only thing that had truly empowered him was... *her.*

Weldir had received a large burst of energy when their bond formed; her living, untainted soul was stronger than anything he'd ever eaten. A byproduct he hadn't been expecting, but one he was thankful for regardless. He knew each use of his power would wane that borrowed strength, but hopefully she would gift him more.

Daekura brought tainted souls through the mist. Sickly things with missing parts and streaked with poison, which he had to then fill and mend. Ghosts, on the other hand, had managed to not be fully consumed, and they remained anchored to something. They *should* give him more power.

He'd collected a few already – the other sacrifices that had been thrown from the cliffs mostly. But they always gave him a burst of energy to expend – which he promptly used to quieten his realm for his own benefit.

Or, rather, he'd place a sound dampener around the consciousness part of his realm to block the screaming from reaching his ears.

If it wasn't for this female and their newly formed bond giving him power, she'd be subjected to those same wails as they spoke. *At least I managed to save her from a harrowing first experience with me.* He doubted she would have been able to sit within it for any duration of time, as he had been for years.

"Okay..." She chewed her cheek faster. "What else?"

"For now, that is all. I have no other use for you."

Her head reared back, her feminine features sharpening. "I don't have to entertain you? H-have sex with you outside of making servants? How often will we have to do that, by the way?"

"Sex? No. That won't be necessary beyond the scope of what I require for servants, and even then, I am unsure how we will do such a thing."

Her dark brows drew together. "What do you mean?"

"I have never done this before. I don't know how I am to reproduce, or if it is even possible between us." He knew he had a special essence, a life-giving essence, but he was unsure how to implant it. Her jaw dropped at his statement, so he added, "We will experiment and learn together. We will create a servant and see what becomes of them before we make more."

Her lips shut, tightened once more, while her eyes squinted into a glare. "Are you telling me you have no idea what you're doing? I thought gods were all-powerful, all-knowing beings! I wouldn't have agreed to this if I knew you weren't as formidable as I thought."

"It's not my fault you made that assumption," he stated plainly, highlighting his disinterest in her words with his tone. "I already told you my power was limited."

"Yes! But I thought you would at least *know* what you're doing. I-I'm a virgin! I don't really want my bits used as an experiment for a god. I thought you'd at least know what you'd produce. What if they're... *weird?*" Then, under her breath, she muttered, "What if they're evil?"

"Evil is dictated by the moral boundaries of the individual," he stated emotionlessly. "It differs between each person and each being's culture. I am unsure what would be deemed as wrong to you."

She picked at the groove of her nail harder, and her expression flittered with all manner of emotions – most he couldn't decipher. All he knew was that he could perceive her heartbeat racing by the way her form pulsated in his darkness, and how her shoulders heaved.

It appears I have upset her further.

"I am not an evil being, so I doubt my offspring will be."

She eyed him but said nothing. She appeared unconvinced.

Weldir wondered what he could say to assuage her worries, but he had little idea. He wanted to be honest, as he had no reason to lie, but he truly had no idea what would happen.

I didn't even know if I would be able to bond with her. That, too, had been an experiment.

Eating her living soul could have killed her. Since she'd been dying already, he hadn't felt the need to explain that detail, but it had been a worry for him. Weldir had been uncertain, but he was thankful that his assumption had been correct.

He could bond with a living being.

I assume my offspring will take on the form of a deity. They could then have any humanoid form, but he was unsure what kind. His mother appeared Elvish other than the gold of her hair, her magical markings, and her constant tears.

His fathers – plural, as it could have been any god – were all humanoid in some form. However, one had the lower half of a bear, his top half was an Elf, and he had antlers. Another looked like a being made up entirely of flora. Another had been made of water, another of lava.

Each male was an attentive partner to the Gilded Maiden, and all of them were her lovers during his conception. Any one of them could have been his paternal father.

And Weldir was nothing like any of them, including his mother.

He only assumed he would make something humanoid in some way due to the evidence of his ancestry. Perhaps they would even look human considering their potential mother was a mortal being given the abilities of...

What is she now?

Weldir's gaze drifted down her spectral form. She wasn't a Ghost, but she wasn't truly alive anymore, either.

His form wavered with unease. *What if she is intangible on Earth?* Then again, he didn't care if she didn't have a physical body, so long as she was able to collect souls and give birth. And considering part of her soul was still intact, he saw no reason why it shouldn't be possible.

"If we are unable to produce offspring, your task will only be to collect souls."

She tilted her head at that. "You don't plan to get rid of me if I can't?"

"No. I still need a servant, and someone who can freely roam Earth."

He didn't care what form they took for that role. He just couldn't leave his mists without fully consuming a soul until it was entirely destroyed, borrowing its immense power for a few fleeting moments. He'd rather not do that, as each time swept him into a slumber afterwards that he struggled to push back.

A deep sleep to conserve energy and slowly replenish it.

"But I have free will? I can go wherever I like, do whatever I like, so long as I collect souls?"

"Precisely."

Her expression mildly softened with relief. "A-and I can use your power however I like?"

He gave a hum of thought. "Yes, and no. I ask that you use it sparingly. If you drain me too deeply, I will sleep to recover what has been lost, and in that time, I will be unreachable. If you die, you will return to me – *that* I have already discovered. I can also feel that I can call you to my realm. I give you my apology that I did not do so sooner to spare you of pain."

Once he came back to his realm after watching her end as she'd originally asked of him, he'd been able to sense he could have brought her along with him. He could have prevented her from needing to wriggle her way off the cliff's edge to have a much less frightening death than being eaten.

He felt rather bad about that, but there was nothing he could do to change it now.

I know I can send her back to Earth in the same way I can go there – via his mist in the Veil.

"What I mean is," she started, tipping her head down while looking at him through her long, curling lashes, "you don't care *how* I use it?"

"No. I don't care what you do with it, so long as you don't deplete me of it entirely. Your tasks are designed to empower me." He lightened his tone and gave it mirth as he said, "Work hard enough, and you can have more. If you have a physical form–"

"What do you mean, *if* I have a physical form?"

This was the first time he'd ever had someone speak over the top of him, and his form wavered in disapproval. His mist spread out only to shut in tight around him, rumbling with what he could only consider a growl.

"Currently you are intangible, we will see if that changes when you go to Earth."

"I'm intangible?" She lifted her arms to inspect them, frowning at the solidity of her form. Then, as if noticing something new, she brought the back of her wrist closer to her face. "Oh wow. I'm a little see-through. Are you saying I'm similar to a Ghost?"

"Yes. Currently you are intangible and untouchable to the physical world. Much like all the spectral beings in my world, I house your soul."

She patted at her breasts, searching for the flame currently floating beside him.

"But what if I want to be solid?" she asked, before her features fell. "How am I to help people if I can't touch anything?"

It sounded as though she wished to use his power to make herself some kind of saviour. He found that commendable, although utterly pointless to the grand scheme of his desires. But if it made her compliant, he didn't care what she did.

If she wished to make herself some kind of hero to her fellow humans, then so be it.

"Like I was saying before you interrupted me," he stated with stern depth, "if you have a physical form, you should be able to collect materials with which I can make you magical items. If so, this will allow us to give you power that isn't borrowed from me. This is what I hope for, that you will have a physical form."

"But Ghosts can't turn solid, can they? What am I then?" Her big, curious eyes then turned large as her lips parted. "Wait! Am I *dead*?"

"Yes, and no." When she gave him a glower, another chuckle slipped from his consciousness. "From what I can tell, you are like me. Alive but dead. Here nor there. Something but nothing. You are on the cusp of both, a limbo of life and death. A... *Phantom*."

Yes, that's what he would call her abilities. She was a human turned Phantom.

He thought it was fitting.

Her eyes slitted in his direction. "Did you just make that word up?"

"Absolutely." His humour-filled tone left no room for her to argue with him or make a statement regarding it.

He was a god; he could make up shit if he wanted to.

"Okay, whatever," she grumbled, lifting a hand to shove it through her long, floating locks of hair. "Is there anything else I should know? Any other rules or restrictions?"

For a short moment, silence befell them as he thought. He truly didn't need anything else from her.

Except one thing. "You are not to fornicate with your own kind. I am unsure how that will affect my own offspring."

He didn't wish for her to make mortal servants by accident

via any potential left behind. Although he knew he had essence that could create life, if there was a residual matter left behind by *living* beings, it could have an impact on what they created.

Her knees knocked together when she snapped her thighs closed tightly. "Excuse me? A-are you insinuating that I would... *betray* you? I would never do such a thing!"

"Betray?" His mist spread out in confusion. "Why would this be betrayal of any kind? I wouldn't care if it didn't have a potential to impact one of your reasons for becoming my mate. If we are unable to produce offspring, then I won't care if you do."

She opened her mouth to say something but promptly shut it. Then she looked down, but he didn't miss the way liquid built in the waterline of her eyes. She bit her bottom lip and said nothing as she looked down at her lap.

"I have upset you. How?"

"Where I'm from, most humans are monogamous. I just thought... I don't know. I thought you'd care more. Wouldn't that be lonely for you?"

"No. Polyamory is normal for me. I don't know who my paternal father is, only that I have many in spirit. There is harmony and unity, which is all that matters, each person having a task to perform to satisfy my mother. She gifts them much affection in return. They also had other females they could attend to."

Well, much of that was true... before his birthing.

His birthing had a great impact on the rest of the Elvish deities. Perhaps one day he could share those intricate details with her, so she understood better. Now was not the time.

"I still won't," she grumbled. "So, that's not something you will ever have to worry about. I always planned to devote myself to my husband fully."

So long as she doesn't affect our offspring, then I have nothing to worry about. But he could see arguing with her on the matter was pointless, as he really, truly, wouldn't have cared if she had many lovers.

Oh well, her sentiment was cute and much needed in the successful production of his servants.

"There is little else for us to discuss," Weldir stated, unfurling his mist and releasing his seated position. "We will begin your duties now."

The female shuffled away from him, and off the little podium of mana he'd given her. She squealed when she fell and then began to float away.

"W-wait! I'm not ready! I don't want to make any babies yet!" she shouted, her arms cartwheeling as she tried to right herself. "Oh gosh. What's happening?"

He followed her so they could remain facing each other, then gave her another podium to support her. Although they were in another direction now, there was no up or down, no left or right in his realm. In the scheme of things, they could be upside down and neither one of them would know it.

Once she was on the solid surface, her fingers curled around its invisible edges with the back of her knuckles straining as if worried she would begin floating and spin off again.

"Although you promised that you would complete your task without hesitancy," he started, annoyed that she'd rejected it straight away, "I'm also not ready. There is much for us to discover first. The unity of our bond is more important. We must learn of your new abilities together, and then we can try."

"So I'll have time?" she asked, her lips trembling like they didn't know what expression they wanted to pull into. "I know I said I would, but I just met you and I'm really nervous. I hadn't expected to be married and making kids right after... *dying*. I just need a little time to adjust to everything."

"You will have time."

How much, he was uncertain.

The trembling in her lips ceased when she bit down on the bottom one. "C-can I go back to my home?"

He didn't have the heart to tell her that her home would no longer exist to her once her tasks began. "Temporarily, while we learn what you can do through me. I also promised you may seek revenge, if you so choose it."

He needed to know the extent of what she could do while wielding his magic, his power. That would allow him to understand how much he could rely on her as a physical extension of himself on Earth. If she could do more than collect souls, then she would be an invaluable tool for him.

He needed to learn the depth of their bond, and what it meant for him to have a female of his own.

A little human, who was a rather pretty thing, and trapped in his hold.

SIX

January 30th, 1689

Lindi would never forget the horrifying first days after she bonded with Weldir, the faceless god shrouded in mist. How they continued to haunt her years later, flickering behind her eyelids like some waking nightmare.

The treacherous hike across a desolate desert, where the heat of the sun had baked her underneath her blood-stained, dirtied nightgown. How the nights had grown so cold from the mid-autumn breeze that her feet were left numb, and her fingers ached against the chill. The way one shoe had blistered the back of her right foot. While the other foot, bare and exposed, had become torn from the dirt and rocks, causing her to limp forward with each step until she lost the other shoe, and that foot had joined in to radiate agony like it was creeping up her leg bones.

How Daekura, what *he* called them, had hunted a defenceless Lindi.

She and Weldir had quickly learned he could bring her soul to wherever he pleased within his mist bordering the Veil on Earth.

Her heart squeezed in anxiety at remembering how each time she'd died and returned to the 'safety' of his realm, she had to restart her journey.

To die. Only to be brought back to full health, as if it was nothing but a horrible nightmare flickering behind her closed eyelids. But each time she knew it was, when she floated in haunting darkness and then was pushed back to light – right next to the canyon where her life had turned to hell.

Where she'd fled from rabid, mindless horrors by willingly slipping off the edge and screaming the entire fall to her death.

Perhaps it was because she was human, but learning to control her newfound ability to turn incorporeal hadn't been second nature to her. She hadn't even known she could will herself to change. It was only after the third time she died, eaten by the very monsters she'd sought to escape, that she began using it as an evasive tool.

Then again, the mind didn't think rationally when one was being chased by predators – and becoming an entirely new being was hard to conceptualise.

Lindi was human. She doubted she'd ever let go of that sentiment, despite the fact that she was now something other. She'd known then, as much as she did now, that she needed to swiftly adapt to the adversity of her new life – one she had *stupidly* chosen.

When she first returned to Earth, Weldir's theory that she would have a physical form was immediately proven right – as that was the form she'd been given. It'd taken trial and error to figure out how to change to incorporeal at will – and it was pure will. The change was as easy as taking her next breath, so long as she remembered to *actually* do it.

Once she remembered this newfound ability, crossing the desert had been easy. There had been no hunger to contend with, even when she was physical. The heat had left her, as had the chill, both lost to the nothingness of her intangible body. The sun didn't scald her, didn't blister her face, and sweat stopped soaking her skin and dirtied dress.

The monsters stopped chasing the only prey they could smell within hundreds of kilometres when there was nothing to scent.

There was freedom in that security, that safety. To no longer exist except for her own sense of self.

A sense of self she feared losing, but had already been turning away from.

Six years had passed since then, and she could feel her mind, her heart, her very *will* changing. Then again, never in her imaginings did she think she'd ever witness the things she had or do the impossible things she'd done.

Or take the vile actions she had.

It feels like forever ago, she thought, as she looked down into the hot wine she drank from. She held the wooden mug with both hands, letting its blissful heat tingle through her fingertips and palms, as she inspected her own features in the reflection of the yellowy liquid.

It was her face; it hadn't aged a day. Yet the solemn expression that stared back felt out of place – as it always did.

She missed the carefree, high-spirited, sheltered girl she'd been. Or, rather, she missed the life that had gifted such a blissfully naïve expression, and the people who had warmed her eyes and lifted the corners of her lips.

Lindi missed her home.

I think I'll always miss them. Her parents, Allira and Nico, had been good, humble people. They hadn't deserved to meet their ends the way they did.

She hadn't deserved any of this, either.

Because after that long and arduous *hovering* walk across the plains and then forests of Austrális, there had been nothing to return to except more pain.

What had taken three days on horseback had taken Lindi *days* to cross, and it hadn't been in the right direction. After reaching civilisation, she'd then had to trek east towards Rivenspire. She'd spent most of it in the back of a horse-pulled cart with her legs dangling off the edge, thankful to rest her tired mind more than her feet.

It had taken everything within her heart for Lindi to not confess the truth about Daekura, worried her companions would deem her insane. Not everyone believed in these devils, and she understood that more people would have to see them before they'd stop being deemed as silly stories to frighten children.

Even in her walks across the desert, she'd only met four – two of which had come a long way to find her by tracking her scent. One even looked... similar to the first one that had been at the cliff that fateful day she'd married a god.

She couldn't believe how wrong she'd been, and how quickly she'd dismissed the rumours to be falsehoods.

Before Weldir had sent her back to Earth from his realm,

Tenebris, he'd told her the truth. There was a portal connected to another world, some kind of Elvish world – not that she knew what an Elf was – and the Daekura were venturing through it. He, apparently, couldn't stop them – although his tone had hinted that may not be entirely true.

He was a fickle god when it came to his answers about himself or the Elvish, or even the Daekura.

Regardless... more were coming.

Every day, a handful of those creepy, snarling devils emerged from that portal, ready and hungry for blood. Weldir believed that human blood was particularly delicious to them due to how they reacted to the Elvish in the past. Before long, the rare one or two that managed to pass over the desert, likely hiding in the shadows of large boulders, canyons, or rocky mountains, would increase.

Soon, no one would be able to deny their existence.

After contending with them, she knew no one was safe. Not her old village of simple farms, whose inhabitants were putting up meagre fortifications, and not the townspeople erecting walls metres tall. Especially not those who were refusing to erect any at all.

Some Daekura were large, some weren't, but they would apparently grow in size, in formidable power, with each creature they consumed. She even saw one trying to fucking *fly*, although it didn't get far with its small, underdeveloped wings.

And Lindi's skin crawled as she'd been carted through the night, with her carriage companions none the wiser that those monsters could be lurking in the shadows. They likely weren't, as they were struggling to cross the desert, but Weldir had informed her that the forest surrounding the canyon was... *growing.*

Some of the Daekura were, apparently, aiding it. Eating away at the desert to offer a path of shade and life for bloodshed.

A few rather notorious beings were also growing the Veil, breaking off the canyon wall little by little – although Weldir was unclear as to how that was possible. It was as if the canyon was alive, consuming the very trees the Daekura were growing, only for those trees to bring more life to the very bottom of the cliff.

She wished he had elaborated more, but he'd said she would

learn more as time passed.

But enough time had passed for her. Enough to reveal that this new life felt rather empty.

She brought the mug of wine to her lips now that it'd cooled, blew on it, and took a sip of its sour sweetness. She tasted it, but it was like ash going down her throat as she lingered on the past six years and what she'd been greeted with when she finally returned home.

The house had felt foreign after what had transpired there, and her mother had been absent. The villagers had been relieved to find that Lindiwe Bernadi was still alive, but their faces had been strained at the same time.

Because what had been her next destination after such a long journey wasn't the loving embrace of her mother's arms, but the desolate seat next to a bed. Allira had never awoken to discover that her daughter was alive and had returned. No, she remained comatose, every day slipping further and further away, her pulse slowing and softening with each passing hour.

Considering her mother's already dwindling health and her weak heart before that horrible night her family had been torn apart, everyone believed that she just couldn't take it. Her heart was too hurt, physically and emotionally, to survive without Lindi and her beloved husband.

Lindi had been both blessed and cursed with just two days of visiting her mother before she'd passed. To be there in support as she'd held her fragile hand in her final days of life, hoping her presence was soothing even if it destroyed her. Although she'd been thankful to be given the opportunity to say goodbye to a living, breathing person, to feel the warmth of a final one-sided hug, it shouldn't have been necessary.

None of this was.

After learning the truth from Weldir, she knew these devils weren't an act of God but just *were*, and no number of human sacrifices were going to save humankind. Lindi hadn't needed to be stolen. She shouldn't have been presented with a choice between dying forever or trapping her soul to a faceless being.

I really should stop calling them devils, though.

Humans had already begun giving them a name – those that were deemed insane by others. The kind of people who made mothers bring their children closer, as they were screamed at about the ending of time, the fall of Earth, and how the sins of humans had brought this upon them. They shouted with panicked, crazed, and manic eyes about the *Demons* that were coming to destroy them and how they must repent – must stay in the Almighty's heavenly light.

To fear the night. To save their children before it was too late.

It was oddly humorous how those deemed insane were completely and utterly correct.

But Lindi knew that was how she'd be perceived if she started spouting the truth, so she kept her lips firmly shut.

She never told a soul about what she'd experienced, seen, or what had happened to her as they buried her mother. She gave her home to the leader of the village, told them she didn't care what they did with it, and left without so much as an explanation.

Instead, she began to hunt.

Her heart had been so sickly, so broken, dripping with agony in every single drop of blood it pumped into her veins, that she swore she'd stop other women from experiencing what she had. Vengeance led her path.

And as much as it was against the teachings of the religion she'd devoted herself to her entire life, she let hate fuel her. She let it fester into a sore wound, one that she scratched at until it was irritated and impossible to ignore no matter how much she, at times, tried to soothe it.

For years she searched until her path had taken her straight to the easiest man to pick from a crowd.

A part of her was thankful that the first of the three men she found, those who had *ruined* her life, was the one who had the biggest impact. The one who, had he not rammed a sword through her father's gut, may have allowed Lindi to return to her loving parents and find them both alive. They could have reunited; she could have spared them of their grief upon her return.

She could have had a semblance of normality within the overshadowing strangeness her life had turned into as Weldir's *pet*.

Not a single part of her felt regret when she finally gained the courage, the very will, to do to him as he had done to Nico. Sure, it'd taken her many days of following him to finally enact the first stage of her revenge, needing to shed away the guilt nipping at her, as well as the fear that the Almighty Father would strike her down for going against his teachings.

She had to remind herself that she was out of his reach and trapped by another, now the wife of a deity who didn't even belong in this world.

So, if her soul was already tainted, traded, and belonged to someone else, it meant her freewill was utterly hers. More so than any other human walking this world. Weldir truly didn't care. He had bestowed no rules or restrictions, despite admitting that *he* was unable to enact such violence.

She was free from his restrictions. She was his freedom now regarding that, a loophole he'd found, and she just hoped he never planned to abuse that through their bond.

She only wanted to end life because she deemed it justice, not because of the whims of a fickle and absent god.

And Lindi found it very justifiable to go around murdering those who left women at the edge of an unholy cliff. She found solace in that rage, found peace in that bloodshed. Giving back the power to the innocent and weak by saving them before they could be taken.

No amount of fury could take back the glory of her innocence, but becoming a waking hell had given her the sharpest teeth.

Sal being her first fatality – she refused to call him a victim – had been a blessing on her subconscious. His strange scars and ugly mannerisms had made him the easiest to track – as she'd been able to garner information regarding his last known whereabouts from his description. She'd offered him no chance to beg or plead. Oh, but did she *haunt* him when he first discovered her in his room at a tavern.

The corners of her lips curled upwards in dark humour as she remembered turning incorporeal to float above his bed and give him the fright of his life. When she finally decided she *would* take his life, she followed him and stuck to the shadows, making sure only he could see her, and disappeared before his companions could.

She wanted him to look deranged to Gregory and Mathews.

To whine and whimper about the woman he'd callously discarded in the middle of fucking nowhere as a sacrificial lamb. Then, when the time felt just right, when she'd made him suffer even just a fraction of the horror she had, she sliced his throat open without a single word.

That shouldn't have felt as satisfying as it did. The blood that had spilled upon her shouldn't have felt so warm and inviting, but finally getting back at him for taking away her entire life, her parents' lives, felt righteous.

She'd followed Gregory and Mathews until they revealed the deeper occult, as she'd suspected these despicable men weren't the only ones doing this. She'd been right. Deranged men and women would gather in secret to discuss what they were doing and babble on about the insanity that they believed. On top of that, they discussed the best women to steal – those who were exposed, pure, and easy to take.

And once she'd picked them off one by one, she followed the leader to another town and repeated the very same thing.

In just a few years, she'd managed to cull their numbers down, visiting different towns, villages, or cities until there was only one left to follow. But there were hundreds more she needed to pick off, and the task seemed endless.

Which was perfectly fine, as she had an infinite amount of time to do as she pleased.

As she did this, she practised with her new magical abilities every chance she had – although as sparingly as possible to ensure she didn't drain Weldir completely, like she'd promised.

Then again, she had a feeling he was using much of it himself.

She'd only been returned to his mist a handful of times since their deal, and it was for an entirely selfish reason on his behalf. Despite knowing that she would have to restart at the centre of Austrális, Weldir snatched her from her location when she'd encountered her very first Ghost.

He made her turn incorporeal and hold its arm, so he could teleport them to his realm. She'd hated the way it'd screamed in terror at her, how it'd squirmed as it tried to rip her hold from it. She'd felt *awful* that she'd frightened it so deeply.

She'd hated it more that there was nothing else she could do but be obedient.

Lindi had just been thankful it turned into a white flame the moment she was encompassed by Weldir's shroud, as if the terrified Ghost no longer existed. It hadn't been hot – the flames hadn't scalded her – but she'd immediately released it for Weldir to take.

When she'd expressed her displeasure towards both the act and that she would be forced to start over her journey, he'd offered her a solution.

Thankfully she'd had a ceramic vial hidden away in her satchel that had been filled with a salve to protect any wounds she gained in her travels. In her Phantom form, she was able to make it tangible to him. He'd emptied its contents and altered the vessel with his magic so it could draw in spirits of the deceased. Then she could ferry them to his mist of her own volition as an offering to him.

Although she was grateful for his creation, she didn't want to.

She refused to return to the Veil when there were more occultists she needed to eradicate. To the very place her life had ended and had been taken from her.

Weldir could wait.

She hoped he waited until the end of time.

Lindi had no desire to be a god's plaything. She didn't want to have to spread her legs for him, or give birth to his children, or really anything that she'd promised.

She would, when the time eventually came, but she just hoped it never did. She hoped he never woke up this time.

It had been over two years since she'd last heard from him, and she did, selfishly, waste a little more magic every day than she should in hopes of keeping him asleep. She used just enough so that she stayed empowered but left him weak enough where he couldn't mould her to his whims.

She wanted to keep this freedom.

She also didn't want to hear him whispering in her ear, reminding her of the task he bestowed upon her. That she must collect souls in her travels in order to empower him when she did return. He watched when he wanted to, and she often thought she could feel his gaze by the hairs rising on the back of her neck

– a completely irrational and paranoid reaction, considering his current slumber.

Even now she felt it, more than usual, and she reached into the hood of her brown cow-hide cloak and rubbed at her nape. A shudder tore down her spine. She brushed some of her bangs from her forehead to clear her vision, before patting down the grey tunic she wore and playing with the ties around her waist. Her burgundy breeches were a little tighter than she'd like them across her backside, but they were designed for men that lacked a woman's round arse.

She'd opted for something looser rather than something that stretched over her generous backside, so the legs and waistband were baggy to compensate.

Although it was proper for a woman to wear a dress, many choosing to wear a bone corset, Lindi had forgone such attire. She needed the comfort of men's apparel, even if she wished to snuff the life from them.

She crossed her boot-clad feet, tucked them under the bench she sat upon, and laid her forearms across the long bar counter.

Grayton Town was simple and small enough that they hadn't heard anything about the Demon rumours. They hadn't begun erecting walls, and a small part of Lindi felt guilt regarding that. She wanted to inform them that they should begin protecting themselves just in case, but she also didn't want to be thrown into their loony cells.

She could turn intangible and disappear, but she didn't want that headache.

She just... didn't see it working out in her favour, especially when her current mission required that she walk through Grayton freely.

Enough so that she could sit in this well-maintained, newly built, large tavern. The Blackbutt gum-tree timber used to build it gave it a cream-grey finish, and much of the same material was used to build the tables that furnished it. Pushed up against the walls, all the seating areas were away from the centre of the long building to allow people to carouse and dance in the middle.

A caged counter blocked occupants from freely taking from the barrels of wine, mead, and ale, with a dim staircase leading to the guest rooms on the two upper levels.

The decorations were minor except for a grand – although plain – fireplace, a brass chandelier with dozens of lit candles, and some paintings of beautiful landscapes. Gridded glass windows allowed subtle daylight to leak in, and could be opened to let a small breeze in throughout the day to help with the stench of body odour, tobacco, and booze.

Since it was late summer, the windows did little more than allow the hot night air to blow out the stuffiness and give onlookers from outside a beacon to follow to merriment.

As much as she would have liked to ask for a pleasant meal just for the taste, as hunger was non-existent for a Phantom, her funds were exceptionally small – despite having pilfered the pockets of all her fatalities. No, this mug of cooling wine would have to do to satisfy her tastebuds. It also ensured she didn't look out of place. With her cloak hiding that she was a woman, she eyed those drinking casually before settling on a well-dressed, unassuming group.

Four men sat in the corner of the tavern, using its busyness and loudness as a shield while they likely discussed despicable schemes. She couldn't overhear their conversation, but she knew them to be of the occult. Their gazes often slipped to a lone older gentleman wearing travelling gear and a wedding ring on his left finger.

Either the father or an acquaintance of their next victim.

Their vile hands would never reach her. At least, not while Lindi was around.

When the lone man stood to leave, the four occultists were swift to exit behind him, with enough distance between them to appear as though they weren't following him. Lindi did the same to her next fatalities. Often using a combination of her Phantom abilities to hide in the shadows, she also let a puff of black mist scatter from her very skin to further shield her.

She pushed darkness beyond her cloak, wasting Weldir's magic with a deceptive reason should he ever ask why.

Since the lone stranger stumbled towards his home on the outskirts of town, she followed the occultists at a meandering pace.

Lindi knew they'd likely steal their next victim another night, but she wished to move on from the town shortly. The occultists were growing wary because of their disappearing acquaintances, who never returned from their adventures.

They had received information that they were being picked off and had begun acting more rashly than before. They didn't know why, most assuming it was Demons reaching towns or bandits. Lindi needed to be faster if she wanted to catch them all – especially when their targets were infrequent and sparse, making it harder for her to track them.

In hindsight, there actually weren't that many men, and she'd already travelled great distances across Austrális. She'd started at Rivenspire, which was far east, then headed due west, and had been circling back ever since. She'd never seen the ocean before her journey, but she'd been all along the coasts of Austrális. She'd like to settle in a town with a beach for a few years and finally feel as though she could take a breath, but that was only something she'd reward herself with if the oppressing evil of the occultists was fully vanquished.

She wished their disappearances were an act of their 'Almighty God' smiting them for their wickedness.

Alas, no, it was just a little human woman.

One that was steadily sneaking up on her fatalities with every quiet, calculating skulk.

The cold blue of the waning moon shone above the intermittent orange glow of the streetlamps against the cobblestones. Avoiding the light as much as possible, Lindi kept to the shadows so her shrouding mist didn't look too out of place. Making sure the ridges of her boots didn't knock against tiny rocks or shift in the quiet, Lindi ignored the two-storey buildings, their small gardens, and their fences, keeping her gaze on the enemy.

The waft of pleasant, home-cooked meals wrapped around her mind, stirring just the mildest nostalgia that never truly faded. She refused to focus on it, not as she neared ever closer.

Once these occultists were far enough from the centre of the town and there were no other pedestrians in the streets, Lindi struck.

Unable to wield Weldir's magic while she was intangible, she turned solid and stepped onto the path behind them. She flung her right arm forward, and a black tentacle of chalky mist and sand shot from between the cracks in the cobblestone. It wrapped around the rearmost occultist's neck, tight enough to stifle his choke, and she pulled her clenching fist to her side to yank him back.

Before any of them could notice his disappearance, she threw him into the wall of a building down an alleyway and walked past it. With his back against the wall, his feet a metre from the ground, his legs kicked and squirmed as the magic strangled the life from him. He clawed at his own neck to free himself, but nothing would save him – just like the bindings she'd once been incapable of escaping.

As she launched her left hand forward to conjure another black tentacle, one of the men noticed her in his periphery. He gasped and stepped to the side as if he'd seen it coming – although it had merely been a coincidence. She figured he was just surprised there was anyone on their path, since they likely wanted their stalking to be shrouded in secrecy.

She was a witness, especially as they'd come upon the lone gentleman's home, and they'd slowed to a crawl. If anyone went missing, and the townsfolk asked for information, she was an unfortunate loose end for them.

One of them drew a dagger while he indicated with the point of his crooked nose at Lindi. They all turned to her.

"You picked a bad night to walk these streets," another one of them stated – not that she cared in the least.

Each of them had different features, ranging from blonde to brunette, bronze to pale, tall to short. Whether they were handsome or ugly was beneath her notice, as Lindi didn't care when she was about to end their breaths.

Releasing the magic tentacle from earlier, the man likely dead now, she threw her right arm forward. It reappeared near her feet and shot forward to wrap around the head of the occultist on the far right. Not quite where she wanted to grab, but she yanked him anyway so he would head-butt the ground.

At the same time, drawing her own dagger of darkness, Lindi sprinted forward. The hood of her cloak slipped back to rest around her shoulders, allowing her long brown locks to flip behind her. With the shroud of a heavy black mist spreading out from her to hide what was about to happen from the eyes of possible onlookers, she held her dagger firm. She lunged the tip forward at the middle man's throat and narrowly missed him when he stepped back in surprise.

The man on the left swiped his blade sideways through the air, and Lindi lifted her forearm to create a magical barrier made of glittering black sand. The blade slammed against it, bending his wrist back, and he let out a pained grunt. Taking the advantage presented while he was distracted, Lindi shoved her dagger hilt deep into the left man's gut.

He spit out a rasp of pained shock, and she let go of the hilt so she could duck when the middle man's fist rushed through the air. Her magical dagger trickled sand as it lost its solidness now that she was no longer holding it, and it glittered to the ground before disappearing completely.

Using her left hand, while still crouched, she created another barrier and swiped it to the side to smash against his ankles. With a quiet yell, he fell to his side and his body thudded hard against the ground, causing her to wince at the noise she couldn't hide with her mist. Extending her right hand, she conjured a shadowy tentacle to wrap around his body and slap across his mouth to quieten any of his yells as she ignored him for the time being.

With him trapped against the ground, there was little he could do.

The man who'd escaped her initial stabbing attempt skulked around, brandishing his knife while calculating her movements to strike. She sprung to her feet, grabbed his fist so it was tight around his blade's hilt, and shoved it upwards. Proving just how much strength and skill she'd acquired in the last few years, she overpowered him and lodged his blade into his own throat. His entire body stiffened. In a matter of seconds, with blood pooling around the blade and rapidly escaping him, his knees buckled inwards before he dropped to the ground.

Devoid of emotion at the loss of this disgusting human's life, she didn't spare him a second glance as she moved her cold gaze elsewhere. She was barely even huffing, as if the exertion from such swift movements was insignificant.

Lindi turned to the final man, and she took in the fear in his eyes. A light, hot gust of wind blew around her form, lifting her hair and cloak to the left as she took a step closer. He shook his head, screaming against the tentacle pressing down upon his lips, and wriggled in his confinements – like how she'd wriggled to the edge of the Veil to fall off it... *willingly.*

He was *frightened.* How dare he be! How many victims had begged and pleaded while they were dragged across the wasteland of the desert? How many women had given him that very wide-eyed, tearful stare as they were pushed off a cliff or gutted to become *Demon* food – as the occultists called them.

He wanted mercy from her, when he would have never given it.

So Lindi straddled his torso, held his gaze with a determined fierceness, and made another magical blade form.

He managed to get the tentacle off his lips so he could spit just one word: "Witch!"

Lindi stabbed her blade into his ruined heart, halting any other foul word that could come from him. Then she proceeded to slam it down multiple times until she left a gaping hole in his chest. She twisted it and let a deranged grin lift into her lips, disappointed that he was so dead he could no longer witness its beauty.

Then, once she was done meting out justice, she hopped off him.

Her heart felt both lighter and heavier. The satisfaction of their deaths twirled with the necessity of having to kill them in the first place.

"Their actions caused your demise," she muttered as a reminder, before she cut his coin purse from his belt. She did the same to the two other dead men nearby.

She didn't savour their deaths. Instead, she looked around at the empty street. *I have to move quickly in case someone comes.*

The black mist would only make the area feel haunted, but a drunken fool might wander through it, thinking the booze was playing tricks on his eyes.

Using three thick tentacles, she wrapped them around their legs or arms and took each man to the alley where the first lay dead. She hid their corpses and evaporated the mist except for in the narrow space. Then she used magic she wasn't particularly fond of.

Making sure there was nothing but stone around them, Lindi

set their bodies alight with a black fire. She didn't need much, just a candlestick's size flame, but it quickly spread out to devour them. No smoke was produced, as if the very fire ate the air around it, and it left nothing in its wake.

No skin, no bones, and even the stone beneath them began to melt into liquid. Much like her barriers, she used black sand to snuff out the fire before it could spread across the cobblestones and set the houses next to the alley alight. If that happened, the fire would spread so quickly that she'd struggle to put it out and it would feed on the entire town.

She'd already witnessed its devastation before and considered it the evilest ability she had in Weldir's arsenal.

She also refused to do it on a living person, as they could spread it. Lindi feared... she'd be unable to control it before she set fire to the entire world. A wildfire that no water could put out.

I'm thankful he is unable to use such magic on Earth, she thought with an emptiness as she looked at the melted stone – the only evidence that she or the occultists had been there.

Because he lacked a physical form on Earth, Weldir's magic was incapable of being tangible there. Not even Lindi could wield it in her incorporeal form, and had to be human and solid to do so.

"I've told you doing that destroys their souls," Weldir's deep and unfairly husky voice whispered in her ear.

No. It wasn't her ear. It was *deeper* than that, like it was calling from the centre of her very being, in the recesses of her mind, quiet but strong enough she couldn't shake it.

She hated the way it caused a pleasurable shiver to run down her spine, and even more so that it was present for her to hear at all. The very decadence, like the smoothest spiced honey, should be a sin. No being, not even a *god,* should have such an ear-tingling cadence to their voice.

It always sounded a little distant when he spoke to her like this, whereas in his realm it was crystal clear.

With a sigh, she lifted her gaze to the side to look at the alleyway's exit. *Damnit. He's awake.* Her right hand curled into a tight fist as she bit the sides of her tongue in annoyance. *Why? I thought I'd been using enough to keep him in a slumber.*

Then she smoothed her features and wore a mask of

indifference.

Although deaths from being consumed by Demons resulted in Ghosts and normal human deaths didn't, the only other way to create them was by her very hands. If his magic touched them, she could obtain their deceased souls.

"I like that I'm able to completely get rid of them, body and spirit," she admitted, lifting her hood over her head to shroud her in mystery once more. "They don't deserve an afterlife, not even in your world."

"But it would empower me." He said it without emotion, yet she knew he was annoyed.

More power, that's all he wanted. It's all he ever wanted. Power, power, power. That's all they ever spoke about.

And she didn't want to give it.

She still didn't know if Weldir was a malevolent entity or not. She didn't know if he was good or evil, and she worried that aiding him meant she was endangering humankind. *If he ever obtained a physical form...* What stopped him from destroying this world on a childish whim?

Old gods were known to be fickle and immature beings. She feared she was aiding one and just didn't know it yet.

Then again, he shared nothing about himself, which gave her no chance to truly trust him. For once she wished he'd elucidate on anything to do with him – alas, apparently that was too much to ask for.

He also obviously cared very, *very* little for Lindi.

Not once had he checked to see how she fared, offered a warm greeting, or even a soothing word when she regrettably shed a tear for her past. With the prolonged silence and the nothingness from him, even when he was awake, he only shared his annoyance that she didn't collect the souls resulting from her kills.

"I'm trying to collect souls, as you have asked of me," she lied coldly, heading towards the alleyway's exit. "I have six already."

She ducked her head out, her curls waving around her chin and neck, and made sure it was clear of people before she walked into the main street. There were no people, and the mix of cold and warm lights from the slice of moon and the widely spaced streetlamps lit the area dimly like before.

It was safe.

The moment Lindi stepped out of the shadows and into the light of a nearby street lantern, her foot sunk. The ground opened up like a yawning mouth and swallowed her whole. Biting back a scream, she fell into pitch-black darkness and floated in its weightlessness freely.

Her hair lifted to flutter around her head, and her cloak wrapped around her body before whisking away. The racing of her heart quickly settled.

"I hate it when you do that," Lindi said as she folded her arms across her chest – although it was only the second time he'd done so.

"And it costs me mana to bring you here, and yet I feel I must do so in order to collect the souls you have on your person," Weldir stated, his voice stronger and no longer a whisper.

He stood vertically while she lay horizontally, and she cut him a slit-eyed scowl. Her arms tightened, since she couldn't argue with him on that front. She also refused to admit the truth that she'd been avoiding him.

No, she'd rather lie.

"Once I'd collected enough, I planned to return to your mist and gift them to you," she said plainly, looking up to avoid peering at him. "I don't want to make that long journey needlessly."

"It is not a gift when it is your task and merely the cost that is due," he answered, and his mist spread out from him until she could see it.

Then six white souls slipped out from the confines of her satchel, despite its solidness, and into his cloud, disappearing completely for him to do whatever the hell it was he would do with them later.

"You know I prefer it if you shift forms when you arrive here."

Her upper lip twitched, but she managed to stem the desire to sneer. Lindi turned incorporeal, which, unfortunately, made her tangible to him. If she remained in her physical form, even in his realm, Weldir was unable to touch her – and she liked that he couldn't force the shift on her.

It was entirely her choice, and she preferred being out of his reach when in his presence.

However, she also didn't wish to anger him, as he *could* remove her abilities from her – which he had once threatened when she'd gone out of her way to not collect souls. She'd thought she'd done a good job of pretending she hadn't seen a lonely soul in the middle of a village, but he'd been watching her and had grown annoyed that she wasn't doing her task.

Perhaps it was her stubborn nature, but she felt slighted by the way he'd wedded her, among other things that continued to vex her. She was waiting for him to be gentlemanly in any way, and not once had he proven to have any amount of soft-hearted decency inside him.

No. Instead, Weldir seemed mostly devoid of emotions. He could laugh, could be irritated, but beyond that, nothing else seemed to get any kind of emotional rise out of him. She was his wife, and he'd offered her nothing regarding that sentiment.

Their relationship was completely stagnant and stilted, and each passing day had her growing resentful of him.

She liked using him, just as he was completely using her. She wanted his power, and he wanted more for himself. That's all their relationship needed to be. Self-serving. They had no need to spend any time within each other's presence, and she disliked being in this empty realm.

It was utter darkness. There was no light, no warmth, just emptiness.

How she was able to see him in it, considering he was made up of black mist, was out of her range of knowledge. The only way she could see anything of him that appeared to be humanoid was by the black chalky flakes streaking across him. It was like someone had flicked the matte, brittle substance upon him, and it'd glued itself to him in speckles.

They moved all the time, sometimes allowing her to see where his hand *might* be by wrapping around the back of his wrist. Sometimes she knew he was seated cross-legged by the shifting pale flakes revealing a kneecap and the ankle bone of the opposing foot.

She rarely saw his face, and when she did, it was part of his lips and nose when he spoke.

His chest, from what she could gather, was leanly muscled, as was the rest of his body. The oddest thing was that his size could differ each time she saw him. Sometimes he was large, as if twelve feet, and other times he appeared shorter than her five-foot-seven height. She didn't know why, and she didn't care enough to ask.

Then again, if they were going to be together forever, she was sure she'd learn all of what she was allowed in due time. There was no need to rush.

She knew nothing of the rest of his features, since they'd never been highlighted by those flaking streaks of chalk. That, or she'd missed the chance to see them.

There's less than usual, she noted, narrowing her gaze at nothingness after peeking at him momentarily to know where he was. All she saw was a cloud and barely any of the man who should be floating within it.

His silence was unnerving, and unless he gave her little invisible slices of magic to lean against, it was easy to lose him if she got turned around while floating. She liked knowing where he was, so she could keep her distance.

"It appears you have become formidable with my mana," Weldir stated, abruptly floating right in front of her so there was less than a metre separating them. "Were they more of those humans that bring sacrifices to the... what do they call it? The Veil?"

"Yes," she answered, cocking a brow curiously.

"I see. You humans are so wasteful of life." His voice hinted at humour, even if the brief highlight of his chalky mouth lacked a smile. "You kill as they kill, yet you consider your actions justifiable."

Lindi pointed upwards at his face and scrunched her nose when anger boiled in her gut. "They harm the innocent; I do not. I am the judge and executioner of cruelty."

"You may be whatever it is you wish, so long as you do what I have asked of you."

Her anger quickly deflated upon realising he wasn't judging her actions but purely commenting on them. She sighed and rubbed her nape before looking down at her hand.

I still find it odd that I can feel in my incorporeal body here, but not my physical one. It was like it flipped for her when she was in Weldir's realm.

On Earth, if she turned Phantom, she perceived nothing but pressure. Here, she felt the softness of her skin, the wetness of her licking across her lips, the tiredness in her eyes. Whereas, if she were physical, she'd only perceive that pressure like being a Phantom on Earth. She wished the ache in her muscles from exertion would fade, but the only way to give herself a reprieve was to turn solid – which he didn't allow.

Much about her abilities and how polar opposite they could be between Earth and Tenebris was a mystery. She would, one day, unfold the secrets, but not even Weldir had been able to shed any light regarding the nature of Phantoms.

It was unknown and new for him, just as it was for her.

"So, the humans have taken to calling the Daekura Demons," Weldir stated smoothly, and like usual, his rich voice tingled in her ears. "Why?"

Her brows furrowed at how he'd come to learn that. *Perhaps he hasn't been as asleep as I thought.* Enough to have overheard conversations in towns while she'd been travelling through them, enough to hear the schemes of occultists to know they called it the Veil.

She shuddered at knowing she'd been watched when she was none the wiser. *Creepy.*

Her eyelids lowered in disinterest. "I guess it's because we would consider them unholy beings."

A sighing sound came from him, but it was utterly false considering they both currently lacked true breath. From him, it came across even more fake. "You humans needlessly tie everything to religion."

"Says the literal god," she pointed out.

"They have nothing to do with faith. They aren't truly evil creatures. They exist to feed and grow, just like a predator. Do you consider a bear evil for taking from the forest?"

"No," she bit lightly, while the fold of her arms tightened. "But they are animals, doing what is natural for them."

"As are the Daekura, as are the humans. It only frightens your people because you are the food source. Yet, you don't seem to see the hypocrisy that you consume things that are smaller and weaker than yourselves. Are you not, then, the unholy beings to the forest critters?"

Lindi parted her lips to refute him, but only the click of her tongue moving wordlessly came from her mouth. She shut her jaw as her features pinched in annoyance.

I hate it when he does that. Weldir could stab, quite swiftly, with cold and unfeeling logic. His perspective seemed to be entirely warped to where good and evil didn't exist – no matter if the actions or reasons were what she deemed immoral.

She knew killing those occultists was wrong, but she also didn't give a damn. She'd shed her opinion on the matter, based on the fact that nothing she did had a consequence in a bad way, only good.

Weldir spoke as if he, and nothing, truly had any consequence except for what humans pushed onto each other.

"I guess it's no different. But humans *are* cruel creatures," Lindi admitted, averting her gaze away from where he was. "What I'm doing is evidence of that. I'm trying to snuff out that wickedness as much as I can."

I want to feel like I'm outweighing the cruelty with love.

She wanted to be a protector, even if no one knew she existed. A hero to women who hadn't yet suffered. She didn't care if anyone thanked her for it, she just wanted every day of her gifted new life to matter. She wanted to know, even though she'd wed a god of another realm that went entirely against her teachings, that she was a part of the good in the world.

Was that too much to ask?

Otherwise... why did she do this? She didn't really want to feel the resentment that sometimes boiled over inside her. She didn't want to feel so... *selfish* for wanting to live, even if it meant breaking her faith and walking away from humankind.

This is one of the reasons I dislike talking to him. He made her think in ways she didn't particularly like, as if it was a game to him. She felt like entertainment, like a puzzle he wanted to break apart and put together in his own imagery.

She refused. Lindi wanted to stay as herself, even if it meant holding onto foolish notions and ideologies.

She wanted to stay human, in heart, in mind, in body, and in spirit.

"Okay," Lindi started, while letting her features relax. "You've collected your souls. I'm ready to go back to Earth now." To just... get away from him.

He'd gained some power; he had no need for her now.

A tsk sounded from all around her. "Not quite. You have another task to attend to, and now that you've mastered your abilities, it's time you give me what I truly seek."

His very words sent a spike of dread through her in an instant. Lindi's skin cooled as a nauseous, nervous pit formed in her stomach and enclosed her heart like a set of frightful claws.

Her eyes widened, and she brought her horrified gaze back to him. *Dear heavens, no.*

SEVEN

January 30th, 1689

Why did I agree to this? Lindi thought, with her face hot like someone had poured smelted ore onto it.

With her knees bent and pressed together, she lowered her hands from covering her eyes to peer down at her bare thighs. She'd been hoping her pants would magically reappear over legs and wrap them once more in modesty. Instead, they floated off into the void in her periphery, making her cheeks flare hotter.

Why did they have to float in the ether? Even a boot was rotating just behind and to the right of where she thought Weldir's head might be.

As if she and Weldir were underwater, it was even more embarrassing to see them scattered around, rather than upon a solid surface!

She would have shuffled away from him when he glided closer to her... if it wouldn't have exposed her pussy to him. No, instead, she tightened her thighs until she felt her muscles lock and ache.

When he told her he required that they enact the part of their agreement where she produced a child, she had agreed to do it. She even removed her boots, socks, pants, and underpants for him, but now she was just... unnerved. Half naked and afraid.

Why did she feel like she was about to do something wrong? Maybe it felt unholy because it was him? *He's my husband, damnit!* She shouldn't feel this way, yet she spooked further when he drifted ever closer.

I'm so glad he said I can keep my tunic on. And it was long enough to come down to the middle of her thighs, which gave her a sense of modesty despite the act they were about to perform.

She didn't want her breasts and the rest of her body exposed to him. Honestly, she just wanted to close her eyes and get this over with. Then she'd pretend it never happened as she carried whatever child they'd produce.

As much as she wanted to blame Weldir, to hate him for pushing this onto her now, deep in her heart, she couldn't.

She'd agreed to do this six years ago. It was the main requirement in her second life, and she'd promised it when she gave him her soul. This was the bargain they'd struck. She'd walked into this knowing what was required of her, and backing out now seemed entirely self-centred and unfair.

He could have found another human woman, one that may have said yes and then not denied him.

She didn't know if she rejected him now, whether he would undo their bond, but... she wanted to continue her mission. Someone else may not have the heart or even the will to hunt occultists. Lindi did, oddly enough, considering her life's path up until her first death.

I can do this, she thought as she lowered her knees from her chest. *I-it's only sex.* Plenty of people did it. Mothers, wives, lovers. It didn't *have* to be a terrible thing; the idea just felt odd doing it with a faceless spirit.

She also didn't know what she'd give birth to, and that worried her.

I wanted my first time to be with someone I loved. Most of the time she felt nothing for Weldir, and if she did deign to have an emotion for him, it was irritation.

He hadn't done anything to change her mind or heart in his cold indifference.

"You must spread your thighs if I am to–"

"I know!" she accidentally yelled, before slapping her hands over her mouth again and wincing apologetically. "I'm just... nervous. I've never done this before and I'm a little scared it's going to hurt."

Ugh, the rumours she'd heard about it had made her want to shut her legs forever! It was one of the reasons she was relieved to wait until marriage to lose her virginity. She hoped they were just overexaggerating, but the fear they weren't was hard to shake.

One woman had even said she heard someone else gushed blood, and Lindi's eyes had widened in disbelief. What had the man done, taken an axe to her?! How barbaric!

"I have never done this before either," he said, and she wished his tone sounded sincere, like he was trying to comfort her. Instead, despite how nice and husky it was, he stated it matter-of-factly.

When Lindi felt just the tiniest pressure on her knee, she looked down to the chalky streak of his inner palm pressing against it. He was trying to push his entire hand against it, but she only perceived that tiny streak. There was strength behind it, strength he could probably wield if he wanted to, but he didn't.

That relieved her, at least. It didn't feel forceful, but more like a gentle coax.

She crossed her ankles in defiance when she looked up at the size of him. "C-can you make yourself smaller? You'll rip me apart like that."

Right now, he looked too big, too tall. She wanted him smaller, so it would be easier.

A streak lining his forehead moved as if he looked down upon himself. "I do not see why my size would matter."

"Because your penis will be too big!" Lindi instantly wanted to die of mortification, but how could he be this... idiotic in this moment?

There was a slight pause from Weldir before a chuckle surrounded her. "We will not be fornicating, human. I only intend to insert a tendril inside you, and nothing more. Perhaps I should have explained that."

The heat, thankfully, bled from her face as her expression dropped, including her mouth. "What? A-a tendril? You really should have told me."

She'd been stressing for no reason then!

"I already told you I have no intention of ever hurting you."

Yes, she faintly remembered him telling her that once, but

this was different! It would have been an accident, like most first times.

She went to bash on his chest – or shoulder, she wasn't quite sure – in indignation, but both her hands went through whatever part of his torso was in front of her. Trying to hit a deity was a poor decision on her part, but her heart was so twisted in relief, nervousness, and confusion that she didn't care right then.

Thankfully it didn't matter since over ninety percent of him was intangible to her.

I would strangle him if I could. She doubted he'd forgotten to tell her, so he was probably toying with her. That, or he was an absent-minded idiot, and she didn't think of Weldir that way.

He didn't know much about their new bond, but he was a very intelligent being. Even if he didn't intend to, he sometimes made her feel small and inferior. It didn't help that he could look into the past of the souls he'd eaten. Earth wasn't a mystery to him, and he knew more about it than she did.

Likely more than she ever would.

Worried his patience was growing thin, and unwilling to learn what the end of that tether looked like, Lindi began to open her legs. She cringed when her thighs peeled apart like they were sticky, and then she was finally revealing herself to him.

When she paused after parting them only an inch, he stated, "More. I will not be able to feel with my tendril, so I will need to properly see what I am doing."

An embarrassed groan croaked from her, and she shoved her thighs apart to get it over with. She then held her breath like that would save her from whatever was about happen. She shut her eyes tightly, bundled her fists near her chest, and waited with her teeth stabbing into her plump bottom lip.

She jerked when something prodded against the lips of her pussy before it glided towards her entrance. The tendril didn't feel cool, or warm, or like anything living. It felt like a foreign thing, almost wrong, and her toes curled in repulsion when it opened her and began to push inside.

Her chest heaved with uncertainty, and she didn't know if this was actually better or worse than the sex she expected. At least that would have been normal; this absolutely didn't feel right. There was no warmth or a body to hold. Instead, she gripped the bottom of her tunic to steady herself through this rather invasive act that felt more like a procedure than sex.

Her inner walls, tight from disuse and tension, stretched around the tip of the thin tendril. Most of Weldir had disappeared, as if he'd focused all his chalky bits into it to keep it solid and stop it from going through her.

Then she gasped at the lightest pinching sensation. She winced, only to immediately relax before her brows furrowed and her teeth released her bottom lip.

Was that it? she thought, wondering if the tiny, quick pain had been her hymen. *Are you fucking kidding me?! That's it?!* Those women had totally been exaggerating! *Gushing blood, my arse.*

They'd just been trying to frighten each other. Gosh, she could imagine them playfully giggling about it behind her back.

Then Weldir's tendril bottomed out inside her. She didn't know why she looked down, not that she could see past her pubic mound or through her very flesh. Maybe she just wanted to truly see that her first time had been complete and that it actually wasn't too bad. She'd wound herself up about it so much that she now felt kind of silly.

That was until Lindi belted out a pained scream when he pushed impossibly *deeper*. Her back arched, her toes clenched in agony, and she reached her hands forward to claw at him – only to grasp nothing.

"Stop!" she yelled, kicking her legs and slapping her hands at thin air. "Get it out, get it out!"

The tendril yanked back. Lindi shoved her hand over her pussy and shut her thighs so fast her knees bashed together as she turned on her side. Tears instantly welled and spilled over as her eyes darted around in fear as she searched for him.

"Y-you said you wouldn't hurt me!" she sobbed out, her shoulders turning inwards as her chest heaved through her shudders of radiating pain. Even though he'd taken the tendril away, her insides continued to ache. "What the *fuck* were you doing?"

"Inseminating you," he stated plainly, but his tone was defensive, like he didn't understand what he'd done wrong. Once more, it sounded like a damn procedure, and it sucked all the life out of it. "How else am I to do that if not inside you?"

"Not *that* deep!" Lindi snapped. "What did you do? Enter my cervix? That hurt!"

"That's exactly what I did," he answered.

Her bottom lip trembled because she'd actually been joking. Her expression twisted as she shook her head at him in disbelief. "That's not how you do it, even *I* know that."

An annoyed huff, with the strangest undertone of a growl, rumbled around her. "Well, how else am I meant to get my essence inside your womb?"

"Like normal! Inside my pussy, not by shoving yourself through my cervix like a fucking jerk. It goes in by itself... I think."

That made the most sense to her. It shouldn't have been that painful, even she knew that. It was like someone had called upon lightning from the sky to strike deep inside her and shoot down her legs and up her groin.

Now I wish we'd just had sex! At least then he couldn't have gotten freaky with her insides in the *wrong* way.

"How was I supposed to know that? I've never seen what happens inside. I thought this was how it was done." His tone finally held some real bite to it, and Lindi did not care one bit.

She didn't care if he was embarrassed or annoyed. She was the one who was hurt!

"F-fine, I get it," she muttered, and then held her breath that he'd at least apologise.

"I'll be gentler," he stated with a sigh in his voice. "I won't do that again."

Then he came forward, and that silly, wriggling tendril drifted near her knees, and she gasped. She tried to scramble away but stopped when she almost fell off the ledge of whatever thing he'd conjured for her to sit on.

"No!" She threw out the hand not covering her privates to ward him back. "Please. I don't want to do this right now."

"I did not finish–"

"I said no!" Then Lindi turned solid, putting herself out of his reach even when she was right before him.

He reached out to swipe through her solid body to test that he couldn't touch her. "Turn intangible, female. I told you I prefer you as a Phantom in my realm."

Her bottom lip pushed forward in annoyed defiance, as she dropped her head and gave him a glare through her lashes. "No," she snapped firmly. "Why should I do anything you ask of me when you can't even adhere to your own promise of not hurting me? That was the one thing I asked for."

"You have asked for much. For power. For vengeance. To return to your home. For time. For the very life you now have." His mist seemed to collect tighter against him, in reaction to the sharpness and curtness of his words. "I have given you all of that. I told you having a mate was new for me, so I'm asking for grace if I make a mistake."

At least he admitted to that, but he had yet to still utter an apology! Perhaps because he was a god, he felt it was beneath him, but Lindi refused to let him get away with it. He needed *her* as much as she needed him, and she had no qualms holding that over him.

It was the only true power she had in their dynamic. He could take away his magic from her, but she didn't actually have to produce offspring if she didn't want to, and her ability to turn physical meant he couldn't force it.

And she didn't know his temperament at all to know if she was truly safe from him.

That sudden realisation made her right eye well with more liquid before another tear fell as her lips trembled. *I'm such an idiot. I should have just let myself die.* So what if she wouldn't have gone to heaven? At least she didn't have to put up with any of this.

Why did I try to hold onto life so much?

For her revenge, despite how fleetingly good that felt? To protect others, who would never know? For her mother, who never woke up to see Lindi safe?

She wasn't actually happy with her choice.

"Just send me back to Earth," Lindi demanded.

His tone was surprisingly dark as he rumbled, "You promised me."

"And I will, but not today." If he wouldn't give her an apology or at least show he cared about her wellbeing, then she would withhold her oath to him until she felt better – emotionally *and* physically.

"Infuriating," he growled. "If you won't give me what you promised, then I will cease giving you anything you desire. Your soul is mine, and I will trap it if I so choose. It belongs in my afterworld."

Then all the wispy, smoky mist disappeared in a flash – as if he... left.

Lindi waited for him to send her back to Earth, but in the lone nothingness, it didn't take long for what he meant to become obvious. Her eyes widened as she peered around into the utter weightless, vast, and empty ether.

"No," she rasped, her eyes widening and frantically darting around. "Don't you dare leave me here!"

She reached for the rest of her clothing so she could at least put her pants back on, but they were out of reach of her fingertips. She wanted them back on – to forget why they'd come off in the first place. With her hair floating and her tunic lifting to the point she had to shove it down to cover her pubic mound, she wished she could swim through his darkness like he could.

"Enjoy your solitude, female," the darkness coldly answered.

EIGHT

A time unknown, but a new beginning

Holding a small leaf, Weldir's coalescing form moved to show solid darkness where he slid the pad of his thumb against its green edge. Pressure radiated across his face, and as usual, he was unsure of the expression that filled it. Perhaps a thoughtful one? He imagined so, considering he was inspecting the leaf and its flaws.

"It still doesn't look right," he murmured to himself, as he dropped his hand and lifted his gaze towards the tree before him.

To his eyes, everything appeared either too fuzzy or too smooth. The leaf was tough and hadn't bent to his touch. He'd witnessed them fold and be rather malleable on Earth. From afar, the bark of the tree – not that he knew the name of it – appeared to mimic those that had formed near the Veil. Up close, however, it was fuzzier than it should be.

The tree's image shifted until smoothness on the tops of the leaves gave a rough sheen, while the undersides remained satin. The bark did the opposite, and suddenly the trunk looked scaley like a reptilian, rather than like tree bark.

He threw the leaf to the side, finding this process to be a nuisance due to his lack of skill and understanding, and it fluttered through the air. It disintegrated before it could touch the darkness below his feet. His gaze drifted along the high, arching roots that wove through the liquid black base he'd given his inner world, his stomach – the place in which souls were held.

The ground looked like black ink that reached on forever.

A feminine roar, like she'd done it through clenched teeth, warbled around him. Although it was loud to him, as if it had come from within the depths of his very mind, the rest of Tenebris – his stomach – was quiet.

"Such a noisy thing," he stated to the air as he looked up. "It's as if she knows I can hear her."

She wouldn't. For what could have only been an hour or so, she'd been yelling at him, about him, to the darkness around her. She spoke to herself, frustrated and annoyed, or sometimes just screamed.

Weldir, try as he might, found her hard to ignore. Since she was in the part of his realm that housed his mind and the depths of his consciousness, using magic to block her was remarkably draining.

So there she floated, constantly being a pest, and he was subjected to listening to her outbursts.

The longer they went on, the more frantic she sounded.

He could even make out her panicked breaths and accelerated heartbeat.

Forcing the tree to shake and offer him a new leaf to inspect, he noted that it still looked wrong. *At least its texture has improved.* He was trying to recreate something he'd never interacted with, and he either made it too thin that it was floppy, or thick and rigid, or sharp enough to slice through the solid parts of him.

He felt no pain, however, and wounds were truly non-existent to him.

"Come back here! I want to go home!" she screamed, only for her voice to soften momentarily as she murmured, "Well... not that I have a home. Just not here! This isn't fair."

Her punishment was entirely her own fault.

Weldir was patient, and had been so for what he knew to be quite a few human years – not that he truly knew the length of time that had passed.

She was not doing the tasks bestowed upon her. Instead of travelling through the desert in search of Ghosts – humans eaten by Daekura – she was in human towns that had no interaction with them. Those she'd found must have been accidents she'd stumbled across in the forests. Or perhaps she discovered them along her journeys each time she crossed the desert when he called her back to the Veil.

It felt like such a waste making her restart her journeys.

He'd like to return her back to where he originally took her from, but he was unable to. He was able to recall her from anywhere, as she was connected to him through a tether of essence, but she re-formed inside his mist – the manifestation of his reach on Earth.

With more power, I should be able to send her back to any location my mist touches.

Yet, she kept using his mana when he told her to be sparing with it. He didn't stop her, but he slumbered more due to it, occasionally waking up and checking on Tenebris, his souls – to see if she'd brought him new ones to consume – and on her.

Always on her.

He watched her through a viewing disc – a flat, oval piece of floating liquid with glittering sand on the outside – any chance he could. She was never where he needed her to be, but he understood this self-imposed task was the result of her feminine rage, and he was giving her time to expend it.

Or, rather, *had* given her time.

He wanted her to fulfil the true reason he'd bonded them. Once they created a servant, she could go back to her vendetta after they worked together to teach their offspring how to do their task. Once they perfected their offspring, he would ask her for more. He could further his reach, his power.

With enough servants, with enough consumed soul power, he planned to encase the entire world with himself. Then he'd have no need for her.

She could do as she wanted, forever, and she didn't have to see Weldir unless she deigned to. He would keep his promise to let her use his mana, and she would have an endless supply of it to play with. She could lay waste to her enemies to her heart's content.

Until then, he expected to be given the things he asked for.

"You're such a jerk," he heard her state, her voice cracking higher an octave.

Weldir looked up to stare between the branches of the tree

he'd created. It was made up of nothing but his mind's interpretation of what he'd seen on Earth... mostly from a distance, until recently. It wasn't alive, it wouldn't grow without his interference, and there was no wind to make it rustle. The green looked too vibrant, the dark-brown bark too washed out, and it still just looked *wrong.*

I truly did not mean to hurt her.

He couldn't see or feel what he was doing, and he truly didn't know penetrating her cervix wasn't how a human female became pregnant. He'd guessed, and just so happened to be wrong.

The tree wilted a little, the colours of it dimming. Now it just looked sad. It looked... disappointed in him.

"He doesn't even have the decency to ask my name!" he heard her scream through the ether. "It's been six years!"

That made Weldir pause.

I have asked her name before, haven't I? He made the roots of the tree shift through the inky, watery ground until they sat more naturally as he thought deeply. *Her name is...*

He didn't know it.

No matter how much he searched his memories – there weren't many, as he'd been asleep for the better part of their time together – he couldn't find her name. He'd never needed it.

If he wished to call upon her, he brought her to his realm.

Has it really been six years to her? He hadn't realised such a length of time had passed for her – he knew this to be long for a human.

The tree wilted even further as his mist swirled tighter around him. The back of his mind thickened with an emotion he wasn't quite accustomed to. Guilt, perhaps. Regret? Shame?

The least he could have done was show a little more care regarding her.

But I have been asleep, he argued in his own defence. *All because she used my mana too much.*

Well, that wasn't entirely true.

The power she'd gifted him through their bond had allowed him to force every soul he'd consumed into a deep slumber. He finally had peace, and he slept to preserve it, giving himself the chance to rest. He'd been letting the well of his mana re-flood enough to handle the constant expenditure.

Without it, he already knew the souls would awaken once more to fret. They'd wail again if he didn't snuff them into a slumber.

I have also been making this tree. Once he perfected it, he could begin making others. He could make... *more.*

I want my own forest. One he could interact with. A proper world in which the souls he'd eaten could wander. He'd like to make mountains, grass, rivers.

He wanted Tenebris to come to life. To *be* life in the afterworld. A place of serenity that even he could bask in.

He wanted his darkness to house beauty. For the yawning loneliness to be filled with distractions. He wanted to pretend that he could breathe the wind he wanted to create, could drink the water, could feel the sunlight.

Weldir wanted to feel as though he existed.

Currently, the only way he existed was through the interactions of a little human female who did not look upon him fondly. She was constantly wary, eying him with a stern regard, and he didn't understand her, or humans, well enough to know how to change that.

The souls here were the first people he'd ever spoken with, and they were always panicked at their deaths. Not quite the pleasant conversationalists. Then there were the sacrifices that were brought to the Veil's cliff, but those conversations, until his mate, had all gone the same.

Confusion at his voice, fear of it, uncertainty of what he offered. Always rejection – or they'd die before they could make up their minds.

He'd never even spoken with his mother.

If it wasn't for the fact that he could talk to himself, he wouldn't have even known he had a voice. He'd been placed in an isolated box; a magical prism.

He'd been hoping having a mate might change his seclusion, but his female wasn't very chatty with him. She didn't seem to like his voice, as she often shuddered whenever he spoke, and she frequently narrowed her pretty gaze at his words.

He thought giving her space would help, hence why he let her adjust to her new life over the years, but that hadn't worked. So, if she would not be his companion, then his servants could be.

That's if I can speak with them.

Weldir forced a sigh from himself, rather liking the way it sounded and how it conveyed many emotions. For now, it was the noise of the guilt that continued to gnaw at him.

Perhaps I should have handled the moment better.

He let the leaf disintegrate and flutter from his hand, and watched as the tree disappeared as well. If it continued to linger, it would eat at his power – he constantly needed to feed it mana in order to keep its presence.

If he wanted to make a permanent world, then he'd need to feed it mana eternally. Some might consider that a constant waste of his power, but there was no one around in his lonely void to judge him.

He could do as he pleased, as he always had and always would.

When Tenebris was empty once more, to the point that even the inky ground faded, he moved his form to another part of his realm. To her.

He found her in her physical form, which appeared ghostly. She still had the same feminine, curvaceous body – not lean and not plump, but with a very defined hourglass. Her breasts were generous, her backside rounded and full. Her dark-brown, curling hair still floated as it waved around her head and rounded ears.

Yet she was entirely transparent to him, which stole away her rich-brown skin, her dark-brunette hair, her eyes a mix of brown and amber, and even the pinkness in her lips.

He didn't understand why she suddenly became unobtainable to his reach and proper view when she was in her physical form. All living beings had this white, transparent glow to him – no matter what kind of creature – but he hadn't expected her to still remain that way as his mate.

"What is it?" he stated when he arrived by her side.

With the bottom half of her still bare, she had her knees tucked up to her chest with her feet covering the intimate slit between her thighs. Her pants and shoes, which were just as translucent to him, since neither she nor he were holding them, had floated even further away.

The human lowered her hands from her face and looked forward. Her gaze darted to the right when she found a trace of his cloud and followed it to where she guessed his head was.

"What?" she quietly snapped.

"Your name. What is it?" he asked again.

Her long lashes lowered as she narrowed her eyes, the emotion in them hot with anger. Her lips twitched as if she'd tightened them.

Her defiance was bothersome, especially as she'd just screamed how he hadn't cared enough to know it. Her refusal only increased his ire.

"I can keep you trapped here forever, female," he stated coldly. "There is no escape for you, or from me. Your suffering here is all within your control."

Her features tightened even further, and he wondered if that was just deepening anger, or perhaps hatred that was beginning to glint in her gaze.

Her tone was sharp, deadly, and more like a snap, as she said, "Lindiwe. Lindiwe Bernadi."

"There, Lindiwe. I have learned your name."

Like usual, the little female shuddered at his voice, and he noticed her skin prickle down her neck. It was a fascinating response to see her body shiver in reaction to him, and he did truly wish it wasn't a negative reaction.

He'd actually like her to find him pleasant.

Then again, I'm not human. Although he sounded just fine to himself, he had no idea how that was perceived by her little round ears.

"You have never said my name," he stated matter-of-factly. "Not once have you ever called for me."

She grabbed the bottom seam of her tunic and pressed it down to keep it covering her when it lifted away from her body. "I've never needed to call out to you," she bit. "Are you seriously trying to make me feel guilty because you couldn't be bothered learning the name of the woman you married?"

"Married? I've come to learn what that is, and our bond is not as fragile as your human custom." Weldir tsked as his mist collected tighter against him. "And no, that was not my intention. Just a causality, that is all. Now, if you have no desire to be in my presence, I will leave you to the solitude you prefer."

Just as he went to dematerialise and go back to focusing on his tree, she reached a hand out. "W-wait."

Weldir did as he was asked. Then, since he was often lax and merely a floating being – his body felt no urge to move due to a lack of muscular stimuli – he folded his arms for her benefit. He wished he could have cocked a brow, as the humans did, but he had little control over whatever expressions his face made – currently.

She didn't say anything, and they did little more than stare at each other. Her expression hardened while she chewed her bottom lip, and he tilted his head to inspect her.

"You do not trust me," he stated.

She stopped chewing. "I don't know you."

"You have never tried to," he reminded her.

Her gaze averted to the side, and there was something haunted in it. "You're a being of death."

"I am not a *being* of death; I am a *facet* of death."

Lindiwe opened her mouth to say something, but promptly shut it. Then she hugged her midsection and crossed her ankles, still hiding her intimates. "Do you promise it won't hurt this time?"

Upon realising his head was still tilted, he straightened it. "I have already expressed my lack of desire to hurt you. We can try again later once you have appeased your anger, as I can see it's still present. I don't intend to coerce you."

Her eyelids flickered, and her gaze slipped to him. "Why do you even care? Aren't most gods self-centred and only care about their own wants?"

"Because I'm not the one who must bear my servants," he answered, not understanding how that couldn't have been obvious. "You are the one who must protect them while you carry them."

Her bottom lip fell as her stare grew stark and wide-eyed. "What are you insinuating?"

"Insinuating? Nothing." He waved a hand dismissively, doubting she could even see its movement. "I'm merely explaining that, although I wish otherwise, my duty ends after my essence is provided. I would like for you to... care for them in my absence, during their creation, and afterwards. It wouldn't do to make you hateful of the process."

Although he didn't think he'd stated anything of significance, her expression relaxed and lost some of its usual edge. It softened the fire in her eyes and the harsh brow crinkle, and made her look prettier. Or perhaps he only found it more pleasant because he'd aided in its loss of tension and it was an improvement on the way her hateful regard made him feel.

"There is no need for you to turn physical in my presence," he added, wishing she'd cease doing so and stay tangible to him. "I do not intend to physically force you, as I have clearly stated. I'd rather look upon you properly."

He'd rather see her beauty more clearly.

Lindiwe's gaze softened even more, as did the tension in her locked-up positioning. She turned incorporeal, which made her tangible to him – and him alone.

"That was my first time, and I admit I didn't handle it too well." She scratched at her left forearm absentmindedly as she looked away. "I was told it would hurt, but not like *that*."

"I don't intend to do that again," he repeated his assurance from earlier. "I'm also sorry for the hurt I caused. It wasn't my intention to do so. My learning shouldn't be above your wellbeing."

As if he'd said something of significance, not that he was quite sure what, her bottom lip trembled before she stilled it by biting down on it. Her eyes softened at him before a more determined expression took over. "Then okay. We can do it."

He doubted she actually wanted to, and just wanted out of his realm.

Seeing there was no point in arguing further about it, Weldir moved closer while forming a tendril. He pulled from the part of him he'd only recently discovered when he first brought a soul to his realm – a place of life he'd never known existed.

It was how he knew he wasn't a demi-god of death, but merely a simple part of it. A soul eater that could, if he so chose it, give life. He could gift spirit – his own.

With her hands balled together near her chest, Lindiwe closed her eyes and parted her thighs for him. Weldir pulled all of his physical matter to the tendril's tip in order to touch her with it –

rather than it merely passing through her. Then, looking down at her mauve slit, he watched as it dragged through her darker lips, and then prodded her pink opening.

She flinched when he slowly inserted it, and her features bunched up further when he went deep until he was unable to go further. Instead of trying to force it deeper by having his tendril mould to her insides, he let his essence go.

A strange light-grey iridescent liquid fell from her hole when he withdrew, and he found that particularly wasteful. He didn't understand how creatures could procreate if the females lost much of it.

The little human instantly shut her legs and turned her head away. "M-my pants and boots... please?"

Weldir wondered how she truly felt about the process as he moved her through his consciousness, so her artefacts were within her reach. She had to turn physical to grab them, as the material had turned solid once removed.

This interaction left him with the same feeling as before, and he wasn't quite sure why. As he looked upon the creature looking off to the side with a shy, pouted bottom lip, guilt nibbled at the fraying edges of his black mist.

Is having a mate always this hard, or is it just because of what I am?

NINE

March 17th, 1689

With a chill creeping down her spine that shouldn't exist in the early autumn air, Lindi gripping the blanket of the bedding with tight fists. Heat radiated through her entire head as she clenched her eyes tight, and she tried her hardest not to bite through her bottom lip against the pain. The bed she knelt down next to, while heaving her torso across it, was her anchor.

Her body flickered between physical and ghostly, her mind fighting to stay present while her body wanted an out. Hot strikes shot down her abdomen and blasted into her thighs during every contraction that assaulted her.

Then, once the invisible pressure at the top of her stomach stopped twitching and clamping, she was given a moment of reprieve.

As she often did, with tears dotting her eyelashes, she looked around the room. It looked emptier than when she'd been here six years ago, and yet nothing about it had changed.

Well, that wasn't totally true, as the bedding was different, and the painting on the wall hadn't belonged to her parents, but it was still set up the same.

Sure, it was dusty from disuse, but their bed with its oak frame remained the same. The white sheets were still unfolded and twisted, as if the last occupants had disappeared before they were to remake them, their pillows dented as if they'd only just laid upon them. Against the wall was her parents' chest, yet it was filled with an abundance of clothes that didn't belong to them. Other than a box, which had acted as a table for a candleholder for her parents, there was little else that had changed other than some discarded bowls and rags.

It was obvious someone had once occupied her family home, perhaps even multiple someones, but it was now vacant. How long, she didn't know, but the evidence of left-behind medicine and bowls hinted at a story of sickness.

The occupant must have died, and the village had yet to place anyone new in it.

It was her home, but she felt so far removed from it.

Her house had barely been touched, as if the village had maintained it in the hope that someone would live there. It had been newly built by her grandfather and her father when he'd been a teenager, so destroying it likely would have been deemed wasteful.

Tithes were due, and she was sure the lord who oversaw this land wanted his payment of crops.

It appeared as though the village had banded together and absorbed the farm. The fields had been worked, fresh crops were sprouting, and even the fences were in good repair.

The only thing beginning to deteriorate was this house.

Part of the thatched roofing was thin in some areas, allowing raindrops to slip through. The walls were a little warped, as parts of the timber needed replacing. The hard dirt ground inside was only uneven in places water had settled for too long.

These looked like fairly new problems, as if the last occupant had not been gone long. At the same time, it revealed that none of the villagers cared to come close enough to maintain it. Even grass grew around the edges outside the house, and she'd seen a few green blades breech inside where the planks of timber and ground met.

When she first came here, she'd been surprised to find her family home empty, and that it hadn't been picked apart for building materials.

She would have loved to know why, but all she'd thought was that she'd been thankful she could return to it. Could hide in it. Could seek shelter when she needed it the most.

Lindi knew she couldn't do what she was about to... in a

town, and she refused the dare she'd placed upon herself to do it in the forest.

Instead, her skin appreciated the comfort of a bed, even if her room had been upturned into some kind of masculine writing space and storage area – most of which was just more clothing, bedding, and some materials she figured had been collected to repair the house.

Her mind appreciated the security and isolation, while her heart constantly bled at the memories that reared their ugly heads harder and louder than before she'd come here.

And her knees... they appreciated the scrape from rubbing against the cold, hard flooring, which was now cushioned with a blanket. Somewhere soft for her and the child.

Lindi clenched her teeth and quietened her yell as much as she could when she felt another downward push against her abdomen. Her eyes slitted with determination at the bare wooden wall as she bore down.

The fact that she was doing this here brought on a well of sadness that pooled in her gut, but she had nowhere else to go.

I don't know what is going to come out of me. She wanted to pretend that her child would be normal, but nothing about her pregnancy had been normal. *It's only been seven weeks!*

This was obviously *not* a human child, and she wasn't going to go to a major town and give birth. It just posed too much of a risk, and she didn't want to frighten the midwives or become a spectacle.

Or be deemed a witch, endangering both her and her child.

And doing it in the forest was even more idiotic.

She also didn't want to do this in a tavern in case something bizarre like a fireball shot from her vagina, as if the gates of hell could open up between her thighs. Especially since it currently felt like her loins were on fire!

Lindi had been given no time to adjust to being pregnant. She told Weldir that she'd talk to him in nine months when it was supposed to be born, and instead her stomach just grew and grew.

The only way to halt it was to turn intangible, as they'd discovered when she'd stayed in his realm too long. They'd both been waiting to see if her body would take his essence, or sperm, or whatever he wanted to call it. Nothing had happened while she was in her Phantom form, and it was only when she'd turned physical that the process began – as if she needed a living form.

Her stomach, which had been unusually quiet the past year, came back with a vengeance. She needed food, and she'd been forced to forage in the growing forest right next to the Veil just to appease the worst of her hunger. That was after she'd vomited so much darkness, so much black liquid, that she thought she needed an exorcism.

And then her stomach swelled faster than her mind could comprehend. Every time she turned intangible for a few days, there were no changes, and she knew she'd halted the process once more. She hadn't grown to full term, and instead she'd started experiencing contractions when her stomach was only half the size.

In the back of her mind, she knew now was the right time. It wasn't coming too soon for it, just too quick for her human mind to wrap around. She'd come to her parent's farm, her childhood home, because of this feeling of impending *doom.*

Despite summer just ending, the house was cold at night. But she didn't want to light the fireplace and risk alerting anyone to her presence. No, Lindi wanted to come and go without ever being noticed.

Even though the property was far from the eyes of another house and the village itself, the smoke would eventually attract attention, and she couldn't have that. When men arrived to sow the crops, Lindi hid in the shelter of her home and didn't make a peep.

They'd ask questions as to why she hadn't aged. They'd want to send a midwife to aid her, especially as she was alone. They'd be angered that she had no husband, but how was she to explain that she did, he just didn't technically reside in this plane of existence?

She didn't want to say he'd died and receive pity, or that she'd had sex out of wedlock, as that would be frowned upon.

She didn't know what to do, but just thought it best she remained undiscovered if she could.

But I don't want to be alone, she thought with a sniffle. Terrified for herself, for the child, she gripped her bedding tighter. At least both it and her should be immortal, considering Weldir had made her deathless and was their parent. *I'm scared.*

She was doing a frightful, traumatising thing all on her own, and the weight of that was crushing. More than anything in the world, she wanted to feel the presence of her mother's warm hand wrapped around her own to help her through this. It was how she'd always imagined it.

Although she'd been resisting it, clutching the foreign bedding tighter and tighter until tension ached in her knuckles and made the skin across them taut, causing her fingertips to hurt, Lindi gave in.

"Weldir," she pleaded so quietly, part of her hoping she wasn't heard and wishing her eyes didn't well up even more. She hated having to rely on him right now, but she literally had no one else in the world she could turn to.

When he didn't answer her, a sob broke before it was ripped away from her when a contraction felt like it was trying to snap her spine in half.

"Weldir," she cried a little louder. Pressing her sweaty temple against the hay-stuffed mattress, she whispered, "Please."

"Yes, Lindiwe?" he finally answered in his deep tone, soft and echoing like usual on Earth.

Her body shuddered against the way his sensual voice uttered her name before she released an exhale of reassurance that settled her insides. The tension in her thighs released, and her backside lowered to press against her heels.

"I see. So, it has begun?"

That was all he had to say? While she was kneeling there, trying to bring whatever he made into the world? If he was physical, she may have thrown something at him.

She'd already learned that Weldir just seemed incapable of feeling. Or, perhaps, he just lacked empathy for a lesser being like a human. Who fucking knew?

"Please do something, anything," she pleaded.

She'd take a pat on the back right now, especially if it made soothing motions against her spine in the process. Even just a wet rag to her forehead would be like a balm to her spirit.

"I can only witness."

Those words, ones he'd uttered before, caused her bottom lip to tremble even more. She pressed her face against the mattress and sobbed, her heart racing as it awaited the next clutch of pain and tension.

"I cannot even be there, as you are outside my mist."

"Th-then bring me to your realm."

"I cannot do that either. You are in a fragile state, and I'm worried we will harm them if you return to Tenebris. You must stay on Earth until you are done."

So, she was truly and utterly alone.

She knew it wasn't his fault he couldn't be there or do anything. From the beginning, he'd told her of that, but right now, she needed a miracle from him. She needed kindness, compassion, and not obliterating emptiness, while she physically felt the opposite.

She wanted warmth, even if it was just words. To be cared for in some way as she did one of the hardest things she'd ever done, in a home where her life had been ripped away from her. She wanted... more.

Just something.

The past seven weeks had been hard. If she hadn't required food, she would have stayed in Weldir's realm, but there was nothing for her to eat there. She'd been forced to eat from the forest surrounding the Veil, which wasn't entirely fruitful and abundant. She hadn't wanted to scrounge in the dirt, but sometimes there were only hares or edible roots for her to eat – and she'd had to learn quickly how to make herself fire from nothing.

At least she'd learned a few survival skills in the process.

She'd gone through a range of emotions, most of them frantic and confused. She'd had no one to turn to, no one to rely on for advice – because who would know anything about an otherworldly pregnancy or the birth of a god's child? She'd gone from sick and terrified, to horny, to sad and angry, constantly rotating on those emotions, but not once had she felt an ounce of happiness or hope.

Yet she'd protected and provided to the best of her abilities, eating in abundance, making sure she was warm and cared for. Lindi, despite her reservations, had made sure it had the best chance of life and health because, even if she didn't love it, the child deserved her best efforts.

It didn't help that Weldir spoke so indifferently regarding them.

She often wondered if he spoke more fondly towards her and about them, rather than calling them a servant or just offspring, whether she may have felt better regarding all this. But he was cold and detached in everything he did, and she didn't think he was even aware of how that made her feel.

She was human. People were full of life, love, and tenderness. To be starved of that for six years, when he could have been something she could have leaned on, was taking its toll on her.

When she'd bonded with him, she'd expected more.

Not once had he truly tried to assuage her fears, which just made her discontented and spiteful. Not once had he tried to learn of her, her life, or anything about her – he hadn't even deigned to know her name until she'd screamed it at him.

She felt like a tool, and nothing more. Not a wife. Not a lover, as she expected. Not even a friend in their forced companionship. Nothing.

Then, just as she was giving up hope, a spark of *something* materialised out of thin air.

Lindi gasped in surprise and rushed to her feet. She backed away when a bright-white light, obscured by black sheer ribbons of material wisping around it, formed inside her room. It coalesced tighter and faster, the light getting brighter as the darkness spread and developed a sandy glitter to it.

Her back hit the wall, shooting pain down her legs, just as a half-being materialised in her bedroom and seemed to fill it at the same time.

Black mist spread outwards as Weldir appeared as he usually did. Except... there was more to him than usual. She could see more of his torso, his legs, and even half his face. And, for the first time, she noted the horn on the left side of head and the short hair flowing around it.

She'd always thought his body was lean, but it looked long and tall – especially since he towered over her as if he wanted the tip of his segmented horn to reach the low ceiling. His left hand, the only one visible for now, was tipped with claws.

His face lacked hair, revealing chiselled features. A sharp jaw was coated in glittered chalk, as was his strong nose, full lips, and high cheekbones. Her eyes widened at the most attractive features she'd ever seen, and it was the first time she'd even seen them!

Even his lashes were unfairly long and fluttery, with more chalky sand easily flickering off them to join the rest of his cloud. His eyes were just two black glossy pools of nothingness, and she had no idea where he was looking as he turned his head to her.

The impression of his face moved, showing her a different part while hiding his pointed chin and lips until his chalky self re-formed there... only to disappear again.

The contrast of viewing him in his darkness compared to the wooden walls and compacted dirt flooring of her home was startling. With her eyes wide and her mouth agape, if it wasn't for the pain, she wouldn't have realised her insides felt like they were ripping as she stared at him.

"You told me you couldn't leave your mist!" she whisper-shouted, barely believing her eyes.

His head cocked, which made the coalesced parts around his horn and short hair disappear until all she could make out was the right side of his face. His brow on that side furrowed, and she imagined the other one had as well.

"Not usually," he stated, and his voice sounded so much louder than when she usually heard it on Earth. It had the same boom and sinful depth to it, like when she was a Phantom in his world. "But I can see that you do not wish to be alone."

Then Weldir signalled his right arm – which suddenly formed like swirling smoke – to part open his torso. The white light from earlier was actually a flame, and it sat between his navel and chest.

"I have consumed a soul in order to be with you."

Her eyes widened further. "You can do that?!"

His head straightened. "Of course. I just choose not to, as it is wasteful and has a negative impact on the reserves of my mana."

When the biggest contraction yet assaulted her, Lindi stopped caring as she braced her hand upon the wall. With the other hand, she kneaded her back with her knuckles as best as she could, almost hurting herself to get through the pain. When it let up, she paced, as she had many times during this, with deep and controlled breaths sawing in and out of her. The ending of this was nigh – she could feel it – but now she limped and hissed between steps.

She flinched when Weldir came closer, like he wanted to steady her when she wobbled on her feet. She went to pull her arm out of his hold, but she went completely through him. The coldness of his form brushed over her skin, making the dark hairs on her arms lift, but there was nothing else.

Not even the more solid parts of him were tangible to her.

"I cannot touch you," he stated with a hint of... something. "That means neither can my mana."

No matter if it was sadness or disappointment in his tone, or even both, for some reason, gratitude radiated through her. At least he'd *tried*. It was more than she'd been expecting.

"I-it's fine." After pacing a little more to work the tension out of her stiff muscles, she returned to her kneeling spot next to the bed and added, "Thank you for... being with me."

"Although I cannot always adhere to this promise, I will always try to be here for you," Weldir muttered quietly as he *hovered* closer.

Then he appeared to crouch beside her on one knee, while facing her, and his body floated a few millimetres from the ground.

Lindi gave him a grimacing nod. His face had disappeared almost completely, before the thickest parts of his mist recollected to give her just an eye, cheek, and temple.

She grabbed the bedding like before and squeezed as she pushed when her body told her to. She rocked back and forth occasionally, often shifting her weight to loosen her body as much as she could. It was impossible to stay still, and her head was aflame – hot and near delirious. The task was gruelling, and being watched by someone who could do nothing to assist left her feeling a little awkward, but she was still appreciative of his presence.

It was nice to know she actually wasn't entirely alone. The fact that he'd done this of his own volition meant he wanted to be there – although she didn't know if that was because he actually cared or if it was just in morbid curiosity.

But it was comforting when he muttered, "You are doing well, little female. They are doing good."

Blowing out and sucking in calming breaths, she eyed his strange form. "Y-you can tell?"

"Their soul is still bright within yours, so yes." Then, as if to demonstrate, he held a hand out and her reddish-orange soul flame appeared. There was a multicoloured spot within its pelvis.

Lindi laid her forehead against the bed, and her lips parted with reassurance. She hadn't known he could see them, but she was grateful to know all was well. Doing this was daunting, by herself even more so, but her worry for them eased exponentially.

Then, when she knew it was the right time, Lindi cupped her hands between her thighs. She bit into her bedding to quieten her determined scream and gave it all her might.

Something hot, bloodied, and solid fell into her awaiting palms. Lindi gulped with relief that the worst was over.

She gently laid them down, her arms weak as her body caved. Tiredness clung to her sweat-slicked body, but at least the worst was done – despite the urge to keep pushing like she wasn't quite done.

She dragged her face off the bed and lifted back so she could peek down at them when she didn't hear a cry. Immediately worried, she furrowed her brows at the strange black blobby creature between her knees.

It didn't look human, although it did have an impression of a baby shape – two stubby little arms and legs, a torso, and a head.

Their featureless, oval face was pointed around their nose and mouth like a muzzled creature. They had no eyes – not even concaves to allude to any – and they had tiny little ear holes rather than fleshy ears. Their little toes and fingers were stubby, with tiny, pointed tips like claws, but they were bent in different directions, as if they were soft rather than sharp and hard. She realised then that they weren't actually black but such a dark grey that they appeared so.

They laid there still as stone but languid. She noticed that although they had the evidence of a cord, it must have snapped or ripped during birth, as the rest was no longer attached to her.

Their stomach wasn't moving.

Gasping in fear, she grabbed her newborn *something* and began rubbing what she thought might be their back. Their body was soft, squishy – as if they completely lacked any bones – and jiggled wildly. At least they were hot to the touch. They flopped for a few strokes before slitted nose holes flared open and they coughed up dark muck.

Lindi had held a newborn before, as she'd visited a couple in her village not long after the women had given birth. She remembered the feel of them, how delicate, fragile, and incapable they were. How their little cries sounded, and the way they looked around sightlessly and mindlessly.

That's what she'd been expecting.

Something that would need assistance in everything they did.

Her child was so tiny that it barely fit into both her trembling hands when she went to cup them around it securely. Despite how odd they looked, the fact that they appeared blind made her heart ache for them.

She lifted her own child so she could hold them, properly inspect them, and... *cuddle* them like she was supposed to.

Lindi didn't expect for them to breathe in, and then for a horrible shriek – so loud it pierced her already ringing ears – to come from them. They leapt out of her hold and lunged within the span of a heartbeat. Lindi screamed when they parted what she originally thought was a non-existent mouth to reveal a hard zig-zagging line of black jagged fangs as they bit her.

Tearing through her shirt, their fangs sliced into her biceps. Terrified, confused, and in agony, Lindi ripped them away from her. Her skin tore further in the process, and she belted out a cry. Before she even had the chance to let go of them, they lunged again, this time biting into her thigh just above her knee.

"Weldir!" Lindi cried.

Her body protested as she fell back onto her arse and started to scramble away with horrified tears welling. She scratched them off her bare thigh when they bit it again, this time taking a small chunk from her. She turned incorporeal before they could do anything more, and they lunged for the blood-soiled blanket she'd originally placed them on.

As they twisted themselves up, burying into the blanket and chewing on it, high-pitched, infant snarls came from the red-and-white bundle.

A black tendril shot out from Weldir's mist. The moment it sunk into the baby *thing*, deeper than just the skin's surface, they turned incorporeal. They also immediately stopped moving as if they'd gone to sleep.

A sorrowful rage had Lindi parting her lips to shout at him, but she was shoved into darkness before she could even utter a word.

The moment Lindi appeared in Weldir's realm of nothingness and weightlessness took over, she turned physical. *What the fuck? What in the absolute fuck?!* As much as she tried to scamper away, her legs did nothing but kick at the emptiness and keep her exactly where she was.

Turning physical removed the ache between her thighs, but she didn't care about that other than covering herself by shoving her shirt down.

"What the hell are you?!" she screamed, watching as her baby was brought to his arm by his tendril.

He *touched* the creature, as if he was able to hold them. Or, rather, the solid parts of him were able to. The chalky parts of him, which had been diluting over the course of the night, rested under the child to hold them.

"I told you," he stated with an emptiness. "I am an Elven demi-god."

"I know what you told me, but you said you weren't evil," she snapped back, wishing she could *feel* the tears coming from her. They floated off her jawline instead of dripping to the ground in this lack-of-gravity place. "You said your children wouldn't be evil."

"We aren't–"

"It tried to eat me the moment I gave birth!" Her shout was so twisted and raw with emotion it was more like a screech. "Do you understand how *fucked up* that is?!"

The parts of his face she could see tilted down to the child sleeping on top of his forearm. "Yes. Well–"

"I gave birth to a Demon! The very thing you said you were

fighting against!"

His head cocked so sharply, she thought most people would have snapped their neck. His nose lifted, as if he greeted her eyes, not that she could tell by the lack of them present currently.

"This creature is not a Demon."

Her bottom lip trembled as she said, "Then what is it?"

His mouth tightened before dispersing, and he looked down once more. "I am... uncertain."

"You never know anything!" Lindi, with her free hand, fisted the messy, sweat-soaked strands of her hair. "You are the most useless god I've ever heard of! You're not all-knowing or all-powerful. How can you not *know* what your own child will become?!"

"Calm, female." He said this, but there was a sternness to his deep tone, a disgruntled demand in it. "You're only upset after your ordeal."

She ignored his ire when hers outweighed it.

"Upset?!" she bit out. "I just spent hours giving birth to your child, essentially alone, and it bit me three fucking times. You can't even tell me what they are. Of course I'm upset!"

Lindi was exhausted. She wanted nothing more than to finish the process – because her stupid body still felt the pressure of an afterbirth – and then curl into a ball and sleep for an eternity. She'd been hoping to maybe cuddle them and take care of them as she rested. Even though her pregnancy had been thankfully short, she'd still grown attached to them.

Maybe her child could have been something she could adore in her loneliness. Now she was just frightened and concerned about whatever evil she may have brought into the world!

"Return back to your Phantom form and I will heal you," Weldir stated. "It's not their fault."

"Not their fault?!" she yelled. She opened her mouth to say they *chose* to attack her, but he spoke over the top of her.

"They are a baby," he stated coldly, and it shocked her silent.

Because he was right...

Yes, it was only a baby, and likely didn't understand anything about the world.

He waved his free arm to the side, and the entire thing evaporated into mist when he finished – and never returned, as if what had been keeping him physical was wearing out. Less and less of him was visible, and the white glow in his chest was growing smaller by the minute.

"I can see that, like me, they are half-formed. I have no idea as to why they attacked you, but they are asleep now and I sense no hostility from them. They may have been frightened from leaving the safety of your womb. Do not judge them so harshly when you, nor I, know the answer."

Lindi blew air into her cheeks until they puffed, and it forced her bottom lip forward into a pout. Okay, so maybe he had a point, and that did make her heart squeeze in pity for them.

They may have been disorientated. Giving birth to them had been traumatising for her, but they'd also just gone through an ordeal.

Feeling rather guilty about her reaction, she turned incorporeal as an apology. To show that she was sorry and that she kind of – not really – trusted him.

She gave him a wincing plea. Nothing reached out to her, but her wounds instantly began to fill with black, glittering sand. It tickled, rather than being abrasive, and her wounds, even the one between her thighs, faded.

Even the blood on her skin and clothing disappeared.

"You have said some hurtful things, Lindiwe." The lack of emotion in his tone made it hard to tell if he was actually upset or not.

"Forgive me for not being impressed, nor impressive, right now." She eyed the creature on his arm with deep-seated wariness. "Y-you promise they aren't a Demon?"

"Yes, as I am not one myself – although my creation is entirely due to them."

Lindi's head tilted at that. "What do you mean?"

If his arm hadn't been missing, would he have waved it dismissively? His shoulder joint twitching gave her that impression.

"Never mind. It is unimportant." The creature didn't stir at all, even when it was brought before Weldir's face to be inspected further. "I have no idea what they will turn into, but I'm slightly disappointed they are not properly formed, nor entirely Elven. I was hoping your mortality would make them whole."

Her nose scrunched. "Are you seriously blaming me?"

"Blaming you?" The child moved to the side in the air so he could look at her. "When did I ever insinuate such a thing? I'm merely stating the truth of my thoughts."

Okay, that was fair. Lindi was just on an emotional whirlwind due to hormones and her terrifying night! She wanted to feel awful about that, but she just couldn't muster up the will to give a shit right then. She was actually relatively calm, all things considered.

"You have done brilliantly in your role. There is nothing more you could have done, and the fact that they at least have a physical form means I am proud. Hopefully they will grow the rest on their own. We will have to wait and see, although it is concerning that they are sightless. Perhaps they have their own way of seeing the world, and more importantly, souls."

Lindi averted her gaze to the side, and tried to not let the strange, half-hearted compliments get to her. Yet, surprisingly, him being proud of her did make her feel better. She was proud of herself and that she hadn't gone insane with how her life had turned. She'd made all these choices, had consented to everything, and she was trying her hardest to wear it all bravely.

She let Weldir inspect them in his own time, while her own eyes drooped. She was tired, and she wanted rest more than anything. She wished she felt comfortable enough around Weldir to let herself drift off, but she was currently not wearing pants and in a place that felt wrong.

There was nothing here, no warmth or cold, but also no scents. It didn't feel real, which warped in her mind that she didn't exist. It was often harrowing, like she was haunting the place just as much as he was. With the way she floated, she often worried her next breath would be filled with water and that she'd been dreaming the entire time as she drowned.

Her eyes slitted from the weight of her sleep-straining lids, but she kept watching him tilt the child one way and then the other.

"I know you will not sleep comfortably here, so I will return you back to where you were."

"I thought you couldn't do that," Lindi muttered softly,

although pointedly.

"I left a small amount of my mist behind so that I may do so. Consuming the soul in the way I did allows me to do small things like this temporarily." The fact that Weldir had thought to do such a thing for her benefit was both relieving and surprising. She didn't think he'd show her any modicum of respect for where she wanted to rest. "I will keep our offspring until you have rested and then return them to you."

Her skin ran cold with fear, but she didn't reject the notion, nor them.

She would learn, and she would adapt, no matter if they continued to be a bloodthirsty thing.

I need to remain resilient.

Even when tears dotted her eyelashes once more, and she thought she'd choke on her next breaths, she needed to stay strong.

TEN

March 23rd, 1689

"What am I supposed to do with you?" Lindi murmured, as she gently prodded the side of her baby's face.

The strange little being sightlessly swiped the air to grasp her forefinger and likely cuddle it, only to miss and start falling forward towards the edge of the table. Lindi quickly steadied them with her palm and pushed them back up so they wouldn't hurt themselves and then wrapped her hand around their back. They laid down, curled into her palm, and nuzzled.

She sighed as she ran her thumb back and forth over the top of their head to give them comfort. Sitting at her family's wooden and rustic dining table, she pouted as she pressed her chin to the top of her fist.

She really had no idea what to do with them.

It'd been days since she'd brought them into the world, and they weren't as bloodthirsty as she thought them to be. Well, kind of. She'd already discovered something about the smell of her fear set them off.

After she'd cleaned up the bloodied mess in her room and rested in her parents' bed for the night, Weldir had eventually sent them back to her via his mist. She was a little ashamed to admit that she'd been so nervous about them biting her that they immediately launched like a bird of prey with a squawk. Then guilt assaulted her when they slammed against the wall because she'd turned incorporeal as a fear response.

But they didn't seem to mind, nor were they hurt, and they quickly got back to their feet and scuttled around sightlessly. She winced every time they head-butted the wall or the bed's leg, but they'd stopped being feral.

Then they started making this cute little whine and her heart, even in her Phantom form, had exploded in sympathy.

She turned physical, and they whimpered as they ran straight for her. It was only when they were at her knees, since she'd lowered to be closer to their level, that they'd started snarling. She turned intangible once more, they settled, and then they started searching for her again.

When they lay down right where her scent was the freshest, she backed up and turned physical again. They didn't attack, and she realised it was her wariness setting them off.

Which made her wonder why they'd brutally bitten her multiple times when she gave birth. The only answer had been because of the blood, and she'd later nicked herself with a knife to test that theory.

She'd been right. They grew enraged, but they quickly settled when she removed the evidence of blood.

Since then, all her fear had faded, and she'd been careful not to injure herself. Due to these precautions, not once had they been a violent little thing.

"You're actually rather sweet," she murmured as the corners of her lips curled upwards slightly.

As if they wanted to answer in confirmation, they gripped her thumb and curled what they could of their small body around it like it was a doll.

Within seconds, they fell asleep. That's all they did.

They sought her so they could lay any part of their heated body against her skin and take a nap. They didn't seem to want to eat, even when she offered them every vegetable she could find throughout the village. They didn't drink water. Actually, they'd squealed in protest at its coolness when they'd knocked the bowl over and it had emptied on top of them.

They just wanted her, and to sleep.

"Surely you eat," she stated, her confidence on that matter waning over the past few days. "Perhaps I should try meat, since you go feral over blood."

The issue regarding that was... all her family's farm animals had been taken by the other villagers, so they didn't cruelly starve, and she felt just downright awful about stealing what little people did have. Lindi knew she should let go of her morals regarding this, considering she had a baby to feed. Her breasts had never evolved to give them anything, but she couldn't shake the nagging in the back of her mind.

Her child also never indicated they were actually hungry, and when she pressed her ear to their stomach, there was no grumbling. Just the sound of a teeny tiny heartbeat and a set of little lungs to go with it.

Over time, she'd begun to see them as delicate and incapable – a creature in need of a mother's love – and she'd been warming up to it quickly. They needed her, they wanted her, and they were openly affectionate.

She wanted to give them everything she could in return.

Lindi turned her head to look outside the window overlooking the garden and then further to the farm. Beyond that, though, the half-built fence her father had started was a glaring eyesore on the beauty of her family home.

Worse still, with everything she knew now, it wouldn't have mattered. After having encountered Demons, with how strong and violent they were, what her father had been building would never have been enough to keep what was truly out there at bay.

If they continued to grow in numbers and actually pass over the desert with ease... humans could see themselves being eradicated. This village would be decimated within a night.

What a horrible thought.

With unease licking at her stomach, she took her hand away from her child and they instantly woke up. They sat up, and their body sagged as if they were gooey, despite how their head stayed upright. With their butt firmly down, their legs bent and out in front of them, and the backs of their hands against the table, they turned their head to the sounds of her voice.

"There's a stream nearby," she told them. "The last person who lived here brought some nets, so maybe I can catch you some fish." She rubbed the top of this strange creature's oval head. "Would you like that, little one? Some fishy fish?"

They gave a happy chittering coo at her and spun to walk on

all fours.

She smiled at herself, surprised that she had the urge to babble at them. Then again, all they could do was smell, feel, and hear her, so a part of her wanted to fill all the senses they *did* have. They seemed to like her voice, and a part of her found it soothing to talk to them.

"Alright, let's go then," she said, scooping them into her hands.

She went to the room that had once been hers and opened the clothing chest that she'd dug out when she first arrived here. The last occupant had discarded it in the corner under house-repairing materials and her efforts to unearth it while heavily pregnant had been a pain.

With her baby attached to the crook of her neck, she changed into a blue dress and cream apron she had stored in her plain wooden chest. Then she obtained a basket for collecting herbs and vegetables from the personal garden and placed the net inside it. She tapped the toes of her boots against the porch to make sure her feet were sitting right inside them, then shielded her eyes against the sun when she looked up. A cool breeze billowed around her, lifting her dress around her calves and making her shiver.

The trek to the stream wasn't too far into the thick forest that bordered her home, about a forty-five-minute brisk walk, but it was completely out of view from others. Her home was the closest to it, and at the beginning of its rush, gifting her parents' farm the best access to it.

The walk was easy, as it'd always been, and Lindi knew the way perfectly. Six years hadn't changed what had been ingrained into her memory from her childhood.

Before long, she came upon the wide, relatively shallow riverbed. It would only come to her hips at the deepest point, unless the area flooded. Loose large rocks made a path from the water to the grass and shrubs that surrounded it. Tall trees reached their branches across the river, shading it from both sides while leaving a sparkling centre of sunlight where it was deepest.

The air smelt dewy from the moss that clung to the bases of trees and rocks, and the sound of fast-moving water rushed in her ears as she placed the basket down on the grass.

Quick to untie the laces and remove her boots, she then placed her child on the ground next to her supplies. They immediately began to climb up the ruffled skirts of her dress, so she carefully unlatched them and placed them on the grass next to the riverbed.

After the third attempt, she puckered her lips in thought as they climbed their way to her hip. *So clingy.*

They always preferred to lie against her chest or the middle of her back, and she had a funny feeling it was due to her heartbeat. In some ways, she found it sweet that they sought that rhythmic sound.

This time, when she pulled them off, she knelt down next to them and put her hands out. A shimmering black barrier formed, the particles so small it almost appeared like mist. It was flat like a disc, and she concentrated to see if she was able to change its shape. With her fingertips dancing just near the edges, she pushed, and they began to fold.

A triumphant smile curled her lips. She'd never tried to change the shape of the barrier before and was pleased to find it was working. In some ways, she was still new to Weldir's magic, and she amazed herself every time she managed to wield it well.

Within a few minutes, she sculpted a dome around her child. She made sure they were able to breathe and unable to escape, pleased that she was able to reach in at will just in case she needed to. She petted them reassuringly before jumping back to her feet.

They head-butted it, then let out a feeble honk of protest. To calm them, she removed her apron so they could lie upon her scent.

Then she rolled up her sleeves, tied the skirts of her dress up near her hips to bare her legs, and picked up the small net from her basket. When her toes touched the water as she stepped in, she gave a squeal.

"Oh gosh! That's surprisingly cold!" Goosebumps spread up her legs as she walked further into the water until it was up to her knees. "You better be thankful for this, little one!"

Little one... it's all she could think to call them other than just giving them the title 'baby.' Lindi had been struggling to name a featureless being. She hoped one day, and soon, they would show her what would be a befitting name for them.

With the water rushing around her knees, Lindi waited for a sign of slippery life. With the river abundant with food, it wasn't long before the first spotty, olive-green fish came near her. Lindi threw her net, tripped, and almost fell in with a squeal.

It swam away, as did the next one she attempted to catch, and the one after that.

A few tresses of her brunette hair fell in front of her eyes, and she blew them away. "Da made this look easy."

He didn't even use a net.

He could do this with just his hands, showing off his skills like that was gentlemanly to do when his audience was just a little girl. Yet, it'd always made Lindi giggle as she sat on the nearby rocks. Thinking of him, and his boisterous laugh after each catch, made her heart pang in her chest, but she squashed those feelings.

With the net firmly in both hands, she twisted her body this way and that while keeping the bottom half of her still, so she didn't frighten the fish off. Then, another trout came right towards her feet, and she threw the net.

It was smaller than she'd been hoping, but she dragged the net around it and brought it out of the river. Water sprinkled over her as it flicked its tail in protest, but she managed to fight against its flinging, squirmy body to get it out without falling over.

Once it was on the grass and had stopped moving, she pulled the net away to properly inspect it.

"I think this is a rainbow trout?" she stated to no one, inspecting its spotty, blue-green markings. In the sun, its hard scales shimmered with a rainbow sheen, which is how it got its name.

Lindi shrugged and pulled out a filleting knife from the last occupant's tools. Placing the rainbow trout on a flat rock, she cut away the head.

"I don't want you to accidentally choke," she told her child while, with inexperienced movements, she sliced it open so she could remove all its bones.

Their blobby form paced at the edge of the dome she'd placed over them, sniffing around, but mostly uninterested.

Once she was done, she sat back. "Should I... cook it?"

Lindi's brow furrowed as she bit at her bottom lip, her eyes bowing in uncertainty. She had no fucking idea what she was doing. None of this felt normal, and she didn't even know if she was doing the right thing or not. All of this could have been pointless, and they may not even eat, but she wanted to *try.*

"If they don't eat it, I'll try cooking it. If that doesn't work... then I don't know," she said as she cut away a slice of meat. "But humans can eat fish raw so..."

Lindi released the dome she had around them. They scampered towards her, their little feet lifting up higher than they really needed to, and she almost giggled at how cute she found it. They immediately started crawling up her leg to nestle against her chest.

She pulled them off to place them between her thighs, her dressing acting as a hammock for them. She held the piece of meat out to them, and they appeared entirely indifferent. Like she'd done with everything she'd tried to make them eat, she picked them up and curled her arm around their tiny torso to keep them steady. She poked their odd, jagged mouth with the meat, and they turned their head away with an annoyed squawk.

"I guess not," she muttered as she went to place them on the ground. "Maybe you only eat souls, like your father?"

It was odd to think of them as a soul eater.

Then they licked at their maw and froze. They licked again, and Lindi accidentally fell to her back in surprise when they gave a screech and launched for the meat in her hand. She had just enough time to let the fish fillet go before they could snap the zigzag line of their hard mouth around her fingertips.

They barely even chewed it as they tossed it around, nuzzling and snarling into it as they consumed it with tenacity and fury. She tried to wrangle them with her hands when they were done eating it and suddenly went for the rest of the fish.

"Wait! You can't have all of it!"

They didn't seem to care. They bit into it and ate a chunk, even with its skin still on. When she tried to pull them off so she could prepare another piece of fillet for them, they gave a cute snarl and snapped at the air towards her. Standing on top of it, their bendy little claws curled backwards to grip it as they warned her away.

They tried to eat it, but only paused to snarl when she approached on her knees.

With a defeated sigh, Lindi let them be and placed her hands on her lap. She tilted her head as she watched them.

"I'm glad I already removed all the bones then." A relieved smile curved across her face when they seemed content with their meal. "Okay, so you eat fish."

Scales, fins, and all.

ELEVEN

October 29th, 1689

"I brought this for you, Miss Lindiwe," Susie said, her straight hair shining bright orange in the sunlight.

Susie's hazel eyes crinkled from the overly large, awkward smile she wore as she handed over a pale clay bowl through the door's threshold. Her stained apron showed its age, despite looking clean, and it helped to accentuate the curves of her thin frame. Freckles dotted the backs of her hands, her cheeks, and even her chest, which was partially hidden away by her plain navy corset and its matching dress.

"You really didn't have to," Lindi said, as she reached out and took the offering. Refusing could be considered rude, especially as readily made food was considered one of the greatest gifts.

Susie's left cheek twitched with nervousness as she gave a laugh. "Well, it was made with one of your chickens."

But all our chickens would have died by now. Did she mean a hen that had been born from one of her family's?

Lindi looked down at the bowl of pea soup that had strings of chicken meat in it. The thick broth was a rather bright yellow, and it wafted with the scent of carrot, parsley, onion, and parsnip.

She figured the chicken had been at the end of her life, unable to lay anymore eggs, and they wanted to eat something high in calories. Edible meat was a rare luxury, since most went to the nobles to eat lavish food. Farmers and peasants, on the other hand, scrounged for whatever food they could find, which mainly consisted of vegetables and fruit.

She even noticed a few wild mushrooms in the bowl. Susie had likely gone foraging for them, as well as the wild herbs, to add taste to their mostly bland food.

Lindi offered her a placating smile.

Why are you here? was what she really wanted to ask.

Lindi wanted to be left alone, as she didn't want anyone to pick apart her lack of ageing. Thankfully, she'd never met Susie before, as she was a new wife to the village. If anyone did ask about her youthful features, she planned to lie and say her mother had always looked young.

"I appreciate it," she answered, hugging the bowl to her side. "I saw Joshua planting barley seeds with two other men today."

Susie was Joshua's wife, and Lindi was thankful he managed to find one, despite his quiet and often shy personality. She seemed similar, reserved and unsure – a perfect match, in Lindi's opinion.

Susie's pale cheeks pinkened. "Y-yes. He told me he saw you when he was working your farm."

Lindi figured the gesture of food was due to the free land they were allowed to farm, with her parents being deceased and Lindi mostly absent. They wanted to show their thanks, even though they didn't understand she was just happy to see all her parents' hard work building this place wasn't going to waste.

Their essence lived on in their land.

"It appears my family's farm has become the entire village's," Lindi said with a shake in her voice. She quickly swallowed the lump of emotion forming in her throat. "Hopefully the yield is good and feeds Rivenspire well."

Susie's forced smile began to fall. "We don't mean to profit off of your loss, but farming the extra land–"

Lindi reached out to grasp the woman's forearm and gave it a tentative squeeze. "I don't mind, really. I don't intend to stay much longer and it's better if it's being used."

She'd been here seven months too long.

Lindi had been discovered not long after she gave birth, and their warm welcome had made it hard for her to leave. Part of her didn't want to, even if that was best. It was her home. She had every right to stay in it so long as the land was being used for its intended purpose and her tithe was given on time.

"Are you sure you can't stay, Lindiwe?" Susie looked at the bowl in Lindi's arms. "Maybe you can marry–"

"No," Lindi quickly cut in. "I refuse to marry just because I have to. I just wanted to get through winter and visit home." She forced a laugh while gripping the bowl tighter, and said, "I honestly thought someone would have moved in by now! No one has told me about who was last here, since I can tell it was once occupied."

There were plenty of couples in the town. With her family home vacant, she expected at least one pair would have wanted to leave the nest and get away from whichever parents they were living with.

Lindi's forced humour wasn't greeted with warmth.

Instead, Susie looked away as she muttered, "We're all a little uncomfortable with the idea... with everything that's happened." Then she held her wrist and scratched at the side of the joint. "People think it's cursed. The man who was living here last grew ill and died of an unknown sickness. The person before that just disappeared overnight and no one knows why. It's... made everyone wary of living in it in case they meet their demise. We were considering demolishing it before you returned."

Lindi's features stiffened, and she looked away as well. *Others have died here?* It made sense, considering the mess of rags and empty bottles of herbal medicine that had been left behind.

People tended to be quite superstitious when it came to repeated deaths. If they were thinking of destroying it, they probably wanted to give it some time before deciding what to actually do with it. Not to mention who would do the job, and what the costs involved would be.

I can't believe my home will be destroyed once I leave.

When she, too, just up and disappeared without a trace.

"My apologies. I didn't mean to share such frightening news about your residence," Susie said, bringing her softer gaze back to Lindi's firmer one. "Joshua wanted me to say hello and offer you some food for letting him tend to the land. Please enjoy the meal."

"I'm sure I will," she answered as the woman stepped back to leave her pathway.

She waved as Susie walked away, and the young woman shyly did it back to her before hurrying off like someone had lit the back of her skirts on fire. *She's probably afraid of this house.*

It hadn't taken long for a few of the men farming her parents' land to realise the unmaintained house had become occupied. She'd probably been spotted from a distance while she'd been outside, as she'd found herself incapable of remaining inside.

They'd come to evict the unwelcomed squatter, only to discover it was Lindi who had returned home.

Then again, one of them would have eventually noticed her peeking through the windows when they were working the field. She couldn't have stayed hidden forever, not with her staying the entire winter so she didn't have to fight the cold.

Once Lindi closed the door to her home, she placed the bowl of food on the table and pulled open the neckline of her cream underdress.

"You were on your best behaviour that time," she said warmly to her child nestled against her chest. "You didn't even make a peep."

She hadn't quite appreciated Joshua and the others calling them a dog, but she had no other option but to let them believe that. When her child had been bashing and growling at the door while she'd been outside answering their questions, they'd enquired about the sound. Then they'd wanted to meet the little puppy, and Lindi had made every excuse under the sun as to why that wasn't possible.

On the odd occasion, Joshua would try to strike up a conversation outside her door. He seemed more confident speaking with Lindi now that he had a wife, as if the potential of Lindi being one had made him nervous. Unfortunately, she would have preferred him to remain hesitant, rather than have her child going feral in his presence, as if they wanted to protect her.

They weren't very keen on strangers.

At least that answered what would happen if she were to enter a town with them – a bad idea.

She wondered if that would get worse or better as they got

older or, rather, *bigger.* It would definitely be harder to hold them back, since they were quickly gaining strength.

They'd grown over the past few months. What had once nestled perfectly in both her hands now overfilled them.

Lindi thumbed the sail fin that had begun to grow down their back, while her fingertips tickled against the softer ones running down the sides of their little forearms. When they breathed, a set of gills against their throat twitched but didn't flare, but their flesh did glimmer with the minutest imprint of iridescent scales.

The changes weren't extensive, but Lindi had grown hyperaware of every little thing about them. The size of them, the shape of them, and even the texture of their dark-grey flesh. They were still soft and squishy, as if they didn't have a single bone in their body, but they were different.

They didn't seem unhappy, so she didn't mind. Whatever worked for them would be fine.

Lindi had grown utterly attached to them. She enjoyed playing with them, to the point that she moved all the furniture out of the way of the living area so they could chase her without bashing their head. She sang to them, cuddled them, told them stories.

Every waking moment was spent with them.

It was nice to have a companion, especially as trying to speak to Weldir had become pointless. He never answered, and she wasn't sure if that was because he slumbered or was just ignoring her.

She had the impression she was being watched, but that paranoia had long become her life. Whether he was or wasn't, Lindi knew currently she was alone. He had no answers regarding their strange child and could do nothing to assist.

He could only witness, which made him useless to her.

I don't need him. I don't need anyone.

She pulled her child from her dress and lifted them into the air. "It's just you and me." They let out a squeal in surprise until she pressed them against her face, and they held on as they nuzzled her back. "Do you want more fish? I'll eat first and then take you to get more."

The smell of the stew was making her mouth water, and she'd adore eating a home-cooked meal for the first time in years.

Then Lindi would take them to the river, as she did every day. Not every adventure was a success, but she didn't mind spending part of her day fending for them. Now that autumn and winter had passed, she found the iciness of the water wasn't too bad, and she enjoyed listening to the sound of rushing water.

She played with them by the river and spent time with them outside, where there was no one to watch. They weren't adventurous, but they were awake a little more throughout the day the bigger they got.

They also associated the sound of water with fish, and they now sat at the edge of the riverbank patiently waiting.

It showed they were intelligent underneath all that nothingness. In some ways, they came across as animalistic, and in others, otherworldly. Even after spending a little over seven months with them, she still didn't know what to make of them.

They weren't violent unless they scented fear or blood, they never appeared hungry despite her still feeding them *just in case*, and they didn't want to do anything but be near her. They slept most of the time, and the time they were awake was in short bursts, and only to crawl all over her until her hair was a tangled nest from them climbing into it.

Then again, it was easier than having a screaming baby to tend to. No, they were rather self-soothing and self-sufficient. All Lindi needed to do was let them cling, and she was able to move around as if they didn't exist.

It gave her a chance to forage for food, trusting they wouldn't scamper off somewhere. It let her explore old paths she'd taken as a child, or practise with Weldir's magic – she'd learned she could carve almost any shape with the barriers she could make, and not just a dome.

Progress was progress, and life had been... easy. Simple.

Lindi still itched to leave and continue her self-appointed mission of destroying the occult, but she had found a purpose for the time being. She couldn't take them with her, considering the smell of blood she'd produce from her justice, but she often pondered on a solution.

She'd never been harmed when out hunting those vile people, since she often worked in the shadows and overpowered the occultists with the magic she could wield. Then there was her ability to turn intangible. If her child remained attached to her as they did now, she didn't see why she couldn't continue for the time being. If they changed, she would adjust to make it work until it was no longer possible.

I really need to figure out how to hide the smell of blood, she thought with a belly full of chicken-and-pea stew and a basket of supplies on her arm.

The walk to the river was as uneventful as it was every day. Her gaze scanned over the colourful spring flowers that had sprouted, and she occasionally knelt down to see if they were edible. She took a few of the nicer-smelling ones so she could liven up her home, and tucked them into her basket before continuing on. The cool air was warmed by the sun, even with the shade of leaves from above.

Insects that had gone quiet over winter now buzzed with life, and numerous pretty butterflies fluttered around looking for a mate. She made sure to avoid a certain tree that had a nasty pair of magpies, as they liked to swoop to defend their nest of newly hatched fledglings. Their whooping calls in the distance made their presence known to all.

Learning to hide the smell of blood would help during my monthlies as well.

Getting her period had become a rather distressing time. She hated locking her child away under one of her dome barriers, but they'd spend the entire time trying to eat her if she didn't. That, or she turned incorporeal so they could venture around her home freely – but that often resulted in lonely, distressed cries.

There was no winning.

I wish it was easier to learn new spells. She'd been practising with an idea but hadn't quite figured out how to conjure it.

Once she reached the riverbank, she placed her child on the ground, and they sat next to her basket. She removed her boots, yanked her sleeves up, tied the skirts of her dress, and entered the water.

As she always did, she eyed them constantly to make sure they wouldn't run off. They often got to four legs to adventure near the basket, sniffling at the ground curiously before sitting or lying down again.

With her net firmly in her hands, she threw it with precision and practised skill, and caught the first fish that came her way. Her child gave a shrill cry, jumping up and down when they heard it flapping around in her hands and then on the ground.

She placed a dome around them as she removed the head and bones, so they didn't choke, and then she released them while stepping back. They ran for it and immediately ate what remained. They licked at the grass for every bit they'd missed before giving a gross belch and sniffing around for more.

As much as she wanted to sit next to them, Lindi didn't move. For a little while afterwards, they could be rather... violent. Only once they stopped searching and came to her, seeking her scent rather than more food, was it safe.

She'd been bitten numerous times. Despite how much it hurt and how scarred her hands and arms were, she forgave them. She figured they didn't mean to, even if it infuriated her or made her tear up from the pain.

There was cloth stored away in her basket to cover any wounds once they stopped bleeding, and she washed them with the river water. She'd also brought a homemade salve that she placed on her wounds to stave off infection.

Sitting down cross-legged so they could nestle themselves in her lap, Lindi placed her hands on the ground behind her. She let the trickle of water lull her mind with the dappled sunlight flickering over them. The wind was soft, pleasant, and refreshing, and she took it in as she watched the river ripple and crash around protruding boulders, sharp rocks, and broken branches.

She patted the top of their head, and her child immediately pushed up against her palm in welcome with their slightly pointed snout.

As much as this all frightened me at first, I can't deny how peaceful this is.

She needn't worry about income, since she had no tithe to pay, nor did she feel the survival need to eat. Lindi wasn't ever at risk of starving or dying of thirst, and she chose to fulfil those needs through the desire to remain human. In reality, there was nothing but loneliness that nibbled at her, but that had started to wane with her child's presence.

I'm surprised I'm content. Not happy, not loved, but content enough to not dwell on the negatives.

With one last face tilt to the sun, Lindi pushed her feet back into her boots, scooped up her child to place them against her breast so they'd cling to her dress, and stood. She swiped up her basket and scrunched up her skirts, not wanting them to catch on forest debris or get dirty, and headed off through the brush to return home.

She avoided the area she knew had the pair of swooping magpies, giving them a wider berth than usual since they were out hunting. Glaring upwards at the sky when one of them flew above her, she was ready with her basket to swat it if she needed to.

Go home. I'm not a danger to you or your babies. They were horrible and mean black-and-white birds.

She walked to the right of a fallen tree trunk to get away from it when it landed on a branch nearby. Leaves crunched and crinkled underneath her boots, and she looked down to make sure she didn't step in a burrow or trip over.

Just as she made it around the fallen trunk and stepped into a streak of bright sunlight, the disinterested magpie flew off.

Her next step landed on something squishy... and alive.

It jolted, exploding from underneath a pile of unassuming leaves, and struck. Lindi screamed and stepped back at the lance of pain when the bottom of her calf was bitten into.

It all happened so fast that by the time she turned around with a limp, she only just noticed the grey snake with bands of cream scales curling itself back for a second strike. And that her child had leapt off of her.

A gasp tore out of her as she swiped her arms through the air to catch them, but she missed entirely.

"Stop!" she screamed, falling to her knees in an attempt to snatch her child away from the death adder.

Its short, thick tail flailed and writhed in aversion when it was attacked. Speckles of her blood were smeared across its maw from when it bit her, and it was what her child lunged for – just as they were lunged at in defence.

They managed to evade its fangs, and the snake was bitten into around the back of its neck instead. With her heart in her throat, Lindi tried to pull them off before they could get hurt, risking damage to her hands and fingers. A yelp of surprise had her falling onto her arse when they released a loud, ear-splitting shriek and lunged for her instead.

The snake wriggled in the leaves, but it was in its death throes. Lindi scampered back as her child climbed her injured leg. Right before they could snap their maw at her, following the scent of her blood, she turned incorporeal.

They fell through her intangible body and gave a roar, then turned back towards their other victim, the last sounds of its movements catching their attention alongside the smell of blood. Within seconds, her child began to consume the much larger snake, like their stomach was a bottomless pit that never ended.

Its neck and body were first, then they turned on what remained of the head.

Eyes wide in disgust and shock, she watched them eat. Then she remembered her wound. Considering they were safe and out of danger, she backed away enough to put space between them and turned physical.

She opened her ceramic jar of healing herbs and slapped it over her wound to hide the smell of blood. Then she wrapped her leg tight enough to stem the bleeding, while also acting like a tourniquet to stop the spread of venom as much as possible.

The smell of blood still permeated the air, because they came for her a second time with a snarl.

Lindi tried to squash the fear that clutched at her chest, but no matter that she cared for them, it was difficult to remain unafraid when a rabid beast was coming for her. She shuffled back and prepared to stand, only to pause with her eyes widening at what she saw.

Her bottom lip fell when a white spine began to protrude through their dark-grey flesh. Starting from between their shoulder blades, which also grew, vertebrae popped up one by one until they reached a set of hips. Their ability to crawl to her was hindered when their little legs began to fuse together at each new vertebrae that formed, going further down past the humanoid body it originally had until a tail formed.

They fell to the side, unused to not having legs to support themselves, and clawed at the ground as arm and hand bones formed. Regardless of their changes, they kept coming for her, flinging dirt and leaves in their wake.

Then white tipped their oval snout. A skull pushed from within their featureless face, and they snapped at her until a bottom jaw appeared. It was split into two pieces, with a sinew of muscle holding them together in the middle, and they parted their maw to hiss with a set of serpent fangs.

They turned into a snake! Well, partially.

Although a viper-like death adder skull had appeared, and a tail had replaced their legs, they still had a humanoid torso. They looked so strange, so monstrous.

Yet, when they fell headfirst into the dirt and were unable to lift it, wriggling and squirming like they were stuck, they looked... vulnerable. The change had been sudden, but it was obvious they were struggling to handle this new form. The skull was too big, too heavy for them, and their body flopped in a circle around it.

As wary as she was, she'd watched their transformation. It was her child, even if they were a little freaky now, and they still needed her.

Since they couldn't snap at her with the top of their flat skull stuck to the ground, she managed to put her hands around them in a way that stopped them from attacking. At the same time, she noticed that all their fish fins had grown – the back fin had split in two to accommodate their spine, while long, soft frills trailed down their tail. Their arm fins flared as they roared at her when she picked them up, but the sound was squeaky and pathetic from such a small thing.

Pain twinged her leg as she stood, and her left knee almost caved in.

"Oh shit. I was bitten." She'd totally forgotten!

As much as she wanted to assess what had just happened, she had a feral creature in her arms, and she had venom coursing through her veins.

Discarding her basket in her panic, Lindi curled her arms tight around their body and sprinted through the forest.

"I need to get home," she muttered through panted breaths. Sweat dotted her brow, cooled down by the wind that whipped across her face. Her forehead crinkled, and she bit her bottom lip so hard she worried she'd draw blood. "I need to get them somewhere safe."

Somewhere that, if she died and disappeared, they couldn't escape.

Lindi hissed in through her teeth at the burning agony that radiated up her leg, and the numbness forming in her toes. She clenched her eyes tight as she broke through the tree line.

"Please," she rasped with a hoarse voice, clinging onto them tighter. "Please answer me for once."

Lindi needed *his* help.

There was no one in her village who could treat venom, and the trek to Rivenspire was just too far. She'd never make it – not without a horse, which she didn't have anymore. All her family's farming steeds were taken.

She knew there was a fifty-fifty chance that she'd die this eve.

The question was... what would happen to her child in the meantime?

Her eyes bowed with anguish, and she held them tighter. *Damnit... I should have been more careful.*

Please answer me, her mind begged, as she opened her mouth to call out to Weldir.

Shivering, Lindi curled her body around a small heat source, and its pulsing radiated against her abdomen. It was the tiniest, most fragile heartbeat, and she found solace in it. A hard bed cushioned them as she wound her arms tighter against her child and drew her knees up to the bottom of their new serpent tail.

Flames crackled in the background, but the fading light barely illuminated the room, and the heat didn't reach her. It did little to take the chill out of the air that clutched at her bones until aches radiated in her joints and up her spine. No matter what she tried, her skin crawled, and she rubbed her sweat-slicked forehead against her saturated pillow.

Her tired eyes rolled as she searched her bedroom for no one, only to turn so she could attempt to warm the other side of her body. She took her child with her, needing their warmth despite the flush in her cheeks, her lips chapped with thirst.

"W-Weldir," she called out, a little weaker than she had before.

She received no answer to her plea and hadn't in the many hours that had passed. Then again, the demi-god had been quiet since the night she'd given birth all those months ago. He was asleep – she knew that. He'd even warned her that he would be falling into a slumber, but she hated that when she needed him, there was no answer.

Cracking her eyes open to look at the fireplace situated in her parents' – now her – bedroom, she noticed its comforting glow. She wanted that billowing heat to engulf her if it meant it would eradicate the illness that had befallen her. Instead, she lay in her bed shivering, incapable of braving the cool air beyond her blanket in case it froze her solid.

She felt awful that she placed her trembling, cold hands against her child, but they didn't seem to notice as they snuggled deeper into her stomach.

It felt like she was dying. Her bones had been replaced with rods of ice, her skin chilled even though her face burned with delirium. Although she'd never asked for it before, she wanted him to bring her to his realm and heal her of this awful illness resulting from the death adder venom.

This made her feel *too* human, too mortal – despite her unearthly station in life now.

Lindi had the power of a god on her side, and she felt like she was passing away. The irony of that wasn't lost on her. Then again, she already, technically, had died multiple times.

Oh, screw it. He's not going to help me, she thought, climbing out of the bed to drag her blanket to the flames. She lay down on the clay ground with her back to the fireplace and hugged her child.

Only then did sleep grasp her.

TWELVE

A time unknown, but awaited

Underneath his toes, grass bent as he set his foot down. He watched each step carefully to make sure it appeared as realistic as possible.

With a soul in his right hand, Weldir peered into it until the human's memories flooded his mind. He observed the way the sunshine cascaded over her face and cast its glaring light upon the world, and how the rain bounced off her tanned skin and caused her eyes to flicker faster to battle the droplets. Wind pushed all around her, which made her clothing billow and rustle around her limbs.

He took in the bark of trees through her gaze, and how the sky's blue hues changed depending on the time of day – or how it splashed the world with fire in the evenings and mornings. There was something notable about the flowers when the woman constantly picked one to press it to her nose, as if they had a pleasant smell he was missing.

Although he couldn't feel, smell, or taste anything, being able to interact with the world through her memories was... heartwarming. It was tender.

He pushed the soul away and called for another.

A man wielding some kind of bow knelt in the gritty sand of Earth to inspect a set of animal tracks. The man brushed the grains in his hand before sniffing them, bit into a reed of some kind, and then looked up to the desert surroundings. Tall, thick bundles of dry grass swayed alongside bushes of white wildflowers – strong plants that could survive what was obviously a much harsher environment. Spindly trees lacking leaves offered little shade, but the man took a moment to rest under a branch's shadow while searching the horizon.

Large insects buzzed near his face, and he swatted them away, only for them to become a nuisance once more.

Weldir moved on, grasping at a new soul. Another male, this time situated around a dinner table, spoke to other humans.

With each new soul Weldir accessed the memories of, the more he learned of the world beyond his own realm. And, with it, his understanding of the environment grew.

Taking another step through Tenebris, the realm within his stomach, Weldir grew grass over the black, inky ground. Wildflowers sprouted as a phantasmagoria of meshing colours, not all of which belonged together. But that was fine. One day he'd learn what matched with the environment he grew; it would make sense once he delved into more memories.

He was thankful that he'd long learned he could actually do more with these souls other than ignore them.

Eating them only gave them a place to roam or, rather, scream in terror. Peering into their very essence was like looking into the reflection of water, but rather than seeing his face, he saw their life. Ripping them apart with his claws split them in two and gave him a large burst of power.

Power came with consequences.

I don't think Lindiwe has forgiven me yet, he thought, as he made a bout of rain drizzle around him. Most of it went through his predominantly absent form. *Then again, I didn't answer when she needed me.*

Apparently the female had called out with desperate need of assistance, but he'd been too deep in slumber to respond. The voice had been too quiet to stir him. He also wasn't used to being called. He couldn't even remember if anyone had the ability – likely not while he was so deep in sleep.

Enfeeblement from the quick and excessive use of his mana had collapsed his very being. Unable to maintain even a body, his mist had spread outwards within his own realm and nothingness swept him under.

He didn't like stealing the essence of a soul to fuel a burst of power, but his quick wit had allowed him to be by Lindiwe's side when she was giving birth. Even though he'd perceived that what he was doing was wrong, he tore that soul apart and consumed it so wholly it no longer existed in any plane.

The consequence of that was an overuse of his natural mana that went with it, as it was also consumed in the process. It momentarily dissolved his strength, rendering him useless except for what kept him alive, his realm quiet, and allowed his mist to remain on Earth. There was also one final task he had to maintain, which was keeping the Demons that passed from Nyl'theria, the Elven realm, trapped on Earth.

If only he could have battled the enfeeblement by swallowing untainted souls. He could have filled in the gap and then given himself more mana to survive on. Instead, what continued to fill the precursor of his realm, his consciousness, were tainted and ruined souls.

Whenever Demons passed through his ring of mist bordering the Veil, he snatched souls from within their essences. But they were sickly, missing pieces, and required attentiveness before he could consume them.

Doing so caused chaotic leaks of mana within his stomach, which rumbled his insides and caused him to throw them up.

Weldir knew better now, but in his moments of physical, spiritual, and mental weakness, he'd been desperate. He'd been hoping having a mate would aid him, but she used far more power than she gave.

She didn't even seem to realise she was hurting him, but he chose to believe that she was doing so to protect their offspring.

Time. He just needed more time, more strength, and for her and their offspring to finally do their duties and aid him. Then, perhaps soon, he wouldn't be brought to such a pathetic state again.

I need more power.

So when she called for him in the future, he could aid her like she needed him to. Perhaps she could even stir him from a slumber, rather than being on the brink of death, in pain and afraid, and managing to somehow survive the ailment of the serpent's venom on her own.

When he had woken up, she'd looked frightfully unwell when he'd checked up on her, as if the venom had lasting effects. Muscle weakness, mental fatigue, and a limp that had not mended itself in the months since she'd acquired the bite.

I healed her, but she still doesn't wish to speak with me.

He'd brought her, and their offspring, to his realm to aid her. She was given back all her strength and health, and he even removed the dark smudges of tiredness under her eyes. Despite this, she'd still been rather pouty.

The edges of his form pulled and shifted as humour flittered through his mind. *She clung to our offspring.* She'd been rather adamant about holding them, even when he'd requested that they be handed over to him for inspection.

She shouldn't have been surprised that would be his reaction, considering how much they'd changed in such a short period of time.

Thinking of her, and them, an oval disc formed with black sand sprinkling along its edges. Lindiwe appeared, as did their offspring. With their serpent tail coiled around her upper arm, they rested their humanoid torso over her shoulder. They slept with the bottom of their white snake skull pressed just below the corner of her stern jaw, and they didn't seem to mind when she turned her head around to look through the forest.

He'd been unable to return them to her family home, as usual, forcing her to reform at the edges of his mist that trickled around the Veil. Lindiwe had not returned to the farm, muttering something about how she thought it was time she left it anyway.

He figured that was due to their offspring, who had tripled in size when they obtained their skull, bones, and tail. *I doubt any humans will find the creature pleasant to look upon.* From the memories he'd flicked through, he'd learned humans were easily frightened by unknown things.

Lindiwe had stated it was safer for both of them to ostracise herself from society until they discovered more about them.

Their soul changed shape along with them. He thought back to when he first held them as they currently were and had been amazed at the change. Their soul also now swirled with more orange, although the multicolours of their spirit still remained.

They were taking shape, were growing, and after watching

her interact with them over the passing months of his waking, he knew he'd chosen his female well. She was caring, considerate, and had adapted to cherishing them in her own way. Her heart had realigned in a way he doubted most humans could.

Surprisingly, the grass and flowers around him wilted, and he paused in reaction to seeing it. He pondered on the reason why, and could only come up with one excuse for their decay.

Perhaps I'm a little jealous.

She spoke to a speechless being, who obviously lacked any understanding, but she refused to give him even a moment of her time. Did humans always stay vexed for this long, or was it just her?

There was something about his voice, or tone, or perhaps the mannerisms in which he spoke, that she found off-putting.

I do have a tendency to be philosophical. Does she find this argumentative? Weldir couldn't quite help his esoteric nature.

The world in which he was born was entirely different to hers. The lifestyle of the Elves was shared with him from the moment he was born, his mother sharing her memories with him while he'd been confined and trapped.

What Lindiwe thought and believed didn't always align with his own morals and imagery. Her belief in higher beings, and her human emotions, ideologies, and morals, often clashed with the lack of his own.

I'll work on this. He would try to be more human for her. *But that'll require I study more souls.* He was not human, nor was he even an Elf. He wasn't mortal, and he knew that meant he lacked comprehension of her capricious emotions. Her heart was tangled and indoctrinated with principles he just couldn't understand, as he'd never felt nor experienced any through generational upbringing.

First, though, he thought, as the grass and wildflowers around him sprouted in vibrancy, and he took another step onto the inky ground and more grew. *First, I must grow Tenebris.*

In the distance, a mountain range rumbled as it shoved through the nothingness and replaced the endless horizon.

I would like to make... a home.

For the souls he guarded, and for himself.

A gust of wind fluttered around him as he tested how to wield something invisible to the eye. It appeared to realistically wave the stalks of grass, rustle the leaves above him, and spread his mist out before it naturally collected back to his incomplete form.

I wonder what will become of our offspring in the meantime.

He kept the viewing disc active, watching Lindiwe as she traversed the world while he created his own. He looked at it often as days, perhaps weeks, or even months bled into each other. He moved as slowly as she did while she explored Austrális, seeming to wander the very horizon available to her with their offspring.

Every day, they seemed to grow, even if they didn't noticeably change.

She continued offering a diet of mainly fish, once muttering how she worried they'd grow too many animalistic aspects and become a conglomerate of creatures. Humour sparked at the notion of what that could mean, as he also thought they'd look odd with too many features.

Lindiwe did find another snake for them to eat, although he wasn't sure what kind. It did reshape their serpent skull slightly, but only in a way that made it bulkier with a stronger crown.

Not once did he speak to her, as he doubted she'd appreciate his intrusion.

He looked away for what felt like a moment as he created and shaped a mountain range properly. The task took quite some time, as it was large, and he had to sift through many human memories to have references for his art.

It was the echo of a charming giggle that brought him back to his disc.

He peered into the mana, to Lindiwe and their offspring swimming in a body of water. Weldir paused his task to give them his full, silent attention, and even made the mana home in on her face while he leaned into the disc.

This is the first time I've ever heard her laugh, he thought, noticing her big doe eyes crinkling at their corners. Her lips were upturned before she squealed and threw her arms up when the tail of their youngling quickly circled and sprayed water over her.

Sunlight poured over them and the moss-covered rocks, sand,

and grassy edges of whatever sparkling pond or lake they swam in. A few dragonflies buzzed around them, occasionally stealing the attention of their offspring as they playfully chased after the sound.

Then, when she stole back their awareness, they pursued her with lightning speed as she attempted to swim away. Considering they were unable to see, they were rather dexterous in the water. He wondered if they were able to smell her through the water, perhaps taste her through their pulsing gills, or if they could feel the vibrations of her movements.

They sunk whenever they stilled and quickly swirled their tail under their weighty body to keep it above water. If they dropped beneath the surface, they did so purposefully and shot out to latch onto any part of her body that they could. They gave a trilling call of delight when they caught her, and proceeded to nuzzle their bony face against any part of her skin they could.

They are very attached to her. As she was to them, by the fact that she grabbed them underneath their armpits and lifted them in the air to spin in the water with a laugh.

His mist tightened around his form until he appeared fully humanoid before releasing again. An emotion lashed his consciousness, and although he wasn't sure if his assumption was correct, he thought he may have felt... gaiety.

Their joy was almost contagious, which wasn't something he'd expected to experience vicariously through them.

It even outweighed the desolation that pervaded his thoughts about being incapable of sharing in any kind of bond. He was an outsider, had always been an outsider, and their companionship brought on a longing he hadn't felt in quite some time.

I am glad she has taken to them.

He tried not to dwell on those negative emotions and let the sound of them exhilarate his spirit as he completed his task. He brought his focus back to the mountains he'd been forming, yet, like he was unable to stay away, his gaze often flittered back to the viewing disc. Especially when Lindiwe babbled playfully.

There was an unknown emotion glinting in her eyes as she held them under their arms and swam backwards. It was not a gaze she'd ever shone upon him – something warm and welcoming. Kind and trusting.

No, she only ever looked upon Weldir suspiciously, and with an unfriendliness that cut through his misty form.

"I think I finally have a name for you," she cooed at their offspring, a smile brightening her features. "Since you have a snake skull, how about... Nathair?"

They softly squealed while straining their clawed hands out to her, since she was keeping herself out of their reach.

"Yeah?" She laughed, bringing them closer so she could nuzzle her cheek against their bony one. "You like the name Nathair?"

Unable to keep himself as apart as he thought he could, he asked through their bond, "Nathair is the name you have chosen, is it?"

Although she kept swimming, her smile instantly fell. She kept her eyes on them, knowing there was no point in searching for Weldir when he wasn't truly there. He almost wanted to wince with how quickly he'd stolen her fun.

"Is that suitable for you?" Her tone was cold, which was such a contrast to the uplifted coos of just a second ago.

Perhaps he shouldn't have intervened after all.

"I take no issue with the name. It's nice that we can call them something proper."

Her features softened and didn't appear so harsh.

"I think so too. I just... it was hard to figure out what to name them, but Nathair means snake or serpent, which I think is fitting for them."

"This is an excellent name, then." He hoped he'd been named with such care by his mother, just as Lindiwe had done for their offspring. "But it has always been your choice. You're the one who will call and interact with them the most."

Her lips puckered as her eyes squinted in that suspicious manner of hers. She placed their offspring upon her chest as she stroked backwards through the water, her expression turning bland.

"Is that why you didn't offer one?"

"Precisely," he answered, as he lifted his hands upwards towards the sky with his palms flat towards the ground, which rumbled as he grew a mountain peak. "I also know little about humans and what they prefer to be called. I don't even know many Elven names."

Weldir knew no one.

Lindiwe was his only friend, his mate.

Only recently had he begun exploring human memories through their souls. He didn't know how they came to be named, if there was significance or not, only that they'd been gifted one and inherited another.

Weldir paused for a moment as he looked up at the black sky of his realm.

"What does your name mean?" he asked quietly, wondering of its importance.

Her lips thinned as she looked down at Nathair, who snapped their maw at her playfully. She was slow to answer.

"Awaited," she muttered quietly. "My mother waited a long time for me, and my birthing wasn't easy. Even though they tried, there were no others before or after me. She loved me quite dearly for that reason."

Liquid welled in her eyes before she quickly batted away her tears. She turned and swam for the shore, and the joy of watching them play was taken from him.

Even though he had an inclination he was the reason she'd abruptly stopped, he was still pleased to have learned something new about his mysterious mate.

I have waited a long time as well.

For someone, anyone, to be his companion.

January 9th, 1690

Oh shit, where did they go?! Lindi panicked as she sprinted through the forest in the direction Nathair had slithered off to.

One minute they'd been wrapped around her shoulders, both of them a little damp from their swim, and the next Nathair had leapt off with a snarl. She'd had a split second to see and hear them thump against the dirt before they shot through a patch of bushes with a rustle.

Even though the shrubbery had been covered in thorns, she'd climbed through it in search of Nathair, but they'd already wriggled away. For the past few minutes, she'd been chasing what she hoped were their long and thick tracks.

She couldn't believe they'd suddenly taken off on her.

She'd been too distracted after giving them their name, and annoyed by Weldir inviting himself to the moment, that she hadn't been listening to her environment. But now that she was searching for them, even *she*, with her weak human ears, could hear the rustle and clomps of an animal's feet in the distance.

Using branches to propel herself forward, and occasionally breaking them to get past, she yelled, "How am I supposed to find them again?!"

It's not like she could call them and they'd come running. Even though she'd finally given Nathair a name, they didn't respond to it at all.

"Calm, Lindiwe. I will help you find them if you are unable to."

She wished that would ease her, but it didn't whatsoever. *What if they get eaten?!* They were impervious to pain or injury, but they'd never been eaten before, and she doubted *anything* could survive that. *Or what if a bird flies off with them before I can reach them?*

With her heart pounding and her lungs wheezing from exertion, Lindi continued to search. Occasionally she'd pause, waiting to listen for any sign of them before pushing forward. She groaned at the setting sun. If she didn't find them soon, she'd lose the light, which would make it just that much harder to find them in the dark.

Their monochromatic head and body weren't easy to spot, so she'd have to hope they came slithering to her.

Weldir's deep voice reached her. *"Their path is slightly to the right of you."*

"Nathair!" she shouted, shifting slightly to alter her course.

"Yes. Keep going that way."

A bird crowed in the distance and a cloud of bats squeaked as they passed overhead. A balmy breeze shimmied the leaves above, as crickets chirped, only to quieten when she got closer. Sweat dotted her brow from the overbearing heat that choked the air of moisture, the summer of early January making it harder to take in hot, dry breaths from panting.

A wet snarl followed by a squeaky roar rang in her ears. Absentmindedly tripping over forest debris and sticks, she followed that familiar little rumble. Chasing the sound of Nathair guarding their prey from something, she was surprised by how far away it was and how quickly they could achieve such distance in such a short amount of time.

She hated that they were small enough to be swept up easily by some kind of bird, which always worried her when they strayed too far. But at least they were ferocious enough to battle most small predators like foxes, and could probably get their fangs into the bird if they were to twist a certain way in the air.

All went quiet before she reached them, and a whimper broke past her lips.

"No. Come on. Where are you?" she muttered, frantically turning one way and then the other.

"To your–"

Lindi sprinted when she heard something not too far away.

Lindi's heart nearly burst out of her chest when a loud roar exploded to her left, and she stumbled that way – heading towards danger rather than away from it. She tripped and nearly fell on her arse, but managed to save herself.

There Nathair sat, their tail coiled around the neck of an animal carcass, with all their fish fins raised in aggression. Their venomous serpent fangs were bared in her direction with a menacing hiss, causing their body to vibrate.

She gave them a wide berth, knowing it was unsafe to approach while they fed. Nathair stamped their hand against the carcass' torso, which looked as though it'd already been picked at by many other animals, and they gave her a second warning hiss. She eyed the milky liquid dripping from their extended serpent fangs. She'd never been bitten by them since they gained their skull, but she had an inclination about the milky substance.

Some kind of brown bird landed on the ground next to the carcass, and Nathair quickly spun to it. They chased it away since it landed too close, but never removed their tail from the dead animal's throat.

Then Nathair dug into their meal once more.

Part of her wanted to stop them, since the creature they were eating was some kind of ram. There wasn't much left; it was obvious other predators had gotten to it first, since there was only a torso and head. But each bite seemed to make Nathair grow even bigger.

Lindi bit her bottom lip with her brow furrowing, but all she did was clench her hands into tight fists.

Although the scene was gruesome, she watched to make sure they were safe and so she didn't lose them again.

It's okay. She didn't mind them getting bigger, but they were already made up of two different animals, and she worried throwing too many more into the mix would make Nathair look even... *freakier.*

They were already an odd-looking being, with a serpent skull and tail instead of legs, a humanoid torso, and fish fins running down their limbs and back. The scales that lined their entire black body shimmered with rainbows and were the only fantastical part about them.

Otherwise, they looked like an omen of death with their skull and protruding bones.

Wincing when they grew so large they could extend their snake jaw and begin swallowing the head of the ram, horns and all, she couldn't help the shiver of disgust that ran down her spine. She finally looked away from her child, who had grown to what must be her chest height in the span of minutes.

I won't be able to carry them anymore. Her heart wept at losing the cute little child she'd been holding onto for nearly ten months. *A-at least they'll be better to cuddle at night though!* she thought to uplift herself, despite it not really working.

Immobile as they swallowed the last bit, each passing second allowed for Nathair to grow bigger and bigger before her very eyes. When the carcass was all gone, they lay huffing on the ground on their side for a few moments, seemingly dazed and fatigued.

They shuddered so hard their tail flicked in every direction, and the coil of it grew with each loop they made. Then sandy-brown growths began to protrude through the top of their skull, while the bone of their head thickened, widened, and grew sturdier.

With their jaw flat against the ground, hooked ram horns grew through the top of their head. Nathair's entire body then stretched, and stretched, extending in length and height, while their abdomen shrank inwards to appear gaunt. They curled their serpent body around their humanoid torso, rolling into a ball and squirming.

Stepping back in disbelief, she bumped into the closest tree with her eyes wide and her jaw dropped.

"What is happening?" she whispered.

A hand shoved through the mass of limbs, more established and rigid than before. Hard, sharp-looking claws dug at the dirt, and Nathair used them to pull themselves from their own tail as if with force. Their snout poked out, and what was once barely the size of her fists pressed together was so big that she'd struggle to hold the very thing with both her palms.

Lindi hadn't noticed how much the sun had dropped beyond the horizon until a set of orbs, glowing bright orange, shone in the dimming light. As if they were birthing themselves from their own form, Nathair crawled out in her very direction and eventually straightened up.

When Nathair rested back upon their lengthy tail, she had to crane her neck ever so slightly, since they towered over her by an inch. Somehow, the gauntness of their body, as if they were starving, made their protruding white bones more prominent.

Their chest heaved, puffing in and out with quick, harsh breaths, and each one flared their fins.

Then they tipped their head back to point their snout upwards towards the sky, parted their split lower jaw, and let out a mind-melting roar that had Lindi screaming as she covered her ears. Pain radiated inside her eardrums to the point that her vision blurred for just a moment.

Nathair twisted their skull to her in a rapid and sudden motion like they'd snapped their own neck. Gasping in surprise, the pain was forgotten when she needed to stumble to the side as their orange orbs flared bright red and they leapt for her.

Instinctually, Lindi shifted into her Phantom form right before they could make impact. Nathair's claws swiped through her body, and they crashed into the tree behind her. It snapped in half, showing the magnitude of their new strength, and broke off thick branches when they grabbed ahold of it. They let it go, their sharp claws leaving deep gouges, and turned on her.

Nathair slithered to the right with a resonating hiss, their fangs bared as they inspected her. The fact that they followed her incorporeal and nearly transparent form told her they could... *see* her. That their red glowing orbs were zeroed in on her, and they found her to be a threat or prey.

Nathair gave a quieter, more menacing hiss that had a growl laced into it. They swiped through her intangible torso, then snapped their maw at her.

Something in the distance caught their attention and their serpent skull snapped in that direction. Within the blink of an eye, they disappeared from in front of her to barrel through the forest in search of it. They thumped against the ground, weaving between sturdy trunks and leaving chaos in their wake.

With her mouth open, Lindi was frozen as she stared at the ground, dumbfounded.

"What the *fuck* just happened?" she whispered, before her wide eyes lifted in the direction Nathair had just disappeared. "They... they grew!"

"Their soul has fully transformed." Weldir's deep, gruff voice swelled within her mind. *"It matched the colour that we saw of their eyes."*

Eyes? Weldir was calling those glowing orbs *eyes?*

"What does that even mean?" she cried, turning physical to stamp her foot and cover her face. "My baby grew bigger than me in the span of minutes, Weldir!"

"From what I can ascertain of their soul... it appears Nathair has become an adult."

She hated how blasé he sounded! Why was she the only one freaking out?! Why was she the only one who ever had a normal damn reaction to the strange and unusual?

"How?!" she growled, trying her hardest not to gouge her face with her nails as she lowered her hands and glowered. "Babies can't just do that!"

"Human children cannot do that. You're forgetting they are the offspring of a god." His tone was stern and detached, and it made her close her right hand into a tight fist with the urge to bash it into the top of his non-existent head. *"This appears to be their evolution, although they are not yet fully complete."*

Lindi looked down as anger, confusion, and... and *grief*

settled across her shoulders. She bit her bottom lip, refusing to let tears fill her eyes despite how much her nose and cheeks tingled with the urge.

Her baby was gone, and she didn't even have time to register it. They... they *attacked* her, and they never did that unless provoked!

"What do you mean, they aren't complete?" They looked pretty damn complete to her.

"There is something missing, but I'm unsure as to what. We will have to discover that in the future, however..." Weldir paused for a long while, which only gave Lindiwe time to dwell.

"Should... should I go after them?" she asked, clenching her eyes shut.

What had attacked her was monstrous and frightful. She hadn't done anything more than stand there, and Nathair had tried to... destroy her. She'd heard it in their roar, had seen it in their claw strike. She opened her eyes to look upon the tree that had been snapped in half, knowing that would have been her – dead within the span of a heartbeat.

She'd never be able to tame or contain Nathair, she knew that. She'd been struggling to do so when they'd been a baby, completely relying on their desire for closeness to control them.

"No. It is best that you don't," Weldir answered. *"They have found prey, and it appears they are going on a rampage."*

A rampage. Her child was much more violent than she'd ever dreamt. Then again, they'd never gone out of their way to hunt before. Now that they had sight, had grown large and imposing, it seemed the cute creature she'd come to adore was lost.

What changed? How did they suddenly grow horns and eyes, or orbs, or whatever?

Her shoulders turned inwards with her desire to go after Nathair despite the danger. To be by their side and in their presence, hoping to return to the last few months she already missed dearly.

Their weight upon her shoulder or chest was missing, and she realised now that she'd come to rely on the very heat they produced. It'd warmed the broken and absent pieces of her heart.

"This has been a failure."

Lindi's brows twitched into a furrow, and she looked up.

"What does that mean?"

"This is not what I wanted," Weldir stated, his deep voice lowering in thought. *"I had hoped once they were fully formed, they would become intelligent, but this creature is mindless. I can see that there is no comprehension, no forethought in the way they move. They are..."*

"Useless?" she spat, and the word tasted like acid.

"That is one way to put it, but yes."

Her upper lip curled back in fury. "So, what? They aren't the *servant* you were hoping for, so their existence is useless to you?"

What about love for your own child? Then again, what would a demi-god who couldn't even step foot in the world understand about forming memories? Nor could he even comprehend how much this was all hurting her because Nathair was *hers*, even if they were weird.

Like always, Weldir was incapable of noticing her grief or supporting it.

She wanted to hug her midsection at the emptiness she felt, but she refused to appear so weak in front of someone who obviously didn't care.

"I didn't say that. Only that they will not be suitable to assist me. Their life is not meaningless, and I look forward to what they become in the future."

"But you needed servants, beings that are intelligent enough to help you gain power."

All he ever wanted was more power. He didn't seem to give a damn about anything else, from what Lindi had observed in the almost seven years that she'd been married to him.

He'd rarely asked about her in all that time, to the point that she'd had to force him to inquire about her very name.

Maybe she was just feeling overtly sensitive right then, but she wanted to give him a tongue lashing and sweep up his mist with a broom to throw it away. He was a powerless, useless god, so how dare he judge his own child for not being the perfect creation he so desired?!

"You are angry, female. Why?"

She turned her head to the side with spiteful indignation, unsure if it actually helped to hide her face or not. "What does this mean for me?"

"You will continue to collect souls, as I originally requested."

Her eyes narrowed. "I mean in terms of children."

A long silence between them was drowned out by the sounds of nightlife flourishing. Crickets grew louder, while something small crunched the leaves on the ground not too far from where she stood. The heat continued to swell around her, making sweat drip down her back and tickle her. It only made the chill that crept down her very being more prominent when she heard a beastly, monstrous roar in the dark distance.

"I have no need for you regarding this anymore," Weldir finally answered. *"If we cannot produce servants that aid me, I would rather not bring mindless creatures into the world that may harm humans."*

"And what of your promise to me? If I can't do this, does that mean you will strip me of your magic?"

"No. Our agreement is still in place. This is not your fault, so there is no need to remove your abilities. You will need them to collect untainted souls for me, and to protect yourself as you do so."

Lindi released her right fist and sighed as all the tension in her body finally bled out.

"At least that's something," she muttered, pushing a few stray hairs from her sticky face. Tiredness washed over her, then annoyance snapped her back into alertness when a mosquito bit her forearm.

She turned incorporeal to avoid the pesky insects, and the itchiness that was sure to come.

"I am... disappointed."

Yeah, me too. This wasn't how she wanted things to turn out with Nathair, but there was little she could do about it. *At least I don't have to go through this again.*

I didn't even get to say goodbye...

THIRTEEN

A time unknown, but in the presence of an unwanted guest

Staring up at the blue sky, the yellow sun, and the white fluffy clouds that passed over and offered shade, Weldir floated above the rocky edge of a deathly fall. Well, not deathly for him, who could not die – nor truly live.

His physical form coalesced, and he perceived the pressure of the oily texture moving. He even saw it when he looked down at his upturned palms. Yet, his mate did not see it, even though he stood barely a metre from her.

Then again, here on Earth, she never did.

Weldir only ever had the capabilities to visit her here, in this world, if she joined him in his mist that bordered the Veil. She didn't do so often. Perhaps once a year, visiting to give him the souls she collected, which he harvested from her person as soon as she entered the cloud of his mana. Then she would leave without offering a word, unaware that Weldir would meet her on the fringes every time – waking from his frequent slumbers to greet her.

It had become a ritual of his over the years.

Lindiwe, his mate in name and spirit, but no longer in body, never saw him, as he refused to use the power of a soul to truly be here. She never heard him, as he never spoke. Not once had she ever sensed he was just out of reach, just out of sight, but he hoped one day she may squint through the boundaries that separated them, the very veils that masked him to her, and reach out.

Like he'd done moments ago, Lindiwe lifted her face towards the sky and let its warmth shower over her.

Although she didn't look a day older than when he'd acquired her soul and trapped her within his realm, she looked... hardened, more mature. The hint of shyness, of innocence she'd often worn, had dissipated over the years. Her eyes were sharpening with each year, growing more insightful. Her hearing had improved significantly, as if she'd been training her ears, so even the smallest twig snapping in the distance had her head jerking that way.

A gloomy downturn had become present in her pretty lips.

Weldir peeked down at her worn boots, noticing that the soles of them had begun to tear. How long had she had this pair? He couldn't quite remember, but they were old enough to appear so frayed.

Even her black leather breeches were worn, the inner thighs of them lighter in colour from rubbing. Her tunic was an off-white and no longer crisp in colour. The cloak around her shoulders was black and light – designed only to shield one from the wind and hot sun, but not enough to provide true warmth. Or, rather, he assumed this from the many human memories he'd sifted through.

Lindiwe stood at the border of the Veil, and the mesmerising deep pools of her brown eyes narrowed at the vast canyon before her. With the sun on them, the flecks of amber were bright, making them appear much lighter than usual.

He inspected them up close, coming right to her before floating around her body to settle behind her. Then she tsked and turned in such a way that the flap of her cloak waved around her and lifted.

His mist reacted to her, spreading out when she passed right through his intangible, incomprehensible form. He would have sighed, but he didn't want to alert her to his presence.

It irks me when that happens.

He didn't like being passed through as if he didn't exist.

She has brought me more souls, he noted, disregarding his ire to hover in a circle and watch her leave. Not once did she spare him or the Veil another glance as she entered the forest and disappeared from sight.

Weldir could have followed her a short distance, leaving his mist for a little while, but today he decided against it.

Instead, he faced the Veil and wondered what had annoyed her so.

Can she tell that the Veil has grown much since she was last here? Just as he thought this, a large chunk of rock broke off and fell towards the ground.

He leaned over the edge to watch as it narrowly missed the trunk of a fallen tree that was already being eaten up by the flora below. The Veil's forest was growing just as rapidly as its sunken home, the area constantly heavy and thick with green-and-yellow magic that twinkled just on the fringe of his sight.

As he often did, Weldir searched for those who were responsible for such growth and change. One being in particular was to blame, his companions assisting by lending him power through a unity of mana.

Jabeziryth's power is becoming formidable for such a young man. The male was barely nineteen and already he wielded much strength. He was surprisingly determined and patient in his creation of this haven for himself and his fellow Demons, despite being a halfling of sorts.

In some ways, Weldir related to Jabeziryth's justifiable anger. He sympathised with a creature who had been locked away as a child, much like Weldir himself. Both were scorned for things they could not control, hated for things they had done without meaning to.

Trapped. Their minds decaying, their bodies in disuse, their mana being stifled with no outlet, running rampant throughout their bodies to whirl as chaotic energy.

He'd never spoken with the boy, but Weldir had been made aware of him – his pain, his suffering, as well as his crimes. He'd also been watching Jabeziryth from the moment he stepped foot upon Earth, since it was that fateful day that also brought Weldir's own freedom.

Although Weldir's freedom was a lie, since he was still trapped, just within his own realm. Tenebris was a prison as much as a haven – one he'd been shaping for what he thought might be close to the past decade.

This world is changing just as much as my own. If the forests surrounding the Veil continued to expand, it wouldn't be long before Demons had the means to cross the land and hunt humans freely.

Even the desert has begun to disappear. Replacing it was more life, more flora, and even fauna.

The Veil had grown exponentially. What had started off as a small crack in the earth now spanned thousands of kilometres in width, and quadruple that in length. Its expansion was beginning to slow, as if Jabeziryth and his companions were pleased with its size.

Along with this, the halfling alone had been growing the forest inside the canyon, while his companions grew the one above the Veil's surface with a mana stone. It was mildly humorous that they had followed similar paths, as Weldir had been doing the same in Tenebris – shaping earth and growing flora, for himself and those around him.

Except Weldir sought to protect the souls that Jabeziryth's companions created.

Something has happened, he contemplated, noticing the uptick in tainted souls that he pilfered off unaware Demons.

More of those void-flesh creatures had begun arriving through the portal Jabeziryth had made to join him on Earth. Weldir doubted it had anything to do with the half-Demon, half-Elf. No, something else was pushing them to this realm.

He had an inclination that it had something to do with his fellow Elven deities.

They can be rather meddlesome.

Perhaps that was due to the overwhelming energy he could currently feel loitering in his mist. Weldir felt everything moving through his essence, and this was far stronger and unearthly than anything he'd ever perceived before.

It appears I'm being sought out.

Rather than going to them right away, Weldir had chosen to greet his mate in one of the rare and infrequent times she – unknowingly – visited him. The loitering entity could wait, just as he'd impatiently waited to be released from the confines of his entrapment.

He was also untrusting of the presence. Why, after over two

human decades, would his fellow Elven deities seek him out? Only once had he ever been spoken to, and that was by the Evergreen Servant. This presence was... different from that flora-encrusted male.

It meant he knew exactly who waited to greet him.

Still, once the beauty of Lindiwe and her mesmerising and confusing expressions disappeared from sight, he finally produced a sigh. Weldir immaterialised in order to travel to another location within his mist, thousands of kilometres passing in the blink of an eye.

Within the floating, although nearly invisible, mass of his cloud, a figure sat cross-legged on the rocky ground with his back turned to the forest. With his eyes closed, blue eyelashes created a fan of shade against his round cheekbones. The same colour of light blue swayed from on top of his head, the hair short except for the two thinly braided tails coming from right behind his long, pointed ears to rest down his broad chest.

Rökul, also known as the god of force, was a rather cheerful male, despite that half his body had once deteriorated from the sickness that had decimated his fellow deities.

A sickness Weldir had brought forth with his birthing.

Now, though, he appeared as whole and as strong as ever, his lavender skin having a pastel hue to it.

His formal midnight robe, which had silver etchings and swirls stitched into it as elegant patterns, covered his entire body. It was tight against his arms like a form-fitting tunic, while the skirt of it was thick as it lay across his folded legs. Black strapping had been placed around his big toes and threaded around his ankles to give the impression of soleless shoes.

Five silver barbel piercings going up the crest of both his pointed ears glinted in the sunlight, while hanging flag-like adornments dangling from his lobes fluttered in the wind, white but appearing as though the ends had been messily dipped in silver. More barbels adorned his face, one on both sides of his bottom lip, each nostril, and one just behind the upper arch of each of his blue eyebrows.

It was obvious by his hair and jewellery that he valued symmetry on his person.

Lean, with only a small amount of muscle beneath his

clothing, he didn't look formidable, despite being quite a powerful deity. Weldir, after sifting through human memories, would say he looked like a tall, slightly muscular bookkeeper.

"There you are, Weldir," Rökul stated in Nyl'kira, the Elven language, with a stiff smile curling his darker lavender lips. "I was beginning to think you wouldn't come."

His eyes flipped open to reveal their ethereal depths.

His irises glowed multicoloured, with a singular silver disc that rotated around each of his circular black pupils to let him see magic and forces that no other could. They often sat on the top outer edges between his pupil and iris border, which could be disconcerting to the mortal Elvish who had been gifted with his presence.

Currently, the silver discs circled his pupils in order to perceive Weldir floating before him, despite his usual invisibility.

Rökul then unfolded his legs, drew his knees to his chest while leaning back, and kicked his feet forward to acrobatically stand. Dark-grey pants were revealed through the flap of his midnight robe, but they were quickly hidden away once more when the outer garment settled. Occasionally they peeked through when the wind gusted around him.

"Why wouldn't I come?" Weldir asked in Nyl'kira, the language instilled into the very fibre of his being.

With his head straightening and his shoulders rolling back, Weldir's floating form held no animosity or dislike. He felt nothing towards Rökul. He was just another being – one who couldn't touch him. He couldn't hurt Weldir, couldn't control him, and they'd never had any contact ever before.

What he knew of this male was through the shared memories he'd been given by his mother.

Rökul's gaze trailed down Weldir's horns, his brow-length hair, down his face, and then his naked torso. Their bodies were similar in their leanly muscular builds, but Weldir appeared taller in his current state – he could change that at will, though. His gaze then trailed down his naked legs, before dipping down to his toes pointed towards the ground.

"No clothes, huh?" Rökul asked while wagging his brows at him.

Weldir looked down and forced his mist to collect around his legs to hide them. "No. I'm not used to needing them, and it is a waste of mana for me to create them."

Rökul gave a small laugh, cheerful just like how he was in the memories of his mother, and placed his hands on his narrow hips. His white teeth flashed behind his lips, the canines of them a little longer than most humanoids.

"Figures as much, despite how much strength you have obtained in just under two years." Two Elven years, he meant.

Weldir tsked. "What I have is barely enough to support what I must maintain on Earth." Not that Rökul, nor the other deities, knew of Lindiwe and how she drained him. He also wouldn't inform them of such a change; it was a secret for him alone to hold onto. "Why have you come here?"

The purple male lifted his arms outwards. "Can I not visit my only living nephew?"

"I am barely alive," Weldir stated, rubbing a hand down his torso. "But that's not what you meant. Your coyness in evading my question, which you will surely answer eventually, confuses me."

A dark glint filled his humour-glazed, multicoloured eyes. "Perhaps I finally wanted to meet you."

"You've had ample time to speak with me – over a hundred years, in fact." Weldir turned his head to the side to gaze over the border of the Veil and see how far it reached into the distance. "I have felt a shift here. I assume you have come to inform me as to why." He brought his face back to Rökul. "You want something from me."

"When Leyfr told me you were rather perceptive, he wasn't exaggerating."

Leyfr, the Evergreen Servant, was the only person Weldir had been granted a back-and-forth conversation with before coming to Earth. He was also the one who had shared with Weldir his required tasks once he arrived here, having taken it upon himself to acknowledge the responsibility cast onto him as a parental figure.

"What is it you seek? I have been doing all I can here, but it has taken building my strength to maintain it."

Rökul's bottom lip pouted forward as he placed his hands on

his hips once more. "Aww, you are no fun. I wanted to play with you a little, but you're just as serious as him. Perhaps he really is your sire."

Weldir didn't particularly care if Leyfr was his father or not. In the custom of his people, he had many fathers and many mothers. Even Rökul was to be part of his shared guardianship as his uncle, as was the way with all young gods and their education.

When Weldir didn't respond, patient for the answers he sought, Rökul grumbled incoherently. His eyes closed as he dipped his head to the side, which made his thin braids sway.

"Fine. Be a spoilsport then. You're correct that you have felt a shift in Nyl'theria. The last Elven city has been struggling to maintain its magical dome. I have granted the mana stone some of my own, but my mana does not mix well with Almethrandra's. I had to stop before I destroyed it and left them without protection. We may be two of triplets, but our powers do not mix well."

Almethrandra, the Gilded Maiden, was Weldir's mother. She currently slumbered, near powerless and devitalised due to Weldir and the sickness his birthing brought forth. Of course, it was also due to her foolish hand in it.

She was the pinnacle goddess in their home. It answered why Rökul had granted some of his own magic to the stone to power it. His mother had been asleep for almost a hundred Elven years, which was just under a millennium and a half for humans. Which just so happened to be how long Weldir had been alive... *and* trapped.

Only the Gilded Maiden could offer such power willingly and efficiently to the mortal Elysian Elves, and she, his mother, continued to slumber.

Rökul lifted his left hand and brushed it to the side. "Leyfr and I have decided upon a different course of action to assist. I have created many portals, each of them touching a different continent in this vast realm. Leyfr has layered a message in the rustling winds of Nyl'theria, telling the Daekura to enter them for salvation – hoping it will seep into their minds subconsciously."

"If you really want to help, why not just destroy the

Daekura?" Weldir asked, seeing this to be the most efficient way of protecting their mortal people.

The smile on Rökul's face twitched before breaking. His blue eyebrows furrowed in deep concern.

"That you would suggest such a thing shows you are so wildly different from us. The Daekura sludge still lives within you. It's altered your very spiritual essence and is why we believe you never obtained a true form."

Weldir's mist collected tighter around his body in disappointment that such words were uttered to him. He knew himself to be different, but to hear it was another thing. He never realised his callous thoughts could be skewed and strange, even to them.

But... I do know that taking mortal life is not the way of our people. They may destroy one or two, but that was usually because that person provoked the gods in an unholy way – like touching gilded ore.

Although the Daekura – Demons – were a violent and horrible scourge, they were still mortal beings. They could form bonds, fall in love, and have offspring. It showed they had hearts and souls that deserved protecting, even if their diets were frightful and cruel. To achieve such humanity to be able to do and feel those things, they had to eat many intelligent beings...

Thus, it created the conundrum of being incapable of destroying them because their lives were valuable but having to watch them decimate the lives of others to stabilise themselves. It left all but Weldir unsure of how to proceed with the problem.

His solution would be to destroy, before their people were decimated. To him it was simple.

"So, you and Leyfr are the reason there has been a sudden influx of Daekura," Weldir pressed on, avoiding what the fully formed god had just said, and how offensive it was. "I have noticed this, but I didn't notice you tampered with other parts of this realm."

Rökul swayed his head side to side. "I wouldn't say *tampered.* We have just opened more doors for the Daekura, but it is solely up to them whether they cross over. Although... you could say Leyfr's whispers might be considered coercion."

"But they will if they believe they can achieve a better life here. You are dooming the humans just to save the Elysians. How is that any better?"

The friendliness in Rökul's features was swallowed up by a stiff hardness. "We have no other option. There are billions of humans, and only a few million Elysians left. They are facing extinction, and I don't really want to be the god of nobody." This time, he pouted in a childish way, like he found himself cute, and ran his fingertips down his left braid. "I'm too... pretty to not be worshipped."

I think he's an idiot. His idea to preserve the Elysians was actually quite remarkable, but his mannerisms were vexing to someone who didn't share in his games.

"There are other Elven realms to garner worship," Weldir countered.

"But these are *my* people." Rökul ran his fingers through the short hair on top of his head. "Perhaps you have no attachment to them, but we do. They are yours to protect as well."

"I can do much more protecting if I lay my mist in Nyl'theria and incinerate all the souls of the Daekura from within their physical bodies. I feel your plight, but I don't agree with your method of salvation."

Then again, Weldir had recently developed an attachment to the sentient and insentient creatures of this world. Viewing the memories of humans gave him insight into their lives, and he found them remarkable in their own way. He also consumed the souls of many animals that had been eaten by Demons, and he'd even spent time living in their simplistic memories.

Each being here, although so different, was... beautiful.

As were Lindiwe and Nathair.

All this endangers my mate and offspring.

Although Lindiwe wasn't very warm towards him, she was still his female. He allowed her to drain his mana without complaint because it protected and mollified her. It obviously gave her purpose to continue her hunt for the human men of the occult, who continued to offer sacrifices – although she was doing a superb job at whittling down their numbers so it occurred less frequently.

More Demons meant she had to defend herself, especially at night. He was rather angered whenever she died and returned to his realm, and she was always irritable in return. She hated having to restart in his mist, more annoyed that she'd potentially lost a lead than her death. She'd grown accustomed to dying, although she often had a faraway look afterwards – a little lost and petrified of what she'd just experienced.

Nathair was a formidable creature on *his* own.

Weldir had been greatly annoyed when Nathair had eaten his first human, but doing so had granted him a gender – thus completing him physically. There was something still missing from him, something Weldir couldn't decipher, something entirely spiritual. His soul had a hollowness to it, and he had no idea on how to fill it.

Despite this, his offspring grew stronger with each meal. He'd stopped hunting and had become a lie-in-wait kind of predator, often lazing in bodies of water or in the forest. He was opportunistic, eating anything that came within a close enough distance that he could quickly immobilise it with a strike of his paralysing venomous fangs and consume it.

Even with their immortality and strength, he didn't want Lindiwe or Nathair to suffer in the real world. More Demons meant more suffering for them, as well as every other creature that lived here.

Weldir could not share this information with Rökul.

He hadn't known if he could obtain a mate, let alone produce offspring. If he didn't, then he doubted his fellow deities did.

And they feared him already.

They didn't need to say it; the scars of history were evident in their avoidance of him. He'd been trapped in a prism crystal for that very reason and freed upon Earth rather than released within their holy realm, Relune. A place where darkness and light touched, where life and death danced, and cold and heat kissed.

Relune was considered a place of perfection, where any element, no matter how obscure or immeasurable, could be found.

Weldir had never seen it, even though his prism had been housed there.

Yet, even now, Weldir didn't hold any ill will regarding all this. He'd been lonely, but he also slumbered for much of his time, gaining strength as he learned to hold his chaotic, immaterial self together.

He'd needed that time alone – and had truly been dangerous.

He wasn't now, which was why Rökul's disappointed and judgemental expression – a furrowed brow and ticking jaw muscle – weighed on him a little more than it should have. It was fleeting, the man shaking his head at Weldir's solution to the current problem, but he wisely let the conversation go.

"Salvation or not, this is what we have begun."

"If it is already decided and already in play, then why do you need me?" Weldir asked.

An easy smile curled his lips, although a little weaker than before. "Since you already barricaded one portal from allowing Daekura that have passed over here from returning, we hoped you would continue to do so, but against many more."

Weldir felt pressure against his face, mainly his forehead, as if he may have lifted a brow. He did so purposefully, just in case.

"Why can't you do it?" he asked plainly. "You are the god of force, so why do you need me? I never understood it when I was given this task with Jabeziryth's portal."

He'd also never asked, but now that he had the opportunity to do so, he wanted that answer.

"The barricade is only possible on the exit side of the portal, which in this case is the Earth side." Then he shifted his gaze away as he muttered, "And, although I can create forces like nature and portals, and manipulate gravity, my abilities are not as... proficient with complex artistry. In the same way that Leyfr is best with healing, and giving life to fauna and flora."

"And my abilities go beyond being a god of death; I'm a controller of my own darkness," Weldir confirmed, now that someone admitted the truth to him. "I can create realms, can consume souls, and use dust to make whatever I want."

"Yes. Your sands allow you to reach magical capabilities we just can't. Your vines are different to Leyfr's. They can consume, destroy, strangle, and heal – so long as they are in your realm, as you lack a physical self to make them tangible. Your weakness is your incompleteness, but you are able to touch essences because of it at the same time."

"And since one must take their physical self and spirit self through a portal, I am able to hold one of those from leaving." Weldir lifted a hand to cease his explanation. "I understand. But how many portals are there? Maintaining just one costs me a great deal of mana, passively enervating me as much as my mist that borders what the humans have begun calling the Veil."

Rökul's brows lifted before he turned his gaze to the canyon beside him, no doubt curious about it. "There are thirteen in total, not including the one here you already barricaded. Some of the continents are quite large, and we've placed down a few to spread the Daekura out and give the humans a chance to survive."

Fourteen... Weldir hummed with thought. *I think I can manage that, so long as Lindiwe brings me more souls.*

His mana had become a deeper well in the past few human years. Even though his own power was finite and nowhere near where he wanted it to be, Weldir couldn't find a reason to reject Rökul's request. Instead, he wondered how he could utilise such reach across this large realm.

Each portal I ward will leave my essence behind. Mist he could access – mist he could use.

"I will accept. Just take me to their locations and I will ward them."

Rökul's abilities allowed him to make permanent portals at will, with no mana stone required.

The male's blue eyebrows furrowed in concern, wrinkling his purple forehead, and his lips flattened. "That's it? You don't have a request or a demand in exchange?"

His mist spread out from him as tension left him. "No. Why should I? I have no need for anything you can provide me. You cannot give me power, nor true life. What could you possibly gift me?"

Rökul scratched the side of his head right behind his ear and above his left braid. He let out a small, awkward laugh. "Surely there is something your realm needs. I imagine all you do is float there. I can give it an up and a down, a left and a right – gravity. I can give you a one-time use portal. There are many things I can gift you." Then he placed his hand over his heart. "You wound me, Weldir. I am a powerful god, a holy maker of much. You can rely on your dear uncle."

Gravity? Weldir looked up to the blue sky, noticing that a cloud obscured the sun and blocked out its light temporarily.

"Perhaps there is much you can do." Then Weldir chuckled as he said, "Let's hope I don't consume you as we try."

Then again, his soul would provide me with much mana. If Weldir were a trickster, he would have lured Rökul to his realm to consume him and the power he held.

Alas, he wasn't that kind of being. And, surely, Rökul wouldn't allow such a thing. He wasn't even afraid of the possibility.

Rökul clapped his hands together and rubbed them as a mischievous smile curled his lips, making his lip piercings glint. "I've always wanted to peek inside that little stomach of yours. Tenebris, is it?"

For someone who was about to be swallowed whole, he looked a little too... excited. His smirk was almost creepy, even to Weldir.

Is this how Lindiwe finds me? Perplexing?

FOURTEEN

August 2nd, 1704

An icy chill stung Lindi's nose, causing it to drip. Stifling the urge to sniffle, she kept quiet as she moved through the forest. The dawning frost had quickly melted under the early spring's warmth, saturating the world in a dewiness that clung to the earth. Forest debris didn't crunch under her boots, but she slowed to reduce the squelch of each step she took, and the suction that happened when she lifted off.

With a brown hood covering her head, the darker fur underneath kept the chill out. More fur lined her thick hide jacket, as well as padded inside her pants that were tied down to her thighs and her calves. Even her boots were padded, ensuring she could survive harsh, freezing temperatures.

Many years ago, such lengths to stay warm had been unnecessary.

Much had changed in the past fourteen years since she, in her heart, had said farewell to Nathair, even if she remained the same.

The distance between the Veil's forest and the green coastlines grew smaller with every year, making the desert separating them smaller. Along with it, temperatures shifted rapidly.

The summers weren't as scorching. They were ripe with flora to ensure more insects, more breeding grounds for animals, and more lakes and rivers that didn't dry up under the unbearable heat. The red dusty soil became nutrient rich, providing plenty of food for all manner of creatures and plants.

As positive as this was, it meant everything was... cooler. Austrális had rarely experienced snow, and if it did, it was generally on its highest-peaked mountains. Now, though, snow fell, only to melt before it landed – leaving the ground wet. Then, after the darkest part of night to the earliest hour of morning, ice formed, making the ground slippery and dangerous to tread across in the middle of winter all day long.

After observing such changes over the past five years in particular, Lindi knew the certainty of something: in the north, and even parts of the south, they would soon see thick blankets of snow in the winter.

It was all due to the land that bordered the Veil. Its forest, likely aided by magic, was taking over the world. Animal droppings and pollinators probably assisted this naturally, but its rapid growth was concerning. As was the forest of the Veil, deep down on the canyon's floor.

There are more Demons roaming, Lindi thought, as she used the cover of a tree and peeked around its trunk to survey the two men walking.

They appeared battle-hardened. Both brandished longswords at their waists, and wore chain-mail armour and metal plates over their bodies.

Her eyes narrowed with spite, as well as to assess their movements, before she crouched to follow them. She ducked behind cover whenever they absentmindedly turned their gazes her way. Neither were fearful with the sun on their backs.

Fools. The Demons run in the shade.

With the desert so small it could be crossed in a single night, those violent, nasty creatures were expanding further and further out.

People were becoming afraid. There had been more attacks on villages, and especially on farms. Terror was beginning to run rampant, causing people to abandon their homes to relocate to walled cities, towns, and villages. Those houses were then dismantled as easily accessible material, often leaving little evidence behind. Soon, the flora would take back what was once theirs.

People were uprooting their lives in hopes of surviving the nightmares that moved through the night. Men worked tirelessly, destroying old homes and moving furniture, while others chopped down timber.

Everyone had heard of the Demons, whether that be because someone they knew had heard someone had gone missing, or rumours from other cities told of terrors. The scent of fear was beginning to blanket the world, so much so that even Lindi thought she could smell it. The children weren't just terrified – even grown men were waking up in cold sweats in the middle of the night.

Which meant Lindi's mission had increased in difficulty. It would surely stop one day, with people too afraid to leave the safety of their walled cities or villages, but the increase of sacrifices to the Veil's canyon had grown. The occult had grown to the point that even civilians were talking about who should be offered.

Idiots. Callous idiots.

With a bow in one hand and an arrow in the other, Lindi followed the two men until she found the best vantage spot. Then she nocked her arrow carefully on her taut bowstring and waited.

"Hello, Lindiwe," Weldir's roguish, faraway voice muttered right in her ear – or rather, it felt that way, even though it radiated from within her mind.

"One moment," she quietly demanded, her tone distracted as she lifted her bow. It creaked when she pulled back on the string and took aim.

"You dare ask a god to still himself?" Mingling in with the darkness of his voice, Lindi was sure she heard humour.

Without responding, she released her arrow, and it darted through the air with a quiet whistle. It pierced into the temple of one man, who instantly shunted sideways on his horse and into his companion.

Before the living occultist could flee, his steed rearing back when he pulled on the reins in shock, Lindi lifted a hand. From the branch above him, black tentacles formed, uncurled themselves, and wrapped around his neck just as he kicked his heels into his mount's flanks. The horse sprinted forwards, while its rider remained in place to choke. Once they were securely strangling him like a magical noose as he clawed ineffectually at his tender throat with blunt nails, Lindi strung her bow across her shoulders.

She eyed the man without emotion, letting him cruelly hang there to his slow death before looking around.

She approached the remaining horse spinning in a circle and cooed up at it with her hands out, hoping to soothe it as she reached for its reins. When she'd controlled and tamed the intelligent steed, she yanked the dead rider from its saddle so she could make the magnificent creature hers.

"What do you want, Weldir?" she asked as she patted its warm, thick neck.

It's been four years since he last spoke to me, she thought, as she ripped her arrow from the corpse now that the horse was calm. *It's never good when he reaches out.*

Mainly he complained that she hadn't visited his mist in a long time, but sometimes he shared new information with her.

I'm sure there is much he is still hiding.

"I often wonder if you will greet me warmly one day, rather than with disdain."

Lindi couldn't help looking down. "I wouldn't say I think of you with disdain."

In the beginning she'd been rather resentful, but now she just felt... empty. Their bond was frigid and lacklustre. He called to her when he wanted something, and there was no point in telling him what she'd been up to – as he'd likely watched. She'd been creeped out by his watchful nature at first but had come to accept it.

Their conversations were often stale and held no warmth.

"Does that mean you think of me?" he asked, and she definitely heard humour this time.

Of course I do. Her right hand balled into a tight fist around her arrow with the left squeezing the reins. *Every time I use your magic, I think of you.* Every time she looked in the mirror and saw she hadn't aged, she thought of him. Every time she remembered the last twenty-one years since she gave away her soul, she thought of Weldir.

After staring at the corpse with a disgusted sneer, she looked up, welcoming the oncoming light gust of freezing wind with her arms outstretched. "How may I assist you, oh great Warden of Darkness, demi-god of some faraway realm, and the consumer of souls?" She lowered her arms and placed a hand on her hip. "Is that better?"

"It seems you have grown rather sarcastic since we last spoke," he murmured. Then humour once more filled his voice. *"I like the praise, and the sudden playfulness. Do go on."*

Lindi rolled her eyes and lifted her palm out towards the dead occultist, knowing the other had likely fallen from his magical noose by now. "Do you mind if I incinerate these two? It's been long enough that if their souls were going to appear, they would have."

"You could always wait longer."

She didn't want to. And, since she knew she wouldn't be reprimanded or punished, she let a flame explode from the centre of her palm. It shot towards the occultist and quickly wrapped him in black fire. She placed a sandy dome over the top of it, having learned that using a barrier stopped the spread.

Once the flames died out, she backtracked towards the other corpse while leading the horse, looking around to figure out where she was. She needed to return to the town she'd been scouting before she followed these two out of it when they were spilling from her grasp.

"How is Nathair?" Lindi asked, evading his statement with a question she asked whenever Weldir attempted to talk with her.

She always thought about him – and how much Weldir had said he'd changed. He'd grown bigger, had gained a gender – although she was displeased that it required eating a human to do so. He'd become strong, and... dangerous.

After being incapable of staying away, Lindi had asked Weldir to help her find him just once. He'd been just as violent as the last time she'd seen him – like he couldn't remember her.

That had been heartbreaking for her, and the sorrow of it weighed on her shoulders constantly. But, in her own way, she still adored him.

He was hers, even if he wasn't normal. Even if he was destructive and what she, in the past, would have considered as evil as the Demons. He was... beautiful, even with his deathly skull and enormous serpent body.

"He is the reason I have called to you," Weldir said, just as she turned to the horse and was readying herself to climb atop it.

She gasped when she got the impression she was falling feet-first through the ground and scrambled to cling to the saddle, to no avail. This was how it felt every time Weldir stole her from Earth. Her heart would leap and squeeze with the stomach flip of inertia, and her hair would lift around her as if she fell from a high place.

In the blink of an eye, she went from bright morning to pitch darkness.

"I really wish you wouldn't do that," she grumbled with the lightest echo as if she was in a vast room, and she slowly threw her arms around to get her bearings in the weightlessness.

"Why not? How else am I to bring you here?" he asked, his voice stronger and louder, and she turned her face in the direction of its owner.

"At least give someone warning before you make them disappear from the realm they were standing in," she answered, turning incorporeal – which made her tangible to him, as per his preference – while taking in his ethereal form. "I also wanted to keep that horse, by the way."

There's less of him than usual, she noted. His physical form was barely a strip of chalk and glittering black sand. It swirled around his legs, his waist, his torso, and arms. Only his nose and cheeks were visible, below a small amount of two-inch-long hair coming from the crown of his head. *He wasn't this powerless the last time I saw him.*

How long ago had that been? Four years ago, maybe a little longer? It'd been a while since she'd died, as she'd grown more adept with his magic. Lindi was able to better fend off Demons now, and she'd never had any issues enacting justice against the occultists.

"I will try to give you warning, then, if it pleases you," he said, mouthless and without eyes to offer an expression. White flames pulled from the satchel at her side and floated towards the part of his hand she could see. "You have collected four souls. It hasn't been that long since you returned to my mist."

"Some Demons are reaching towns." With spite, not aimed at him but at the changing state of the world, her jaw muscles knotted when she ground her molars. "It means there are more people – more *Ghosts* – for me to find."

His face tilted back, as if to look at some non-existent sky. "So... that time has come, no matter how much I have tried to prevent it."

The outer corners of her eyes bowed with discontent and worry. She knew what he spoke of.

"I know you opened portals to bring wildlife from other lands here," Lindi stated, remembering how he'd told her of such details. She'd even seen them – an abundance of prey animals and predators that shouldn't exist here. "Can't you just... do it again?"

A sigh flittered around her. "No. That was not my power, but another deity's. It was only ever meant to be a temporary solution."

A few years ago, Weldir had informed Lindi that he'd opened a portal and moved it across the world at will. With it, he'd brought all manner of creatures here to Austrális, as it didn't have many to begin with. A wide range of prey and predators were introduced, although mostly the latter, in the hope they'd whittle down the number of Demons naturally.

He'd also done it to give the Demons things to hunt and eat other than humans. In those few years, and currently, those animals had grown in numbers at a startling rate. The expanding forests of Austrális gave them plenty of life to fuel them, although there were a few hiccups regarding predators harming some humans who hadn't yet moved to walled villages.

Brown and black bears were a new thing, and they were rather large and frightful beasts, especially during mating and offspring season. New species of deer, antelope, and hares had been introduced, giving everything something to chase – although they were easily startled and fast. Wolves, large cats, and even foxes had begun making their homes across the land as well.

So, so much has changed. From the fauna to the flora, and Lindi was witnessing it all, ever stuck with the knowledge but unable to do a damn thing to help.

She still felt so human, despite all her new abilities.

Learning Weldir was trying, pointlessly, to help, eased how

she felt about him. Did she like him? No. But she couldn't dislike a stranger when she could see he was attempting to help in his own way.

He wasn't as evil as she'd thought him to be.

Turning to him, since she'd been staring at him from the side, she pushed her fur hood back and let her hair wave around her. "You mentioned something about Nathair. Is he okay?"

"He will always be okay. He is immortal, just like his sire," Weldir stated plainly. The spray of his chalky mist spread out, but as he consumed the souls she'd given him, each one whole, the ribbons of his body revealed a little more. "It appears I was wrong. I have use for you, after all, in the terms of our original agreement."

Lindi's brows twitched, confused, before they drew together. "But you said that there was no need to... to do *that*. That he wouldn't be useful as a servant."

"And by all regards, he isn't. He is ill-tempered and uncontrollable." He lifted a hand, appeared to look down at it, and then closed it. "However, he recently visited the Veil of his own volition. With it, he brought many souls – enough to stir me from slumber."

"He collected souls for you?" she asked, pushing a few of her floating strands of hair away from her eyes. "Why? How?"

"It appears my offspring is a soul eater, much like me, after all. Except that he is naturally able to heal the souls of humans that have been consumed by Demons."

"How do you know they were eaten by Demons? What if he ate them?"

Just thinking about a child she brought into the world consuming humans made a shiver ripple down her spine until the fine hairs on her arms and legs stood on end. Lindi pushed the disgust and fear down, especially as she'd been trying for a long time to just accept it.

He was what he was. A serpent monster, destructive and magnificent at the same time. Something mighty, strong, and... beautiful.

"I have been inspecting the memories of all the humans that I have eaten. I bore witness to their final moments, and they were not at the claws of Nathair – although he brought me a few that were."

"And you want to create more of him in the hope that they'll bring you more souls?" Unease churned her stomach, and she placed her hands over it in an attempt to soothe it. "They may just attack humans, like the Demons. We could be adding to the problem."

Weldir turned, his visible body leaving his mist before it swiftly followed to encase him again. "That is a small price to pay. A few offspring hunting an unwitting human when they have shown they can massacre many Demons, in turn preserving human life, outweighs their cons."

"I don't think I can agree to this," Lindi rejected, chewing at her bottom lip until it swelled and stung. "And as much as I care for Nathair... knowing he's harmed humans makes me feel sick."

"And yet it is that very thing that is making him intelligent."

"What do you mean? Nathair isn't intelligent. He's a wild beast." She hated talking about him that way, but that was what he was. A mindless, bloodthirsty beast, chasing after anything that moved in his radius.

Not even Lindi could get close to him without being struck at by his venomous fangs. *If he bites them, he paralyses.* She'd avoided such a fate, but Weldir had kept her informed of the properties of his magical venom. It kept his victim alive but incapable of moving, just so he could eat them at his whim – well... in theory, if he didn't consume anything that bled within seconds.

It meant he could fend off multiple opponents, rendering each one immobile until he was done. Then he could take his time. Nothing escaping, nothing safe.

"Actually," Weldir started, his tone uplifted even if his face was stiff as stone as he spoke, "his mannerisms have been changing. It took me a while to notice the difference, but I can see thought behind his actions now. There is... change. I believe each human he consumes aids his mind."

"Like he is gaining humanity?" she asked with a hopeful tone.

She pushed her hands back through the air, and she propelled herself forward slightly – a new ability she had in his realm that developed a few years ago. It apparently had something to do with some Rökul person.

Reducing *some* of the distance between them, she came close enough to better see his partial features. Which was very little. It just meant she could see minor lip or brow twitches whenever his coalesced self moved to reveal them.

"Does that mean he may one day stop hurting humans?"

Weldir shrugged. She'd never seen him do that before, but Lindi figured he attempted to mimic human actions for her sake.

"That would remain to be seen, but possibly. Either way, if he grows more intelligent, and continues to consume and heal the souls of humans that have been eaten by Demons, by in turn eating them, then our offspring may passively assist me. They are too mindless to not have their own free will. I doubt I can acquire loyalty from such beings, but if they pass through my mist, I can take the souls that have clung to them. They will be servants without knowing it."

Lindi's mouth open and closed, one moment wanting to refuse, the next wanting to agree.

The fact that they would destroy Demons, aiding their plight, was so beneficial she wanted to say yes. They were immortal, and if the others were like Nathair, they would be formidable and fierce.

But I would have to look after them, carry them... birth them. At least now she knew what to expect, but doing it all again sounded just as frightful. What if something different happened, or there were unknown complications?

Looking down at her hands, she picked at her nails. *I'm nervous, but...* She looked at Weldir through her long, dark lashes. *He's not asking, not really.* She'd already agreed to do this.

It was part of their deal.

"Why do you look so concerned?"

Her lips parted, and she looked up in surprise that he would even ask. She shrugged her right shoulder in answer.

"You can choose their animal variations. Perhaps when or *if* they gain enough intelligence, you can rekindle a bond with them, teach them your ways, and how to act human. One day you may even be able to speak to them."

She hugged her elbow and hid her face behind her hair,

confused as to why, after so many years, she still felt so unsure in his presence. He was the only one who made those innocent feelings arise, even when she tried shedding them. She was older, more mature, even if she was stuck in this body.

"I guess I didn't consider that."

"I know you have been lonely in your solitude, Lindiwe. You have not made any lasting companions and only speak to other humans briefly."

"What is the point in knowing anyone when they grow older and I do not? That seems foolish."

Weldir came closer until he was less than a foot away from her face, as if he wanted to see it through her curled tresses. "Yes, but from what I've seen in humans, such isolation can twist one's mind."

"I'm fine." She tried to laugh it off, even though her lips didn't smile, nor did her tone indicate anything more than panic for the conversation to end.

"Should I speak to you more?"

I'd rather you didn't speak to me at all, Lindi's mind retorted callously, although she'd never utter that.

"Whatever you wish," she muttered, stifling the urge to curl her upper lip in distaste. "If you want more children, then that's what we'll have. That was the deal. In exchange for life and your magic, I would collect souls and make you... *servants.*"

"That is all very true."

"Then why bother with the explanation?" Lindi stated coldly. "Just tell me what you want from me, and I'll do it, rather than making it out as if I have a choice."

As if her words struck a touchless being, he flittered away from her swiftly with a grunt. "This was your choice to begin with. I told you the requirement."

"I know," she bit back in a whisper. "And I'm doing it."

Doesn't mean I can't complain the entire time. She'd grin and bear it because that's what she had to do. Because Lindi *did* stupidly make the decision to agree to all this, and that wasn't his fault, but hers.

She wouldn't punish him for her own mistakes.

A sigh slipped from him, just as his mist sprayed out from his humanoid form. "So be it. We will do it like before. Do you want to undress, or should I just evaporate your clothing?"

Lindi gasped and lifted her arms to look down at her winter gear. She quickly crossed an arm over her breasts and covered her pubic mound with her other hand, as if to further shield them from him, like he could peer through her clothing. She sincerely hoped he didn't have that ability!

"What? Now?!"

His head cocked to the side so sharply it didn't appear like a natural movement, but a forced one. "Why not now?"

Give a girl a chance to wrap her head around the idea of being impregnated! The man, or god, or whatever, had no decorum!

She cringed. "Couldn't you just give me a few days?"

"What does a few days matter?"

She could ask the same thing!

She shied her gaze away when her cheeks flared with heat. "I'd like some time to process this."

"The sooner we do this, the sooner we can create another offspring. If their development is the same, then I can begin finding additional mates, knowing this is a tried-and-true process."

Other than her eyes growing wide, Lindi stilled. She froze to the point that she thought even her hair wisping through this floating realm halted. "What... did you just say?"

"This was never meant to be a lone burden," Weldir continued, his tone as nondescript and emotionless as ever, like he spoke of nothing more than the weather.

Lindi stared at him, gobsmacked. Surely the words he'd just uttered were a joke! But in the small silence that followed, he didn't say he was jesting, and the reality sunk in.

"Y-you plan to have other wives, mates?"

Oddly enough, his coalescing form chalked around his face in time for her to see his brow pinched together. "Why do you sound so surprised? I have told you that we deities, and even many Elves, have synergistic bonds. I would have had many fathers and mothers, had they not all been eradicated."

Lindi *vaguely* remembered such a topic, but she hadn't known *she* was pulled into that type of bond!

She didn't understand why her chest felt like it'd been lashed with a whip of betrayal, but it branded her all the same. Anger and hurt mingled together until it all rolled around in her stomach like a sickening wave.

"Then no," she bit out spitefully. "I won't do it."

"What do you mean, you won't do it? This is what we agreed upon."

"Marriage to me is valued differently. Under my beliefs, under the god I grew up with, only two people could be married."

"But that is not how it is done–"

"I don't care!" she yelled, clenching her eyes shut and fisting her hands. "I wouldn't have agreed to any of this had I known! If that is what you plan to do, then I don't want any more involvement. I will not live a second life bonded to someone who has many others. I'd rather go to hell, or disappear forever, or whatever *fucking* happens afterwards."

"Lindiwe, this was always what was planned. You were merely meant to be the first, especially now that there are many lands that my mist, and therefore servants, can occupy."

"I was the first, but I don't have to keep doing this if I don't want to." Lindi turned physical so he couldn't touch her even if he wanted to, then gave him a glare so foul she wished it would burn him to smithereens. "And you can't make me, even if you try."

His tone darkened as he said, "I can leave you by yourself forever."

"I'm always alone because of you! I've lived in solitude for the last twenty-one years, and not once did you care enough to fill the void. I'd rather rot here and go mad than let you touch me while you have other women."

She hated that tears welled in her eyes, but she couldn't stem them even if she tried. Her bottom lip trembled as her sinuses tingled, and she had to hold back a shuddering sob when the dam of her emotions threatened to give way.

She was tired and already felt hollow inside. His 'plan' just made her feel all the worse.

"I don't care that you're a demi-god from a different realm, or if it's done differently there. I don't want this anymore. This life, this power, you can have it back. I'd rather you kill me than be subjugated to a pain I know I cannot handle, even if your absent presence already leaves me with sorrow."

I've already sacrificed so much. Years, in fact, for a selfish Elven god that likely didn't even know how his words could hurt.

She was thankful he wasn't physical. It allowed a barrier between them where Lindi had the control over her body, her will, and there was *nothing* Weldir could do about it. All of this, even if it left her annoyed or irritable, was *her* choice.

Lindi didn't have to keep doing this anymore.

The suffering, dying, wandering, and sadness. She didn't need to hold onto such a pitiful life.

She hadn't realised she had such power, such control, until this very moment. That, in reality, she really did have a choice, just one she'd never wielded before, nor cared to. Somewhere in her heart and in the back of her mind, she'd always been okay with their shaky companionship and her duties, but she was also fine without it all, even if it meant her eventual true death.

I hope when he truly eats my soul, he stares at it with regret.

The dark world around her rumbled, wobbling and warping as if shadows of light just beyond her periphery had always been present and could be skewed. A growl reverberated from everywhere, and it spread across her skin like the tickling threat of razor claws.

It was *his* growl.

A snarl, a warning, so terrifying it could spread the ice of fear into one's veins. Something that demanded wordlessly that one should bow their head and obey.

Lindi, on the other hand, sneered. He could bark as much as he wanted to, but he'd never be able to bite.

Within the span of a heartbeat, Weldir disappeared into thin air and materialised in front of her. Lindi gasped in surprise and reared her head back, especially as he'd blinked into the space less than an inch from her nose.

With the back of his skull missing, his entire face was visible for the very first time and, in such proximity, it was as handsome as it was frightful. Behind a chiselled jaw, high cheekbones, an attractive eyebrow arch, and a slightly rounded nose tip, was the sneer seething with anger.

His pitch-black eyes, lacking in any white sclera, were like pools of glossy voids, endlessly deeper than the ether in which she floated.

His lips, with the bottom one fuller and poutier than the thinner top, were curled back to reveal a set of sharp canine fangs on the top and bottom. A set of smooth, although segmented, horns pushed back over the top of his two-inch-long hair, making him look like a devil.

"Not once have you ever tried to erase the barriers between us either, little human," Weldir snarled. "The only cold I have experienced is in your gaze, and your reach for me is as barren and vast as the deserts you once crossed. Yet you throw my lack of attempts at me when you make yourself impossible to court?"

His left cheek began to crack and wisp away, as if he was losing his hold on his face being visible.

As much as his words struck with truth, Lindi narrowed her eyes further. It was his fault as much as hers. Perhaps they just weren't compatible for anything truly lasting.

"I will *never* turn into a Phantom again in this realm, Weldir, if that is your intention," Lindi stated, refusing to acknowledge his accusations which deviated from the current issue.

"Your first reaction is to put yourself out of my reach and shout at me, rather than discuss," he bit, his lips twitching into a scowl. "You have a nasty habit of speaking over the top of me, human. It begins to tire me."

"The topic is not up for debate," Lindi snapped, resisting the urge to falter. "I will not *discuss* something when there is *nothing* you can do to change my mind. Leave me here, for all I care. Break our bond, do whatever it is that you must do, but I will not be moved from this."

"I don't know how to break our bond without destroying your soul entirely."

"Then do that!" Lindi waved her arms in the air as a show of petty annoyance, hiding how much her heart was racing at the idea of true death. "Dead is dead. What will it matter to me if there is nothing beyond? It is better than being stuck here, in your empty, desolate realm, alone."

A tsk sounded from him. Then he pulled back as the entire left side of his face broke apart like the falling pieces of a hollow statue and moved to fill other parts of his body.

"I don't want to do that." He folded his arms, from what she could visibly tell, across his naked chest. Then they loosened so he could cover his face. "Is having a mate always this hard? Female, if you are discontent, you merely need to voice it. We can *discuss* issues, rather than dramatise them."

Lindi shrugged her shoulder while snorting in disbelief. "Why? So you can pretend I have a choice in such matters? You are a *god,* Weldir. Our histories tell tales of their mannerisms. Your kind do what you want, and us humans can do little more than bow our heads and accept it. We are powerless and our voices matter little."

"I am not one of your gods!" Weldir bellowed with a beastly roar, and once more, his realm warped – more intensely than before. She flinched, and stemmed the urge to cover her ears when they ran from the loudness of his yell. "Lindiwe, do not lump me in with beings I know nothing about other than from tales in the memories of humans who have never seen them. I am not like them, nor am I even aligned with my own."

Averting her gaze to the side at the strange and unwelcome swell in her stomach, she covered it with her palms once more in an attempt to soothe it. It was true she thought of him like all others she'd heard of, but why shouldn't she? She had no knowledge of him, his people, or his desires.

In reality, she had nothing but her assumptions to work with, and even human men who wanted more wives couldn't be moved. Although, admittedly, they tended to do so for sexual gratification and variety, whereas Weldir, in all the years they'd been together, hadn't attempted any kind of intimacy with her.

She understood that his want of this was simply strategic for the one thing he did desire: power. Did that make it better in her eyes? Sure. But she still couldn't swallow it, and nothing would ever make her.

Her values were just too deeply ingrained in her mind.

Still, after what he said, not a word crawled up her throat. He was right; she'd gotten upset without even listening, and she was making assumptions based on her own lived history.

Lindi bit her lips and waited for whatever he said next.

Seeing she wasn't going to be the one to break the silence,

and was refusing to look at him, he moved into the path of her sight. She almost childishly looked away with a pout, but she didn't, not wanting to be perceived as immature – especially for a woman who was nearly three and forty in lived years.

"This task I have bestowed upon you was always intended to be shared. Having to create many servants and offspring, all at my whim, was a heavy responsibility that I thought you would not want to bear. That is my reasoning."

Her heart twisted, and she lifted her knees to her chest for comfort. "Okay, I understand. I still won't be a part of it."

He moved away from her sight with a sigh. "Then so be it. You will have to wear it entirely on your own."

Her lips parted, and her eyes flicked open wide. She followed him by swaying her hands around. "What do you mean?"

"A matehood is designed to be on as much even footing as possible, regardless of who and what beings partake in it. You merely need to share your desires, and I will try to abide by them as much as possible. Nothing is to be forced. You wish for this to be a singular bond, then that is what it will be, but then you must carry out the duties set out for you – just as I do my own in sharing what power and life I have with you."

As she opened her mouth to agree, this a much more fitting solution to her, he lifted a hand to make her pause.

Then he seemed to gaze at her, as if with dismay. "But, Lindiwe, you must *actually* fulfil your promises. No more hunting the occultists, rather than hunting for souls for me to consume. Revert your energy to assisting me, as you initially promised. I have been ignoring you not performing them."

All the tension in her body evaporated. "It's really that simple?"

She could barely believe it. Lindi never thought he'd actually *bend* to her will. Not so easily, at least.

"Yes, little human. It is that simple." Then his voice softened as he muttered, "But... it would be nice if you *tried* to be a part of this bond, rather than so detached I can do little more than witness you."

"Fine," Lindi conceded, tipping her head side to side while holding back her groan. "I'll try to be more forthcoming and cease my wanderlust."

"And try not to be so presumptuous. It irks me greatly. Heed that warning now." His deep and gruff voice held the smallest rumble at the end.

Just like that, her anxiety and worry evaporated, not just for the conversation, but for some of the weight she'd been holding since she first met him.

Not all, but some.

"It only took us twenty-one years to have such a conversation," Lindi murmured as she scratched at her forearm, embarrassed now by her outburst.

This was the first time they'd truly communicated or connected in any way. She was to blame for much of that, but it took two to talk, and he hadn't been very open either.

I guess we'll be doing that strange tendril thing he did last time. To say she wasn't pleased was an understatement, but she'd deal with how uncomfortable it made her without complaint.

"Has it been that long on Earth?" Weldir laughed, and it sounded much more jovial than she could have mustered with the awkwardness that clung between them. "For me, it has been a little over a year."

Her head reared back at that. *What?*

FIFTEEN

September 3rd, 1704

Running while she thought she might be the equivalent of six-and-a-half-months pregnant might not have been the brightest idea, but Lindi couldn't resist. When she saw four figures emerge at the edge of the cliff not too far down, she needed to act fast – jiggling, rounded belly be damned.

She hoped her child was okay in there being bounced around.

With one of her hands supporting it, she sprinted as hard as her aching and heavy body could handle. Her winter gear caused her skin to flush with heat in the balmier spring air. She tolerated it and ignored the sweat clinging to the inside of her jacket and tickling down her temple.

There are occultists near the canyon. Although she'd promised Weldir she'd cease hunting them, it didn't count if they came right to her! Right? It's not like she went out of her way to do it. *I can't let them sacrifice the woman.*

When she saw them approach an area of the cliff not far away, she'd just been about to enter the trees and leave this forsaken place. Honestly, it was a miracle she'd seen them at all, and it was only the call of a bird that brought her gaze that way in the first place.

Then she'd bolted into the forest to hide her presence and chase after them. It was after a few long strides that her stomach had clamped up with a contraction, and she'd held it to soothe her muscles, knowing it wasn't *that* time yet. Just her muscles tightening in protest and her inner walls stiffening to protect her unborn child.

Lindi redirected her path slightly when she heard voices and brought herself closer to the border of the Veil she'd just left.

Drawing close enough that she could almost make out their clothing, she ceased running to slow and approach strategically. She wasn't at her optimal strength, was pregnant, and needed to make sure her child was safe above all else – including the woman.

Usually, Lindi would have crouched when she wanted to be hidden, but she just didn't think her aching back and tired knees could muster up the will to do so. Instead, she lightened her footsteps and was careful as she moved around low-hanging branches.

One of the three men was making some grand speech with his hands towards the air, so she had time. The other two were holding back a frightened brunette woman, trying her hardest to escape now that she looked at the yawning depths of death.

Bright sunlight showered over the Veil, helping to take away the last of mid-spring's chill. It was bright against her pupils after being in the thick shade of the forest.

Squinting, as if that would focus her sight, she lifted her hands to ready Weldir's magic. As always, she was thankful for it and that she still breathed.

The past two and a half weeks had been her wandering the forests surrounding the Veil in search of any left-behind souls. She'd only found one in that time, which she brought back to Weldir today since she planned to leave in order to give birth. It was a show of good will, and that she'd adhere to the promise she made when she was last in his realm.

Their argument had been enlightening, although their relationship remained almost the same except for a little more chatter between them. The conception of their child had been as impersonal and strange as the last time, but her chest had been swarmed with the emotional high of their disagreement and she barely registered the awkwardness of it.

She'd agreed to do it immediately, since he so graciously adhered to her will regarding the sanctity of their marriage... matehood.

Lindi had chosen to forgive, putting it up to a clash of culture. He hadn't stated his desire for other mates maliciously or because of a dislike of her. She was not a problem, or unsatisfactory, and that made her feel better about it. He'd also chosen her and her wants over his own.

That was the best outcome possible.

I wonder how close I would need to be to the Veil's edge to be in Weldir's mist. Unless he was directly watching her right then, he wouldn't sense her nearness. She needed to be standing in his mist, from what she gathered.

He hasn't said anything...

She took in a long, steeling breath, one that helped cool her from running, and readied herself for a potential battle. The men were standing in the sunlight and likely felt safe from terrible beasts.

Unfortunately for them, Lindi was the most menacing thing that could possibly be there, and she sought vengeance for womankind.

Just as Lindi was about to wield her magic, hoping she didn't accidentally hurt the poor woman due to the inaccuracy of using it from a distance, a figure shot from the tree line. Taller than any *living* being she'd ever seen, as Weldir and his changeable sizes didn't count, a person shrouded in a thick, brown cloak struck.

A bloodied, dirt-stained white tunic covered their torso, while their legs were encased by brown pants that had a side flap, making them appear half like a skirt. They didn't seem to wear shoes, even though material was wrapped over their feet. The hood of their cloak never fell from their head, even when they lunged or spun.

There was no glint of a weapon as they slashed across the throat of one occultist from behind, instantly killing him before anyone could register their appearance. The short choke and blood splatter, and the resulting thump of the man's corpse as it was carelessly dropped, made the two still-living men turn.

The disgusting, unholy chant stopped.

It gave the sacrificial woman an opening for freedom, and she willingly took it. She shoved at the man still holding her, who was then attacked, but Lindi wasn't quite sure how. It looked as though the taller figure bit into his throat like a grotesque vampire.

The occultist fell to the ground, holding his throat when it squirted blood, just as the taller figure pulled back with a snarl. It was in that moment Lindi got a peek of a young, masculine face in the shade of his cloak's hood. The woman screamed in reaction to the gnarly death and blood and tripped back to fall onto her arse. Leaning on her bound hands, she scrambled to get away, struggling to find her footing when she kept stepping on the skirt of her dress.

At least her feet are unbound. Unlike Lindi, when she'd been brought here to die.

The final occultist, who had originally been chanting, placed his hand on the scabbard of his sword and spun to the attacker. Before he could even draw his blade, he was booted in the chest so hard he was sent flying metres through the air like he weighed nothing to the shrouded man. He hit the rock once before a single roll sent him over the cliff's edge with a yell.

In less than a minute, all three were dead.

The strange man turned to the woman on the ground.

Lindi could hear her sobbing even from a distance, and she was shaking her head in what had to be utter fear. Standing over her, he looked like a daunting tower, and even his thin frame didn't make him any less imposing.

Staring down at the woman, he cocked his head to the forest, and the message was clear: *run*.

She wasted no time. She yanked her snagging skirt to the side, got to her feet, and sprinted into the forest with her bound hands leading the way. She ran straight towards two other people waiting in the shade of a tree, screaming as she dodged around them before heading into the forest.

The strangest part was that all three people stood at least a foot and a half taller than the woman who'd just fled. Lindi had seen a rare giant of a person, but to see three congregate together was out of place. And here, at the border of death?

No, something was wrong. Especially with the strength and speed the shrouded man possessed.

"Weldir," Lindi muttered quietly, so as not to be heard.

"Yes, Lindiwe?" Then before she could unravel her thoughts to actually ask a question, Weldir gave a low hum. *"I see. I didn't*

realise you had noticed them and returned. It's unsafe for you to be there."

So, he did *watch me enter his mist.* But that wasn't what made her eyes narrow in suspicion. "You know who they are."

Placing her hand over her belly when a welcoming and comforting kick came from within, she winced and braced her weight against a tree trunk to steady her breathing from running.

What a waste of energy. *At least the woman is safe, not that she needed my help.* She wiped away the sweat on her brow and fanned her face with the neckline of her coat, pleased that the cool air was refreshing.

"Yes. I know who they are. They come to the edge of the Veil often."

When the man who attacked the occultists stood before the two remaining corpses and lifted a set of gloved hands, she braved sneaking closer. She couldn't help herself, just too curious – and the fact that Weldir didn't instantly give her more information told her something intriguing was afoot.

She couldn't believe that the man had killed three occultists so swiftly – and she thought she was fast! She could tell it'd required little strength on his part – both mentally and physically. Even his final kick still had her in awe. She had to use Weldir's magic to cart and fling heavy things around effortlessly.

"Lindiwe," he warned, when she closed the gap between them – enough to see their faces and mark out their expressions.

"Oh shush," she muttered. "I can protect myself, and if I am in danger, you can just call me back to you."

Now that she could properly make out the figure standing in the sun, she noted the quality of the thick brown cloak covering his body. Odd points jabbed upwards from the back of the hood like he wore some kind of hat underneath it. He turned to the side and neared the Veil's cliff edge, his gloved fists in front of him as if he held something precious.

He separated his palms and something glowing bright red floated between them. A charging pulse washed over her, and the strangest energy gliding across her flesh caused goosebumps to prickle down her limbs. Then the wall of the canyon exploded like an invisible, gigantic being took a sledgehammer to it.

Lindi blinked in surprise when she noticed the difference.

The wall seemed to be disappearing into dirt and dust, rather than just purely breaking off! Like it evaporated into nothing, leaving a whole section gouged out in the shape of a sphere. Rocks lost their support, and a few pieces broke off on their own, crashing to the ground below.

Another pulse surged energy through the air. It didn't change the wind, didn't brush hot or cold over it, but it was there. A tiny vibration that scattered across her entire being, tingling deep into her bones.

This time, the torsos of the two occultist corpses suddenly slumped over the edge of the cliff. One quickly toppled off, and the cloaked figure lifted up the leg of the other with a foot, ensuring the last occultist fell over the edge as well.

Lindi, with eyes so wide she thought they'd pop from her skull, stared at the glowing red crystal hovering between his gloved palms. *This is how the Veil has been formed!*

This person, with their strange stone, was the reason!

In the direction of Lindi, he moved down the cliff's path to do it again, causing another section of wall to vaporise into dust and settle below. This time, a tree resting close to the edge was also dealt the same fate. Exploding into smithereens by unseen energy, it cast sharp fragments of bark, sap, and debris outwards to catch the wind and flutter downwards.

"Who–" Before Lindi could finish her question, she ducked behind the tree next to her when the person cocked their head in her direction with shocking swiftness.

After waiting a few seconds, she peeked around it. His eyes darted around her general vicinity without focusing on her before he turned back to his task.

"They are Demons who grow the Veil every day from a different part of the land," Weldir said, stating what she'd already guessed. *"The young male with the mana stone is Jabeziryth."*

A mana stone? I've never heard of something like that before. She eyed the red crystal with deep interest.

"The other two standing inside the tree line water the earth and grow the forest on the surface, while he uses that mana stone to destroy the earth. Then he alone wanders the ground below to grow the forest. They have been doing this for as long as I have

been here, alongside many other companions."

She wanted to ask how long he'd actually been on Earth, as she didn't know, but she didn't want to risk being heard. *I should have asked when I first learned he wasn't from here.* It must have been years before she and Weldir met, considering the Veil had already started to be shaped.

It definitely wasn't this grand. She couldn't even see the other side anymore.

Then again, this Jabeziryth person was expanding it rather quickly before her very eyes.

After a brief pause, Weldir added, *"These are dangerous beings, Lindiwe. Demons who are intelligent and cunning. Never approach them. The female is fast enough that you may not have the chance to turn intangible before being struck."*

She nodded in understanding.

After another shove of energy crashed through her without making even a single leaf rustle, the red stone in the air ceased glowing. The man caught it before it fell, and he swiftly rotated on his left foot to walk away from the edge. He walked out of the sunlight to meet his companions.

Pushing back his hood, he revealed a scalp that had just the lightest dusting of white hair, as if it'd recently been shaved. Curling back above it were two black segmented horns that didn't twist like Weldir's, nor were they smooth, but had a roughness to them. Long and pointed ears poked up from the sides of his head, and they were brown, along with the rest of his skin.

From what Lindi could tell from a distance, he looked younger than her frozen age – roughly between the confusing twilight years of eighteen and twenty. He also had red eyes and strong, handsome features.

"You look tired," the woman standing in the shade stated, her hair white like his, her eyes a brighter red than his, and her skin a dark brown. She stood only slightly shorter, even though she had antlers that towered over his height, and her body was lithe and agile beneath a similar attire. She looked to be similar in age, if not slightly older. "You need to take it easy. It's already big enough."

"No," Jabeziryth answered with a shake of his head, slipping the stone into a pouch tied to his waist. "More Daekura come every day. Once this is over, I can purely focus on growing the forest, our home, while you all create a path to the sentient creatures above. The stone is almost out of mana anyway."

Lindi's brows furrowed when she realised that their mouths didn't match the words they spoke – as if their speech was being translated somehow. As they continued to talk amongst themselves, she shrugged, figuring it was Weldir's doing. *I'm just glad he's letting me eavesdrop.* She would have been annoyed to learn he had the ability to translate and childishly hadn't let her overhear because he obviously didn't want her to.

Another man stepped forward, braving the swaying edge of the shadows to approach Jabeziryth near the light. He appeared much older than the other two, although much more muscular beneath his black long-sleeved clothing and cloak. A short white beard was unevenly cut, like it'd be shorn with a blade, and his medium-length hair was tied back into a low ponytail.

"I've noticed they always chant the same words. What do you think they mean?"

"I think they've begun calling this place the *Veil*," the woman stated, her pointed ears twitching as she looked out over the gaping chasm.

"Yes, I noticed this too," the older one stated.

"The Veil, huh?" Jabeziryth mumbled, turning to face the canyon too. "I kind of like that. Little do they know this place sits between two worlds – theirs and the portal that leads to ours. A barrier and a haven from the sun."

The woman's features crinkled into a frown. "How do you know what it means?"

He shrugged. "My stepfather was a linguist. He made me learn many languages, most Elven and some Earthly. I'm not proficient, though. I can only catch a few words."

"We'll have to begin learning their language. It could prove insightful," the woman stated. Then she folded her arms and poked her chin at the edge. "Why'd you save that female? She could have been food for the other Daekura."

He sighed before turning to her and shrugging his lean shoulders. "I don't know, Lettie. Just felt like the right thing to do." Then he looked *beyond* the canyon, as if he was trying to find something far away on the horizon, his gaze forlorn and... listless. "I guess I took sympathy on her. You can go after her, if it matters all that much to you."

Lettie folded her arms, cocked her hip to the right, and snorted a huff. "You're too soft-hearted. Just because you've forgotten how we sought refuge and they strung us up in cages doesn't mean I have. They don't deserve our sympathy." She sneered as she muttered, "Look at what they do to each other."

"I haven't forgotten," Jabeziryth bit, before digging his bent foreknuckle into his left ear hole to wiggle it as though it itched. "I swear my ear still rings as a reminder. Just leave me alone. I'm not in the mood."

"You're never in the mood." Lettie, with her arms still folded, poked her tongue out at him.

The older man placed his palm gently on her shoulder, causing her to loosen her arms, then lifted his other hand out to Jabeziryth.

"She's right. You still carry the gentle nature of the Elves. You won't last long being so forgiving."

Jabeziryth's features went from soft to hard within seconds, souring further as darkness crept into the dark-red depths of his eyes. "Don't compare me to them. I haven't forgiven anyone. I let a female, someone likely innocent, go. So what?"

"You will need to learn how to face needless death. Killing is in our nature. We must hunt and eat what is available."

"I killed those males!" he shouted, tensing his fingers in front of him with obvious anger. "What more do you want from me? I have fed those below."

The shorter male's wrinkles deepened as he gave a stern yet sympathetic furrow of his brow. "You need to remove that gentle, empathetic heart of yours if you wish to be king."

"Uh! Not this again," Jabeziryth huffed, throwing his hands up. "That is your dream for me, not mine, Yusel. I have no interest in governing mindless Daekura until they evolve into intelligent beings. If you wish to have them safeguarded and controlled, *you* do it. You have more years, more experience than me."

"But you have more prowess with mana than anyone I've ever known, and as a young boy too."

His upper lip pulled back in a spiteful sneer. "I'm not a boy."

"My point is," Yusel grumbled with a weathered sigh, "with training, both in wielding mana and in strength, you will be formidable. If you control them, you can build an army and take the revenge you seek."

Jabeziryth's head tipped to the side with a petulant groan. "I don't need to be a king to do that."

"But it would help. Take control. Be a lead–"

"Enough!" Jabeziryth roared. "I tire of this conversation! I'm returning home. You two tend to nurturing the earth to make a path."

Then he swiftly sidestepped them both to enter deeper into the forest.

When he was gone, Lettie turned to Yusel. Her features were crinkled in concern. "I don't know how many times I have to tell you, father. He doesn't want this. Stop trying to force it."

"You are both too young to understand that what he desires doesn't come easily. I have experienced war in Nyl'theria, and someone must take up the mantle and be a leader. There are many Daekura chieftains, and they all fight to claim territories. If he settles himself into one of those positions *before* more come, and we defend that title, he can unify us all under one rule. *That* is what will garner peace within the blessed night, while we figure out the best course of action against the Elysians."

Her gaze drifted to where he'd disappeared into the brush. "But he's right. The Daekura will not follow a half-Elf. He will constantly be targeted because he's different."

"And that difference is what makes him stronger." He folded his arms, as if to show he wouldn't be moved from this. "Once again, you are both too young to see his potential."

"Wouldn't someone wiser or older be better suited? Someone like you?"

"No one would follow me. I'm not a warrior, and he can't just command an army with someone else issuing all the demands. Like all of us, he would be forced to follow them. *He* needs to garner that loyalty. With enough training, he will be strong enough to convince all those who would question his blood to follow him and then destroy all those who won't. He's young enough to train for it."

Her eyes crinkled as she slipped her hand under her chin-length hair and rubbed her nape. "As much as I like him, his mind still isn't well. I think he was trapped in that prison for too long, father. I'm not sure if you see it, but he swings from calm to unhinged within the blink of an eye."

"He comes with his issues, but they can be overlooked."

"He mutters to himself, and he often forgets where he is when it's dark. The only thing that keeps him focused is expanding this canyon and growing the forest. He... may not be the right kind of person to lead anyone."

"Lettie, my sweetling," Yusel stated with another sigh, this time placing his hand on her shoulder. "Only the insane can lead. And it's the heartless that hold their place. He will learn. He has to. For all of us."

Both Lettie and Yusel continued to speak, expanding on this apparent war they wished to initiate. They wanted retribution for the hurt the Elysians had caused, both of them enraged that they were kept locked away. They felt as though they'd been lured into the pretty Elven city to be punished for merely what they were, despite the fact that they were trying to change their lives and become more civilised.

Lindi listened in, soaking up as much information as was being unwittingly offered. Later she'd ask Weldir about it all. Now that she was learning about that world, she thought it may be useful to know more.

I should have asked Weldir years ago about what is really happening. She knew a Demon had opened a portal to Earth, and that Weldir guarded it, stopping them from returning, but *why* had one been opened here? And why was Weldir stopping them from returning home?

Why was Weldir here at all, requiring all that he did from her?

Lindi placed a hand on her swelling stomach as unease settled in her chest. There was so much she didn't know. So much she hadn't *wanted* to know.

I have to ask from now on.

If she was going to do his bidding, be his eyes, ears, and hands in this world, then she couldn't cover her ears and hide under the blanket like a child anymore. And the moment one question came, she knew she had hundreds for him.

"You are far from home, female," someone said right behind Lindi.

Holding in a scream, it came out as a sharp gasp that clumped in her chest. She spun around and came face to face with Jabeziryth.

Standing over her by at least a foot and a half, his dark-red eyes bore into her brown ones. His head and gaze followed her when she stepped back and to the side in an eerily watchful way, as if silent cunning simmered beneath the surface. He was so tall his lean body appeared stretched, which made him look just as inhuman as his horns, and he smelt oddly of herbs.

His very presence was daunting, given Lindi's five-foot-seven height.

"S-stay back, Demon," Lindi demanded, putting her hands out to ward him away.

His head tilted to the side, causing the very short hair on top of it to catch a stray of sunlight. His ear twitched in the light before he hissed and drew his head away from it.

"De... mon?" he mimicked in English, only to continue speaking the foreign language from before – and it was stranger up close to see how his lips didn't meet his words. "I've heard this term a few times. I can't quite remember what it means."

"I'm going to call you back to me," Weldir warned.

She'd gotten him to agree to asking before he just plucked her out of thin air.

"N-no. Don't," Lindi said, slyly taking a step back while refusing to disconnect her gaze from his. When he followed, she shoved her hands up. "Stay back, or else."

It was only when he grinned, which pulled his lips apart, that she noted what monstrous fangs he had. All of them were sharp and pointed, and revealed he had a bite that could kill in an instant.

He easily looked away before nodding in the direction of the others. "You're not the female from before, so I wonder what you're doing here. You don't smell like the other sentient creatures of Earth."

Did he find me because of my scent? Damnit. Had she known that, she would have spied on them while being incorporeal.

As he continued to approach, Lindi had two options: attack with her magic and reveal all her powers, or...

When Jabeziryth reached out with sharp nails, Lindi turned incorporeal. He halted, as did she, and he tilted his head with a white brow cocking.

"Interesting." He waved his hand through her form and then pulled back to inspect the lack of her on his fingers when he rubbed his thumb against them. "I didn't know there were magical beings here."

Once more, he wriggled his fingers through her before leaning back to stare at her with a dull expression.

He didn't offer her any more words, as if he thought she wouldn't be able to understand. She didn't speak either, instead slowly letting her intangible body sink further and further away from him.

Now that she'd been detected, she wanted nothing more than to escape.

"Jabez?" Lettie called from within the forest, the name shorter than what Weldir had told her. Her footsteps were loud and crunching across the leaves as she pushed rattling branches out of her way. "I still scent you. I thought you were leaving."

"Come here, Lettie," Jabeziryth said, lifting his gaze up and away to the other Demon. He waved her closer. "I found something odd."

While he was looking away, Lindi shunted back into the tree right behind her. She peeked one eye out just enough to see that when he looked back to where she'd been, his features twitched. His long, pointed ears flicked back as his eyes darted around in search of her.

"She disappeared."

"Who disappeared?" Lettie asked, breaking through the brush to occupy the space Lindi was just standing in.

His lips pursed, and his brows drew together further. "I saw a female, but she was untouchable."

Lettie's expression hardened as her brown complexion – slightly diluted in saturation, giving it an inhuman grey tone – grew even more ashen. "Are you sure?" Then she laughed, leaned forward to get under his face level, and grinned with her hands clasped behind her back. "Or is this another ghost of the past?"

Folding his arms across his chest, Jabeziryth rolled his eyes with a low growl. "Ugh. How dare you," he sneered quietly.

He gave one last look around the area before shaking his head, dismissing her and the situation between them that just took place. As she watched them leave, both bickering like friends who liked to bully each other, Lindi had this overwhelming feeling.

One that sat forebodingly in her psyche.

I doubt that'll be the last I encounter those people.

SIXTEEN

December 19th, 1704

"Are you sure he's this way?" Lindi asked out loud, knowing Weldir was listening in.

Climbing through the brush, she pushed back the thick foliage, eager for it to thin out once more. She was careful of any spiderwebs and any potential nasty traps their owners could leave under unassuming dry leaves or under flaps of loose bark. The rough trunk of a nearby tree brushed beneath her fingertips as she steadied herself to step over a cavity in the earth.

Insects flew through scattered rays of sunlight penetrating the criss-crossing leaves above, soaking in the summer heat as they emitted a cascade of different sounds: buzzing, flaps of wings, and many even sung. Butterflies chased each other right in front of her untrodden path, while a mosquito haunted her every movement until she almost slapped herself in the ear, trying to swat it before it could sting.

A harsh gust of wind made branches creak, clack, and groan, but Lindi lifted her face in welcome as it blew past her. The cool air was a reprieve from the scorching heat. She also searched beyond the brush for whom she sought.

This wasn't Lindi's first time walking through the forest below the Veil's canyon, and she was thankful she was on the fringes of it near the cliff wall. The forest was still rather sparse due to the young growth. In due time, it would mature, thicken, and be impossible to see any light through the crossing branches like further within the Veil.

She was nervous about walking through it, but not enough for it to stop her. Lindi just kept a wary ear out for danger.

"Yes. I'm sure," Weldir confirmed. *"I can feel your spirits drawing closer to each other, but I can't tell you exactly where to go. Just the general direction."*

Watching her next footfall, Lindi blew a sweaty curl from her forehead, only for it to fall exactly where it'd been.

"I wish there was an easier way to travel," Lindi complained. "I also don't like being on the ground here."

A shiver tore up her spine in worry, and she flinched whenever something snapped or rustled in the distance.

"You could try a horse again."

She *almost* rolled her eyes at that, but she did huff. "No. Horses are exceptionally intelligent creatures. I think that's why they spook whenever I have one of our children on my person."

Plus, she could only imagine how she'd get a horse to willingly descend any possible path along the cliff walls to the bottom. She'd only tried to utilise them for transport in the previous years when Weldir no longer wanted children from her.

Lindi had acquired a few horses, but that was in between her first and second child. They refused to let her near them with Nathair when he was a baby, and she imagined it would be the same with the one who currently had their nose to the wind over her shoulder. Many were also wary of her, although she was a natural with a horse due to her family owning one to sow their crops. She had a feeling it was something to do with her magic abilities or the fact that she was actually half dead.

"Can't you just... I don't know, give me the ability to move from one location to another in the blink of an eye?"

"I don't have such abilities, Lindiwe."

"But you do it all the time in your realm!" she argued, keeping her voice light.

His answering soft chuckle had her ears warming. It was too decadent and rich, and it always unnerved her how quickly it could send a pleasurable shiver across her skin. *"That's because my realm is me. As you can touch your nose, I can move to anywhere within me. On Earth, I would have to walk if I wasn't trapped in my mist."*

Lindi turned her head to look at the baby currently clinging to the back of her brown tunic with their head over her shoulder. "He isn't being very helpful, is he?"

Hearing that she spoke to them, their little oval nostrils flared rapidly in her direction. They gave a bawk and leaned closer – but Lindi leaned back, unsure if they would playfully nip her or lick her nose. This child happened to be much feistier than Nathair had been.

"Let me dwell on a solution," Weldir offered. *"I may not be insightful about Earth, but all Elven deities are aware of all spells that the Elysians learn. There may be something in my memories that I can find."*

But I want something nooow! She didn't dare utter her childish pout, but she did stick her bottom lip forward slightly. Then she moved them onto the current topic at hand.

"I'm still surprised he's in the Veil," Lindi commented, noting the trickling water in the distance.

"It seems he favours a particular lake."

A lake in the middle lands of Austrális... After wandering the desert for years, she wouldn't have thought such a thing was possible, until now.

She couldn't help lifting her gaze to the twinkles of sunlight shining through the gaps of lush green pine needles. At any point, the sky could turn grey, and they could be in the middle of torrential rain. The development of such chaotic weather was new, and she already surmised it had something to do with the forest that had been unnaturally grown both within and around the Veil.

Something had to keep it all healthy. She didn't know yet if that was by the intervention of Demons, or if the growth of flora forced the sky to change. Either way, Lindi had been rained on countless times during her pregnancy as she'd clung to the forest.

Her family home... it'd been destroyed quite some time ago. The resources were given to Rivenspire, and already the earth had begun to take back the land, cleansing it all in rot. In another decade, she doubted it would even look as though there had been a home there at all.

Rather than finding a safe house to dwell in, Lindi had made the forest her home.

She'd learned much about camping and making a temporary shelter out of branches and animal furs quite some time ago. A farming girl had turned into an adventurer in her wanderlust; hunting occultists had been an arduous journey of travel.

Since Weldir had intended to call her back to his realm right after birth, she'd made herself a soft and safe nest beforehand. All she'd been thankful for was that it had been mid-spring, not too hot and not too cold, while she'd felt like her body was splitting in two.

Since then, Lindi had been nurturing her little forest buddy.

They'd travelled away from the worst of the Veil to avoid the rare sighting of Demons – although they were becoming more frequent as the months passed. She was often at the fringes, in places like the last bit of desert in the west, taking in its red-dusted beauty before it disappeared forever.

It also so happened to be where she found an echidna. And, curious to see if her child would obtain its features if she let them eat it, she gave it to them – while first removing its head. If she was going to be able to choose what skulls her children obtained, she wanted them to have predator ones so they could defend best against Demons.

She'd learned that she was correct.

Although no bones had formed, this child obtained echidna spines from eating it. It was only afterwards that she was thankful they were pliable and non-dangerous like their bendy claws – otherwise she would have been constantly pricked by them.

She thought they looked kind of... *cute* with spines. She often played with the ones going down their back, forearms, and calves by brushing her fingertips in a soothing manner. They always curled their back in delight, as if they adored the sensation.

After a little more trudging, Lindi's ears rang from the familiar sound of crashing water. She followed it, hoping she'd find what she sought at the end of it.

That sounds like a... The forest opened up to a waterfall rushing from the surface into the Veil. Ironically, a rainbow glimmered in front of it, as if the world was lying about the beauty it was pouring into.

The churning froth collected in a large body of water so deep she couldn't see the bottom of it, which connected to a thin river that ran deeper into the Veil. The midday sun allowed the entire area to be bathed in sunshine, and she placed her hand above her eyes to shield them from the worst of the blazing light. Lindi searched to find it empty.

She noted the towering, rough wall and how it grew convex just to her right. *He could have told me it was next to the cliff wall.* She'd been wandering the Veil for no reason!

With those spooky... Demons.

Not all were as human-looking as Jabeziryth, Lettie, and Yusel. Actually... most were so inhumanly pitch-black they looked like a glossy void, as if they didn't have flesh. And Weldir had confirmed they didn't – their outer bodies were made up of energy that kept all their internal organs in.

It disappeared as they grew actual flesh. It thickened, hardened, and they could morph into any shade that humans were born with.

I don't see him. Other than the waterfall, the space was vacant.

"Weldir, are you sure this is the right–" Before she could finish, a giant wave of spraying water flung in her direction, right as something leapt from the middle of it.

Instinctually, Lindi backed up and turned intangible, and the child attached to her turned ghostly as well. The creature, perhaps eight metres long, landed right where she'd been standing. With a snarl, his long, coiling serpent tail slithered and splashed, remaining in the water as he warded back thin air with a menacing hiss and his long serpent fangs bared.

Then, leaning on his hands, he looked up at her Phantom form.

Unable to form tears due to her intangible nature, Lindi just offered a heartfelt, shaky smile. "Hello, Nathair," she whispered.

His snarl softened to a growl, and his angry red orbs shifted to dark yellow. He tilted his snaked skull and sniffed at the air. Nathair snorted a deep huff when he no doubt smelt nothing, as her baby was scentless.

It hadn't taken Lindi long to learn that his orbs could change from their natural orange hue to a variety of colours, depending on his emotions. Red signalled anger or bloodlust, and dark yellow likely conveyed curiosity. She had yet to see any other colours, especially as he'd always warded her away in the past.

It was difficult to remain at the side of someone who tried everything in their power to claw, bite, or envenom her. She'd also been causing him distress by doing so, and she'd drawn away for his comfort more than her safety.

When it had been long enough, Lindi materialised her physical body, allowing her worn boots to touch the wet grass. Nathair lowered on his arms and gave a deep growl, but she held firm.

That was, until the child on her shoulder attempted to leap forward with their own snarl. Lindi, already prepared, caught them in the air before they could get far. They barked at him while snapping their strange maw of teeth, and Lindi was forced to hold their rabid, wriggling form out from her torso, so they didn't accidentally bite her.

They were warning Nathair, and he, funnily enough, reared back in surprise. All sounds halted from him, and his head tilted to the side as though he was perplexed by the tiny creature before him. Then, with his orbs still yellow and non-threatening, he leaned forward while ducking low. He sniffed the air about a foot from them, reared back with a snorted huff, and then came even closer.

Lindi was ready to turn them both intangible at the first sign of danger, but it never came. He kept sniffing, kept snorting, until he eventually touched them, and incidentally, the backs of her fingers while he investigated.

Don't you dare attack, she mentally warned him, although she had this motherly intuition that he just... wouldn't.

Instead, Nathair dropped even lower to get a good look at them, his head moving this way and that. Even though they were still growling, he didn't seem to mind, like he could sense they were defenceless. They tried biting his skull, but couldn't get purchase no matter how wide they pried open their little mouth.

Lindi held her arms out until her muscles shook with exertion and threatened to collapse from holding their light weight, but she held on for as long as she could. This was the first time she'd been this close to Nathair since he'd formed his hooked ram horns, and it was also the calmest he'd ever been.

Even with his lack of intelligence, perhaps... somewhere, deep down inside that thick skull of his, he knew this was his sibling. She hoped there was that kind of spiritual bond, even if they never recognised it for what it was. Or maybe he liked that they were scentless and unassuming.

Only when Nathair finally inspected Lindi, sniffing at her arms before going around to almost inhale her big curls, did she bring her baby to her chest. They clung to her before going up to get between herself and Nathair while pushing at his bumpy closed maw. They swatted at his face with an upset mewl, and she huffed out a giggle at their possessiveness.

Not far from Nathair's lake rested a tree with three decently large boulders underneath it. Lindi sat underneath its shade with her butt firmly resting on a boulder and her back against the trunk, watching Nathair laze upon the ground. With his little sibling crawling all over him, Nathair was quick to catch them before they could fall into the lake.

He was fine letting them roam the area – as was Lindi.

A small handful of weeks had passed since she'd first come to visit Nathair, and she'd grown comfortable in his presence, as had her baby. They never strayed too far, often scampering between her and Nathair, obsessed with cuddling her and playing with him.

As much as Lindi wanted to join in on their fun, Nathair wasn't... exceptionally welcoming towards her. In a cold corner of her heart, she knew her presence was merely being tolerated due to her encouraging their siblingship.

She had a feeling it was because of Nathair's interest and curiosity that he was fond of her baby. Now that they were used to him, and less aggressive and protective of her, they just enjoyed the active freedom. They were curious as well, sniffing anything that they could crawl to, so much more alert than when they'd been clinging to her.

They were still wary about Nathair coming too close to her,

often giving a cute little growl of disquiet. Their protectiveness could've also been the reason Nathair was convinced she was acceptable. They trusted her, so he was choosing to have faith in their trust.

Honestly, she'd take anything she could get.

It was enjoyable being able to witness them together while just being near Nathair again – no matter that he was so different from before. Her sweet little serpent child was no longer either of those things. He was big, he was cautious and standoffish, but he was just as beautiful as before.

She spoke to him often, filling the area with the sound of her voice, although she never expected any kind of response.

Since it was unsafe to sleep at night in the Veil, she often greeted Nathair with a 'good morning' after sleeping through most of the day. In the middle of stretching one day, she swore she almost broke something in her spine from stiffening in surprise when he mimicked her greeting.

He'd spoken! Used his own words to say something, and she almost fell over in disbelief. Sure, it sounded like he'd tried to talk with a throat full of gravel, more beastly and monstrous than truly coherent, but she didn't mind learning his inflection.

Since then, she'd been attempting to teach him how to communicate, and it was part of the reason she refused to leave despite the weeks passing. He was slow to learn, as he didn't appreciate her nearness, but it was... *something*. So, in the background as they gently played – which was really just Nathair chasing his sibling over his body with his big hands or tail tip – she taught him things by pointing to them and stating what they were over and over.

He was listening, even if it didn't seem like it. His orbs would spark with dark yellow, and his snout would drift towards her before becoming distracted.

Lindi knew what her task was. She was supposed to be growing this new child so they could go off into the world and be a violent menace.

She'd originally come here to make sure Nathair wasn't in danger within the Veil, and perhaps even cunningly convince him to follow her out of it for his own safety. If he wouldn't, she'd had every intention of leaving, as she figured that's what he'd want.

What she hadn't been prepared for was how fervently he'd protect what he'd taken as his territory. This waterfall, the lake, and the immediate cliff around it was his home. He often swam in the water, and it was much deeper than it appeared. Lindi couldn't swim in it long before irritating him, as if the lake was his most precious haven.

No amount of encouragement on her part could get him to leave, and she'd given up. But with how warmly he'd accepted his sibling, Lindi had chosen to stay just for a little while longer.

She missed Nathair, even if he was all snarls and maw snaps. Participating in his life, even if it was just for a moment, nibbled away at the loneliness that had been burning her chest. Being able to be the one to teach him, as a mother should, gave her a purpose she hadn't even realised she'd needed.

Educating Nathair could only be helpful, as he could teach the others in the future.

He could be the starting point. If they all accepted each other like this, then they could all help each other. Lindi wanted to nurture that possibility and let Nathair be the leader for them all.

With how long his body had gotten, she thought he might be big enough to keep them all in line. That serpent nature of his, patient, calm, even-tempered except to defend, may be what made him so tolerant of her. If others in the future were less so, they could lean on him instead, with Lindi paving that path now for them all.

She constantly worried about the future. It was undecided, so uncertain, and growing more dangerous with every new Demon that crossed the threshold.

Lindi would set down foundations everywhere, hoping in the many decades to come that one of them would stand up like a tall building – even if others failed and came crumbling down.

She'd been floundering for so long, her heart rejecting all this. But she'd finally decided to take action, even if it was merely pointing to the ground to explain to Nathair what grass was.

All the while, she tried to stem her triumphant grins whenever he looked at whatever she was pointing at, then opened and closed his mouth as if to silently mimic her.

SEVENTEEN

December 30th, 1705

In her incorporeal form, Lindi grimaced deeply and closed her eyes at the gruesome scene before her. Holding her baby in her crossed arms, who was still dark and featureless besides their quills, they remained asleep despite all the blood and fighting.

Lindi had never been more thankful that turning into her Phantom form always put them to sleep when they were an infant. She didn't need them joining the fray and getting hurt.

Although he was much thinner than the roaring adult brown bear, Nathair fought it off all by himself with utter tenacity. He was barely strong enough to lean back much lower than normal on his tail to match its nearly six-foot height, but he held back its swiping paws by swiftly catching them. Every movement he made was jarring and quick, like a striking snake.

When Nathair gave a strong push, it landed on its side with a loud thud against the dirt and gnarly roots. He charged while it was down with a resonating hiss that would have set Lindi's teeth on edge, if she wasn't incorporeal.

Just as Nathair went to lance it with his venomous fangs, it managed to smack him across the face with its meaty paw. His head snapped to the side under its formidable power. With his orbs long ago red from being swept into the fury of bloodlust, they brightened in their hue, and Nathair roared, causing whatever wildlife remained to scatter. He tackled it around the shoulders to smash its back into a nearby tree, causing leaves to detach and flutter around them.

The bear bit into his shoulder with ferocious stubbornness, but it was no match for Nathair's razor-sharp claws gouging down its back. Its fangs parted with a bellowing roar, giving him time to strike it around the neck with his fangs.

The injected venom was utterly pointless when he proceeded to rip its throat out, causing blood to splatter against the patches of tall grass stalks nearby.

There was no point in Lindi intervening, even though she'd wanted to. Not only did she want to protect her child, who had flaring claw wounds going over his shoulder and opposing side, but the bear hadn't deserved the violence, nor death. It was merely protecting its territory, as Nathair did for his lake each night.

He was the trespasser.

She peeked at its genitals from a distance, making sure it wasn't a female and could have a cub nearby. *It's a male,* her mind registered with relief.

She may have tried to raise an orphaned cub until it was old enough to be on its own, otherwise. Which would have been a struggle with the baby in her arms.

Remaining in the form that Nathair wouldn't be able to sense as he ate, Lindi thought back on the last few days.

When Nathair had left his lake, she had ended up following since she was curious about his intentions. Being summer, the land was hot, the air balmy, and he seemed restless to move. He looked over his shoulder often to check on her, and she had no idea if it was because he didn't like being followed or if he wanted her to come.

He never tried to stop her, though.

He'd initially begun to travel with his sibling attached to him, but she doubted he'd known that. They'd been asleep at the time, and they were scentless and light, often clinging to his scales like they'd passed out while playing. Sometimes she didn't feel them on her, although she was hyperaware when they moved for those very same reasons.

After she stopped him and removed his sibling from his scales, Nathair had set off with Lindi quickly following.

When he revealed a semi-safe path to climb the cliff wall,

Lindi floated up it in her Phantom form. Since then, he hunted while she took the opportunity to teach him what everything was called. Walking ahead of him in his predicted path, she'd grab a leaf and relay its name before going to a flower or touching a tree branch.

If he diverted in a new direction, perhaps annoyed with her company, she just inserted herself into his line of sight and continued. This was how she'd been teaching him for the past few weeks.

He still said little more than greetings, and never attempted a proper conversation. Yet his orbs were always dark yellow, and sometimes she'd find him staring at her when she spoke. She tried to teach him how to count, and on more than one occasion, he'd slyly – as if trying to hide it – use his fingers to mimic her.

At his lake, she'd managed to obtain silent permission to sit a little closer, and she'd drawn in the dirt more complex things. The sun and moon and how he could use them to count the months passing. How seasons worked. She'd also drawn animals and had relayed their names.

Even if it didn't seem like it, he was always listening, watching, learning.

She had no idea how much he actually retained. He mostly mimicked, so even if he learned what something was, she doubted he understood any significance regarding it. He didn't appear to be intelligent. More like a creature that could learn tricks; like a bird that could learn to talk by copying sounds but not truly communicate.

But she intended for all her efforts to be foundations for later. So when he gained more humanity – to her disgruntled complaint – all the pieces would eventually come together.

Lindi had no idea how many humans he'd eaten, but there were many for him to gorge on in the vast land of Austrális. She just hoped he never came across a town full of them. If he could take down a bear relatively easily, she didn't want to know how many people he could slaughter before needing to flee.

That's if he fled at all. He could easily take on an entire town and decimate its population throughout the course of the night *and* day. Unlike Demons who would need to escape the sun's touch.

When Nathair nearly decapitated the bear, Lindi grimaced in disgust, only to stare at its furry head for a long while. Then she eventually dropped her gaze to the child lying limp over her folded arms.

Well... I did say I wanted to give them a predator skull. A bear was pretty formidable. *And it is about time I start letting them grow.*

Since her children didn't seem to feel hunger, even after many months of not eating, she didn't need to feed them. She could pick and choose when it suited her, or when opportunities arose.

With a nod and her arms tightening, Lindi decided.

She backed away from Nathair and his large meal until she figured it would be safe. Then she turned physical.

The child in her arms immediately went berserk. They squirmed, twisted, and tried everything in their might to get to the source of blood permeating the air. Heat surrounded her from the scorching air, causing sweat to trickle down the back of her neck and hairline. She struggled with them until she had a strong grip on their barking, snarling body.

With his side facing them, Nathair paused and gave a wet growl as his snout remained buried in bloodied meat. She gulped when his orbs seemed to flare an even brighter red. Lindi stepped out of his line of sight and took a few more steps back until he stopped making a noise of aggression and resumed his meal.

Then she sent out a tentacle of black sand and wrapped it around the bear's furry snout. Inch by inch, she slowly shifted it away from Nathair, trying not to alert him to what she was doing, until it was at her feet.

She placed her baby on the ground, and they scampered to it with quick little feet and hands. Their fangs were surprisingly sharp and strong as they destroyed the bone bit by bit. They happily smacked their maw after each bite, regardless of it being mainly bone.

Wanting to give them something meatier, she also stole a back leg from Nathair when he pushed his meal around and exposed its rump to her. He never noticed. Then again, he seemed more interested in its middle than its limbs. She gave the leg to the baby at her feet, whose white skull was already starting to form through the crown of their head.

They both managed to finish their meals at relatively the same time, preventing any need for her to intervene if one wanted what the other had.

Nathair's length had grown exponentially, but he didn't seem much thicker than before. The child at her feet, on the other hand, now looked like a small toddler – perhaps no larger than a one-year-old.

Along with their bear skull, little pawed feet had developed, with cute claws to match them.

She chuckled when they struggled to pick up their heavy skull after it drooped to the left, then they overcompensated and it fell to the other side, only for it to thump backwards on the ground. With their legs and arms flailing in the air, they rolled back, and she crouched down to help.

Supporting the base of their new skull, she picked them up, and they squealed in delight, their hands waving through the air to grab onto something.

"I think I already have a name for you," she said, when they managed to grab a handful of glossy curls in their right fist. "How about Orson, my little bear cub?"

Her eyes softened as a small, loving smile curled her lips. *It's the name my father would have given his son, if he'd been presented with the opportunity.*

A strong, sturdy name for someone treasured.

She thought it was fitting, and a wonderful way to honour someone she missed dearly.

EIGHTEEN

January 1ˢᵗ, 1706

"How long do you intend to remain there?" Weldir asked, his quiet voice distant through their bond.

Throwing Orson into the air in the shelter of a shallow cave, only to catch his happily squealing torso a second later, Lindi shrugged. "However long is necessary to teach Nathair all he can learn."

Light rain pattered beyond the mouth of the cave, into Nathair's territory within the Veil, and splattered against his lake. The waterfall was stronger than usual, but it was difficult to hear its roar over the *shaa* of rain.

Where Lindi sought shelter was still within his territory. Although he rarely huddled in here, preferring to sleep in the lake where he was safest, he defended it ruthlessly. She eyed the noticeable claw marks on the walls. Nathair had been digging out this cave, perhaps to make a home outside of the water as much as within it.

It wasn't very large, or deep.

With her back against the wall, the dying rain sprinkled on her toes and seeped towards the threshold as a growing puddle. Water continued to trickle down the cliff wall and threatened to put out the fire she had next to her. Its heat was unwelcome this deep into summer, but it's light much needed with the moon obstructed by the dispersing clouds.

"Is that an issue?" Lindi pressed, masking her attitude with a nondescript tone.

"Not at all," Weldir answered, catching her off-guard. She was surprised he didn't seem to be in a rush for her to shoot out babies, like her womb was a living catapult. *"I have no concept of your earthly time. I don't know if it has been a few weeks or many years. I'm just curious as to your intentions."*

Or just trying to strum up a conversation.

"I always forget that you don't feel the impact of time like I do," Lindi admitted, lifting Orson up, then lowering him back to her face so they could rub noses. "Does that not bother you?"

"I cannot be bothered by something I have never experienced any other way."

Understandable. Lindi had learned to... slow down.

There was no need to rush, not when there was so much time for her to expend. It'd taken many years, well over two decades in fact, to alter something that was fundamentally set in her very spirit. To not feel the flow of time, as she was outside of it.

I struggled for so long to accept that concept. She still did, in some ways.

It made being at Nathair's side, with little to do, far more bearable. Sometimes she just stared at him, enchanted by his odd beauty and how she was part of his design. Now with Orson, who bore their own skull and quill features, she sometimes emptied her mind to just let herself witness their moments together.

A witness. Just like Weldir.

Something that didn't need to interact with the world, even if she sometimes longed to immerse herself in their play – but was always coldly rejected.

I guess it's different, though. She was able to experience everything that Weldir could not. The grass, the sun, life. *I don't think I would be able to live as he does.* To be outside of a world, to see it but not grasp it.

It sounded too painful for someone who had always been able to touch the delicate petals of a flower, take in its floral scent, and do more than just watch it wilt from a distance. There was loneliness in being able to merely pluck it from its bush and take it with her as a reminder.

"How long has it been?" Weldir pressed, and the note of mild

curiosity was evident.

"Almost a year," Lindi admitted.

It'd been eleven months since Orson was given their name, their skull, and not much else had changed. They'd consumed a few Demons with Nathair, both gaining a little more mass each, but that was all.

Last summer, Lindi had followed Nathair as he wandered. He'd fought against that bear, and then all manner of other creatures that strayed into his nearby path. He had no direction, from what she could tell, but just seemed to have an instinct to move with the heat on his back. As autumn came, and the world grew chilly, he'd returned a slow path back to the Veil. Once the winter frost had settled above the surface, although not so much on the ground of the canyon, he'd been reluctant to leave the lake.

I think he finds the water more agreeable in the cold.

Perhaps he was able to handle it better when he breathed through his gills, as if a physiological change happened. He only left to sunbake for a few hours of the day and then returned to the water like a hibernating animal.

Lindi had remained, only because there was no point in her leaving. Winter was cruel and was growing colder as each year passed. The Veil appeared to be warmer, so hunkering down where she had somewhere safe and protected seemed like the wisest choice.

Then, like the budding flowers of spring, Nathair had emerged. His lessons had resumed, his playfulness with Orson continued, and he'd carved out this cave. Lindi had attempted to help with a sharp rock, trying to show him she just wished to be helpful.

When he'd allowed it, she'd grown more audacious with her closeness to him, while a triumphant grin had curled her lips. He'd been benign and welcoming to her, in his own strange and quiet way, and she'd pushed the boundaries as much as she could with the aim to eventually win him over.

But, like always, no matter that little had changed – and Lindi not at all – summer had returned to bake the world. She always found it the hardest time to have a clinging child – especially one that was so large now they were the size of her torso. They were heavy, they were unbearably hot, but at least they could hold up their skull now, which gave her tired arms a break.

Lindi lifted her gaze to the calming sky to greet the stars that were beginning to wink through wisps of clouds as the rain subsided. A thin, barely noticeable barrier at the cave entrance kept the horrible mosquitos at bay while she enjoyed her evening of nothing but her thoughts and Orson.

At least, that had been her intention. Weldir's voice continued to ring, even after his silence.

She was alone, without anyone truly sentient to speak to even after a year, but she didn't feel as lonely as before. Lindi had come to accept this forced solitude, basking in its carefree nature. She did have her two children, no matter that they were so different to her and not even human.

How lonely it must be to rule a realm filled with only the dead.

The least she could do was offer a branch of 'friendship.'

"Weldir," Lindi started, before licking at her lips nervously.

"Yes, Lindiwe."

"What have you been doing all this time?"

"I have been... creating," he answered slowly, like one might do when they were looking over a hobby they'd been working on and had been interrupted mid-task.

A star seemed a little brighter, a little redder than the others. She inspected it as she crossed her legs to settle Orson into her lap, then stroked their back quills gently. "Creating what?"

"My realm."

Her upper lip curled up to one side, disliking that he was being vague as usual, and she rolled her eyes. Before she could tell him "never mind," Weldir surprisingly continued.

"Tenebris is within my stomach" – she already knew this – *"and it has been as empty as the rest of me, which you have seen. I am working to rectify that, especially after Rökul's assistance."*

She could only imagine what he meant. "Are you making stars?"

Is that how the ones above her had been formed? Had a divine being really made them? And was she simply resting in their stomach as they spoke? To create one's own realm, what would that entail?

"I... have not tried to make any. I can. I don't imagine it would be hard to make glittering dots in the distance."

"So you don't know what the stars are made of?" she asked, looking up at them in the inky sky with wonder.

"I do. Most are giant balls of hot hydrogen gas, although they can be made of other gases. Science is an encouraged study among the Elysians. Some of it I know, some of it I don't. I only received trickles of information within my prism."

Prism. She'd heard Weldir use that term before, but had never asked about it. She wasn't going to ask now, either, not when she had other questions.

With her cheeks heating because she didn't understand science at all, or what hydrogen was, she asked, "Can you describe for me what you're creating then? If not the wonder of stars."

A small silence bled through the bond.

Lindi's ears began to heat instead. *Is it because I've never done this before? Or never really tried to speak with him?* Although she tried to be more forthcoming, Lindi still found it hard. She didn't know him, wasn't all that trusting of him, and he felt so, so far away.

It was hard to talk to someone she couldn't see, couldn't touch, couldn't smell. All she could do was hear him, but his detached nature made even that difficult.

"Sure, Lindiwe. I can describe what I have made of Tenebris so far."

Lowering her head to hide her face behind the curtain of her unbound tresses of her bangs, she watched Orson curl their back to get comfortable as she waited for Weldir's decadent voice to bless her ears.

It was like being read a story.

With every detail Weldir described, he watched his mate's eyelids slowly droop before eventually drifting shut. She fell asleep to the sound of his voice, and something about that left a tingle in the back of his consciousness. It was something pleasant, and he hoped she'd enjoyed the narrative of his world, while he also tried to ignore the nagging doubt that perhaps he'd bored her.

If only I could reach through this viewing disc and lie her down comfortably.

She looked cramped with her back against the wall and her body slipping to the right, which was the way her head had fallen. Orson remained cuddled in her lap with her lithe arms around them to keep them secure.

He looked over her summer outfit, consisting of a dirt-stained cream tunic and brown breeches. From the memories he'd sifted through, women wearing such masculine attire was uncommon for the humans – although not so for the Elvish. He figured she'd forgone dresses for ease of travel.

Her boots lay next to her, sheltered from the wet that had long passed. They were exceptionally worn. Her hair was neat, recently washed and brushed and, although her bangs were down, the rest had been thrown up in some kind of simple updo that created a fluffy cloud on the back of her head. She'd seemed content to use its softness against the hardness of the uneven rock behind her.

With his mind, he directed the disc to zero in on her relaxed face so he could inspect it in closer detail.

Her long, dark, and curling lashes created a fan of shadow over her cheeks. Her round nose tip had the tiniest mar of soot on it, likely from some stray ash fluttering away from her dying campfire. Her lips were open just slightly, revealing even teeth and a pink little tongue as she gave light, steady breaths of sleep.

Her cheekbones were high, her jaw subtly defined, while her brows were arched and prominent. Her features were... distinctive, from what he could gather, and exceptionally feminine. Made more so by her full, soft-looking lips, and the smooth quality of her brown skin.

Her beauty is quite beguiling. The further he looked through human memories of the souls trapped within Tenebris, the more he found her incomparable.

Even her eyes, although hidden from him in that moment, were such a rich brown with amber flecks in them that they looked like pools of molten liquid.

And that gaze of hers... he'd seen it harden over the years.

She used to appear so wide-eyed and bewildered, so lost and unsure. Now, her eyes held a steadiness in them he found quite attractive. She knew what she wanted, what she wanted to do, and no longer seemed to be denying herself.

Lindiwe's eyes flickered open just long enough that she, half aware, repositioned herself so she was lying upon the rock on her side. She gathered Orson to her chest and snuggled them with her nose buried into the back of their neck. Once more, her eyelids drifted closed with her knees pulled up around Orson.

I like watching her interact with our offspring.

She gave them both affection, despite Nathair's unwillingness to reciprocate or allow her close enough to even pat his back. He appreciated the lengths she was going to, tending to them in her own way, as it was more than he had expected of her, or any human mate.

She's keeping this one young to remain with them for as long as possible. He found that oddly tender.

He eyed the line of her hourglass figure, and how her new position made her side more curved than normal. Her backside was round and tight against her pants, and he tried to appreciate it like many other human males seemed to.

He found it to be a pointless endeavour. He'd never be able to feel its 'squish' in the palm of his hand like a physical being.

Once her light breaths resumed and she grew limp, he saw no point in peering into his viewing disc anymore. He waved to dismiss it and turned to the pink flower in his hand. The petals had a satin finish, and he wondered if it was supposed to be that way or if they should be glossy like a leaf. He inspected it with a brush of his thumb, watching the way it moulded to his touch.

Every detail of his realm was scrutinised thoroughly.

Every new flower species, every different blade of grass, to even the way a mountain was formed and the kind of rock that created it, was carefully sculptured. Such attention took much of his time.

He strived for perfection, as he was an imperfect thing. He wanted utter completion, as he was an incomplete being. He wanted it to be real, despite neither of them really being so.

It felt like he'd only just finished his first thumb stroke when Lindiwe's voice rang loud and clear. His name, a linked call, was the only thing that could break through his concentration.

He only hastened his pace to bring forth the viewing disc at the frantic tone of his name being called a second time.

"Yes, Lindiwe?" he asked, before it fully formed – the image of her murky but steadily clearing.

"They're gone!" she shouted, her hair heavy, wet, and clinging to her neck and shoulders as she climbed out of Nathair's lake. "Orson and Nathair are gone!"

From what Weldir could tell, in the mere second he'd been inspecting the pink flower petals, many hours had passed. The sky was clear of clouds, revealing bright stars and a falling crescent moon. The area was bathed in light, rather than shaded by an encroaching new night.

"I'll find them," Weldir informed her, whooshing his mind forward to create two more discs.

In his periphery, Lindi's drenched form knelt on the side of the deep lake before she shakily rose to her feet. She lagged, her clothing clinging to her torso and limbs, as she wrung the water out of her hair before pushing it away from her worried, crinkled face. Had she dived into the lake in search of Nathair, only to find him missing? It wouldn't be the first time Nathair had tried to bring Orson into his favourite place, although Lindiwe was usually quick to stop him.

With his family bond to his offspring, despite the distance and skew of realms, Weldir was able to locate them. The discs brought up their images, overlapping to show they were so close to each other that there was no gap between them.

"They are together. Orson clings to Nathair's back as they travel through a forest. There is a mountain range in the distance to their right."

Weldir was unable to tell whether Nathair was aware he had his sibling on his back or not, or if it had been intentional.

He also observed how far the strings of their essences were from Lindiwe, being forever intertwined with her.

"They are quite a distance from you," he told her. "Northwest from where you are."

Lindiwe turned to the cliff before her. "How far?"

"I cannot give you a correct estimate. Perhaps a hundred kilometres, or slightly less."

Her jaw dropped as her eyes bowed in obvious distress. She turned incorporeal to float up the side of the cliff. With her face lifted towards the sky, he could tell by her clenching and unclenching fists that the pace was too sluggish for her.

"How did they get so far in only a few hours?" she muttered in a grouchy whine.

"You forget how fast Nathair can be. He must have left with Orson not long after you fell asleep."

And not long after Weldir had stopped watching her.

When Lindiwe finally reached the top of the cliff, she didn't turn physical. Instead, she used the ease and freedom of her Phantom form to cut through trees rather than go around them, saving time as she sped through the surrounding forests.

No matter how fast she was, it was slow in comparison to Nathair, who chased after a scent on the wind.

"Are they safe?" she asked, peering up at the moon occasionally to ensure she was heading in the right direction.

"They are together, but Nathair's orbs are red. He is hunting."

"Damnit," she snapped, seeming to go faster than he thought possible. "Do you know what he's after?"

In the intertwined discs with black misting borders, it wasn't long before he watched them come upon a herd of cattle, unfenced, free, and wild. They lazed in an open field asleep, only to spook at Nathair's growl, and they scrambled up on wobbly legs in a rush to flee.

He tilted his head as he inspected the mostly brown, bulky creatures. "I believe humans call them cows?"

A creature gave a lowing snort and tossed their head as they presented their large horns to ward Nathair back. It was the only one with horns on its head, and Weldir assumed it to be a male for that reason, although its bigger size compared to the others of its herd was another indication.

It protectively charged when Nathair slithered closer.

The battle was over quickly; the bull, although large and strong, was slow and easily caught with a mere tackle and fang lance. Yet Nathair, struck with excitement from fleeing prey, was quick to charge after the females.

Orson, attracted by the scent of blood coming from the male, was left behind when they leapt off to scuttle towards easy food.

They stayed behind to eat.

The discs unlinked from their conjoined state so both his offspring could stay in his sight. Nathair seemed set on a particular female cow, while the others ran in opposite directions, the night filled with terrified lowing.

Weldir's mind was able to soak in the information from all three discs effortlessly, and he watched them all at the same time. Nathair claimed his prize, and without any of the other cows in his line of sight to distract him, he began to consume it. Lindiwe continued to float through the forest, but Weldir could tell that she wasn't close by.

"Lindiwe, Orson is..."

"No," she whispered. "Are they okay?"

"They are eating a horned male. If Nathair doesn't come to claim his prize, then they will consume it in full. They are already growing quite large."

"Fuck!" she screeched, throwing her hands up with rigid fingers. Weldir's mist collected tighter, unused to this usually prim female swearing so ferociously. "I wanted to be there when they gained their horns. Is there anything you can do to stop it? Anything at all?"

No, there was nothing.

"I'm sorry, little female."

"But..." Her voice broke, leaping an octave higher, as her eyes crinkled in obvious sadness. "But I wanted to say goodbye to them as they are."

The right side of his face tightened with pressure, and his reflection in the disc showed he'd winced. *She merely wanted to be there in their final hour as a youngling.* Weldir couldn't fathom what it was like going through all these different ordeals, especially as her emotional ties to them were so much more profound than his.

He was just as detached as they were.

Nathair, finished with his meal, slithered back towards the carcass his sibling ate at. He didn't fight them for it, as if he didn't even seem to notice their very presence or perhaps didn't care.

The cool hue of the moon's fading light glistened upon Orson's white bear skull as their newly formed tail, long and thin with a furry tuft at the end, flicked to the side. They swiftly ate their way to the bull's upward-jutting horns, quick to consume them before Nathair could steal the head for himself.

NINETEEN

June 21st, 1709

Keeping her arms pressed to her chest, Lindi grimaced as something thin, smooth, and wiggling slid out of her pussy. She tried to ignore the trickle within when it threatened to spill from her and closed her knees to shield her privates.

Her face remained heated from the awkwardness of having a shadowy tendril inserted into her. At least it was never painful, since Weldir treated her with the utmost care regarding this now.

"Hopefully this time it takes," Weldir commented, withdrawing so completely from her as though time and space were closer to each other.

"I think it's due to how closely the last attempts were to my monthly blood," Lindi admitted, hating how her cheeks flared even hotter and she felt the need to be elsewhere. But there was no denying it.

This was their third try for this child, once before her monthly, once afterwards, and now. *At least it isn't always a one-shot event.* But he seemed to be hyper-fertile, partially to her dismay.

She'd like more time, more attempts, to ready her mind for the next child. To learn that she would not only be inseminated by a gross tendril and then pregnant a few days later, and a mother again in around five weeks, was a lot for her to swallow. She'd hate having to do *this* part of the procedure repeatedly, but at least it'd give her time to settle into the idea.

Then again, spending the last month near the Veil was gruelling. She stayed near Weldir's mist because there was no point in venturing far if she was just going to be brought back to it. Which then brought on the issue of her smelling like blood with Demons nearby when her monthly cycle came.

There wasn't really any winning for Lindi.

He did give her a year before asking to create another child, though. She'd needed a break, and to rejoin society temporarily to learn what had happened in her absence. In the year she'd spent with Nathair, the desert had almost disappeared, and Demons were running rampant throughout Austrális.

No one was safe anymore.

In the year and a half since she left, she'd seen the devastation up close, and it was heartbreaking. But as much as she wanted to dwell on it and grieve for humankind, she couldn't.

She had her own problems to contend with. Some human, some otherworldly.

Lindi swished her arms to swim towards her floating pants and turned physical to grab them. Once donned, she shoved a boot on, then the other. The sole of the left snapped, and her toes peeked out from the ruined tip.

"Curse these infernal things. Why can't a good boot last more than a few years?" she whined, pulling it off to check the damage. She came to the conclusion that it was irreparable. She ripped off a strip of her tunic in order to tie it together until she obtained new ones. Then she smacked the rounded toe. "And slippers are far worse."

With his hands clasped behind his back, Weldir looked down at her from a distance. "You could always forgo them, like the Elvish."

Her nose scrunched as she darted her gaze to the right to look at him. "Why would I do that?"

"Well, the Elysians do so in order to feel the ground beneath their feet. They feel the vibrations of magic and must be touching the earth in order to wield it."

Lindi lowered her eyelids in false annoyance. "You forget, Weldir, that I'm not an Elf. There are all manner of dangerous things to step upon when treading through Austrális. Doing so barefooted is just asking for your death."

Did she seriously need to remind him of the time she almost died due to a snake's bite? *And let's not talk about the spiders.* She almost shuddered in reaction.

"Says a deathless being to another deathless being."

With one finger raised and her mouth open to refute him, she paused. Then she narrowed her gaze before her brows cocked upwards as she looked away.

"I just prefer to wear shoes." She thumbed the tied cloth, sighed, and then slipped the repaired boot on. "I'll have to buy some more. I can't even count how many I've owned now."

"The new land you will be going to may have something more long-lasting."

Lindi's head perked up at that, and she turned to him with suspicion. "What do you mean 'new land'? I'm not leaving Austrális."

Weldir, with his arms still behind his back, hadn't moved an inch. Only his constantly shifting form and shroud of mist – both as minimal as they'd always been – had changed. His solid form was spottier than usual, rather than a ribbon coalescing around his body like it was struggling to contain him.

With his tone dull, the sinful cadence of his voice couldn't battle back how his next words caused her skin to prickle in fear.

"Austrális already has two of our offspring. I would like to extend their reach by having this one roam another land of Earth. I already have the destination in mind."

Her brows drew together. "Why didn't you tell me sooner?"

"I saw no reason to until we had confirmed your pregnancy. What does it matter if I told you earlier or now?"

Lindi opened her mouth to argue, but promptly shut it with her heart tightening in her chest. Wringing her hands in front of her twisting stomach, she looked down at the nothingness.

"Am I allowed to refute?" she asked in a tiny voice.

"I'd prefer if you didn't. When I spoke of other mates, I had intended to obtain one from each continent of Earth." Then he pulled an arm forward to shrug with it. "Like I said, this responsibility now lies completely on your shoulders. Austrális is the most impacted, and it's also one of the largest continents on its own. We can keep most of them here, but I would like many servants collecting souls all over the world."

The sinking feeling in Lindi's chest grew more cavernous, like the fall was never-ending.

Lindi didn't know how she felt about the idea of her children being so spread out across the world. It was a struggle just to travel to them across Austrális. Only with Weldir's help, by having him call her to his realm and then back to his mist, was she able to cross great distances quickly.

On foot, it took gruelling and tiring weeks. By horseback would have been better, but the distance was just too great, and now too deadly with the Demons that travelled at night. Horses spooked easily, and she didn't have the time nor skills to train them into not bucking her off if a Demon chased after them.

Thankfully Nathair remained within the Veil at his lake, returning to it whenever the summer passed. She could easily reach him in very little time because he was, essentially, in Weldir's mist now. Orson, on the other hand, went wherever they wanted. They came back to Nathair's territory during the winter, as if sensing they had a safe place to rest during the frosty months, but they and Nathair fought a lot while there.

Nathair was prickly about having an adult sibling in close proximity, and his venom put him at an advantage, as did his strong, mobile tail.

It was only after the fact that Weldir had told her Nathair had removed Orson's head from their shoulders. She'd cried into her hands for only as long as it took for Weldir to inform her that they were still alive, their soul connected to their skull and still living. Twenty-four hours later, they emerged again, their body re-formed and entirely healed in a show of gooey black sand.

It had been one of the hardest days of her life, and there had been many.

Orson had been a little warier of Nathair after that, but still remained until the winter passed. Then they'd left again... only to gain their male gender by hunting down a poor, unsuspecting group of humans who didn't believe there were any Demons roaming the world.

The rumours of them were spreading faster and faster, and humankind was growing more afraid with each passing year. Not enough to fully move into towns, though; many people still chose to remain in the quaint, small villages all over Austrális.

Sometimes information was slow to trickle throughout the country.

Many also thought they could simply fight them back like they did with the new wolves, bears, and large cats that had suddenly appeared 'out of nowhere.' Fools, the lot of them.

Lindi and her family would have been those fools if it wasn't for what happened to them twenty-four years ago.

"Lindiwe," Weldir called, his voice deepening in what could only be anger, when she hadn't responded for quite some time.

"Okay. Fine," she reluctantly bit. "If that is what you desire, then so be it. I will make do."

"I don't understand why this bothers you so."

Many things bothered her about this, including the slip of his essence finally leaking from her and soaking her undergarments. She squirmed, uncomfortable with the way it made the material cling to her pussy.

Making children was surprisingly messy. And there was never any fun in it for her.

And now... she had to embark on a journey to an unknown place, pregnant of all things, and figure everything out all at once. It was a hard ask.

"So long as you help me reach our other children when I need to, or if they need me, I will do as you have asked. Just... let me stay there for a while before asking for another. Let me understand the world beyond the borders of Austrális."

She finally lifted her gaze to Weldir, who stood floating like an unmoving statue that had been broken into pieces. If it wasn't for his cloud and chalky spots constantly shifting, she wouldn't have thought he was alive. Maybe he wasn't, and that was why he lacked such a heart.

He dipped his head slowly to show her the top of his horns. "As you command, Lindiwe."

TWENTY

August 22nd, 1714

"How are you going with that poultice, Lindiwe?" Karlann asked, peeking over her shoulder from across the aisle where she ground amethyst crystals in her mortar and pestle. If she leaned back any further on her heels, she was sure to fall.

Both Lindi and Karlann worked in a warm, spacious laboratory with two tables parallel to each other to create an aisle. Both their tables were tall enough to meet their midsections, made of Northern Elm, and had a perfectly polished red-brown colour to them.

Although they were neatly put away behind ornate wooden shelves, an array of tools and ingredients were available for any person to use at any time. More could be accessed from either side of the table, as there was a walkway around each one. Large bay windows on one side lit up the area, whereas decorative lamps, with scenes painted on their cloth shades, had been bolted to the walls and lit up the rest of the room.

Lindi placed her hands around the handles of the iron pot she'd been stirring, filled with a green, grainy, and seed-like concoction, and took it to a heating stove that ran perpendicular to their workstations. It was large, spanning almost the entire wall, and made of iron. Its magnificence had daunted Lindi at first, as she'd never seen such a large cooking hearth before, but she'd long come to appreciate the extra space and utility of it.

Incense seeped through every nook and cranny, and was a

pleasant aroma that filled the entire temple, including this room.

"It's going well," she answered, wiping her dirty hands on her colourful, pleated apron skirt. "I just need to heat it now and add the final ingredients."

Lindi then wiped the sweat from her forehead, the area a little too warm and humid, and peeked at her companion for the morning. Her gaze immediately darted to her forehead before shying away, and she fumbled for the next ingredient. She cleared her throat when she'd been caught, and the woman laughed.

"You don't have to be so shy about it, Lindiwe. We really don't mind if you stare."

Lindi offered Karlann a wry smile.

Karlann's short black hair reached to the base of her neck and was as straight as an arrow. It framed a cute, round face with a smattering of freckles that dotted her light complexion. Her nose was small, her lips as well, but her eyes were large and warm. Her eyebrows were slightly crooked, her jaw prominent and strong.

She was as pretty as she was curvy and tall, though her loose-fitting changpao hid the majority of her plumper figure.

Although most of the people in this country wore colourful clothes made from bright silks if they were richer, and hemp and ramie if they were poorer, these people predominantly wore white. Well, except for their leader, who was the only one who wore black to signify her station.

In their temple, the only colour came from the polished wooden walls, the painted cloth tapestry art, and their aprons.

Even though she was in a foreign land, those here in this special place were even stranger. The people within this temple all had different-coloured hair, different complexions, and varying body types – as if they were gathered from across many lands and brought here to Sing Dynasty.

But they weren't. They weren't just foreign to the country or this continent, but to this very world.

Lindi met Karlann's pink eyes, which seemed to shimmer, before she couldn't help dart a peek at the third one sitting horizontally above the middle of her brow.

Once more, the dark-haired woman laughed. "You would

think after a year, you would be used to it."

"I can't help it," Lindi muttered, turning away to stir the now bubbling and revolting-smelling poultice. "I know all three can be looked upon, but it feels impolite."

"It's only because you deem it so. Do you take issue with me looking into your eyes?" Then Karlann grasped her shoulders from behind and leaned over one to peek at the side of Lindi's pouting face. "They are rather watchful."

Lindi shrugged her off and poured in crushed blood powder, and the poultice glowed bright yellow for a moment. "I must learn, and watching is the best way."

Karlann rolled all three of her pink eyes before stepping away to resume her task. She ground the purple crystals further to ensure she created a fine pale dust. The granules were sharp, and Lindi hated doing Karlann's task – she always found a way to rub some into her eyes.

Beyond their walls, someone played a musical instrument that was a mixture of a harp and a drum – nothing like anything she'd seen from this world. Lindi didn't know how one could manage to strum a note and make pounding noises at the same time, but it required the assistance of magic to do so.

I still wish Weldir had warned me of the arrival of Anzúli. Then again, the demi-god had his many secrets, all of which he claimed were, in fact, not secrets – just things he hadn't yet told her. So his time delay and bouts of rest often meant he had to play catch-up with her in their conversations.

Then again, I'm sure I just missed the notice of their arrival in Austrális.

These strange people had been on Earth since the creation of the other portals, but Lindi had withdrawn from most of humankind by that time. She'd been fixated on the occultists and her children.

She'd thought the Anzúli priests and priestesses were just another fanatic group rising from the ashes of destruction. How was she supposed to know they were legitimate sorcerers and alchemists?

Their titles were capitalised outside these walls, as those were their names to humans, and they offered nothing else to them; not their faces, not their names, or where they came from. They were meant to be a mystery, which was what safeguarded and protected them.

As did the magical wall that surrounded their beautiful yet ominous temple. Not even Lindi, with her keen eyesight, could see that barrier, but Weldir had allowed her to see past their façades.

She'd stumbled upon their newly built temple a little over a year ago.

In this part of the world, they liked to make thick walls of fast-growing bamboo to hold the Demons back. Even the Anzúli had done so, although theirs was more for aesthetics, as they hadn't roped them together to make it impossible to get through their tall and thin hollow shoots. No, the Anzúli preferred them loose so they could hear the pleasant noises they made as they creaked, swayed, and rustled. They also didn't prune them, as they didn't fear Demons climbing them.

Honestly, when she'd first spotted them from a distance, Lindi had been curious about the shoots, as she'd never seen anything like them before.

When she'd walked through their circling forest of bamboo and their barrier without issue, as though nothing was amiss, it had alarmed them all greatly. She'd walked right past the open gates, into their lush courtyard, and immediately halted in her tracks.

They hadn't expected a visitor, so none had been adorned in their masks to hide that they were inhuman. The base of the expressionless masks was white with white mesh covering the eyeholes, and each person embellished theirs with painted colours to identify themselves outside these walls. Many had put up glamours to hide their shimmering eyes of pink, purple, green, and yellow, as well as their third eyes, but Lindi had seen through all of it.

After many months of silence, Weldir had finally offered his voice. He'd explained who and what these people were, and how they may be a little disgruntled to know she existed.

How her magic came to be was to remain a mystery. She couldn't inform them of her attachment to him, which left her with many questions. Why not? Why was their relationship to be kept a secret, as if what they were doing was wrong?

The Anzúli's ability to converse with each other across not only Earth, but their home world, and possibly even with the Elvish, meant everything was to remain well hidden.

Weldir gave her the ability to see through everything, while gifting his translation magic to allow her full transparency in their presence. After a few questions to her, and much interest in her abilities, they'd accepted her.

In the last few years, Lindi had learned enough of Mandarin to eventually forgo the translation spell. She'd always been a quick learner, especially when she did little else but study.

She studied the language of Sing Dynasty, she learned of its history, of its landscape, and the proper etiquette regarding society. Not that she intended to enter any place that remained untouched except for this temple.

The Demons had come through and caused ruin.

Not just here in this country, but everywhere.

From the day that Lindi stepped foot on this land, newly pregnant, it had been ablaze with violence. There were so many natural forests, so many mountain ranges, that freedom within the shadows was perfect for the biting, snarling vermin to flourish.

Lindi was unsure if Sing Dynasty was lucky in the sense that there was a great and vast man-made wall of stone separating them from one portal, but it did mean they were alone and trapped with another. The Demons could still climb over the wall and leave, digging their claws into the edges of the bricks, but why should they when there was plenty to eat on this side? The humans couldn't flee to other lands easily, and the water had quickly become just as treacherous to sail.

Lindi had underestimated just how quickly the Demons' influx was hastening. There were scores of them rapidly making their way through all the forests in the world to decimate and destroy everything in their paths. Austrális was just fortunate that the desert surrounding the Veil had kept them at bay for so long, as travelling in the reflective sunlight coming from the moon was painful for those void-flesh creatures.

But that moment of peace was ending even there.

Humans had already begun to flee, but the droves of Demons entering into the water meant no one had seen a boat returning to shore in at least three years. Pandemonium had truly set in, and everyone was terrified, which only fuelled the rabid beasts to be even hungrier.

And thus, the Anzúli making themselves known beforehand, warning all of the impending doom, had ensured they were at the pinnacle of the most trusted.

Those who had disregarded them, namely other religious leaders, were now thrown out as incompetent. Who would trust them when they so fervently denied such dangers were arising? Either their gods were not talking to them, or they didn't exist in the first place – quickly becoming the mutterings of the disillusioned in a time of ruin and chaos. Faith was being turned on its head, and with the Anzúli offering up no gods to worship, they themselves were becoming the very beings to follow.

Yet they offered no followings, no teachings. They weren't here to rob the faithful of coin to create beautiful temples of glory. No, their temples were merely homes. Places for them to practise their magics and alchemy, as well as create medicines, protective salts, and other much-needed tools in this time of destruction.

The Anzúli didn't want pretty, flowery words, or grand gestures and glittering baubles. They even denied offerings, whether they were items of beautiful artistry or servants.

They could be harsh and cold people. To outsiders, they were callous and as sharp as a knife, and only soothing when needed.

In Lindi's case, the temple inhabitants trusted her cautiously, so she was brought into their fold. She had magic. She was set apart. They knew she had lived a full lifetime and still appeared the same as the day she turned two and twenty.

To them, she was not human, and stranger than them.

Nothing will take away my humanity, Lindi muttered in her mind, stirring the frothing pot until the seed-like consistency shifted to only grainy. *I'm human, even if they deem me otherwise.*

She kept telling herself this, but she believed it less with every year that passed. They said she was sanctified and touched by their magnificent god, whose magic was just as black as the glittering sands she wielded. Since she played ignorant, claiming she didn't know how she obtained such power, she let them believe what they wanted. But Lindi knew better.

She'd been touched by the lukewarm hand of a demi-god who lurked in shadow and mist. Well, his tendrils, really. She'd never been touched by Weldir, other than when he made her stomach swell.

She often thought about how their god and hers were similar in their dark makeup. She often thought about Weldir, and her life, in the many years that had passed since she last stepped foot on Austrális.

I wonder how they are doing out there, Lindi mused, looking up at the wall in front of her. It was a shame the wall itself was partially blocked by the hearth, since it was so beautiful.

It'd been painted with a landscape she wouldn't have believed was real, if they hadn't told her that their home, Anzúla, had floating pillars of rocks. Dragons and wyvern were in flight, each having a gemstone of dragonite glinting in their foreheads – oddly enough, in the same location the Anzúli had their third eye.

One creature on the mural caught her eye. A fanged beast with thin antlers bearing only one off-shooting tine on them.

"You always stare at the siluk," Karlann commented, drawing Lindi from her thoughts.

Her answering response was quiet. "They remind me of something."

Or, rather, someone. Then again, it was difficult – impossible even – to not think of her children, especially as she'd only parted ways with her third one three years ago.

Dymphna was a little different to their brothers, Nathair and Orson. When Lindi had come across a fanged deer, she'd mistaken them for a predator and had hunted the creature to feed them to her new child. How was she to know water deer were purely herbivores when they had such menacing fangs? She was in a new part of the world, had never spoken to another human here, and she knew little of the landscape, its people, its culture, or its animals.

She eventually deemed their tusks cute and helped them obtain their antlers from another deer and let them run wild when it felt right. Which had taken her over two years, as she wanted to navigate this part of the world first and ensure their safety in her placement of them. Once she deemed they had plenty of food, considering the number of Demons sniffing after Lindi's meat, she let them go.

Her pregnancy had been dangerous. She'd spent much of it trying not to be incorporeal in fear or to escape danger, especially as that prolonged the length of how long she was to carry them. It was an adverse side effect. If she was in her Phantom form, she was technically dead and it halted the process, to her dismay.

What had only taken five weeks with Orson had been stretched to nine with Dymphna because of the way Lindi fled most altercations in the wilds. Nowhere had been safe, except behind walls that were still being built.

And she'd known not a lick of the language.

Thankfully the people were so petrified, nobles and commoners mixing in the chaos, that a stray Lindi had barely been noticed.

She'd stolen food and water from the already hungry, needing to fuel her body that only desired nourishment when she grew new life. Her child preferred hearty, meatier foods, which were being kept hidden in stores for the truly selfish members of society, but they were no match for Lindi's ghostly hands.

Lindi ate abundantly, pitying those who couldn't, but unable to do little more than offer biscuits to a child who had lost her parents in the great city. No matter how she tried to help them by holding their little hand as she searched, she couldn't find the kid's parents. Her stomach had become so large she'd needed to leave the city before she could complete her sympathetic task, but she'd given them as much food as they could hide on their person and had just hoped someone else kind took them in.

Then, once more, Lindi was left to the wilds, in danger as she gave birth under a protective dome with Demons bashing to get to her.

It'd been a frightening time, which had only been eased by Weldir giving her haven in his realm. With her newborn in her arms and biting at her, she struggled to hold on until she was safe there, and she finally felt relief. Lindi didn't think she could still be traumatised after so many years, but she'd proven herself very wrong that night.

Why had her body decided to give birth in the darkness?

As always, Lindi shuddered at the memories and looked down to return to her task. She gasped and quickly stirred the pot that was bubbling over.

Karlann tsked in the background, came over, and removed the pot from the fire.

"Seraphina won't be pleased if you burn this," she stated firmly, her third eye darting to Lindi while the other two concentrated on stirring in her stead. "We only have so much dragonite powder. You know how rare this is."

Lindi's lips flatted into a hard line. "You have an entire room of it," she argued, although, in her heart, she knew she should have just apologised.

"An entire room to last us however long we are on Earth." Karlann raised her dark brows. "There are no deceased dragons here for us to grind the bones of. This is all we have, and it's our best conduit. It's the one item we cannot be wasteful of. We also don't know when the Elvish will be gracious enough to give us another portal to resupply, if ever."

"I'm sorry," Lindi said with a sympathetic wince. "My mind has been elsewhere of late. I think I've been studying too much."

"If you're sick, take rest. The humans will get their medicines when they get them. We can only do so much with only a few dozen of us here."

Lindi offered an apologetic smile. "I'm fine. This is part of my learning."

Karlann huffed in annoyance and scrunched her nose. "I don't see why you insist on the teachings of concoctions and poultices to be one of your firsts. There is little mana on Earth, so what you learn in this room won't be useful. You won't have the right ingredients in your future travels."

"But there are many that will work," Lindi argued, pushing her out of the way with a hip bump. Then she gave a dark laugh. "Back home, the people there would call me a witch if they ever saw me standing over a bubbling cauldron."

Karlann snorted. "This pot is hardly big enough to be considered a cauldron." She waved a hand in front of her nose, fanning away the waft of smelly steam. "You'd stink of one, though. You should work with the other teachers. Your magic might be better suited for it. Try Elis, he is proficient in earth-based growing magics."

"It hasn't rained in a few weeks." Lindi checked the poultice, making sure it had survived her blunder before adding in medicinal weeds that could be found all over the world. "Elis believes my growth magic is best with all the right components. Dirt, seeds, and rain."

"You're the only person I know who needs rain to grow their plants. We need sunlight."

Lindi quietly sighed and ignored her teacher as she brought the pot back over the fire. "I think it has something to do with the origins of my magic. It's like it runs from the light."

Her magic was strongest when there were shadows. She wondered if that said anything about Weldir.

Karlann picked up her mortar to shake the crystal dust into a jar, and the sound of chinking ceramic echoed behind her voice. "No matter what Seraphina believes, I don't think it's our holy being that has blessed you. Yes, she works best in darkness, but it's the light she loves. She blessed us in the sun, in the beauty of colour, and we are merely her vessels."

It's why they all mainly wore white to act as colourless conduits for her addition of mana hues. Their leader, their robes black as night with purple emblems written along their seams, was the overseer of her whims. And, when colours splashed upon them, it seemed even more vibrant with the contrast.

They believed there was beauty in darkness, just as much as light. In death as much as life. In decay as much as the bloom of a newly sprouted flower.

I think Weldir and Uxos would get along well.

"Speaking of the Elvish," Lindi muttered as she tucked a curl behind her ear coyly. "No one has told me yet why the Anzúli are going out of their way to help them by protecting Earth."

Karlann's eyes, all three of them, narrowed on Lindi. "You're evading the problem."

Lindi grinned. "So?"

The woman tsked at her before giving a weary sigh. "You could consider it a transaction of trade. When the Elves first introduced themselves to our realm via a portal, we traded knowledge and minerals. They were interested in our magical

conduits and alchemy, and we their magic and mana stones."
Then Karlann turned to her mortar, now devoid of the ground-
up dust, and put the pestle back in it in order to move it all away,
only to pause. She merely stared into the mortar's bowl. "We
need their stones. It's now a way of our life, as we use them to
power our cities. When the Daekura came and they were forced
to shut down their portal to protect us from being infected, we
lost that valuable trade. When one of their gods recently opened
up a portal and offered us mana stones in exchange for coming
to Earth, it was difficult to refuse."

Both Karlann's expression and dreary tone sunk into Lindi's
heart. "You were forced to come here?" she asked, her voice
sympathetic, part of her wishing she could hug the woman.

"Huh?" Karlann's head shot up, and she darted her face to
Lindi. "Not at all. I couldn't think of anything better than leaving
Anzúla and coming here. Everyone who came to Earth was a
willing volunteer, and there were many of us who were
interested in the humans and their culture. I came here because I
had no ties to Anzúla, unlike many others." She then offered a
bright grin. "Don't worry. We're here because we want to be,
however long that may be."

"I'm sorry," Lindi grumbled, turning away when her cheeks
warmed in embarrassment. "I didn't mean to assume the worst."

"It's fine. I understand why you might think otherwise. Most
considered it insane to willingly run towards the dangers of the
Daekura, but I guess that's what makes us brave." Karlann then
smacked the mortar on the table to grab Lindi's attention, which
she graciously gave. The woman placed her hands on her waist
and cocked a hip. "Now, no more avoiding your terrible skills in
my poor alchemy laboratory. Why don't you work with Furir?
Her primary skill could be within your reach."

Lindi almost groaned out loud that Karlann had brought them
back to this discussion – when it was so obvious she'd been
avoiding it.

I don't even know Furir or what their primary ability is.

Primary abilities. Every Anzúli had proficiency in just one
skill. Karlann was best with medicine and poisons, Elis in earth
magic, and there was a sage who could make fire with nothing
more than a snap of his fingers. The last had stolen much of

Lindi's time, overly curious about her black flames and their cruel and destructive prowess.

She'd been the centre of unwanted attention from many, and had been poked and prodded one too many times than she cared for.

"I have not met Furir," Lindi admitted. She inserted her hands underneath her apron skirt so she could safely lift away her pot from the hearth. "I didn't even know there was someone here by that name."

"You haven't?" Karlann lifted a hand, and with a curled finger, she tapped at her pursed lips. "I guess I shouldn't be surprised. She often hides from the rest of us, as if we're an eye or ear sore. She seems to be more beast than anything these days."

Lindi cocked a brow and gave her a judgemental head tilt. "Is that nice to say of another person?"

She lifted her hand away with a frown. "What? I only speak the truth. With her ability to animal shift, she spends more time digging in the dirt as a mouse than cleaning like the rest of us." Karlann rolled her eyes. "Though she 'claims' she's using her nose to search for useful herbs."

Lindi paused just after she settled the hot pot down, and her gaze slid to the woman. "Animal shift? She can turn into an animal?" A shaky laugh slipped from her. "You're playing with me. No such thing could be possible."

"Of course I'm not playing. It really is a primary skill, as rare as it is." Then Karlann waved to the strips of bark in a ceramic pot. "She's the one who helps us seek out ingredients that are magical conduits that even humans can utilise. Some humans don't even realise they're already using them! If it wasn't for her, we couldn't have been able to share such information with other sectors who don't have an animal-shifter."

Seers and scryers allowed all the Anzúli to speak to each other from across the seas through various mediums, such as mirrors, waters, flames, and crystals.

Lindi lifted a hand to her lips and drummed them with her fingertips. "Shapeshifting... I never considered..."

"Neither had I," Weldir stated through the bond, his voice distant as always. *"But this is something you should explore."*

Lindi didn't jump, but she did startle after so much silence from him. It'd been a year – upon her arrival here at the temple, in fact – since she last heard from him.

The walls were too thin for her to speak with him freely, and being caught muttering to herself as though she wasn't sane was unwise. So, they never conversed to preserve the lie that she had no connection to the being who gifted her magic.

She turned to Karlann and raised her arms in supplication. "If you're so ready to get rid of my presence in your precious laboratory, can you introduce me to Furir, then? I'd like to meet her."

A smile slowly curled Lindi's lips. It must have appeared menacing because Karlann's eyes narrowed into suspicious slits. The woman then laughed, used to Lindi's oddness and playfulness, both often wrapped into one unique bundle.

TWENTY-ONE

July 7th, 1717

As black glittering sand encompassed her entire body, Lindi grunted a scream through grinding teeth. Eyes clenched shut and hands balled into fists near her midsection, she put all her might, all her determination, into her magic.

Heat clung to her clammy skin from the muggy atmosphere, but she didn't dare wipe her soaked temple against her shoulder. She hated how hot and heavy these thin white robes could be, and how unbreathable they were, but she always persevered.

When she couldn't hold onto the magic any longer, her body gave out before her will.

With a rain of black mist falling around her, Lindi collapsed into the mud and ruined her clothes within an instant.

"No!" Furir roared, her high-pitched voice somehow shifting to a baritone. An ugly baritone. "You must *feel* the fur. You must become the animal. Think mouth changing to snout, hands shifting to paws."

"I can't," Lindi rasped through pants, shaking her head as she stared at her hands in the squelching earth. "I just don't have the ability."

A set of stained white robes and boot-clad feet stopped in front of her, and Lindi looked up to the towering, thin woman before her. For someone who was six inches shorter than Lindi's five foot seven, she shouldn't seem so large. But with her hands on her small hips and peering down her large nose at Lindi, Furir looked like a giant.

Her three yellow eyes, unsteady and cold as always, sneered down at Lindi. "Get up and try again."

"What is the point in pushing this?" Lindi made it to her wobbly and lethargic legs without Furir ever offering out a hand in assistance. "We've been at this all day."

"You begged to learn to animal shift, so you must train."

"It's been three years!" Lindi shouted, her nose bunching as she scowled down at the blonde woman.

Her three eyes glared back at her. She was young, not a single wrinkle upon her sun-kissed face, but she had the personality of a commanding elder. She also had the mind of an unhinged madperson.

She was truly a beast.

"It's because you don't think like an animal. You hold onto your humanity, like it makes you superior!" Then Furir waved her hands in the air with a screech of uncontrolled rage. "You all do! This is why animal shifting is such a difficult skill to learn. Impossible, even, unlike the other skills." She smacked against her large bosom, hitting her own chest right where her heart was. "You are born with the ability to sniff the earth, to see beyond what normal eyes can't, to touch what no one else can. From the moment I was born, the shift felt freeing. It felt righteous. I spent most of my youth as a creature because it's better."

"I can't change what I am!" Lindi yelled back. "I am *trying*. I don't look down on your teachings or your ways, but you're right: I'm human."

Furir snorted a laugh while lifting her nose to snub Lindi. "A human you are not. You reek of *other*, no matter how much you deny it. I can smell it on you from a distance." Then she tapped at her own temple with two fingers hard enough to shove at her own head. "No, your humanity is in here. Your mind. You must let it go if you wish to be free. Perhaps it's just not possible for you, but your will is as much a barricade as your magical capabilities."

Lindi lifted her arms in a wide shrug, wishing the hot sun would go away and the rain would return. She was tired of overheating outside with Furir and wanted the woman to imagine what it was like to not be *her*. She didn't seem to feel the heat or the cold – not even when the ground was blanketed in a thick layer of snow.

No. She was merciless in any temperature and every season. Rain or shine, windy or calm, it didn't matter to her.

"Then what would you have me do?" Lindi asked beseechingly. "You make me train, yet we both know that this endeavour has long run its course."

In retort, Furir folded her arms. "Perhaps it has. I tire of watching you fail in the mud."

Then the short woman lost her focus when a shadow passed over them, causing her to dart her gaze up. Her yellow eyes glimmered, her third one glinting with purple, as she licked at the corner of her mouth. She muttered, not to Lindi but to herself, or to no one.

"Look at it fly." Her gaze narrowed, perceptive and yet lost, as her neck craned to follow a golden pheasant's movements, twitching when its large wings flapped like she could hear it when Lindi couldn't. "One of its wings has only newly healed. The feathers... they're not streamlined. Wait for its squawk. It will tell me what it seeks."

She lifted her right hand and her fingers twitched near her jaw, before the other lifted to do the same. Her head jerked in an unnatural way.

Lindi sighed and rubbed her straining neck. "Furir, please. Stay with me."

The woman's three eyes widened, and she darted her face back to Lindi. Her cheeks pinkened in embarrassment, but Lindi looked away to pretend she hadn't noticed her lapse of lucidity.

"Sorry. Please don't mind me," Furir grumbled awkwardly.

It was a curse for all animal shifters that their minds be a little chaotic. If they weren't careful, if they spent too long as a creature and not enough time as a person, they could lose themselves completely.

The eccentric, boisterous, and flamboyant Furir, who was only six and twenty, was already at risk. So young, they feared. She'd been ordered by Seraphina to remain humanoid until the worst of her lack of lucidity faded.

Nobody had prepared Lindi for the messiness of the woman's mind, and she truly seemed to be part beast despite her small, mostly human appearance.

Unfortunately, the curse had already progressed to the point that she changed into an animal from a stray, intense emotion. Anger, happiness. Sometimes even extreme fatigue could slip her away. Her dreams were pests to all, as she could be heard scampering about in her room – or, rather, destroying it.

Furir brushed back the stray blonde hairs from her dirt-smeared face. She was dirtier than Lindi, who had just kissed the mud. Those hands of hers had messed many books, an avid reader in her downtime, which once surprised Lindi that she had such focus after first meeting her.

Her peculiarities were often startling, and she had a keen eye for others.

Like now, when she peered around Lindi's still huffing form to cock a brow. Lindi turned to see what Furir was looking at before darting her gaze away and to the ground with her shoulders lifting nervously.

"I think it's odd that you have captured Evart's eye," Furir stated absentmindedly. "He is usually so reserved and pensive, but he makes this as obvious as a weed, rather than a truffle."

Lindi's cheeks heated at Furir once again making it known that Evart was watching her. She wouldn't allow Lindi the ruse that she was oblivious to this annoying attention.

His black curly hair went from longer on top and gradually shortened to the skin just above his ears and at his neckline. The Anzúli called it a low, tapered fade, not that Lindiwe had heard such a term or seen such a style before. His hair on his head was much fuller than the dusting of curling hair on his brown face. His jawline was prominent, chiselled even, and it matched his high cheekbones and thick brows. He had full lips and arresting brown eyes. His body was lean, and a little taller than Lindi's.

He was a very handsome man, despite the oddity of his third glowing green eye. She'd found her gaze often shying away when he had the top half of his robes folded down around his waist as he worked out with the rest of the Anzúli people in the mornings or evenings.

"I've already told you all that I have no such aspirations here."

Even if she wanted to, she'd made a vow to Weldir to keep

herself closed off to other men. Not in friendship, as she made many friends here, but romantically, physically. Even Evart, among a few other attractive men here, was given a more appreciative eye for his form, rather than anything desirous.

Not even her mind could cross that barrier and be playful, but it was also entirely barren when it came to any lust pertaining to Weldir. He had not sowed that seed, and thus, there was nothing to tend to in her special garden of desire.

"Yes, yes. Something about the sanctity of marriage and remaining untouched until then. So unfair on the maidens of this world." She placed her fists on her hips and shook her head. "Virgins. What an annoying concept. Who cares if she bleeds her first time or not? It does not matter to one's cock when it hits deep in hot wetness."

Lindi shuddered at her grossly forward speaking, fearing her ears would disintegrate with the searing heat of embarrassment. It also made her pussy clamp up and tingle, and the fact that Furir's nose was sharper than anyone else's was disconcerting.

The woman's lips curled from the mischief she knew she'd caused. "Be a ripe flower and take his nectar." She winked. "I'm sure he'd like it, and it smells like you need it."

"Oh, do fuck off," Lindi snapped while rolling her eyes.

Furir placed her hands on her hips, threw her head back, and barked out a grating laugh. "You amuse me, Lindiwe. Truly."

Lindi brushed off the drying, caked mud from her hands and lifted her head nonchalantly. "I think today should be our final lesson. It's obviously pointless and I won't be subjugated to this mortifying torture any longer."

"Yes, I think that's a good idea." Furir's smile went soft, reaching her eyes with fondness. "But I hope that you will continue to converse with me. Uxos knows how much the other Anzúli bother and bore me."

Lindi smiled in return.

Just as she opened her mouth to accept, liking this mad woman's company more than most, Weldir's echoing voice halted her.

"I have another way to give you what you seek."

Lindi swallowed. *How much of our conversation did he hear?* His tone didn't hold any note of jealousy or concern for

Evart, but she didn't like him thinking her promise was at risk.

Her gaze slipped to Evart sitting on the stone fence separating the training areas from the vegetable garden. As if he could feel her eyes on his lithe and tall form, he lifted his nose from his notebook. His expression didn't change, but he held her gaze with strength.

Quiet and stoic, the temple's architect and craftsman by nature was able to see beauty in many places – even in someone human.

Lindi shied away from him.

Maybe I wish Weldir would grow a little jealous.

The idea of someone being jealous over her left Lindi with the want to moan in satisfaction. Instead, she was only given the desolation of nothingness, interspersed with a few sparing words, most of which had nothing to do with fondness.

Although she wasn't a vindictive person, she'd considered fanning the flames of Evart's interest. He was handsome, a great conversationalist, and she thought she would've been interested had she no other ties. But that wasn't fair on Evart, nor did she truly wish to upset Weldir.

I doubt he would care anyway, so long as I keep my body to myself.

How bad would a kiss be? A simple grasp of hands? The brush of affectionate fingertips on her cheek?

Her nipples pinched under her robes at the idea; not with Evart, but anyone. *I've never been kissed.* How long had she been alive? Fifty-four years? Not once in that time had she had a taste of any kind of passion and Lindi... *longed* for it.

The only affection she garnered was from her children, which was why she adored them so quickly. She often yearned for one of her father's too hard and too long hugs, or her mother's gentle cheek pat where her thumb would run up and down the side of her nose.

Here, no one touched her beyond anything brief and platonic. No one offered her sweet words or sentiments.

Her heart and body were so touch and attention starved she feared if another person were to simply hold her hand, she'd dissolve into a puddle. How pathetically saddening.

"I was hoping you would be able to learn this ability," Weldir

continued, so uncaring or oblivious to anything that truly pertained to Lindi, her thoughts, or her needs. *"But it appears it's out of our reach with the Anzúli. I have scoured my memories for a solution, and I believe I have discovered one."*

At least he was willing to help in this regard, so that was something.

"I will always converse with you, Furir," Lindi stated with warmth, offering the woman a small smile. "I enjoy your company as well."

Her yellow eyes lit up in return, so different to the glare she'd worn when they'd argued.

"You've been there many years, Lindiwe," Weldir's rough voice muttered in her mind. Her smile began to fall at what he was insinuating, and what she knew was coming next. *"It is time you returned."*

Time she withdrew from a society once more... to be his breeding mare. Lindi shuddered at the mere thought. She knew that wasn't what he meant, but Lindi had grown fond of these people. She didn't want to leave, didn't want to go back to her lonely and isolated life.

The resentment she'd given up on threatened to rear its ugly head once more, this time wielding fangs and claws.

"There will be a treacherous journey for you to take," he stated plainly. *"But I think this is the best course of action."*

Those fangs bit deep, while the claws rent down to the bones of her spirit.

TWENTY-TWO

July 15th, 1717

Rubbing her hands down the side seams of her trouser-clad legs, Lindi shifted her weight from side to side on her booted feet. Her tunic – loose and allowing a breeze to flutter its way in and keep her cool – felt foreign wrapped around her torso.

She'd been wearing robes for so long, she'd almost forgotten what it felt like to wear these. In fact, she'd struggled to find where she'd tucked them in her room all those years ago.

Lindi had left Sing Dynasty's only Anzúli temple a week ago, to her heart's dismay, and had travelled south. She'd come across one of their other temples in her travels, as they had six main temples on this massive and seemingly unending continent that spanned hundreds of countries.

Each temple was situated close enough to a portal that led to the Elven world to be able to assist humans nearby in surviving the oncoming monsters.

Lindi stood in front of one of those portals with nervousness slipping down her spine. She nibbled on her bottom lip with trepidation that a nightmarish creature would slip from it.

No matter how long she stood in front of it, the centre of it swirling like water and transparent enough for her to see through, nothing came from it. The outer edges of it were yellow and sparking like lightning, giving minor creaks and zaps that reached her ears.

Situated over the very middle of a tiny spring that had a wall of dirt and roots beside it, the portal floated just above the muddy ground. Tree branches gently swayed above it, while rivulets of water trickled between rocks beneath it. The forest was so thick that only the minutest amount of sunlight shone on it, and Lindi cursed its location for that very reason. If only it was in a meadow – then perhaps many of the Demons could have scorched to death upon exiting it in the daytime.

Her skin prickled in aversion, her soul – her very *being* – telling her to run. To flee as far as she could.

A stick snapping in the distance had her gasping and turning incorporeal, so whatever might be hunting her lost her scent.

"Are you sure I have to go in *there*?" Even her floating essence seemed to tremble in repulsion and fear, despite that she could no longer sense her increased heart rate or rapid breaths.

"It's the only way."

Gosh! Couldn't he offer some kind of moral support? A little nudge of encouragement would be much appreciated right then. A little 'I believe in you' wasn't asking too much, was it?

Seeing as there was no other way to avoid it, Lindi turned physical and took in a strong, calming breath. She tightened her satchel over her shoulder, kicked her newish boots to make sure they were sturdy, and let out an expire of shaky determination.

Coldness touched her nose as she stepped through the threshold before it spread all over her.

Blinking through the muted light from a flaming torch, Lindi tried her hardest to see better in the swallowing darkness as clangs against the rock wall reverberated all around her and down the tunnel.

Each one sent terror through her heart, yet she continued to bash her handheld drifting pick against the rock. A clang sounded, along with a crack from the earth, but the rock wouldn't relent. The only thing that guided her to what she sought was the faintest blue glow, and she kept her focus on it. She didn't dare take her eyes from it, worried if she blinked for too long, she'd lose it and be stuck here even longer.

Another clang rang out, and her lungs clamped up when an

answering animalistic whooping answered from beyond. Lindi bashed faster, wishing she had the strength behind her impacts.

"Control your fear, Lindiwe. You only bring them upon you."

"Don't be afraid," she whispered to herself, smacking her pickaxe again. "I'm not afraid."

She was utterly terrified.

Then again, being however many metres below the ground, deep within the darkness, in a world overrun by Demons... who wouldn't be fucking afraid? It didn't matter that she had magic and abilities that she'd honed over the years with the Anzúli.

Instinctually, her body sensed the malevolent presences all around her, crawling in the shadows of the earth like disgusting worms. Her body breathed in their haunting violence, as if it was so thick in the air it tainted the very oxygen.

Even with barriers on either side of her, Lindi was wrought with unease. She also didn't like how the tunnels were so small, and how the edges of her vision wavered as if the rock around her was closing in on her. She never knew how suffocating being underground could be.

When the animalistic whooping grew closer, she smashed her drifting pick quicker.

"Come on." Smack. "Come on." She smacked her pickaxe so hard it bounced off the wall and the recoil threatened to send the other pointed end into her shoulder. "Come on!"

The rock finally relented, just as multiple somethings bashed against the wall of her barrier. Lindi gasped, held her prize to her chest, and turned incorporeal. She began to float, and she almost screamed when her sight blackened as the top of her head went through the ceiling. She waved her arms down, even though the control was all in her mind, and she sank beneath the rocky ceiling once more.

Red eyes, illuminated by the burning rags of oil-soaked cloth on the ground, tilted when the Demon dipped their head curiously at her. She stared back at their semi-humanoid face, noting their long, pointed ears, and their odd muzzle of lips on a small snout. They were grossly meshed together with some kind of creature, with little horns no bigger than an inch pointing out from their forehead towards her. Their arms and legs were digitigrade, like a dog's limbs, yet their hands and feet were humanoid, which just looked strange.

There were others around it, some more animalistic, but she couldn't look away from *that* one. Especially when it opened its mouth, which flared into a triangle as its chin separated.

If she wasn't a Phantom right then, she may have shuddered.

"You have the mana stone, Lindiwe," Weldir stated, stirring her from her staring.

Lindiwe looked down to the clump of rock in her hand, as transparent as her, and noticed the sky-blue crystal was no longer glowing. Her gaze drifted to the other bits still shining in the wall.

"Are you sure this is enough?"

She'd hate having to come back here.

Traversing underneath the gigantic trees, foreign grass, and treacherous mountains of Nyl'theria was terrifying. It seemed everywhere she went, there was a clan of Demons, factions of them spread out everywhere.

She'd even passed two clans locked in a cannibalistic battle of blood and flicking gore. This world was more overrun than she could have ever imagined, even with the thousands that had already begun to enter Earth.

Everywhere she'd turned, there'd been a monster in the shadows, just waiting for something to feed on. No wonder the Elvish had pushed them to Earth, as there seemed to be as many Demons as there were trees, which left the entire realm nearly covered in shade.

"I will not be certain until I inspect it myself," Weldir answered plainly, not giving her an ounce of faith.

Lindi returned to the rock wall and wanted nothing more than to expire with mental exhaustion. Instead, she sucked her lips into her mouth and bolstered strength and determination from the pit of her very spirit. She turned physical, ignored how that sent the Demons into a frenzy, and mined another chunk. Each bashing thump against her barrier made her flinch, but it was the eery scratching of claws against the rock that sent her teeth on edge.

Fearful tears welled in her eyes no matter how much she tried to bite them back, and they trickled down through her dirt-stained face. The taste of salty, wet dirt thickened in her dry mouth as she licked at her shaking lips to remove the evidence.

"Lindiwe," Weldir rumbled, and she was unsure if it was pity or a demand to control her emotions. Right then, she was so frazzled that it sounded like both.

Her heart was racing so fast that its panicked *ba-dumps* made her vibrate with stress. Any more of this, and it was sure to give out or explode right in her chest.

"I'm not afraid," she repeated to herself, wishing it were true. Her tears fell faster.

She needed to learn how to not fear the Demons.

She was alive, but she'd never die. Not truly, not forever. She'd always come back. That should be enough to still her rapidly beating heart, yet...

It was the pain of their teeth and claws that struck across her memories like hot iron. How many times had she been eaten alive? How many more times would she have to scream until she faded into dust through her bond with Weldir? The sound of smacking lips, tearing skin, and crunching bones – her own – still gave her nightmares, no matter that it had been well over a decade since she'd experienced such a thing.

Her hands shook as she swung her pickaxe and lodged the pointed end into the wall to wiggle the unyielding rock. She drew it back once more and hit that same spot, then dug again, and the rock popped forward just enough that she could wedge the point of her axe head behind it.

The relief that washed through her when it came free and landed in her hand was overshadowed when she turned towards the Demons. There were more, all of them fighting each other to get to the front of the line in this cramped, small tunnel. They bit, clawed, and struck each other just for a taste of *her.*

"Please, Weldir," Lindi cried. "Please take me away from here."

Within an instant, the swallowing, choking darkness was replaced with one that was quiet, weightless, and pleasant.

She embraced it, and how it meant Weldir had surrounded her.

"You did well," Weldir stated, his voice stronger and no longer echoing.

Her frantic eyes found him, and she wished the sight of his

barely visible form calmed her. His words, although a compliment, did little to soothe her.

Being the literal hands of a demi-god came with challenges, and more than ever, she wished his own could touch the world... and would reach out soothingly, rather than rest unfeeling at his sides.

She wanted to feel protected and safe.

Lindi would never get that with him.

TWENTY-THREE

August 28ᵗʰ, 1717

Closing her eyes, Lindi took in a deep, steadying breath through her nose and released it through her mouth. She flipped her eyelids open and spread her arms to the world.

Before her lay the Veil: vast, dangerous, and seemingly unending. At her feet, merely a hair's width away, was the deadly and frightful fall of the canyon's cliff edge. Rocks broke off under her boot tip and, if she wasn't careful, the ground could come apart underneath her.

In the seven years she'd been gone, it looked so different. She hardly believed her eyes when she took her first look at the ground far down below.

It was as though thousands of trees had not only newly sprouted, but had fully matured. Moisture clung to each leaf with such richness and lusciousness, breathing life and creating a cloudy white mist that spread all throughout. It reached everywhere, touched all of the Veil, and gave it an eery, haunted atmosphere.

Along with it, Weldir's black mist had thickened and descended into the canyon like the pour of a waterfall down each wall face. To a normal, unsuspecting eye, they wouldn't see it, but Lindi had begun to pull apart the very fabric of life and see beyond into the shadows that lurked even in the shade. The mist was there, growing, as was his power.

She'd seen it in the forests surrounding the portals she'd

passed in the northeastern continent she'd wandered.

So much has changed in thirty-two years since I gave my soul to Weldir, she mused, as she looked up to the dusking sky. *And I've witnessed so much of it.*

She'd seen wonders and horrors. She'd pitied people she encountered, and was thankful for the strange ones who had taken her in. She'd killed, and she'd adored. She'd cried, and recently laughed. She'd shed blood, sweat, and she'd sacrificed.

A splash of orange set the horizon ablaze while dusting the clouds with a mesmerising purple. It somehow made the horridness of the Veil seem less imposing and daunting, reminding her there was much beauty left in the world. That there was, truly, light in this dark age.

It was a beautiful evening.

So beautiful, even, that she leaned forward as though she dared an attempt to grasp it. The cloak around her shoulders caught the wind in her movements and opened as she fell off the cliff...

Lindi didn't scream; she didn't even fret.

Instead, she closed her eyes against the cold, invisible wind cutting across her face and the frightful rush of the incoming hard ground. She ignored the reminder of the only other time she'd done this, which had ended in her very first death.

Feel your skin change. A certain boisterous and mad woman's voice rang in her ears. *Your heart must be open, your mind clear enough to allow another's instincts to enter.*

Lindi felt out with her mind to touch the air and harness the way it rustled within her shapeless, masculine clothing. Heat collected against the middle of her sternum between her collar bones as her cloak ties choked her. A sharp whistle pestered her eardrums, but it was drowned out by harsh teachings.

It was a long fall. Forever seemed to pass.

The ground had to be closing in.

I've done this fall before.

It felt like eons ago. That day she fell to her first death, only to awake in a realm of weightless shadows.

"Lindiwe," Weldir's dark warning rumbled, calling even louder through her thoughts than normal.

As she opened her eyes, Lindi twisted in the air. Everything changed all at once. Her eyes sharpened to the point that she could see the blades of grass below her, rather than the murk of just plain green. Her ears dulled against the wind, but the scamper of something, a monstrous void creature no doubt, scratched in her mind despite the distance.

Her hair shrunk in length, as black feathery hardness sprouted across the bridge of her nose and moved like a wave. It spanned across her face, over her head, and then down her neck and back. Her spine changed to support much larger feather growth as a tail formed, while her feet changed shape into taloned claws. Her hands, loosely spread out behind her, thinned as her fingers lengthened into wide arches, just as thick, strong muscle formed between her armpits and wrists.

Just before she hit the treetops, Lindi flapped her lengthy wings. They caught a current of air and she caused the leaves below her to sway and rustle in her wake as she shifted into a glide. She opened her shiny dark-grey beak to release a caw.

Something snarled in answer from the ground, but it was swiftly left behind as she continued on.

Then Lindi banked left to head west. She darted towards the cliff wall until her wing tip almost brushed against it, but she skilfully avoided it.

She looked down when she passed over water to see the reflection of her black feathered form. White irises stared back, and she cocked her head for a better look.

Although she knew it to be hidden beneath her feathers, she felt the sky-blue mana stone against her sternum. Its warmth was comforting. She never imagined something so small and light could be so powerful.

It was no bigger than a tiny riverbed pebble, yet it gave her the power to harness a spell that had been interwoven into the very cloak of feathers she'd worn upon her fall. Of course, many ravens, and even a crow, had needed to die in order for Lindi to be granted the use of their frock. Hunting and collecting them for Weldir had been a long and arduous task, the creatures cunning and wise enough to flee her before she could pounce.

But it was done, and in their death, Lindi was gifted freedom.

Lindi, as her raven self, cawed as she brought her wings close to her body and spun like a vortex in the air, only to spread them once more. She flew up and away from the Veil that passed at lightning speed below her.

She was swift, her body still large and her same human height. She crossed meadows and passed over newly erected walled towns in no time.

"It seems you like your new form," Weldir stated through their bond. *"Should I call you little raven now instead of little human?"*

Mirth was evident in his tone; Weldir found humour in the way she took in this new power. Without Weldir it wouldn't have been possible, as she couldn't create such a complex and interwoven spell, but it was now all hers.

The mana stone was physical, and she could take it anywhere. It didn't need him or his magic to fuel it. She thought Furir would be proud, and perhaps one day Lindi would return to her to show her what she could become.

However, until Furir, Lindi was limited to this raven form, so long as she didn't lose any of its feathers. If she did, she would have to hunt for another and have Weldir fix it, otherwise she might not transform properly.

If she wanted, she might even be able to create a cloak from furs and shift into that instead, but she could not choose without making arrangements. The stone and spell could only handle one animal type each time.

They were arrangements she doubted she'd make.

Now that she'd tasted the wind, felt it in her blood, her bones, she knew she'd always choose the liberating openness of a bird. Why be planted on the ground when she could reach unimaginable speeds like this? She didn't even feel the cold, and the wind wrapped around her like a blanket of security.

I could reach Nathair's territory in no time.

To prove that, she banked to the right to cross back over the expanse of the Veil.

What would take a month on foot should surely only take a mere day, if not less, if she didn't rest. She chased the darkening horizon with the last of the sun on her back, watching as a crescent moon, pale blue and gorgeous, rose before her.

Her dark-grey beak was hard and immobile, but she felt her smile within her very soul.

If I could, I'd never turn back into a human. No wonder Furir found this so addicting.

TWENTY-FOUR

April 6th, 1726

Standing on top of the lantern of a great cathedral, Lindi noticed the broken section of stone beneath her talons. The cross that had once been fixed to the very top had been removed forcefully, and there was evidence of its fall lower down on the building.

Beneath the stone lantern she was perched on top of was a great dome, and below that a rectangular building. Off to one side were two towers, one of which had a great clock on it large enough to see from a mighty distance.

The clock was well maintained, possibly so that all the occupants of this large and vast city could count down the minutes of their demise. The cathedral, once a pillar of a mighty religion, was in disuse for such a reason and had been repurposed into a different temple.

These people needed it.

With so many injured soldiers and builders, as well as sick people, the city of Londinium required much support.

Below her talons was the home of the Anzúli who resided in Londinium. Anything that looked to be of the old religion had been removed, giving room for new paintings, glass windows, and glorious artefacts. Deeper within its bowels, materials from another world were stored away and constantly monitored.

But of course, Lindi was the only human who knew such immense changes had been made within these stone walls. Not even the current king had been inside. Then again... he rarely left his newly built estate within the city, too afraid to step outside past the guards that surrounded his home.

The Anzúli within Sing Dynasty had used their communication scries to let all those on Earth know of Lindiwe Bernadi, the strange human *witch*. Someone touched by Uxos, even if that was an unconfirmed blessing.

She was welcome everywhere.

And she was here, in the great Englian. Not that it was so great, considering its morose state.

I hate that I must stand here and bear witness.

Because the current situation was that Lindi had somehow found herself being pushed into the role of a pillar of hope. Her black downy feathers and large bird form reminded the Anzúli of one of Uxos' forms, a large phoenix-like creature with black flames coming off its feathers.

The fact that she was human sized and large enough for most to see, even from a small distance, had been a good omen to them. Most animal shifters morphed into the size of the animal, perhaps with a small amount of discrepancy. A bird of her size was impossible, and yet here she stood, massive.

With warm night pressing in against her, Lindi shifted her talons on her perch to drift her gaze elsewhere.

It was hard to watch, no matter where she looked.

This large city, one of the biggest in terms of congregating people, was at war. Hundreds of thousands of humans were suffering at the hands of Demons. Night was the only time they could rest, but sleep eluded many with the sounds that scratched, howled, and rustled in the night.

Before her lay houses that separated her from a large river, and more buildings spanned to the right and left as far as her raven eyes could see. Behind her were more homes and then acres of much-needed farmlands – not that it was enough to feed so many.

Her feathers ruffled as she shivered at who stood on the fringes of this city and bordering the river that spanned five or so kilometres. A string of Anzúli *desperately* tried to keep the monsters at bay. Walls made of magic, varying in colour, shimmered in the night – each one belonging to a different caster. The other side of the river was left to ruin, all those that once lived there eaten and their homes occupied by inhuman beasts.

The river did little to keep them at bay, and the bridge that separated the two lands had been purposefully burned down.

Lindi wished she could leave. She had done her part for Weldir for these two main islands that made up Englian. Even just thinking of escaping had guilt slicing into her gut.

The Anzúli were doing their best to keep up a linked barrier, but they could only do so much with fifty of them. There were more across the country, others helping other towns and humans, but this was the largest city.

The humans up north were strong, hearty people, but they, too, needed assistance even with their kilts and axes. Thankfully they had many rolling hills and mountains, but they also had many forests and woodlands to contend with.

Like those people, those of Londinium had taken up arms. First it was just men who had taken up muskets and swords, willing to fight for their women, children, the old, and the sick. But as they fought back against fang-filled beasts and swiftly died, even women had taken up arms.

The societal restrictions and silliness had been shed in the wake of destruction. They all worked together to build a wall that encompassed the entire city, which had been a painfully slow endeavour.

There was a shortage of resources, their walls first built of stone being swiftly extended and reinforced with wood to fill in the gaps. Their muskets were now lacking in bullets and there was only so much gunpowder left. Citizens were hungry and thinning from famine, giving room for disease. They had access to the river, their only drinking source, but it wasn't in the healthiest state.

Those who left throughout the day to chop wood and search for herbs were few. In the shade, hungry beasts lurked and took their opportunistic meals when they could, picking off workers or soldiers one by one. People had acquired resources in many ways, such as taking from ships that were afraid to leave harbour when the debris of other shipwrecks came back down the river in pieces.

They were unable to go to the mines to find ore, halting any progress they had quickly been achieving. The technology they had here had already far surpassed that of Austrális, but they were now shoved back decades into the past.

The Anzúli were doing all they could, but there were limitations. They could only expend so much of their magic, reserving it for use at night when the city was most at risk. In the relative safety of day, human soldiers stood guard around the perimeter while builders shed blood, sweat, and sometimes their lives to quickly construct defences and repair infrastructure. They restored much of the city that had burned down, people working tirelessly to give homes to those without.

The Anzúli offered medicines, which were far superior to anything humankind had ever made. They aided the farms in growing food with thrice the natural speed. They were there, helping, but they were mortal beings, and not impervious to exertion.

Thus, Lindi had not only become a pillar of faith that their god was there watching over in the form of a feathery blessing, but she was aiding. She had a powerful magical source, and though it was finite, it did not drain her.

It drained Weldir.

When she had explained their collective cry of desperate need to him, and how much she wished to be a solution – unable to witness such a slow mass destruction of people – he'd granted her full use of him. Which meant he had been shoved into his slumbering silence, as he slept during the overwhelming usage of his abilities.

Weldir slumbered to allow Lindi to cast a barrier of chalky sand against the length of the river each night, giving the city a wall of darkness to protect them. It gave many Anzúli time to rest or work on other means of aid. Throughout the day, and if it rained – which it did often here – she grew vegetables so they could tend to rearing animals in a more efficient way.

The city council pushed back the perimeter of the city, wanting more farmland since they no longer needed to rush their building of the wall. With her help, they could make the city's border bigger. She burned corpses with scentless black flames, ensuring the horrible and frightening stench of meat didn't cling to people's noses and minds, while also removing the potential of disease. It seemed a more humane means of removing the dead, with the Anzúli praying for their peace as they moved onto the next life.

There was one final task – one which was solely reliant upon her to take care of. One that happened at each dawn.

There was so much more she wanted to do, but it was her body's demand for rest that prevented her from doing more.

And, in her sleep, Lindi transformed into a raven to stand upon this cathedral to close her weary eyes. To be a pillar of hope, letting the Anzúli wrap the humans in a comforting lie like a warmed blanket.

At night, she awoke to bear witness to the plague of Demons scratching at all their barriers, hers spanning the furthest along the river. They howled, squawked, and yelled. They were relentless, baring their teeth just for a scrap of meat.

The sorrowful state of not only this city, but the world, was ineffable. She'd seen such devastation everywhere, but this was where she had been planted for the past seven years. This was the worst she'd seen in person, but surely other cities faced such destruction, with the Anzúli doing all they could to prevent total annihilation.

How pitiful.

I can only be here. This is where the Anzúli had reached for her help, and she couldn't be in many places at once. *I am only one person.* She couldn't become many, no matter how much magic she could access.

And, as sunrise crawled its way closer this day, pink and orange splashing across the sky, Lindi grew tired. But she couldn't cease her assistance. She could not close her eyes against the heavy weight in her lids and rest.

Her next and final task before rest awaited her.

Lindi unfurled her wings to the oncoming light and lifted off to search through the slow retreat of Demons. The wind rustled her feathers as she soared higher into the sky and then banked to the left to glide through the air.

She sought a monster, but not one that matched the throng of others. Something else. Something far more dangerous and beautiful.

She circled the city until a tiny speckle of white made itself known among the glistening blackness of bodies. A creature sniffed at a glimmering, translucent wall, unable to pass through to hunt the humans within, but unafraid of the oncoming rays of sunlight.

In the past six years, it'd been seen by many humans who loitered at the barrier to get a peek at what horrors lay on the other side. This creature, although menacing, aggressive, and just as nightmarish as the others, was obviously different.

Here it skulked every dawn and reappeared every dusk. Stepping through the light without burning and dominating the night as it fed on Demons foolish enough to come near. Like a shark, it was always circled by prey, but wasn't always lucky enough to feast on what was just out of reach.

Lindi, in her raven form, landed behind it.

Orbs flared bright red, and it turned to her with a boisterous and ear-splitting roar. An otter skull, mighty and large, snapped its intimidating fangs, while a deep-purple tongue curled with saliva dripping from it. Roe deer antlers jutted up from the crown of its head, and the creature tossed their head to present them.

The humans hadn't known what to make of it at first, only knowing that it was dangerous and would eat them like the Demons. Yet, the fact that it stood here with the sun on its back while skulking on all fours caused fear to quake in their hearts.

They'd given her child a name, and she found it to be rather suitable. Especially considering their abilities to march wherever they desired, in whatever time of day they liked.

Duskwalker.

The Anzúli had relayed the name to other sectors, and the term was swiftly spreading throughout humankind – especially in the places where her other children had been spotted. They would find more in far-reaching places, as she already had four in three continents.

There would be more, as per Weldir's wish.

This child was young, a little over eight years old, but rather formidable. Not long after she'd given birth, she'd discovered the state of Londinium and had quickly found their skull and antlers to grow them. They had yet to consume a human and find their gender, but Lindi knew if they were to travel north rather than relentlessly returning to this barricaded city, they would stumble upon one eventually.

Lindi sighed as she transformed from a raven to a human before they could step a single humanoid hand forward.

"You have done well tonight, Odie," Lindi complimented, noting the carnage they, her child, had produced throughout the night. "But it's time for you to return to the forests."

Just as they charged, likely seeing her as another enemy, black tentacles made of glittering sand shot out from the ground and wrapped around them. Odie fought with all their might to be freed, but little could be done against the magic of their father. They could snap and snarl all they liked, could fret and squirm with all their might, but Lindi wouldn't release them.

Instead, she turned and began to walk away from the city, with them being dragged behind her. Odie got a hand free to claw at the ground in an attempt to stop her, tearing up grass and dirt, but all they did was rend the earth.

She took them away from the scent of humans, otherwise Odie would cause devastation while they built in the daytime. They would kill soldiers, and she couldn't allow it.

As much as I cherish you, I must bind and move you from my gaze.

Odie would one day eat a human, but not under her watchful raven eyes.

TWENTY-FIVE

A time unknown, but the seeds of conversation begin

With his energy slowly replenishing, Weldir stirred. Darkness met darkness as he opened his eyes, but there was an illusion of light in his periphery, allowing him to perceive his own sight.

With his palms facing upwards, he looked down at his hands and clenched and unclenched them. *It seems she has ceased using too much of my mana.*

He opened his mind to feel all along his selfs, checking the realm within his stomach. Tenebris was exactly how he left it, mostly finished in creation except for what he would change for the departed souls he held for safekeeping.

He moved his consciousness along. He felt his mind, and how he had tucked himself at the back of it to rest.

He checked within his heart, finding Lindiwe's soul's citrine flame bright and exactly how he left it. *It still has impressions of darkness.* He noted the black charcoal around its heart and streaming from its brown eyes like flaming tears. With its arms crossing over its torso like it was hugging itself, its legs were slightly bent in the weightlessness. It never looked at peace, but the glare in its gaze had faded, now just appearing solemn while alert.

It reminded him of her, especially with its large curls flaming above its head. He found it just as beautiful as her.

Weldir moved on to the fringes of himself and then let out a weary sigh.

So many souls.

There had to be thousands of white flaming souls waiting to be consumed. He materialised his body to the area in which they floated and reached a hand out. The closest soul to him was in a horrible state.

Unlike the mess of scarring that could come from a human's life being present on their very spirit, those consumed by Demons were different.

Rather than the grey spots lingering deep within their soul from sickness, or the charcoal spots that snuffed out life like mental decay, or even the evidence of pale scars, those eaten by Demons were in pieces. He brushed his fingers over the torso of what appeared to be a woman and cupped his hand under it.

Cracks of red, like burning lava, streaked across her body like it had been struck by lightning. It did not show how she died, but he knew from the memories of others it must have been frightful and painful.

Weldir didn't have a name for the sickness produced from being eaten by a Demon. All he knew was that if he were to consume this soul before healing it, that lightning would spread to him and fester by eating away at his mana in hungry sparks.

So, Weldir enveloped the woman's soul in his hands and concentrated. He glued the pieces back together with the use of the spiritual side of his mana, while drawing away the toxin into his own body. Once taken into his black right hand, making it appear to have lava cracks throughout it up to his wrist, he threw his palm out to the right. He expelled the toxin out into his mist on Earth, ridding himself of it and letting it disperse into the air.

Even holding onto the toxin for a short period of time chipped away at his mana as much as piecing the broken souls back together did. Already the mist surrounding him thinned, and he grumbled in annoyance. He quickly assessed if the woman's soul had any tethers intertwining with another spirit to see if he could give it a joyful place to rest in his realm.

There was a connection present, but that person had not yet been consumed. Their flame floated somewhere nearby, not yet in his stomach but ready to be eaten.

She will rest in my valley of souls until that person greets her memories with their own.

Not wanting to waste any more time, he opened his mouth, pressed the soul to the cavity he created, and shut his lips around it. He swallowed, and it descended his throat and entered Tenebris.

He floated towards the next listless, drifting soul, passing the hundreds around, above, and below him. His direction was always different as he picked a soul at random to heal it, expel the toxin into Earth, then consume it.

Each time he healed one, he lost a little more strength, the toxin's festering stronger than the soul's replenishment.

But, unlike the toxin, which was a fleeting wound, he would have a deeper well of mana with each new soul he added to his collection. It would go further, so long as he rested. For now, it only debilitated him.

Weldir one day may go through their memories, wanting to visit their life out of curiosity. He'd learned many languages, and although he could not leave the reach of his mist, he'd seen many places. He'd been on ships setting sail across the ocean, had dug his hands into dirt as he farmed, and he had even sat at a table putting ledgers in order for a business. He'd poured drinks for dreary patrons, as well as danced with a man in the rain as his flowy, sodden skirt swayed around his lithe, feminine calves.

Every new spirit pieced together the many kinds of life for a human and granted him more understanding with each one. He chose what he valued or what he didn't care for, and dismissed a lot of superstition, moral ideologies, and faith, as they had no room in his already-filled consciousness.

He had no use for them.

He could not count how many sickened souls he consumed until he eventually came across one that wasn't lava-veined.

It appears one of my offspring has healed a soul for me and returned to my mist. Oddly enough, it had curly hair, and he was once more reminded of his mate. He thumbed its chest, finding the female's body to be less curving than Lindiwe's, inspecting it closely with a hum of thought.

My mana is small right now; this is a welcome change.

If he continued to do this task without finding those not destroyed by Demons, he would have consumed many souls but would also risk slipping himself back to sleep. Each one ate at his power little by little, and their aid to him was often delayed and only effective upon rest.

Which would be no issue normally, but he had no concept of how long it had been since he'd last been awake. He looked down at the white flame in his grasp, and how it bore a striking resemblance to someone dear.

I wonder how my mate fares.

Rather than do his duty, he allowed for a moment's distraction.

Weldir looked to his right when he made a viewing disc form, his consciousness focused on the tether connected to him and a pretty little female. Suddenly she appeared, staring off absentmindedly before her.

With her gaze far away, she popped a slice of plump orange and white pith into her mouth. While she chewed, Lindiwe spat the seeds into a handkerchief. She sat on a patch of grass near some trees bearing round fruit – an abandoned orchard, from what he could tell. More orbs of fruit lay in her lap, her legs out straight in front of her.

Her black cloak of feathers was in a disarray, many of the plumes bent and unkempt, with patches even missing. He shifted the disc to view her from the front, noting the old dirt stains that she couldn't remove from her blue high-quality tunic and black breeches. Her boots, brown and new, had been removed so she could air out her feet and likely give them rest.

Next to her was a small satchel, and he had no idea of its contents.

A subtle, light breeze moved her tangled hair around her shoulders. He rather liked the windswept appearance of the coiling and kinking strands, finding it flutterier and more voluminous.

Her face was as it always was. It had not changed, but his appreciation for it had grown during however long they'd been bonded. There was a prominent edge to her jaw and cheeks, and a gentleness in her brow. She dabbed her pink tongue along her full brown lips, licking along the darker line that circled them to collect fallen juice. Her nostrils flared when she took another bite, as if smelling while tasting what she ate, and her expression proved that she found it delicious.

Her body was hidden beneath her clothing, but Weldir knew it quite well from watching her bathe in streams and waterfalls in the past. An hourglass figure blessed this female, her breasts full and her hips wide.

From the memories of humans he'd seen, most would deem her body sinful and her face lovely.

Like them, he noted how the sun shining on her medium-brown skin gave it a wonderful golden glow, which then gave her darker hair a reddish hue. And how that light sparkled in her doe-brown eyes and gave a glimmer of spiking amber around the pupil.

Most would have been mesmerised by her beauty, even if her state was a little wilder from traversing the world freely.

Her dark, curling lashes fluttered when a sudden gust cast pollen and dust into her eyes, and she shut one to protect it. It wasn't enough to stir her from her thoughts.

"Your cloak is looking quite worn, Lindiwe," Weldir stated, wondering if he could be the one to pull her from staring down the hill. He tried to hide his humour, but even he heard it mingling in his tone. "You haven't taken care of my gift."

Lindiwe didn't flinch at his voice, but she did pause momentarily to take it in. Then she continued to pop a slice of orange into her mouth.

"A gift well used is a gift obviously well treasured," she answered freely once she finished chewing. "Consider it proof of my appreciation."

Weldir placed his hands behind his back, ignoring the floating white souls around him to give her his full attention – not that she would know.

"How do you fare, little human?"

She snorted a curt and false laugh. "I'm coming to realise I'm barely human anymore. I haven't been treated so in quite some time." She shrugged a single shoulder. "Then again, talking to you always reminds me of my origins."

Weldir cocked his head curiously. "Is that a good or bad thing?"

"Just a fact. I don't mind feeling human, especially when my grasp on it appears to be fading."

"You didn't answer my first question."

Lindiwe looked down at the peelings in her lap. "I'm well. Tired, if anything."

"You do look as though you have been living largely. How go the humans you attempted to save?" The reason for his likely lengthy sleep.

The corner of her lips twitched, as if she were close to offering a smile. "They're good. Londinium is still standing, and I have helped many other towns and cities since then. How was your sleep?"

Weldir stood a little taller, surprised she would ask, as she'd never done so before. He was pleased she was interested in his wellbeing.

"It was the same as it always has been. Uneventful."

Grasping a new orange orb, she drifted the side of her thumb back and forth over its thick skin. "You know... I've always wanted to ask, but do you ever dream?"

He cocked his head, once more surprised at her intrigue regarding him. "Dreams? No, I have no use for such things. But I do remember the past, as it was, without alteration or fantastical perception."

Lindiwe's brows drew together. "What does that even mean?"

Weldir offered a small chuckle in return. "I have seen humans' dreams, and they are strange. They dream of things that are not possible for them, or things that have not happened and never will happen."

"I dream," she quickly interjected. "Like you, I remember, but then the memories run away from me and become something else. I think it's human to dream – maybe that's why you don't."

"Perhaps," he answered, hoping she heard the shrug in his tone. "How long have I been asleep?"

She was slow to answer, and she rested her chin on her right shoulder as if coyly. "Almost fourteen years, since I started helping Londinium."

"I see. So little time has passed, then."

Her lips twitched before she rolled her eyes with a lengthy sigh. "Really? That is actually a long time, Weldir. I expected you to be furious with me."

"I see no point in being angry with you. I have collected many souls from Demons, our offspring have brought me several that lack any toxin, and I can see you are content from aiding the humans. I've never had a better waking."

"I'm glad you're pleased."

Lindiwe peeled the orange and cracked open its pieces to take one.

"Why do you eat when you have no need to?" Weldir asked, curious about this and finally desiring the answer.

"Eating reminds me that I'm human. It tastes refreshing and I miss doing it." Then she used her long thumbnails to split apart the membrane to reveal the pulpy insides. "I'm also collecting the seeds."

His gaze slipped to the off-white seed she'd revealed. "Why are you doing that?"

"I never know when I'll need them, or when a town could use a new source of food. Oranges, in particular, stave off illnesses from malnutrition such as scurvy." She let out a sigh and turned her face up to the sun. "I've actually collected quite a store of seeds, and the Anzúli have taught me how to preserve them forever. There's the means to grow lemons, apples, cherries, and oranges, to name a few."

"I was surprised when the Anzúli took you in with such welcome."

Her lips pursed and her eyelashes lowered when she narrowed her gaze. "I still haven't forgiven you for not informing me of their arrival on Earth."

Another chuckle slipped from him. "As you said earlier, such time has passed. You hold onto your grudges fervently, little human."

"I can't help it. It's how I've always been."

"I see no issue with this. I enjoy your peculiarities."

They were harmless to him, and they had forever for him to knead out her disquiet with him... Although, that did come from a place of hope that he was actually able to.

Weldir was grossly aware she was discontented with him, and she was not very forthcoming as to how he was able to mend that. It was difficult to repair something that had never existed in the first place. Trust was something apparently to be earned, and he knew she trusted him distantly.

"Says the most peculiar being I've ever met," she commented quietly.

Their conversation lulled, and Weldir took that as the chance to continue his original task. He finally pressed the untainted soul his offspring had procured for him into the cavity of his mouth, and swallowed.

He received a small burst of strength, finding true replenishment without punishment. His mist thickened and collected tighter against him in relief.

He then reached out for a new soul while keeping a careful eye out for any more that weren't sickened, so he could gain mana without any cost. He kept the viewing disc up, peeking at her occasionally while he worked in their shared and comfortable silence.

After some time, when the sun reached its highest peak and shielded her under the shade of the orange tree, she finally broke the tranquil quiet.

"Weldir? Are you still there?"

"I never left."

She nibbled on her lower lip. "Thank you for letting me help Londinium, and consequently many other cities and towns."

"You're welcome, Lindiwe. I don't wish for the humans to perish, same as you." He also had no issue aiding her in her endeavours, and he hoped she leaned on him more in the future. "Where are you now, if not near Londinium?" he asked, unable to tell when much of Earth's environment appeared similar.

She could be all the way in Austrális, for all he knew.

"Near Orange. It's a town in Francia."

"Is that far from where we last spoke?" Weldir asked.

Her shoulders turned inwards, and she looked around nervously while chewing her bottom lip. "A little? It's actually across the water and on a different land not too far."

"I wasn't expecting you to leave there..." But he wasn't stunned that she'd flown so far, considering her wings. "I don't have any offspring on that continent yet."

Which was something they should change soon. Eyropea was large and encompassing many countries like Francia and Polen, much like the Middle Eastern lands.

As if sensing where his mind had gone to, she tucked her

seed-filled handkerchief into her bag, and asked, "Is it possible for you to fix my cloak? My flight is unsteady with so many missing feathers."

Weldir looked away from a tainted soul to the disc and found her awkward gaze roaming everywhere – as if she wanted to avoid him. She didn't know from which direction he was watching her, and the playful side of him was tempted to follow her eyes' motions to always be before her.

He didn't, as that was a waste of his time and efforts.

"Of course, Lindiwe. All you need to do is bring me more feathers. We can then bring another servant to life in the very place you currently rest your feet and wings."

Her nose crinkled before a deep groan croaked from her.

Weldir almost laughed at her reaction but wisely kept himself quiet.

One day I would like to truly tease her. But he didn't think she would be receptive to such attention welcomingly just yet. Or maybe never, depending on if she ever came to see him as anything but a god that asked much from her.

November 3rd, 1732

Lindi's toes curled when she felt Weldir's tendril leave her pussy, and she tried, and failed, to stop herself from grimacing. She squirmed like usual as she snapped her legs closed, doing everything in her might to avoid looking at him.

With her cheeks and ears so hot she feared her head would combust, she croaked, "Do we have to do it this way every time?"

Turning physical, she reached for her trousers and donned them quickly, ignoring how the seams on the inner thighs were so thin from chafing that they were threatening to unravel. She'd lost many pants from split seams and frayed material from her strong thighs rubbing.

As she continued dressing, her eyes followed the retreating dark tendril, and she cringed at her own wetness on it before it dispersed in a puff of mist.

"How else should we do it?" Weldir asked plainly, as if what she insinuated wasn't obvious.

It doesn't seem like he cares for desire. He'd never attempted it with her.

In the beginning, Lindi had actually been relieved about that. She hadn't wanted to be close to someone she felt no affection for, and who obviously didn't truly care for her in return.

But, as their many years together passed, her body was dying on the inside. It craved touch, to the point that even a subtle feeling of someone's knuckles brushing against the back of her hand felt naughty. She wanted someone, anyone, to hold her in an embrace, to be teased with light caresses or even hard kisses.

She couldn't believe he was making her spell this out to him!

"You know," she grumbled, her face somehow growing hotter as she rubbed her upper arm awkwardly. "Sex? Your tendril feels weird, like a worm."

So often the Anzúli said she came across as candid and assertive, yet her gaze fell to his partially visible face with shyness. It allowed her to see the way his brows furrowed, as if what she asked was absurd.

"A worm?" A new tendril appeared, just so he could wiggle the tip of it... much like one of those little creatures.

Lindi shuddered at the mental image, especially as it'd been inside her not even moments before.

"I thought doing it this way would be best, which is why I have never attempted another way," Weldir stated. His black eyes, completely lacking the white sclera, peered into her very being. They were shiny in comparison to the matte appearance of his chalky, misty body.

Lindi tilted her head. "Why do you think that?"

Like usual, Weldir barely moved, his expression light and fleeting, as if it was forced. He always floated in his emptiness, his body lean and long, stretched and motionless other than his coalescing form.

It made reading him difficult. Like now, when additional body movements may have helped her decipher how he felt.

Had he ever thought about having sex with her, or was it just Lindi who wanted something a little more? Then again, she was so touch-starved she may have turned to a cactus for pleasure if it would offer it.

"I didn't think you would like being close with me. I assumed you didn't want that."

"Oh," she rasped, lifting her hands so she could interlock her fingers to play and fidget with them coyly. She lowered her gaze to look at him through her lashes while hiding her face. "Does that mean you want to?"

She could almost feel her heart coming up her throat in nervousness. They were married, and this should be normal, yet it was anything but normal between them.

Lindi no longer knew what normal felt like.

"It's never truly crossed my mind," he answered dully. "Whichever way this act results in what I want is all I care about."

In the back of her mind, Lindi played out a scene. One in which she grabbed an invisible dagger and shunted it into her heart and played dead because... his words were so detached and callous he may as well have felled her. She even heard her imagined cry of pain as the blade dug deep.

Instead, she bolstered herself with courage, and a touch of her outrage. How dare he deny her pleasure under his lack of care? A woman had needs, and so should a man! Even if he was a freaky shadow being.

She lifted her hands in annoyance, almost like a shrug, but also like she could reach out and wring his non-existent neck. "Don't you want pleasure? Human men seek it constantly, even going to places to find it."

Even doing it themselves, her mind grumbled.

After inserting herself into different societies, Lindi was learning that the belief system she'd grown up in wasn't a shared one. Men still preferred pretty virgin maidens, but not all societies made it a requirement, and not all shared that same sentiment. She'd blushed at her first brothel, and the first set of tits she'd seen paraded in public with no one batting an eye like it was strange.

A lot of what she learned was that customs could be contextual, and they differed between people and backgrounds.

Then again, she may have also been sheltered by her parents and their isolated farming lifestyle.

Learning all this made her mind fill with different fantasies, and her body thrum with need. Over time, it was worsening. She'd been alive for almost seventy years... and her lust was building. Her need for affection was stifling, and if she had to be subjugated to another wormy tendril, she'd claw at the ether and murder his undying ass somehow.

But he's a man, of sorts. Hopefully he'll...

"Coitus seems like a pointless activity, since I'd find no pleasure in it. This way is faster."

Lindi promptly shut her fallen jaw, and her features tightened in dismay. She fisted the bottom of her blue tunic, unsure if she wanted to weep or scream at him. Instead, frustration bubbled in her chest and Lindi didn't know how she wanted to release it.

She bit the sides of her tongue as she gritted her teeth and lowered her eyes to look at anything but him. She found his toes and mentally cursed him to stub the pinkie ones at every chance the universe permitted it.

Her anxious heart changed and swirled with rage instead. Undenied, lusty, needy rage.

"Have I upset you?" he asked, as if he was uncertain. "Is this something you want?"

"Obviously, if I'm bringing it up," she muttered as low as possible, her face twisting up further. She tried to smile to show it was fine, but she knew it was more like a horrible cringe as it pulled tightly across her face. "But don't mind it. Forget I asked."

"Lindiwe," he warned, just as she reached out to grab one of her boots.

"I'm rather embarrassed now," she admitted, shoving her foot into it before grasping the other. "And I'd like to leave."

Weldir waved his hand towards her raven cloak floating beside him – intangible to her currently in her physical form – as he secured it with a tendril to it to keep it solid for him.

"I have yet to fix this. I thought we agreed that you would stay here until I have completed that task."

"I will go without it for now," she stated, while turning her head away from him defiantly. "If you place me near Nathair's home, I will spend time with him."

"We can speak on this, if you'd prefer."

Lindi threw her hand out. "I would sincerely rather not. If it's not something you want, then I see no reason to convince you otherwise."

She'd also never beg for it.

I wish I didn't ask, she thought, craving nothing more than to crawl into a hole and die of mortification. *Gosh. I'm so embarrassed.*

She doubted he understood how much courage she'd gathered, and she hadn't expected to be rejected so coldly or outrightly. But she wanted something more from him, even if it wasn't true affection.

Just something to feel like she wasn't as alone as she sometimes felt. Something to look back on with fondness, and to remind her body that it could be loved physically, even if emotionally it felt impossible. She couldn't – nor wouldn't – offer it to anyone else, even if he hadn't made that a requirement.

She was his wife faithfully, even if it was a distant role in all ways.

Mum and dad said I would be a spinster if I continued on my lack-of-marriage path. She felt like one, except she somehow produced children, like by a sexless miracle.

Weldir was barely her friend. At most, he felt like a lifelong acquaintance she couldn't shake from her tail.

In reality, she wasn't all that upset with Weldir.

She was just disappointed, and that emotion could be rather crushing to one's spirit. She was angry at the situation, that was all. He didn't even seem to truly understand how or why she was hurt, and it was just another case of Weldir being Weldir.

A god who lacked comprehension of what it was like to not only be a human, but someone with needs, wants, and longing.

But the long silences and absences were more painful than she was ever willing to admit, especially as she had no idea how to strum up a conversation. Worse still, on the odd occasion that she tried, he wasn't always there. Such things would warp the mind of most humans, so how she'd managed to retain a semblance – let alone an abundance – of sanity was beyond her.

"I don't feel anything, Lindiwe."

She closed her eyes, wishing for the conversation to end. "Yes. I gathered that," she snapped out a little harsher than she intended. "You're very detached. You always have been."

She hadn't expected him to feel affection or a sickening ache to be near her, but she'd been hoping they could at least find pleasure together. Their bond was apparently forever, so why not find enjoyment in it somewhere?

Still, Weldir admitting that he didn't feel anything was just another blow her psyche couldn't take right then. Maybe somewhere in her mind, she wanted to feel adored emotionally, but she'd been willing to settle for at least physically. She didn't like that he was so open about how little she meant to him, considering all she'd done for him as his wife and *servant*.

She turned from him when she felt the inevitable well of tears forming and made sure he couldn't see it when she palmed her cheeks to keep them from falling.

"I'm hoping Orson will be there," Lindi continued while forcing an uplifted tone in her voice, trying to distract from the conversation and hoping he would just allow it. "I haven't seen him and Nathair since you made me leave Austrális last."

Weldir's following sigh wrapped around her entire body, seemingly exhausted with her and her human emotions. "As you wish, Lindiwe."

By her next blink, she was transported to his mist within the Veil, and a cascading waterfall in the daylight thundered just before her. The rainbow that greeted her was too joyful and bright for the despondent pain that clung to her lungs.

With her hands bundled into fists, she looked down into the Veil, and Nathair's lake.

Why do I feel like I keep being punished for giving him my soul?

TWENTY-SIX

A time unknown, but a time of discontent

Weldir peered into the viewing disc before him with his legs bent and crossed beneath his floating form. Four other discs surrounded him, each one showing someone in motion.

The two behind him were of Nathair and Orson, their discs overlapping as they were in direct proximity to each other. The one to his right showed Odie, the otter-skulled *Duskwalker*, while the other showed Dymphna with their skull of a water deer.

They were all safe, either resting or in the middle of battling with Demons and collecting the souls that were unwittingly clinging to them. He felt no need to watch them as intently as he did with the one that held Lindiwe and their twin offspring.

With a blanket covering her from head to toe, she lay on her side. The bed beneath her looked lumpy and uncomfortable, the blanket fibrous and itchy, and the pillow hard. She often complained of these things out loud, yet not once had Lindiwe moved from her spot.

Winter screeched outside the abandoned cottage she'd taken for herself. White snow fell upon thick blankets of snowpack, with not a single sprout of green flora visible. The building was small, some peasant or commoner's house made of wood and brick, with mansard slate tiles.

She'd evicted the occupying Demons when her stomach was overly swollen and much larger than usual.

Weldir had found her waddle rather cute, despite how she grumbled about the aches and pains in her bowed back and tired knees. Her ankles never swelled, but she complained about the brain fog, the back pain that never relented, and the way one of their offspring seemed to rest on top of her cervix and knock lightning through her groin.

He'd been rather concerned when she'd spent the beginning of her pregnancy constantly expelling darkness from her stomach, only to eat like her life depended on it. Which then caused more to come up, this time with her partially digested food. This symptom, although reoccurring, usually only lasted a few days at most.

Weldir wondered if the fact that she had carried two had made all her symptoms far worse than usual. She wasn't usually so unwell, fatigued, or absent-minded. She even struggled to cast magic, and being in her raven form was near impossible to fly in. She'd been unsteady in all ways.

She'd nearly stumbled her way to this cottage, but she did hunt and gather food when she made it her temporary home. That had ceased from the moment she'd given birth, once more falling back to not eating since her being a Phantom meant she didn't need to unless growing life.

Since then, she had not left.

Weldir wasn't usually so concerned for her wellbeing. She had a rather determined, spritely spark to her personality. She'd proven, time and time again, that she was tenacious and resilient. She could be teasing when she was in the company of others, and she could be playful with their offspring.

So, to see his mate become lacklustre towards life had drawn his ever-watchful gaze.

She rarely left the bed, preferring to lie there in a half dream-like state while it was clear her mind was elsewhere. Lindiwe barely interacted with their offspring, letting them roam around the cottage freely or all over her. She cuddled them, which helped to settle her shivers from the cold outside, but she didn't cling to them when they desired to scamper around or play with each other.

Despite how much she rested and slept, the dark impressions under her eyes never faded and her gaze just appeared lost.

Seeing the complete flip in her personality, Weldir had attempted to console her. Lindiwe, for the most part, was unresponsive.

When he asked about their offspring and their potential to escape, she reminded him of the barrier she had permanently placed around the cottage. When he asked her why she looked so solemn, she'd mumbled something about how many women faced a depression after their pregnancy.

He didn't know if she was being truthful, or if that was just an excuse to avoid speaking of the last conversation they'd had in his realm, the one during which she'd asked to leave abruptly. She refused to speak of it, even after Weldir had done some reflection on it.

Although he didn't feel desire, he realised that many humans required affirmations within their relationships. Physical, verbal, and perhaps even spiritual. He truly never thought she'd deign to be intimate with him due to her rigidness around him, but her simple request showed she was actually quite the emotional creature. And, as always, lionhearted when she set her mind and heart to something, even if she was shaken and unsure.

He appreciated that she'd asked, and thus, he allowed his regret to fester and eat at him over how he handled the request.

Weldir wanted to find a solution.

Although true that he didn't feel anything, he did have emotions, perhaps not as strong as humans, but they did exist. Her throwing at him that he was detached was another truth, but one he could work to change.

Before Lindiwe, I'd only ever been alone.

The only conversation he'd ever had was the one during which he'd been given his tasks, and then he was moved to Earth. She was his first and only companion, and he was learning much from her and the memories of humans he'd been diving into.

He could ask for some grace regarding what he lacked, but he thought it may be an insult at this point. Many years had passed for her, and they were no closer than when their bond was first formed. He'd been so consumed by building Tenebris, gaining power, and creating his servants, that he'd not stopped to truly see how Lindiwe had fared.

Then again, what had really brought on his deeper reflections was how she'd responded the last time he'd tried talking to her. The memory of it played out in his thoughts, and his mist vibrated in what could only be an outright, full-body cringe.

"You are always welcome to call for me, Lindiwe," he'd finally told her. "I am here for you to lean on, should you want someone to talk to." He, himself, wanted someone to lean on, to converse with... for someone to fill the quiet he'd come to cherish with the music of their voice.

For *her* voice to fill his void, even with the distance between their two realms.

"What's the point?" she'd muttered with her gaze lowering, lacking any flare of anger or snark. "There is little warmth in your words and all you can offer is sentiments. I desire none of those things."

Weldir was struck by how austere her words and deep tone had been. Rendered speechless, he'd completely lost his voice since then, no matter how deep into winter the world crawled.

He'd realised then that his words within his realm had caused a burn that was even present on her soul. The charcoal of it had spread, covering her entire torso and face now.

The silence between them was stilted. He thought he'd enjoy the peace of it after so long of living in the sound of disarray from screaming souls, but between them, it felt stuffy. Were matehoods usually this strained between others, even those that had a transactional occupation to them?

Perhaps I was not designed for matehood. He'd hurt his own female unintentionally and without truly understanding how.

He'd acted and spoken in ways he thought best, and it constantly caused strife between them.

Weldir blamed it on his godhood, and that he didn't have a single experience they shared. There was no common ground, no familiar scenarios in which they had lived. There always had been, and likely always would be, an imbalance between them, and that would never change with his form this way.

He was intangible in all ways that a mortal creature, one which came from another world to him, was not. His ideologies often didn't align with hers, his opinions differed in ways she found unsettling, and his mindset was firm with the teachings of his mother and fathers.

Worse still, Weldir was deeply aware she thought of these as failings in him.

Lindiwe was attempting to unravel a being who had been alive for over fifteen hundred human years, and she was a being he could not relate to. The space between them was vast, not because his realm was not part of hers, but because who and what they were would never be one. They would always be misaligned.

All they shared was their bond; it was spiritual but lacked anything else.

So how to change this?

Is it possible to give her what she seeks? Surely he could do this... be intimate with her.

Oddly enough, Weldir found it daunting.

He could barely hold onto the physical parts of his form she *could* touch. He was mere ribbons to her, even though he could see and feel all parts of himself. He'd seen humans conjoined in coitus. There was much grasping and holding, which they could not do. Not unless he finally reached true strength, something he'd never achieved and had been reaching for with each soul he collected.

But could he at least offer the pleasure and tenderness she sought in some semblance? *How?*

It took much focus just to control a single tendril, and for even a small length of time. How was Weldir supposed to give her something more substantial to cling to, and how was he meant to claim her without dispersing into mist from within her?

These were questions that plagued him.

What you have asked of me feels near impossible.

But Weldir was set on trying, for her sake.

Because, even if she didn't believe it, Weldir did care for this female rather deeply. She was the mother of his offspring, and his hands and feet in a world he could not be in.

He found her beautiful. Even though it hadn't changed in the many years, his appreciation of her continued to evolve and deepen. Her personality was gallant and charming. Her care for others – their offspring and other humans alike – inspired him, and it made him inclined to let her have her way, even if it meant he was drained of power and suffered for it.

Her soul was bound to him, and he knew he must nurture whom it belonged to.

I must do better.

But with Lindiwe in this state, unreceptive and reclusive, it was impossible.

She did not want his words, and that was all he currently had to offer. Until their twin offspring were grown, there was little he could do.

And so, he would bear witness, joining in with her suffering, even if she never knew he was there for her should she choose to reach out.

October 2ⁿᵈ, 1733

Readjusting her newly repaired cloak of black raven feathers, Lindi stepped out from underneath the shade of a tree and into bright sunshine. Spring had fully bloomed in this part of the world, melting away the snow and allowing small yellow weed flowers to sway in the light wind.

It always surprises me that the northern and southern hemispheres differ as to when their seasons happen. She'd just left early autumn in Eyropea, whereas here, in Austrális, the spring was cool and inviting. *If I wanted to, I could avoid harsh winters forever.*

Then again, she found the cold desolation of white snow could feel rather tender-hearted. The world could be rather cruel in the most heavenly ways.

She hummed in thought as moss cushioned her steps when she sprung over a small river, making her way to two individuals. One lay on the wet grass, letting his black scales soak up the heat as the sunlight gave them a rainbow shimmer. The other lay nearby in a small huddle – not close enough to hurt his companion with his quill spines, but his thin tail and tuft swayed against him.

The moment her boot crunched against the crisp grass, they both reared their heads out from their individual cuddles to inspect who came near.

Orson, with his orbs flaring a deeper red, let out a growl. His quills jutted up from his back and limbs as he quickly got to all four paws. He arched, going low to ward her back. Nathair, on the other hand, tilted his head with his orange orbs shifting to dark yellow.

Then he held his scaled hand out in front of an aggressive Orson to halt him. Nathair was ignored as Orson snapped his fangs at his fingers, silently warning him not to intervene. Orson tossed his head, presenting his bull horns, and stamped a forepaw in her direction before gouging at the ground as he swiped back with his claws.

Lindi paused as a stinging heartache wrapped itself around her chest. *Is he going to charge me?*

After the last few terrible months, Lindi just wanted to be greeted warmly by her children for once. Taking care of a set of twins, and a horrible depression at the same time, had taken its mental toll on her.

She'd managed to shake the worst of it once the winter snow passed, finally feeling less listless after months of immobility. Guilt constantly nipped at the back of her conscience at how she'd essentially ignored her little blobby children as they ventured around the cottage and her. Thankfully, they didn't seem to care at all, happy to explore the confines, play with each other, and snuggle up to her freely.

Even though she embraced them whenever they desired, it didn't make the nagging doubt in the corner of her heart go away. She... felt like a bad mother, even though she couldn't help it at the time.

Once spring had come and melted the world, Lindi had then felt renewed and set off to help them find their skulls and horns. She'd spent enough time with them that she didn't delay this task, although it took nearly nine months from when she gave birth to them. She wanted them to be utterly perfect in her choices, but they were also a large handful together.

She just didn't have the skills to keep them calm and with her once they gained their skulls. Even without their horns yet, they'd just been too much.

She still didn't know if it was okay that she let them go off on their own, but they'd gained their horns at different times. She constantly wondered if she should have waited in case they were bonded, like Nathair and Orson seemed to be in their own way.

But, like before, they didn't seem to care.

The moment one was gone, the other seemed to forget their very existence. Guilt nipped at her harder for it, yet in some ways, it was a good thing. It allowed her to drop them off in two different locations, spreading her children across the continent of Eyropea. Hopefully that meant Weldir wouldn't need her to carry another child for that area – at least for some time.

Afterwards, she'd felt this loneliness twisting in her stomach. And, with the fact that she wanted little to do with Weldir, someone who offered nothing, she wanted affection. She longed to feel wanted, and not have the space next to her feel so empty.

She didn't find it with Odie, who immediately tried to attack her. At least they'd ventured north and away from Londinium. She didn't know when her mindset about human death had changed, but she couldn't wait to find out what gender they'd end up being. She wanted to see their personality flourish.

She felt that way with Dymphna as well, who was a little stronger and a little less chaotic in the mind.

Lindi wanted her children to grow and evolve. She wanted them to become like Nathair, who bashed the bottom of his fist against the top of Orson's head to stop him.

Orson spun to Nathair and roared in his direction.

"Stop," Nathair demanded, his orbs flaring red.

Orson snapped his fangs at him in response, shaking his head from side to side before nudging his nose in Lindi's direction.

"No... st...op," Orson croaked, obviously not confident with speaking. Honestly, it was hard to decipher, like his mind and throat were full of gravel and shards of rock. *"Danger."*

Lindi couldn't help the proud smile that parted her lips. "You've been teaching him how to speak!" Lindi exclaimed, her heart racing with joy.

Every opportunity she had, Lindi had been teaching Nathair how to talk. He wasn't amazing, but he could string together enough to make basic sense. She suffered little regret that it was likely due to how many humans he'd consumed that he had the ability to speak.

She was proud that Nathair was teaching Orson, just as she'd always hoped.

Maybe I can figure out a way to get him to travel to other parts of the world to teach the others. Her chest blossomed with warmth when he snapped his serpent jaw at Orson, who backed down with a disgruntled snarl. *Look at them snapping at each other like real siblings.*

Nathair then twisted towards Lindi, and skulked low on his hands and slithering tail to approach. He was wary, but hopefully somewhere in that disjointed mind, he knew she was safe. That she cared for him, even if he never understood the depth of just how much.

Her bones tingled with the urge to reach her hands up and greet his skull with a loving, cupping hold, but she snuffed it. Every time she'd attempted to do that in the past, he'd reacted very negatively. If she kept her hands down and in plain sight while moving very slowly, especially at a small distance, she was permitted to stay nearby.

It wasn't enough to quell the depth of her loneliness, but it was enough to make it ignorable for a short while.

"Hello," Nathair grated, his voice a tremulous ripple, deep and gruff, and almost close to being indistinguishable to someone who wasn't used to the beastly tone.

But Lindi was able to decipher him clearly, and she looked up to his towering height with a smile. Orson frantically paced behind him on all fours with agitated stomps, constantly flaring red in her direction as his bull tail whipped to the side. Her cheer almost fell, and she wished he was more amicable and approachable, but unlike Nathair, he was always unable to be soothed.

He always seemed to be... angry and unapproachable.

"Hello, Nathair. Have you been a good boy?"

Nathair tilted his serpent skull, and his dark-yellow orbs deepened. "Nath... there?"

Her lips twitched as they unfurled from their smile, and her brows drew together. "You forgot your name again?"

"No," he grumbled, tossing his head around as his orbs flared a reddish pink. "No forget name *again.*"

She gave a mild laugh and placed her hands behind her back.

"You're turning out to be a big liar, Nathair." She repeated his name, hoping one day he would remember it. She'd keep doing so until then. She pointed her chin towards the one skulking agitatedly behind him. "Have you been nice to Orson?"

Nathair snorted through his nose holes before a big huff came from them, close enough to billow hot air over her. He didn't answer, instead clacking his jaw together. It was his way of saying he didn't understand what she'd said.

Then he leaned forward to sniff around her curls, and cool bone brushed against her cheekbone. Her stomach tightened with tension, wary of his nearness and how quickly he could violently strike, but her chest aching with the unintentional affection was more prevalent.

Every part of her very being wanted to nuzzle into his snout.

"Smell different," Nathair muttered. Then he reached out to lift a few feathers from her cloak with careful claws. "Different."

"Yes. I smell different. I'm using a scent-cloaking spell to hide my scent." When he pulled back to inspect her as she spoke, she played with her cloak. "Feathers. These are black feathers, from a raven."

"Raven?" He tilted his head, only to lift his arms up so he could lightly flap his hands to the side. "Like bird?"

"Yes!" she exclaimed a little too excitedly, causing him to spook and recoil backwards.

Nathair's orbs flashed white momentarily, and he settled low on his palms, dipping his chest down so that it almost brushed the grass. His long tail shimmered in the sun as it looped and made figure eights behind him with wariness.

Orson lunged forward and skidded to a halt in front of Nathair defensively with a snarl. Drool dripped from his fangs when he parted them, warding her back with a stomp of his forepaws. His spines were flared to their highest points, while his tail was lifted and swatted from side to side with agitation.

Her brows furrowed as hurt crinkled her features.

Lindi stepped back, giving them much-needed space.

They're so animalistic at times, Lindi bemoaned. *Orson, in particular, is distrustful of everything.* It was like he was a skittish dog that had been trapped on a lead attached to a spike in the ground, just waiting for the cord to snap so he could attack with a ferociousness.

"Is fine," Nathair claimed, pulling on Orson's shoulder where there were no spines.

"Stay back," Orson barked, his voice much deeper and more beastly than Nathair's. *"Protect."*

"I don't understand why you aren't welcoming of me, Orson," Lindi rasped, shaking her head. "Why don't you remember me at all?"

"Smell bad," Orson retorted. *"I no know scent."*

I wonder if it's the scent-cloaking spell. It was apparently sweet to the nose. It just made it painfully obvious that Nathair remembered at least her face, and Orson didn't. *But why? They were born not many years apart.*

Is it because many humans began to hide behind walls by then? Orson may not have eaten as many as Nathair.

The humans of Austrális, in the grand scheme of things, were actually relatively lucky. Although she hadn't known of them because she'd pulled from society by that point, the Anzúli hadn't needed to convince people of the arrival of Demons. They already knew about them.

The Anzúli had merely confirmed their existence.

The people living in Austrális had already begun to build walls and fortify their cities. Coupled with the fact that Demons had struggled to cross the desert except on moonless nights – the connecting forests not grown yet – they hadn't been overrun when the flux of them did arrive.

Not many lived within the centre where the Veil had formed; most settlements were nearer to the mountains and meadows bordering the cooler and more bountiful coastlines. When people fled, they didn't have to travel far.

It was the natives of the country, the farmers, and those who chose to live in isolation that had needed to pack up their lives and travel to the closest large city, village, or town. And because they'd been given ample time to build their defences, everyone had been welcomed, as there was plenty of space. Most mayors had rightly assumed there would be many seeking refuge, and they accepted everyone.

No matter who they were, where they came from, their

beliefs, or if their lives had been vastly different beforehand.

Many had to learn how to adjust, especially those who didn't understand each other's languages. It'd been a stressful time for all, but it ensured that, even though the number of humans living in Austrális had been much fewer than what she knew of the rest of the world, they'd managed to mostly retain their numbers.

There were already reports of Duskwalkers being sighted in Austrális, but neither Nathair nor Orson travelled far to the coastlines, preferring to stick close to the Veil. It was likely that neither knew of the existence of towns or that humans congregated together. Otherwise, she doubted the town, no matter how tall its walls, would have survived.

There were people who still chose to live on their own – far too many, in fact. Somehow, even after years, they continued to survive with the help of the Anzúli offering protection charms and herbs. People were hidden well under these magical tools.

These things meant that Orson would struggle to reach Nathair's humanity, despite them only being a decade or so apart. It was disheartening, and even though she knew it was wrong to think this, she was disappointed for him.

I want to spend time with my children.

Why did she have to be treated like an outcast by them when she was the one who brought them into the world? Why must they be so beastly? Why did Orson have to get in the way of her being able to reach out to Nathair – the only one who welcomed her?

Her eyes bowed with sadness when she could tell that Orson was refusing to settle, no matter how much Nathair tried. And when he turned his long body towards Orson with a soothing head pat – not afraid of his snapping fangs – and retreated for both their sakes, Lindi knew there was no point in staying.

She'd return later, when either Orson ventured off on his own like he occasionally did, or when he had gained more humanity.

Nathair kept his skull on her, watching as she backed into the shade of the closest tree, and she held his stare. Then she pulled her hood of feathers over her head and willed the shift to take her.

His orbs morphed from orange to dark yellow at her raven form, and even Orson halted his growl with a confused head tilt.

Lindi unfurled her wings and swiped them down, taking off into the sky and away from them. She was thankful that, like her Phantom form, she was unable to produce tears when in this form.

I wish this didn't have to hurt so much.

That she didn't have to constantly hurt inside.

Sometimes I wish I could just keep them all as babies. Then maybe Lindi would forever know love and be needed in a tender way.

TWENTY-SEVEN

January 4th, 1738

Cupping her hands, Lindi dived them into the cascade of a frothing waterfall. Finding the water more bearable than she first anticipated, deliciously cooling with the oppressive summer heat, she braved ducking her entire naked body into its fall. Closing her eyes, she tipped her head back and let it wash her face and down her skin in harsh rivulets. The pressure was intense, but she found it all the more cleansing.

Even though this waterfall actually started above the surface and fell into the Veil, linking to a swamp just a little ways west, she wasn't afraid. She had no reason to be.

Lindi was so quick with her Phantom abilities that she hadn't been killed by a Demon in decades. Her borrowed magic was also a tool she wielded with practised skill, and she knew what to listen out for. Most Demons were loud, snorting and snarling long before they were even in view.

Even over the roar of the water, she'd hear them, be dressed and then gone before they could reach the top of these steep rocks.

I'm glad I found this place, she thought, taking in the lukewarmth as she rubbed down her arms.

The spray coming off the cascade pushed away Weldir's thickening black mist, allowing her to feel as though she wasn't directly under his gaze. For now, she didn't think he was watching her through one of his viewing discs, since he'd been quiet for quite some time.

It was a private moment she was allowing herself on the border of the Veil, and within it.

Weldir's mist, although thin and mostly transparent except to her keen and knowing eye, was growing. It didn't encompass the entire Veil, but at least a quarter of it from the edges inwards.

His silence often made her want to call out to him to check if he was asleep or not, but she never did. She worried that if she did so, she'd somehow stir him awake and then she'd be forced to have a polite conversation she wanted no part of.

She'd barely spoken to him since before the separable twins were conceived. She probably shouldn't have taken what he said and how he treated her to heart, but her grudge wouldn't waver, no matter how she tried.

His rejection had been so instant that her ego had taken a massive hit, and she felt like she was undeserving of any attention. That she wasn't pretty, or worth anything more than what they were now.

A servant and her master. A god and the human he took advantage of. A husband that saw her as nothing but a person who did not deserve even the lightest, brief caress.

That kind of insecurity could really bruise a person.

Lindi never thought she was capable of feeling that way. She wasn't utterly beguiling, but she thought she was beautiful enough. Her parents made her feel that way, as did the boys in her village when they tried to court her.

The word ugly or unbecoming had never been uttered in her direction, but his actions allowed those pestering doubts to fester. They ate at her and left a wound within her chest that she'd been struggling to fill.

It was getting easier every day, resigning herself to this fate, but it still kind of... well, it kind of fucking sucked. Although his tendril had been inside her numerous times, she was still practically a virgin after seventy-six years.

What a depressing thought, and one she'd been trying to ignore for the better part of six years. She gave birth to their children, suffered horrible post-partum depression, and then asked for a small reprieve from this duty to collect her thoughts.

In this separation of time, the lack of child rearing made it easier to ignore this pain. It made it easier to forget.

She didn't want to speak to him, and she hadn't called out to him once. She didn't want his support, just his magic. He'd painted a clear line in the sand, and she would adhere to it. There was no point in kindling a friendship when it offered nothing and often left her dismayed.

She was better without him.

I don't need anyone, she thought, washing her curls by following her usual routine. She reached down to the hair products she'd brought next to the falls so she could apply conditioner to her hair, gently combing through the strands from the ends to the root. *I don't even need people.*

Later, when her hair was dry, she'd focus on using a special oil to make her curls glossy and springy, finger-styling them for definition. Sometimes she would style them into a single thick braid, as she often liked to do. Even though it was in frequent disarray due to her adventures through the wilds, Lindi liked to take care of her hair.

She had ample time to tend to her physical needs and took comfort where she could.

There was a hot spring not far from where Lindi was – at least not far by flight. It was probably a few days' walk south, though.

Sunnet Hill's Headsprings was a small mountain village connected to rocky heat pools. The humans who still lived there, refusing to leave their homes, claimed the water had healing properties.

Lindi had visited a few times just for the comfort of a warm bath, but she hadn't felt much different after a 'therapeutic' soak. However, her muscles did relax, which helped to make her tired and weary bones ache less. Her mind also found a way to untwist itself, at least for a little while. Perhaps that's what they meant by healing; it was more to one's psyche than their body.

But, as the years passed, and Lindi found herself withdrawing more and more from who she was and humankind, she'd rather bathe in this barely warm waterfall in the Veil.

It felt... simpler. Better.

No one could ask her questions she couldn't answer. She didn't have to politely ask the name of a person she'd surely forget, just as she'd forgotten the thousands of others. There was no such thing as a friendship for her, not when her presence was fleeting, and her life a secret.

She didn't want to play pretend. Lindi was tired of doing so.

Checking her surroundings now that she was clean, she sat down on a rough, jagged boulder right next to the cascade, with droplets continuing to spray her legs and feet. She took the moment of tranquillity while she could, peering into the lake below to watch its ripples and how it frothed. Shaded by the cliff wall, moss clung to the rocks and looked darker in the lack of light.

The air was cool here, despite it being summer.

If she didn't know better, she could have mistaken this for a picturesque rainforest brimming with quaint life. There was no white condensation that was present throughout the Veil, nor was there Weldir's darkness. Not a Demon had come along to make a peep or peek at her naked body, and it looked peaceful. Beautiful, even. Definitely serene.

I hate admitting this, but the Veil has its charm.

It was quiet, and only eery when she considered the danger that lurked – danger that she didn't *truly* have to be frightened of. The forest was now lush and full, barely any sunlight able to touch the ground except for near the centre. There were plenty of flowers, and even some trees bore fruit.

If only the Demons didn't exist, she thought, moving her gaze away from the pleasant scene so she could lean down to her feet.

She lifted one after the other, cleaning them thoroughly. She cringed at the state of them, finding them dry and calloused. *At least the soles are thickening.* After so long of not wearing boots, she was finally adjusting to being barefooted.

Shifting to her raven form usually allowed her clothing to be hidden, but her boots remained. It was uncomfortable to wear them as a raven, and it was difficult to walk or stand in them with her bird feet and talons inside them. It was impossible to perch.

After years of obtaining new boots, only for them to be worn to the point of holes, Lindi had finally given up on them. She had a pair of flats tucked away in her satchel for if she ever needed them, light and not taking up a lot of space. She'd been training her feet since then to handle walking over sharp sticks and rocks, and, unfortunately, to be dirty.

She washed them every opportunity found, even if it was an inch-deep stream. *I wish there was something else I could wear, though. Oh well.*

Just after she finished cleaning them and was about to lean back, a strange awareness tickled the back of her neck. All the hairs on her body raised, like she was being watched, just as her ears picked up on the softest breath.

Surely, it's just Weldir.

"Hello," a masculine voice greeted from behind.

Lindi screamed, covered her naked breasts, and had to stop herself from bounding over the edge of the fall. She turned to look behind her as she got to her feet. A man's face was less than a foot from her own before she put space between them, but he creepily followed her.

How did someone get behind me?! She'd been watching! Okay, maybe not when she'd been cleaning her feet, and a little before that, but she should, at the very least, have heard them!

Red eyes, sharp and observant, narrowed as he halted and watched her move away. He straightened, raising himself to his full height, one pointed ear flicking through the few inches of white hair around his head. It almost brushed against one of his black, segmented horns that ran over the top of his head.

Noting exactly who it was, she immediately turned incorporeal. She made sure her breasts and the apex of her thighs were covered with two arms as she lowered her lids into a glare.

"Yes, I remember you can do that," Jabeziryth commented with a grin curling his lips, exposing his shark-like fangs. Humour lifted into his eyes, making the youth in his face even more present. "Did I spook you?"

His accent was layered and thick, reminding her of the pale man she'd met who came from the north of Eyropea – Pryssia, she believed it was called. When Jabeziryth had learned English, she'd never know, but he appeared to speak it confidently. It'd been many years since he'd first spoken to her.

He looked almost the same, except for a few minor changes. *He looks my age.* Maybe even a little older than her frozen two and twenty. His white hair was a touch longer, a light wind swaying the few inches around his ears.

He lacked the black cloak from last time, but his attire was similar. A cream long-sleeved tunic was tucked into his brown breeches that looked to be fitted to his long legs. He was still lean, but he did appear to have slightly more muscle than what she remembered.

If it wasn't for his pointed ears, red eyes, and horns, he almost looked human. Although his height was alarming, as he now stood well over a foot above her.

Wanting to keep her distance, Lindi chose to back up further until a bundle behind him drew her attention.

Shit! My clothing. She was nude, and she doubted she'd be able to grab them before he could stop her. Not that she knew why he'd try to.

Regardless, she'd rather not be physical in his presence after everything Weldir had told her of him. She knew about Jabeziryth, why he'd come here, the portal he'd opened, and how he'd brought the first Demons to Earth. He wasn't to be trusted. She also knew of the death and chaos he'd instigated on his way out of the Elven city of Lezekos.

To be bare in front of him, and without her animal changing cloak... Lindi wanted to groan.

"I mean you no harm."

"Says the Demon," she finally said, staying where she floated partially inside the waterfall.

"Yes, I remember you used that term last time." His head cocked to the side as he eyed down her body before drawing back up. "I wonder if you know you inadvertently named us all that very day."

Her arms tightened around her body, wishing her clothing would magically wrap around her. Her knees turned inwards, and she hoped it wasn't obvious. It alarmed her that she was naked in front of a man, no matter *what* he was.

"What do you mean?"

When he must have noticed where her gaze had drifted to, he looked behind him. He cocked a brow at her clothing and bag and then turned back to her. Her features dropped when he took a few steps towards them instead.

"I looked up what that word meant when I learned your language. I found it to be rather fitting, like what the Elysians call us. Daekura means 'shadow beasts,' but your version – 'something insidious and harmful; an evil spirit or devil' – sounds more like what we can be when we are not evolved. Cruel and evil. Something from the very pits of hell." He lifted a single arm to shrug with it before kneeling next to her things. "Then again, I'd rather not be titled anything by the Elysians."

"You'd rather be called something so offensive?" she couldn't help asking, watching him slowly reach down.

His shoulders lifted. "Only if we think it's offensive, which we do not."

To her horror, he opened up her satchel, and she shunted her ethereal form towards him. She didn't dare reach forward and uncover herself. "Hey! Don't touch my things!"

"You know, you can garner a great deal of information about someone by the artefacts they have on their person."

"I said stop!" she whined, refusing to move her arms and expose her body or turn physical to pull on him.

He reached into her bag and pulled out a pair of black slipper flats. He placed them on the ground since they were the bulkiest items in her bag and then continued his rude delve. He inspected a glass perfume bottle, opening it to smell the sweet osmanthus flowers before putting it back to open her pouches of seeds. Next he inspected her glass vial of precious hair oil, sniffing its contents before giving a hum of approval. Then he carelessly placed it back down, and it rolled so close to the edge of the rock that her heart would have clenched if she wasn't incorporeal.

"No food or water?" he commented, raising a brow in her direction. "Do you have no need to eat? Your ghostly appearance makes you look dead. You don't appear to have aged at all, either."

"I'm a Phantom," she admitted, hoping that would make him stop. She was the only one she knew of, and she doubted he'd know what it meant.

It didn't halt his progress, and he dug down further. He pulled out a special ceramic vial that usually held the souls she collected. Worried he'd break it, she kept just enough distance to stay out of his immediate reach and turned physical. Then, while covering herself with her arms, she put up a solid, flat barrier between them, and willed tentacle limbs to shoot out from the ground.

They coiled themselves around his arms and throat, and she pulled him back. He fell off the side of the rocky ledge with a yell, and Lindi dived forward. Panicking and fretting, her hands shook as she quickly shoved her undergarments on, then her clothing.

She just managed to poke her arms through the sleeves of her tunic before he crawled his way to the top ledge she was on. She grabbed her bag and returned her jars and soul-collecting vial, but gave up her shoes since she doubted she had time to shove them back inside. Just as she reached for her cloak, she and Jabeziryth grabbed it at the same time.

"I truly won't harm you," he swore, and Lindi didn't believe him.

She pulled with her right arm, wincing when she heard his nails – or claws, or whatever – tear into her cloak, and she gave it some slack again. She lifted her left hand with her palm facing him. "L-let go, or I'll use more of my magic."

She worried if she turned intangible, her cloak wouldn't come with her since he was holding it. She couldn't let him have it. It was a precious gift, the only thing that allowed her to shift into a raven, and she needed it. If he kept it or ruined it, she'd be heartbroken.

"You're making me out to be a bad guy here. I only wish to talk to you."

Then, as if he wanted to prove he was harmless, despite his claws, fangs, and ridiculously tall height, he yielded and let her cloak go. The issue was, Lindi wasn't expecting him to. She squealed when she stumbled backwards from the lack of resistance and began to go over the ledge of the waterfall.

A massive hand wrapped itself around her wrist, warm and surprisingly gentle, and pulled her back onto solid ground.

Lindi yanked her arm away and drew her feathery cloak to her chest. His red eyes followed her, and they seemed to lack any hostility or callousness. They were observant, and she hated to think how much of her body he'd seen while she'd been bathing.

I can't believe I didn't notice him come up behind me. He'd been quiet, freakishly so. *He probably snuck up on me on purpose.*

She shuddered to think what that could have meant for her if he'd had ill intentions.

"Some of the more... intelligent Demons have noted you using this waterfall to bathe in the past few weeks. A large raven that isn't a Demon flying over the Veil is odd, and cause for concern."

Lindi's blood ran cold. *I was watched?*

"What do you want?" she snapped, stepping back from him as she donned her cloak. She was now ready to escape if she needed to. "W-why did you follow me here?"

"They gave me your description, and I thought it might have been you. You look human, but you don't smell like one, just like before." Once more, his gaze flittered down her body, and she realised then that it had always been observational and nothing perverted. "I've never heard of a Phantom. No human has ever been able to turn into some kind of spirit or bird before. Are there more of you?"

Her lips tightened. Should she give him any information? *What harm is there?* She knew what to keep hidden and what she shouldn't. At least, she hoped she did.

"No. I'm the only one."

"As far as I knew, only Anzúli can use magic." He tapped a pointed claw at his forehead. "You don't have a third eye like them."

Swallowing thickly, she said, "I'm not one of them."

"Then how did you come to be here?"

Lindi bit the sides of her tongue and stepped back a little further, her eyes narrowing.

"Not a question you'll answer?" Instead of looking annoyed, Jabeziryth leaned forward with his arms behind his back. His short hair swayed around his pointed ears, as if the strands had caught a light gust of wind. "There's only one being I know who can wield magic such as yours, and it's doubtful he can touch this world. I had my suspicions then, but *seeing* you use your magic in person..."

Her expression became more closed off, and she tightened her hand on her satchel while curling her fingers around the neck of her cloak. She prepared herself to flip her hood up and transform.

He might be fast, so I'll have to jump.

The shift was near instant, so she doubted she'd touch the lake below before she shifted.

"Phantom, you can either admit your tie to him or not, but you're a half-dead creature who can wield shadowy magic and does not age. You reek of magic that doesn't belong to you." Then he straightened and grinned before cupping his broad chin. "Actually, this is perfect. He doesn't answer my call when I stand in his mist, and I have been trying to speak to him."

He's a lot more intelligent than I could have ever given him credit for. He'd managed to surmise her bond with Weldir with such little information.

"Why do you want to speak with Weldir?"

Jabeziryth was slow to answer, as if he wanted to be careful with his next words. "I just want to talk with him. Perhaps even obtain his assistance. A mutually beneficial agreement, if you will."

"I will never help him," Weldir stated through the bond, and she almost wanted to groan.

The moment she uttered his name, she should have known he'd come.

"You should leave, Lindiwe."

"He has warned me to keep my distance. He will never help you."

Oddly enough, Jabeziryth let out a small, genial laugh that seemed true and soft. "He's worried because of what has happened, but he and I have faced the same prejudices and experiences. I want to see what we can do for each other."

"My answer remains the same."

Lindi opened her mouth to relay that, but then shut it. *Should I be letting him know that Weldir can speak directly to me?* She didn't want to be trapped in some way because of it. *Who knows what kind of magic the Elves have?*

So, instead of speaking for Weldir, she asked, "How do you want to help?"

Jabeziryth brought his hands out from behind his back and shrugged. "He and I are both outcasts, shunned in horrible ways by the Elvish and their deities. I seek his help and wish to offer my own." He tilted his head while his eyes narrowed on the centre of her collar bones, and she wrapped her nimble hands around the mana stone there. "If there is only one of you, there is only so much you can do on your own."

Lindi shrugged a shoulder with a rude snort of laughter. "What can a bunch of Demons do to help?"

"But I'm not a Demon, at least not a fully bred one." He reached a hand out to her like he wanted her to take it or show that he was harmless by offering his palm. "I'm the only one of my kind. He is the only one of his kind, as are you. It's a lonely existence, one which we can all share."

All the humour and warmth faded from his face, and replacing it was something Lindi had been struggling with for years. It made his young face look much older and strained. Sorrow and the pangs of isolation, of loneliness. Worse, it seemed genuine, his brows furrowing in a similar way to how hers often did, his lips curled in and tighter, like he had unshed words but there was no one to listen.

Her heart betrayed her, and she softened towards his plight.

She remembered how she'd overheard his companions in the past pressuring him with things he didn't want to do, and how they said he was different and would struggle.

It didn't help that he aged slowly and looked to be similar in age to her physically. No one else in the world was like that. No one understood the deathlessness that she was facing, or what it was like to see everything changing as she remained the same.

And, true to his word, he hadn't hurt her or grabbed her when he had ample time to try.

"I haven't introduced myself," he said, his hardened expression shifting to a calmer one, losing its tension as if he was used to wearing it. "My name is Jabez."

"I thought it was longer," Lindi muttered, giving him more of her side as she looked at him awkwardly, unsure of what to do now.

Should she flee, as Weldir told her? Or should she stay like her heart told her to? Her curiosity had also become a rather starved beast over the years, and she tried to unearth all the mysteries she could to feed it.

His pointed ears dipped back. "I'm guessing Weldir told you

my true name, but I prefer not to be called it."

Although it was the reverse for her, Lindi understood that, as she didn't want anyone who wasn't close to her to say her nickname. Not even Weldir knew it. It was for her, and her parents, and her long-dead childhood friends.

"I'm Lindiwe," she answered, her shoulders losing their tension. She fiddled with one of her feathers as she stood next to the falls, trying her hardest not to look at his face.

It was handsome, and human-looking, which made it easier to forget all the parts of him that were different, like his Demon fangs, eyes, and horns, and his Elvish ears. He didn't look mean, or even rabid, like the monsters that lurked in the shade.

He didn't look... evil. He was just a young boy.

"Lindiwe, you should leave," Weldir said, his deep voice tingling her senses. His words sounded like a suggestion and a command all in one, and that made her want to do the complete opposite.

So when Jabez hooked his thumbs into the waistband of his trousers and turned to look over the Veil, she found her feet rooted to the ground.

"I come here a lot," Jabez commented, his eyes scanning across the treetops that went for as far as the eye could see. "It's my favourite place in the Veil. It's quiet, other than the comforting sound of the waterfall, and there's never anyone to watch you. That's part of the reason I was surprised when they told me someone else, something other, comes here."

"I feel the same way," she answered in a small voice, letting her gaze fall to where he did.

"It's nice to know I'm not the only one who seeks an escape in this place."

He made her jump and gasp when he sprang into action and stormed towards her. Lindi turned incorporeal before he could reach her, but he only went around her and under the falls, where there was a semi-dry section to walk, and moved to the other side.

Curious, Lindi followed while intangible, so her feathers didn't catch any wetness. On the other side, Jabez climbed slightly higher so he could seat himself on a ledge that was perfect for perching oneself. With one foot planted on the edge so his knee was bent and the other hanging, he watched her from above.

"Well? Are you going to continue to look like a frightened mouse, or are you going to sit and enjoy the view? Stay in your ghostly form, if it makes you feel better."

"Why do you continue to stay?"

I'm not a frightened mouse! She hunted Demons and occultists with ferociousness, like a mountain cat!

Lindi ignored Weldir and braved turning physical out of spite towards both of them – Weldir because she didn't want to listen to him, and Jabez for calling her something so weak. Did she trust him? No, but she trusted herself to escape any danger should she need to.

She wasn't afraid of him, just wisely wary.

She climbed higher and found herself a perch that was a safe enough distance away. She lifted her nose slightly to snub them both.

Weldir produced an unnerving growl that rumbled in her ears, causing her to fist her cloak in worry. Her shoulders lifted nervously, since she was blatantly violating his wishes.

"Fine, Lindiwe. Do as you want."

Strangely enough, he went quiet, when she'd expected him to spout furious words at her or childishly growl some more. She and Jabez shared a silent, tranquil – although tense – moment as the sun dipped further behind them. The area grew more shaded by the moment, but she also felt more at ease with each second that passed.

All she could hear was the chirp of a few birds, bats beginning to squeak as they woke and prepared for their nightly flight, and the sound of crashing water. Each noise bled into her being and soothed her, lulling her when she should have more wisely stayed alert.

Only when Lindi chose to speak, as if that was what Jabez waited for, was the silence broken.

"I used to be afraid of the Veil," she said quietly. "I thought it was evil. But the longer I see it and the more I find places like this one, the more I appreciate it. It's... picturesque, in its own way."

"It's the mist," he responded. "It makes it eerier than it's supposed to."

She huffed a laugh. "Yeah. But that just means it's really healthy. Plants need water to survive, and there's so much of it here in the air that you can see it. I think most humans would think it means something haunted might peek out from behind a bush."

Jabez chuckled at that. "That doesn't happen here. I've only seen one or two Ghosts, and they tend to be above on the surface, or attached to an item belonging to a deceased human a Demon has brought in."

So there are Ghosts in the Veil. That was handy for her to know, as she'd been collecting them. *Then again, Weldir's mist has been drifting further into the Veil.* Surely at some point he'd be able to collect them himself.

The reminder of him made her wonder if Weldir was still watching or if he'd chosen to completely ignore this. She lifted her palm to produce a black flame, checking to make sure he hadn't momentarily rescinded his magic.

He hadn't. *At least he isn't* that *childish.* She would have rolled her eyes otherwise.

"How long have you been alive?" Jabez asked nonchalantly. "I've been here for almost a hundred Earth years. Time seems to pass so quickly here."

Her eyes widened, and she turned her head to him to find he'd leaned back on straightened arms. It gave him a boyish air of indifference.

"What do you mean, *quickly?* I've been *alive* for almost eighty years and it feels like forever!" She wanted to fall back and pretend to faint with fatigue at how long it'd been.

His eyes crinkled as he let out a boisterous laugh. "For a human, maybe. My kind can live an exceedingly long time in comparison. I think I've lived around three hundred human years, but I'm almost twenty-two."

Ah, so she'd guessed his age pretty well then.

She pouted. "I was two and twenty when I stopped ageing."

His lips drew back into a grimace. "Who the fuck says their age like that? That's so complicated."

Her cheeks heated in embarrassment, and she threw her arms up. "I don't know?! Humans, I guess? It's how we've always said it."

"Why not just say the number? I hope you don't count to a hundred that way." He let his head fall to the side. "By the blessed night, that would take forever if you did. Three and fifty, four and fifty... End me now."

The gentle needling softened her more. It reminded her of the banter of her childhood friends, especially Marcus, who had always been a bit of a jokester, incapable of having a serious conversation.

"You make an excellent point."

"Of course I do. Anyone with sense would make that distinction."

An accidental laugh escaped her, and for a moment, Lindi completely forgot what he was, Weldir's warnings, and a few of her troubles. He sounded so normal, and not like the Demons she'd come to know. He felt like another person, just one who wasn't human and bore a strange accent.

She'd matured so much that it was nice to feel young again, like her physical age. She'd almost forgotten what it was like, and how human it made her feel. She'd only ever felt that way with the Anzúli, but they weren't usually so carefree or light-hearted.

They were rather stern people, all on a mission to help the humans.

"So, why come to the Veil when everything in it wants to eat you? Bathing here seems suicidal," Jabez quipped while tilting his face to her. "Although the view wasn't unwelcome."

When she gave him an untrusting glance, his lips pulled back into a mischievous grin, and not even his sharp fangs prevented her from unwittingly letting her ire fall. He even gave her a cheeky wink.

He seems so much more human and personable than Weldir.

Jabez was playful and suave in a way that made it hard to dislike him. If Weldir had been even a fraction this approachable, she may have shaken her distrust and anger at him long ago.

Lindi rolled her eyes. "Don't you know it's rude to sneak up on a woman bathing?"

"Must I point out the irony of that when you chose to do it out in the forest? How is that my fault?"

The fact that he was right had her grumbling, and had she been any more immature, she may have poked her tongue out at him. But it was that same annoyance that made the urge to smile tickle its way into her face.

What harm is there in making a... friend? Even if it was likely temporary, as she had to continue with her bound duties.

Even to Weldir's dismay.

Actually, that very reason was why her butt stayed exactly where it currently rested.

Keeping her wings stretched and rigid, Lindi circled around where she wanted to land. She flapped her wings once to keep herself airborne, and the person below turned their head up to watch her.

She let herself descend to a rocky ledge, one that was a little too close to the cascade of water, and it wetted a few of her feathers. She shook them as she shifted and drew her hood back to uncover her face.

"I wasn't sure if you'd come," Jabez commented, remaining seated where he was the previous day.

"I wasn't sure if I was going to," Lindi admitted, which made him grin in appreciation at the truth, even if she sounded a little pouty and surly.

His red eyes glinted with mirth. "Why? Didn't we have a good time yesterday?"

She wiggled her head side to side to pretend what he said was debatable. "All we did was talk."

"We did laugh, or did you forget that? Or is the issue Wel–"

Lindi cut him a sharp look. "Don't. Don't say his name. It may call him, and if he isn't watching, he will."

His lips shut, but his grin remained. It morphed into something more mischievous. "So he does talk to you."

Her nose crinkled as she took her seat. "Yes, but don't expect me to talk to him on your behalf. I'm not a messenger bird."

"No. Just a raven, it appears." He placed his right hand on the rock and leaned towards her, bridging only a slight amount of the large gap between them. He nodded his nose at her cloak.

"How did you obtain such magic? You have a mana stone. They can only be obtained in Nyl'theria."

Her brows furrowed and Lindi held the neck of her cloak, where her stone was threaded to it. "How did you–?"

He shrugged. "Comes with being an Elf. We can see magic when it's active, even if it's particularly obscured. You didn't have it the last time I saw you."

She figured he meant all those years ago.

"*He* helped me. Told me where to go to mine, how to get there, and what I needed to search for." She fiddled with some of her feathers in hopes that it would help her stifle the repulsive shudder that was trying to tingle down her spine.

The memories of that time still haunted her.

"But going to the mines is impossible, even for me." Jabez then pushed his fingers between the drawstrings of a pouch tied to his waist to open it and pulled out a few different-coloured stones. "I collected my stones from the ruins of a city. I barely got out alive, and that wasn't within the nest of a mountain."

One of her eyes twitched at how easy he made that sound. Apparently an infested ruin was easier than a mine, and she would have much preferred that over the claustrophobia she'd suffered alongside her terror of the Demons snarling at her.

"I saw you used one to make the Veil's canyon," Lindi muttered, resisting the urge to give him a nasty eye.

"I don't have such destructive magic. I can grow a tree with my Earth mana, but only one a day without a stone." He leaned back on straightened arms and let out an exhausted sigh. "It's taken me so many years. I think if I look at another seed again, I'd rather eat it and choke on it. Could you imagine?"

He wrapped a clawed hand around his throat and bounced up and down as he began to feign choking. He stuck his tongue out, and the roundedness surprised her. She half expected him to have a forked appendage.

She sucked her lips into her mouth and bit down on them to push down her desire to laugh.

He made it all too easy to find humour in what he said, his nature light-hearted and calm. He never moved from his spot, as if he knew it would spook her. And even though they'd spoken until dark was almost upon them the day before, he never asked her anything more about Weldir or anything too personal.

Why didn't he, if he wanted so badly to speak with him? She didn't know, but she kind of didn't care.

He doesn't seem so bad... or evil like Weldir made me believe. He just seemed like a normal person, despite all those features that definitely weren't human.

Lindi had questions about Demons, about the Veil, and... about him. She hadn't asked any of the latter. She gathered Weldir had told her most of it, but there must be more below the surface. Why did he turn on his people? Why did he hate them so much he wanted to build some kind of army like she'd overheard? It sounded like he wanted to start a war.

She was curious about him, just as he was about her.

"How did you ever come to find yourself bonded to a demi-god?" Jabez asked, holding her stare as he lifted a hand and offered a one-sided shrug. "You would have needed to be near the Veil, his mist. There were very few humans near here back then."

Her features tightened as she looked down at her feet, and subsequently, at the water below. *Should I answer that?* What harm was there? He already knew she was tied to Weldir – what did her story matter?

So why did she feel this guilt when she opened her mouth to answer? "Remember the day we first met?"

She shyly met his gaze, and he raised a singular white brow.

"I wouldn't say we met. There was no introduction."

She tipped her head up to give him a bland look at his facetiousness, and he chuckled in response.

"Okay, yes. You were spying on us. Eavesdropping is a nasty habit, although I guess it didn't matter, as I doubt you understand Nyl'kira."

Lindi swallowed and managed to cool her features, not giving away that she'd overheard everything by Weldir's translation spell.

"That wasn't on purpose. I just so happened to be nearby," she answered with a harrumph. She looked back down at the white foam collecting on the surface of the water. "Well, you know how you saved that woman? I... was once her, but I didn't have anyone to save me."

"That's technically not true."

Ugh! She knew exactly what he meant, and she wanted to kick him for it. "Yeah, I know *he* technically saved me, but I mean before that. Before I had to make a choice between dying or not."

"Making a decision that goes beyond lifelong, when under duress, is barely passable. Feels like trickery to me," Jabez muttered while cupping his chin, a thoughtful hum present in his voice. Then he lifted his shoulders. "Then again, I doubt he would have had any other way to find a mate."

The fact that he agreed on how *unfair* it was she'd had to make the decision under duress softened her even more to him. She wanted that validation. For someone other than herself to think it, believe it, say it out loud so she didn't feel so wrong about her feelings.

Still holding his chin, Jabez tapped a claw against his cheek. "I've always wondered why the humans threw each other into the Veil. Such a custom is unknown to us. Even Demons wouldn't do such a thing."

"It's this whole idea of a virgin sacrifice," she bit out. "Offer the pure in hopes of protection."

His head reared back, then he scratched at his short hair behind his ear. "Why always women? Men can be virgins too."

Lindi threw her hands up, enraged and perplexed at the same time. "It's just the way things are. They can 'prove' a woman is pure, whereas with men they can't. It's all bullshit."

And their 'proof' wasn't always valid, nor correct! It was flawed, all of it.

"Sounds like a flawed and misogynistic system."

Lindi smiled at that, as his words managed to touch a wounded part of her heart. "It really is." Then she held his gaze as she said, "Thank you. You know, for saving that woman. I was already on my way to do it when you stepped in. I'd been hunting the occultists for a long time to put an end to such madness."

Obviously uncomfortable with her gratitude, Jabez looked away, fidgeted in his seat, and shrugged. "It's mostly stopped happening, from what I can tell. People are too afraid to come here. Which poses a problem for my fellow Demons."

The hairs on the back of her neck stood on end when she realised what he meant, and it sent a horrible chill down her spine. He *wanted* his kind to eat more humans, like a humanity-growing food source. It reminded her of the danger he did possess, even if his words were kind and his expressions were warm.

He saved one woman, but he saw no issue with the deaths of many more. Then again, that had been a long time ago and his mindset may have changed. If it happened today, would he have saved that woman like he'd done then?

Who knew? But maybe watching him do that for a stranger, a female of a different species, someone weaker, was why she had returned to this waterfall when he asked it of her. It still resonated with Lindi, and had since that day.

I don't think I should keep coming here, though.

It did pose a lot of risks, and she didn't actually know what his motives were. It could all be a ruse, and she knew she'd find that more hurtful than she wanted to believe.

With that thought in mind, and the fact that an all-too-comfortable quiet fell upon them like it did the day before, she looked out across the Veil. Where they were was just high enough to look over most of the trees, giving her a view of endless green. The sun shone over much of it, although where they were was in the shade to protect him.

I guess it feels wrong defying Weldir like this. Her gaze slipped to Jabez, who was looking out at the forest as well. *Then again, I'm not really doing anything bad.*

They were just two people sitting there, sharing a few breaths and space.

Lindi looked down at her lap as she fidgeted with her fingers. "Do the Demons live as long as you?"

"Hmm. Most. We are noticing those who have eaten more humans than Elves are ageing at a much faster rate, though."

"I see." She chewed the inside of her cheek. "I'm finding it difficult to return to humankind, or even the Anzúli, for that reason. They... age so quickly, and yet I remain as I am."

"Because you're not the same, Lindiwe," he answered in a dark tone, one that dripped with stoicism. "It comes from being other. No matter how much you look the same, you will always be set apart because of it."

He said it with so much weight, and the truth of it settled heavily upon her already weary shoulders.

Becoming a Phantom came with its pitfalls.

She couldn't reveal what she was to other humans who didn't have a large Anzúli influence. She couldn't make genuine connections, as she'd inevitably leave to continue her duties for Weldir, and the likelihood that they'd be much older and almost a new person by the time she saw them again was what she found off-putting the most.

Even with the Anzúli she felt like an outcast.

They easily brought her into their fold, but there were secrets she wasn't privy to, and there were rituals she wasn't allowed to attend. She was other – to them, to everyone. Even to Jabez.

And especially to Weldir, who barely understood her humanness.

"It's isolating when you're the only one," Jabez continued, leaning forward to interlace his fingers between his spread thighs. He kicked his feet subtly back and forth over the ledge. "I know that all too well. Even if you're accepted, it's only to a certain degree, whether that's because you put up walls or they do. I've felt that here, as well as in my home realm."

A small breeze made her curls sway around her shoulders and shifted his short hair around his ears and horns. She looked at their hard, tapered lengths, wondering why they didn't bother her as much as they should.

And when his red eyes connected with hers, she didn't find them as sinister as other Demons.

Why do I feel drawn to him?

Why did his red eyes not feel evil, but rather seemed to hold a note of kindness in them?

Or am I seeing things that don't exist because I want to?

"Will... you tell me how you came to be on Earth?" Lindi muttered, refusing to avert her eyes. It was a question she'd once asked Weldir, although his answer was rather vague.

His mist gave him the ability to touch this world, and another deity opened his prism near the portal at the centre of the Veil to allow him to spread it here. She didn't understand how that was possible, and why that meant his realm was connected to this one.

He'd merely concluded his puzzling explanation with, "That is how it was done."

Jabez's gaze darkened, hardened, and revealed that his aloof personality could be twisted at times. "I imagine he's already told you. Why ask me to bring up painful memories?"

Lindi shrunk a little under his piercing, cold crimson eyes. "Because sometimes people layer biases in their version of a story. I want to hear it from you, to hear your side."

His full lips tightened into flat lines, and he looked away. "Let me consider it for a bit. It's not something I've spoken about in a while, and my memories are... unclear."

"It might make me trust you more," she said with a playful grin so large it revealed all her flat teeth.

"Trust through pity is the saddest form of bonding." His eyes slipped back to her, and when they connected gazes, they held each other's with strength. His nose wrinkled on one side and he groaned. "Fine, I will tell you *part* of my story." Then he pointed his index finger right at her face. "But if you give me a sappy fucking look, I will cease speaking and leave."

With a hand over her heart and her grin returning, triumphant now, she said, "I promise I won't."

She wouldn't, simply because she'd hate the very same thing.

TWENTY-EIGHT

A time unknown, but a dark day

Why does she keep returning? Weldir thought, as he watched Lindiwe and Jabeziryth converse next to the waterfall.

It was what he counted to be the fourth day cycle of them falling into this strange and unwarranted routine. Every day just past noon, when the sun had faded a little and shaded the area, they both returned.

Either she would be waiting for him, or he was already there.

They always made some snarky retort about the other being late, or that they had shown up at all, before easing into a conversation. Or silence, which they shared pleasantly.

On this day, Jabeziryth climbed the steep, jagged rocks to her, his clawed toes easily finding purchase as he ascended the most difficult path. For a moment, Weldir wondered what it felt like to have mossy rocks beneath the soles of his feet, if they were as wet as they appeared or dry, if they were slimy, or even cushiony.

Perhaps I should add such texture to my realm. Weldir was always adding to Tenebris and changing it in the minutest of ways to improve its realistic qualities.

Rather than taking his usual spot, Weldir glowered when Jabeziryth took a seat closer to her than normal. He was slightly in front of her and down a level, but if he reached out, he could potentially brush her left ankle. Maybe even her right heel, since her feet were crossed.

Weldir was uncertain if they knew he'd witnessed all their

interactions, ever watchful of his mate. He'd remained silent after his initial attempts to warn her and she'd refused to respond to him in Jabeziryth's presence, skilfully hiding her reactions to his demands that she stay away.

"I swear you get shorter every day," the little half-Elf teased, leaning back to look at her with a shake of his head. "You probably couldn't even climb these rocks if you actually tried."

"I'm a pretty normal height for a *human* woman, thank you very much." Then she scrunched her nose up at him and sneered. "Do those horns of yours go deep into your brain to make you this thick of thought? You're the *odd one out here*, sir comes-from-a-different-world. We were here first!"

"Watch out or I'll show you how thick they are by ramming them into your forehead."

"And I'll show you how quickly I can wield a dagger. I'm just as sharp of tongue as I am of sword."

Jabeziryth burst out with laughter. "That I'd have to see for myself, little *Phantom*." Then he stabbed his empty fist forward multiple times as though he had a blade. "I could just see you trying. You're pretty prickly, you know."

"Prickly?! I think I'm as sweet as a puppy!"

"A puppy is a small dog, correct?" He offered her a dull and serious expression. "I eat those for my first meal."

Her mouth gaped. Then a ripple of discontent pulsed across Weldir's misty being when she let out a mild, although genuine, laugh.

"No, you don't," she answered with a chuckle.

She smiles and laughs so freely with others, but never with me.

Even that Anzúli male, Evart, had gained her fondness in easy conversation. She'd always been awkward around Evart, and avoided him as much as possible, but when they did finally speak, it was always with the enjoyment of each other's company.

It showed Weldir felt something tender for this human female, even if it was small due to a lack of nurturing on both their parts. He had developed a possessiveness when it came to her, since she was his mate, and especially as her beauty was beguiling enough to draw the gaze of *many* men.

She was entirely oblivious to it.

She made companions where she saw fit, not realising a male's gaze would remain on her with keen interest whenever she was not looking.

It wasn't her fault, but it had stirred some peculiar unfamiliarity within him. Although he doubted she'd do anything to betray him, it also didn't mean that he didn't have a right to be vexed by it when he thought the person had ill intentions, no matter what they may be.

It had never truly bothered him that she spoke with other males until now. Then again, he'd never attempted to intervene before. Nor had it been with someone he detested.

I told her to stay away from Jabeziryth and she defies me.

Why? He'd told her of the halfling's past, what he'd done, why he was on Earth. Weldir had told her he was the very reason Demons were now throughout her realm, causing mayhem and death. Jabeziryth's desire for revenge was not unknown to him, although he had yet to truly understand what that entailed.

Likely a war, one that pitted Demons and the Elysians against each other.

I could remove her, Weldir thought once again. *I can call her to my realm by force.*

He doubted that would go well, and he didn't wish to be on the sour end of her ire. She already seemed displeased with him, and he had yet to be given the opportunity to correct his mistakes. To gain her favour once more.

She always required time between tending to their offspring, which he'd been granting her.

When a conversation opened up about how she'd been to other parts of the world, something that drew Jabeziryth's keen interest, annoyance flittered through him. *She speaks freely, as though talking with a long-lost friend.* They joked in ways that Weldir had never experienced with her, although on a few occasions he had *tried,* to no avail, to gain her humour.

Is that what she considered Jabeziryth? A friend? While Weldir was trapped in his realm, unable to garner even a modicum of her attention or affection? She'd barely known the male for less than a few days and already their companionship lacked the strife Weldir and Lindiwe's possessed.

He found it... demoralising.

The easy laughter, the smiles, the depth of emotion they shared in their stories, the fact that they were able to experience all this in a world he could not touch. Weldir was so far from her, their realms didn't even collide unless he made it happen by bringing her to him.

He wished he could experience such things with her.

So although her defiance irked him, as he wanted to protect her in his own way, it was how she was with Jabeziryth that truly had his mist agitated. Or maybe he was bothered because she was this way *while* blatantly defying Weldir, likely knowing it upset him.

And the fact that this child of a male was encouraging her did not leave him pleased.

Jabeziryth had no reason to return. He had many fully evolved Demons to familiarise himself with. He had companions, surely.

He didn't need to be sniffing around Weldir's out-of-reach mate.

The half-Demon pretended he understood her plight, but he and she were not the same. Lindiwe truly was other. She was *his*, and that made her special. She was stronger and more beautiful than the Demons or humans when she wielded his magic for those very reasons.

What does he seek from her? Surely he was there under the guise of false pretences. *It cannot be for companionship. Not truly.*

They both rarely spoke of Weldir, which somehow made the situation worse in his eyes. They were tiptoeing around her bond with him, as if it was something to be avoided, or perhaps ashamed of.

But Jabeziryth did occasionally, although rarely, mention him. Like now, for instance.

He leaned his lithe body against a wall of rock, folded his right leg so his ankle rested over the opposing knee, and placed his interlaced fingers behind his head to cushion it.

"So, how does one do 'it' with a spirit of the void?" Jabeziryth asked casually, dipping his gaze up to the cloudy sky.

"Excuse me? Firstly, what kind of name is that for him?"

Lindiwe blanched, causing her nose to scrunch up in a rather cute way and her tongue to stick forward slightly. "And secondly, how dare you ask me something so... so personal!"

He rolled his head to the side to look at her with a cocked brow. "Oh, come on. If you're his mate, I'm assuming you both have done the nasty. Like how does one fuck a spirit that you can't touch?" Then Jabeziryth waved to the horizon of trees before them. "Do let the world know. We're all curious; I think anyone would be."

A growl rumbled through his realm, deep and quiet.

Why would he be curious?

If he attempts to touch her – whether it be as platonic as her ankle – *I will bring her to me before he even has the chance to lay a hand on her.*

"I'm not going to dignify your rude and violating question with an answer!" Lindiwe yelled, reaching down while lifting her feet until she found what she wanted. She grabbed a rock and launched it at his head, which smacked him in the temple.

"Ow, fuck!" he barked when his head shunted to the side. "There's no need to throw things at me like an ill-tempered child."

"Ill-tempered child?! I should wring your neck." Then she stood and pointed at him. "You know what? I'm going to do just that."

He let out a laugh as he tipped his head back, arms once more going behind his head in a relaxed position. He wiggled his back into the crevice as he said, "I'd like to see you try– Uk!"

A thin tentacle shot out from the ground and wrapped around his neck, swaying him side to side. One hand reached up to claw at the choking limb, while a band of Elvish words glowed around his right wrist when he placed his palm against the ground. A combination of grass and moss that was present in the cracks of stone grew. They climbed up her ankles and tripped her so she'd fall to her backside.

Once they both yielded and released their magic, they stared at each other for a short while. Then they both burst into laughter.

"If you must know" – she put her hands up to make air quotation marks – "the 'spirit of the void' and I have never actually done it. That question will likely forever stay unanswered."

She settled back onto her boulder, just as Jabeziryth's features twisted into a look of disgust. "Seriously? That's fucking boring, minus the fucking part." He placed his hands behind his head once more and reclined. "I figured he'd want offspring or something to help him, like what he makes you do."

Lindiwe opened her mouth, but promptly shut it. She turned away to look at the forest.

She never corrected him, and that at least drew some of Weldir's faith in her. *She still doesn't trust him.* When he looked back on their conversations, she'd wisely shared very little about their bond, their deal in it, or anything that could be considered useful.

She was keeping him emotionally at arm's length and uninformed, at least in some regard.

But Weldir still didn't like any of this.

And when Jabeziryth reached into his bag to offer her some kind of fruit, and she willingly took it, both of them sharing a meal he'd never be able to with Lindiwe, he wanted this all to cease.

He didn't like that behind all his crankiness and annoyance, the root of the issue may actually be...

Am I jealous? he thought, looking off into the darkness behind him. *I cannot do any of this with her.*

He could not sit next to a rushing waterfall in the physical realm and feel the breeze together with her. He couldn't sit with her and experience the sun or shade, or the water spraying against his skin until tiny droplets collected upon it. He could not share in a meal or offer her such a fruit.

He'd never been able to, nor may it ever be possible to experience such ease with her. She was further from him than ever in every way, and closer to Jabeziryth in ways he didn't appreciate.

Yet neither had done anything to warrant such envy, other than sharing in each other's amicable presence. He felt all this entirely on his own.

Although it upset him because he'd never made his dislike of Jabeziryth unknown to her, she obviously wasn't doing any of this to cause such an emotion. She was seeking a personal connection, something that Weldir couldn't give – or, rather, hadn't been giving. Something he didn't quite understand.

And realising that somehow made guilt roll with his jealousy, making his mist collect tighter against his form until there was obvious strain.

But I want these things.

It pained Weldir in his own way to be separated from the physical world. He was so different, and sometimes it felt as though he didn't exist in reality.

He wanted to be able to share in her laughter and bring it forth from her. The more he thought on it, the more he wanted to bridge the vast gap between them, and the more he realised she'd been trying to do just that in her own way when she asked to deepen their relationship physically.

And then he'd been detached and callous, as she no doubt already thought him to be.

He looked back at the viewing disc as a heaviness settled over him.

"I will speak to him," Weldir said through their bond, his tone more annoyed than he wished it to be.

Lindiwe paused just as she was about to take a second green lumpy fruit. With her hand out and touching it, her features twisted into something pained before she took it.

"Why now?" she whispered, looking away from Jabeziryth when the male's sensitive ears twitched in reaction. "You said you didn't want to."

"It's what he seeks from you," Weldir stated coldly.

Because it will surely reveal the truth about his intentions. And then Weldir would get what he wanted, which was her absence from his presence.

I would like to have your attention back. Even if it was disjointed and stilted. *I would like to show you I can do the things you sought from me.*

"Is he talking to you?" Jabeziryth asked, tilting his head and leaning forward with abject interest. Too much interest.

She nodded to him, yet answered Weldir with, "You don't know if that's true."

No, Weldir was making the assumption despite no longer knowing if it was true or not. But he wanted to separate them, and he would use any means necessary in his power – *without* potentially upsetting her. Doing so forcefully would gain him no ground.

Then once I have proven I do seek a deeper bond, I'll place her in a different part of the world.

Somewhere, anywhere, that was as far from Jabeziryth as possible.

Especially as he had no desire to give this male what he wanted, and he didn't wish for Lindiwe to be caught in the middle of it. If his assumption was correct, then she could potentially be in danger if Jabeziryth and his Demon companions turned on her.

He wanted to prove to this female, this human, his *own* damn female, that he was... trying. That he would like to give her the things she sought – like companionship in ways he could not fully achieve – even if he found little value in them for himself.

In his own way, he wanted to make her content, like she'd been at this waterfall for the past few days. To protect her, even if he couldn't do so by his own hands.

TWENTY-NINE

A time unknown, but one of failure

She is cross with me, Weldir thought, as he floated before his mate with his arms folded.

Hers were also crossed over her chest, and she refused to look at him since he brought her here. Her pretty face was furrowed with deep lines, while her shoulders were raised and tense.

Yet he couldn't help finding her bottom lip pouting forward cute, especially as he felt infinitely better now that he'd stolen her away from that half-Demon.

He'd take her being cranky with him over the disgusting pit of emotions he'd been floating in earlier. He wasn't used to feeling them, and he thought that may be why he found himself to be much more sensitive than usual.

I don't like that I will have to make that male reveal his true intentions. That their companionship was fragile, and likely only reached the end of Lindiwe's usefulness to Jabeziryth. In his heart, that male was a Demon who had cruel and violent intentions, even if he was only a mere boy in Weldir's mind.

I do not wish to hurt her, but she will see when I speak with him. The result of that conversation should irreparably damage their useless friendship.

Yet he felt his mist unfurling itself with her presence near and safe, and the vicious tangle of emotions quickly pulled away. She floated in his weightless shadows, completely wrapped up in him.

That was all that mattered for now.

"You continued to meet with Jabeziryth, disobeying me," he stated with a deep tone of displeasure.

"He doesn't like to be called that," she grumbled. "And you likely heard him say so."

A swirl of confusion wrapped around him.

He didn't see why she cared, or why he should.

"But that's not his name."

Her arms tightened. "Doesn't matter. Are you going to use a soul to speak with him?"

"I don't see why I should?" he stated, a question underlining his voice as he tilted his head to the side. "I can talk to him through you."

Her jaw dropped, then she threw her hands up, obviously more annoyed with him than just a second ago. "I will tell you what I told him. I'm not a messenger bird!" she exclaimed with a hateful spark of fire in her eyes. "Talk to him yourself. You have the ability to do so."

"In order to speak to him properly, I would require the use of a soul. I have no desire to waste such energy on a petulant child."

Then again, calling Jabez that *was* a little unfair, considering he was a fully fledged adult. Just something that was young on the scale of unending time Weldir had lived and would live.

"I'll happily be there to mediate, but I don't want to talk on your behalf."

Weldir sighed. Was he being childish? Perhaps a little, but he had his reasons, however selfish they may be. "You once told me that the gods you know of were fickle beings. I am choosing to be fickle."

Her brows drew impossibly closer, and her gaze much sharper. "Then speak to him in your mist, like you first did with me."

"If we do that, then you will not be there, as there will be no point."

"No." She placed her hand over her chest. "I want to be part of the conversation, since it apparently impacts me."

"Then you will speak on my behalf." When she opened her pesky mouth to argue and refute, bold as usual, Weldir darkened his voice. "*Enough,* Lindiwe. I have taken your disobedience lightly over the past few days, but my patience does have an *end*."

She promptly shut her lips, and then her pretty features pinched into a displeased expression. She looked to the side, away from him, as her hands bundled into tight fists.

Seeing as this was a losing battle for her, he sighed. *I'd rather her not be there for her safety, but she is stubborn and she must see the error of her ways.* Especially regarding Jabez, and what he knew to be the truth. She seemed to have more faith in a total stranger than acceptance that Weldir could foresee the likely outcome.

He wanted her there *only* for that reason. To know, with irrefutable proof. So she couldn't argue with him about it in the future, and would do anything in her power to avoid him from then on.

"There is a portal in a large rainforest, which has given the Demons a plentiful home," Weldir continued, refusing to entertain the notion of her changing his mind. "Once we are certain you are carrying another of our offspring, I will speak to *Jabez* through you and then remove you from Austrális."

"Whatever you want, Weldir," she snipped. Then, with her expression relaxing into something crestfallen, she muttered quietly, "It's always whatever you want."

It was almost like he'd taken a toy from a creature that did not want to relinquish it.

What I want is for her cheerlessness to fade.

Although he'd taken her from Austrális – he could have had this conversation through the bond – he had good intentions. Namely, to keep her safe, within his reach, and finally enact something he'd been wanting to try for quite some time.

And his desire to do so had only strengthened over the past few days.

His mist collected tighter around him, as the oily solid parts of him moved a little faster around his body. Nervousness skittered along the edges of his being; he was unsure how to instigate such an interaction.

He knew now, more than ever, that he must be determined. Her response to Jabeziryth's personal questions proved there was a missing link between them, one that may be paramount for a matehood. One he'd never considered until she brought such a need up.

She wasn't making it easy with her closed-off body language.

Should I ask? That felt disingenuous. *Don't human men usually do this from a strike of passion?* He didn't know how to emulate such behaviour when he lacked the emotion necessary.

In the memories he'd looked into, usually the woman helped to instigate intimacy. With Lindiwe's arms folded and her body slightly turned from him, Weldir felt out of depth within the ocean of his own darkness.

It was a strange feeling, really, as he was always calm and in control here.

"Lindiwe..." Weldir started, before his words lost him in his uncertainty.

"Yes. Yes, okay," she snapped out.

Then she unclipped her raven cloak and began to fumble with the ties of her trousers with agitated movements. She was preparing herself, as she usually did, without giving him a chance to say more.

Rather than shunting himself forward through the darkness, Weldir reached his clawed hand forward and yanked her to him. Her gasp of surprise echoed throughout his realm, and her hair floated and waved as she was brought right to him with barely a few centimetres parting them.

"Do you ever soothe?" he asked with an exaggerated, false sigh.

With eyes wide in puzzlement, and her hands waving backwards in an attempt to put space between them he didn't allow, she rasped, "Excuse me?"

"What I mean to say is: *how* does one soothe you?"

"Well, I don't know," she grumbled, her bottom lip doing that cute pouty thing. "I don't think I'm all that difficult, if I'm being honest."

"So it's only me who irks you?" His tone was deflated, and he wished his question didn't ring with so much truth.

Her eyes slitted into little cute glares, and she bore them right into his gaze. "People usually listen."

"I listen," he rebuffed.

It was all he could do. That, and witness.

She rolled her doe-brown eyes, giving up on swimming backwards when it was pointless. "Yes, but they *understand.* They compromise."

"We compromise plenty." When she gave him a dull look, emphasising that what he said wasn't favourable, he quickly added, "I can try to do better." He'd been trying all along, even if she didn't realise it.

She let out a long, solemn expire. "You are what you are, Weldir. You don't know what it means to feel like a human, and I doubt you ever will. I've started to accept that."

He tsked. That wasn't the answer he'd hoped for; he didn't want her to just settle. "But there is always room for improvement. For change."

Her lips pulled down into a frown and she shook her head, as if she couldn't comprehend what he was trying to say. She pushed back the tresses of her hair when they swam in front of her face as her gaze flicked side to side over his form. Then something seemed to register in her mind and her eyes widened.

She cupped her hands to her stomach, as though it became unsettled. "Weldir... you didn't think I was trying to make you jealous out of spite, did you? I'm not that kind of person." She bit down on her bottom lip and then nibbled it. "I just... it's nice to have a friend who understands what it's like to be alive for so long, to be... different from everyone else. I would never..."

Weldir would have rolled his eyes if it were possible; he lacked any whites in his eyes for such a thing to be noticeable to her. "I've never doubted *your* intentions, Lindiwe. I see no reason as to why you would betray our deal, and with a Demon, no less."

She shook her head while rearing it back. "Then I don't understand what the issue is."

Tired of going in circles when it was just easier to *show* her, Weldir forced all of his physical self, no matter how little it was, to fill his face in its entirety. Then he leaned forward and pressed his mouth against hers.

She flinched, winced, and seemed to gasp all at the same time. Her head ducked back to escape him. Caving in on herself did little to stop him until he pulled away, only because she started shoving her arms through his intangible torso to no avail.

He tilted his head when she covered her mouth with her cheeks lifting into a cringe. "What are you doing?" she mumbled past her hand.

"Attempting to give you what you asked for."

I thought that had been obvious.

Her cringe, although semi-hidden, deepened. "Was... was that supposed to be a *kiss*?"

"Well, I did press my lips to yours, didn't I?"

"Yeah, but it felt like I was punched in the mouth by a brick." She brushed her fingers over her full lips, like she was trying to soothe them. "Why was your mouth so hard?"

Weldir's mist spread out before quickly sucking back in, as discomfiture trickled through him. "Was it? I can soften my form."

He stopped the physical part of him from pulling in so tight, and pieces of it flaked off to stick to the rest of his body freely. He leaned in closer to try again, and Lindiwe put her palm over his face to stop him. Inadvertently, she poked his left eye, but he felt no pain, as he never did.

"There's no need. You said this was something you didn't want." Then, with her head to the side, she pulled her hand from his face and grumbled, "You even said it was pointless."

His essence winced at hearing those words said back to him.

Giving himself a reprieve from using his magic to fully form his face, he let his oily self streak across his body like normal. "I admit my words were callous, and I did not give the idea more thought before speaking."

Lindiwe peeked at him, her eyes slitting mistrustfully for a moment before softening. "Is that your way of apologising?"

"In some way, yes." He gave her a little space since she brought her gaze to him fully. "Lindiwe... I am an imperfect being that has no experience with any of this. Matehood. Humans. Emotions. Even just sharing a casual conversation is out of the realm of my aptitude."

"Then why this now?" She offered a mild laugh, but it lacked any humour, then she went on, "It's been years since we married, or bonded, or whatever it is you call it. And when we spoke of it..."

Weldir had an inclination that his next words would be

important and would weigh heavily on this moment.

"You... have sacrificed much for me," he started slowly. "You may not realise it, but I do wish for you to be content in this bond. This is something you desire, and therefore, I wish to give it."

Her brows furrowed with a pained emotion, which gave him the impression he was in trouble and had not said the right thing.

"But you won't enjoy it." She fidgeted like she often did when embarrassed.

"I didn't say that." He didn't *not* say it either. "We don't know until we try."

He may derive pleasure from it in some way, much in the way he could perceive his emotions. Perceive his world. But yes, largely, this was for her.

I seek for us to form a proper bond, Weldir thought, reaching out with a tendril to push a few of her curls from her eyes. *At one point, we had an amicable time when we spoke. I would like that again.*

He didn't want to feel like an outsider with the only person in any existence he was connected to. It never bothered him until her, but he tired of that. Of being alone, totally and utterly, even if he would always remain so.

Because, even with her presence, his lack of true form made anything real entirely impossible.

When she didn't reply, nor pull away – instead cupping her hands to her chest shyly – Weldir read that as he could continue. This time, when he pulled his physical self to his face, he didn't yank so tight, so the impacted layers weren't so hard.

He was slow to lean in this time, being ever watchful of her reaction to know if he should stop. Other than her shoulders turning inwards nervously, Lindiwe didn't back away even when he pressed his mouth over hers much more gently.

For a moment, they did nothing, and he had no idea how to proceed.

When her head moved but didn't dip away, revealing she'd done *something* in return, he realised he had no idea what was going on. He separated his consciousness from his physical self, and like an out-of-body experience he was all too familiar with, he viewed how his form and surrounding mist interacted with her.

This should help...

January 8th, 1738

Lindi flinched when his lips touched hers. She closed her eyes, unsure if she wanted to run away or stay.

Her heart felt as though it was beating a million times per second, her stomach fluttering with butterflies. Uncertainty and nervousness skittered beneath the surface of her skin, causing heat to flush throughout her body.

His mouth wasn't so hard this time, giving under her lips rather than crushing them against her teeth. When it didn't hurt, and he hadn't moved, she tentatively brushed her lips over his to instigate more and see what it was like.

He feels like... nothing.

Although she could feel him, his body lacked a temperature. She was glad he wasn't icy or too hot, but she'd expected some warmth, maybe a little bit of wetness. It was only when their lips locked and moved with each other a few times that her saliva made things slippery, and more enjoyable.

She peeked open her eyes to find his were wide, and she internally screamed before shutting them again. She'd rather just pretend he wasn't watching her so intently.

But he leaned to make it deeper, and she melted a little.

Okay, so my first kiss kind of sucked, but this is... She almost wanted to moan with how nice it felt, how it pleasurably tingled her lips.

But it was her mind that ran rampant, throwing her images that had plagued her for decades. She flinched at them, but didn't push or evade them, letting them play behind her eyelids to help her lean into this. She parted her lips a little further and wetted his by lightly slipping her tongue forward to taste him – again, nothingness.

Dear lord, am I actually going to have sex? Like actual sex and not some weird, freaky, wriggly little tendril doing its thing?

Her stomach unknotted itself as a pool of warmth began to grow, subtly dripping down until wet heat spread between her thighs. Not unfamiliar with the sensation, Lindi only squirmed due to the anticipation that began to build.

She hated admitting how quickly she caved for this. She'd been wanting to know what it truly felt like for a long time, and she couldn't believe it was finally happening. Suddenly her anger vanished in the wake of the touch she'd been craving, and the hopeful promise of more.

A little of her loneliness ebbed, and her annoyance about Weldir getting in the way of the friendship she'd been making dissipated with each foray of his mouth. She'd rather *this* companionship – to reach for the person she was tied to, rather than a total stranger in desperation.

Letting out a raspy moan when her nipples budded against the coarse material of her tunic, Lindi reached out to wrap her arms around his neck. She wanted to cling to him, to deepen their kiss and let him know she was ready for more.

Her arms wrapped around air and fell forward, making her smack her nose and forehead against his. She sucked in a gasp while pulling back to right herself with a struggle as she pushed *through* his intangible body.

"There is only so much of me right now," Weldir stated.

Her gaze flicked down to his lips, glistening and wet from her, and it felt naughty. Heat rose in her cheeks when her own felt a little puffier than normal, like they were swelling.

"Try again. I will give you something to hold."

When glitter shimmered against his chest, but the consistency looked different to the chalkiness of his face, she reached out. Cool hardness met her palm, and it reminded her of the barriers she could cast.

It wasn't him, not like his face.

He's trying.

He was making this work, despite the constraints of his abilities and form. She appreciated that more than he'd ever know. She could be disheartened that she was merely touching a magic barrier and not him, but the fact that he was doing this was enough.

She ran her hands up his chest and wrapped her arms around his neck. Only when Weldir leaned in did she meet him halfway.

This time, she moaned when his lips gently brushed hers and

she instantly deepened the contact. Lindi kissed him hard, trying with all her might to ignore how her heart attempted to betray her by uttering painful truths in her ear she just wanted to disregard for now.

That she didn't love him, nor truly desire him. That she was touching someone intimately out of curiosity and physical need, rather than because of lust for him. But even if every single little thing about their relationship was fucked up, he was the only person she trusted.

And that trust was superficial at best.

At least she knew he'd never hurt her; that had always been a constant.

M-maybe we can change that. Maybe this could be a start to more.

She wanted that more than anything.

When they kissed for too long, and her body began to painfully thrum for the next step he never took, she pulled back just enough so she could talk. She kept her gaze on his wetted lips to avoid his glossy, pitch-black eyes.

"A-are you going to touch or undress me?" she asked with a raspy, shaky voice.

She didn't want to seem pathetically needy by stripping on her own. Then again, she was suddenly acutely aware that Weldir was always... naked.

"Do you want me to touch you *or* undress you, Lindiwe? I cannot do both at the same time," he said, and she thought she heard the mildest humour in it.

Dear heavens, his sinfully rough voice wrapped around her senses more than ever. She couldn't help the shiver that cascaded across her skin, causing goosebumps to form in a wild wave. Even her pussy clenched when he said her name.

When his lips tightened, she looked up to greet his gaze just in time to see his brows knit together.

"Would you prefer if I didn't speak? You always seem to have an adverse reaction to my voice."

Her eyes widened. "Pardon? No." She hated that her face flushed with shy heat once more. "I actually like your voice very much. It's deep, and kind of rich."

"I... didn't know that." Then, parts of his face broke away

like ash and collected somewhere else on his body. "You don't make the truth of your thoughts obvious, and it's rather infuriating. You should have told me."

When fingertips danced against her skin just above her waistline, her stomach caved in and her unstimulated body went chaotic. She'd been craving touch for so long that even in its mildest form, the merest caress, she had to hold back her moan and the way she shuddered with his hand ghosting back and forth just above her pubic mound.

The drawstring of her pants was pulled on, and the band loosened around her waist. Lindi drew her legs up to help remove them, and for the first time, she noticed how the material tickled her thighs and calves on the way down.

My body feels so sensitive. Unusually so.

Her breaths were short and shallow, her skin hot to the point of nearly sweating, and her heart thumped so hard she felt it in the sensitive parts of her body, like her wrists and eardrums. It was as if she'd been sparked alive after being deadened for so long.

He undid the ties of her underwear – a thatch of material covering her privates like those worn in Sing Dynasty. It was much easier to wear underneath her trousers, and she'd adopted it rather than the pants women wore underneath their frocks.

"My physical self is lacking due to my mana being so low," Weldir said as he pulled it away. "My barriers are not dexterous, so I can give you my torso and legs to hold, but things like my hands, face, and cock will require what little I have. Would you rather look upon my face or have me touch you at the same time as I'm inside you?"

Oh gods, just the word *cock* had her thighs clamping with need.

"I-I have to choose between your face or hands?" Her heart raced a little faster, and her eyes slipped to the parts of his fingers that were visible. Then she darted her gaze up to what little there was of his face. "I don't really want to have sex with a headless person."

A deep and surprisingly pleasant chuckle rumbled around her. "My head is always where it's supposed to be. It's just not physical or visible if I move my outer layer from it."

Lindi nodded to say she understood, and his fingers pulled her thighs open, parting her so he could come closer. Wisps fluttered over her skin, parts of him that were physical pushing against her while other sections moved through her. The sensation was odd, like rare droplets of oil sluicing over her body.

It felt nice, and her toes curled when they sensually brushed or moved across the sensitive line of nerves going down her inner thighs. Reaching up, she placed her hands over the barrier's curve where his shoulders would be to hold on as she looked down.

She didn't know what kind of cock she was expecting, but she should have known it would be hard to see. The darkness of his realm often shadowed him, and it was only possible to see him due to a strange grey glowing silhouette. She saw a phallic shape, but without closer inspection, she couldn't note its details properly.

Widening her legs more to make it easier for him to get closer, she bit down on the inside of her bottom lip.

It looks a little... sm– Lindi gasped in surprise when his hips shunted forward and he managed to skilfully enter her in one move.

Her pussy lips pressed against his groin tightly, squishing her folds in a way that felt nice against her clit, making her instantly want to rub it against him. However, the rest...

Lindi stretched a leg to the side as if that would suddenly give her the ability to see what was going on inside her. *I thought it was supposed to hurt. Is it because he already broke my hymen?* But wasn't she supposed to be all tight and narrow?

Her lips twisted as worry nibbled away at her confidence. Women couldn't be too big down there, right? Or was Weldir undoubtedly small?

But he feels only a little bigger than his tendril. And his tendril was barely half the thickness of her pinkie finger.

Big, small, average, Lindi didn't mind the size of his penis, so long as *she* wasn't the problem. She just wanted to be close with him, to feel wanted and desired. She wanted to be touched, and she thought what was inside her could be pleasurable if he moved it back and forth. It was already pressing against a spot that was hot and swollen, making this feel far better than usual.

She just didn't know if this was a normal size for a man, as she'd never even seen a human penis.

"You look concerned," he said, causing her gaze to drift up to what remained of his face. Barely his left cheek, brow, and eye could be seen, although his lips and chin were entirely visible. "I can make it bigger."

Before she could answer to say she was fine with it, as she didn't want to change him if this was his natural size, her answer tore through her chest as a choking, pained, and quiet scream. White flashed across her sight as her back arched and her whole body locked up. Immediately she kicked as she tried to push him away, anything to get him away from her, from inside her – only to push at fucking air!

She'd never felt anything more painful, not even like the first time he'd foolishly penetrated deeper!

Lindi whimpered. *It feels like I'm being torn in half.*

"Too much?" he asked, just as the pressure let up and she whimpered again in agony. "I'm sorry, Lindiwe. I am... struggling to make myself the right size for you by only what I can see."

By what he can see? That didn't make any sense.

Tears welled in her eyes and her lips trembled, even when magic glowed around them and he healed her. She tried to give him a smile in gratitude, thankful the pain was quick, but her arousal had been ripped from her and trepidation replaced it.

I'd rather take too small than too big any day, she thought, as her legs relaxed around the physical parts of his narrow hips.

She thought anyone would feel that way. She'd rather his tiny tendril than to feel that burning, sharp pain again. Especially when a droplet of red floated up near her face, and she knew for certain that he'd torn her enough to bleed.

His voice was low and quiet as he asked, "Should I stop?"

Although thankful he'd asked her consent, Lindi shook her head.

"N-no. I'm okay now that you've healed me," she answered in a croaked voice.

To test their fit, she wiggled her hips side to side, finding she was much fuller now, and that it was comfortable. Actually, it was kind of nice, just stretching her enough so she could feel it.

She'd lost some of her confidence in him, but a few hiccups along the way were fine. Things didn't have to go perfectly their first time, so long as there was pleasure by the end.

Apparently if he moves just right, it will feel good.

Except, the moment he pulled back and quickly thrust forward, Lindi drew her knees up with a sharp gasp. She resisted the urge to recoil, hoping it was temporary, but each time he slammed in, flashes of white-hot pain sparked across her vision and through her very being. She felt it all the way down to her soul, which she didn't even own anymore.

After the third time, Lindi let out a cry.

"Stop." She shook her head with her nails clawing into her chest, knowing there was no point in grabbing him when she'd likely touch nothingness. "No more."

"Too hard? I can go softer."

Lindi grimaced and shook her head, not daring to look upon his face so she didn't have to see his expression – nor him see hers. She was thankful when her curls waved around her face and partially obscured it, wishing they'd cushion around her body as well, like a soft shield.

The next words that fell from her tasted meek and weak-hearted. "I don't want to do this anymore."

She'd completely lost her desire for the act and just wanted it all to cease.

And she felt awful about that to the point tears gathered once more, this time from the sting that was still present between her thighs, but also the one against her heart. She knew it wasn't his fault, that he wasn't doing this on purpose, but she'd built up so much anticipation for this and it was... ruined. It just felt awful to be repeatedly hurt, even by accident.

All at once, everything relented.

The pain faded, as did the pressure of him inside her, all in a puff of smoke. He didn't withdraw, just vanished entirely.

Lindi let out a sob when she realised he'd vacated the area completely, and he only ever did that when he was upset. Did she hurt his feelings, no matter how lightly he felt them? Was he as mortified and embarrassed as she was?

With regret roiling around in her stomach, she turned

physical. She reached for her undergarments and trousers and put them back on, wishing to be clothed again and pretend all this never happened. Then she grasped the floating handle of her satchel and yanked on it to draw it to her chest and hug it. She felt so awful for him, and depressed for herself, that she pressed her face against its leather and cried with shuddering breaths.

I want to go home, she thought, despite not having a home. What she really wanted was just a safe and comfortable place to digest this horrible moment in private.

To swallow the hard lump of loss and cuddle herself, since no one else would do it.

Despite everything, she still felt a familiar trickle leaking from her. For once, she was thankful for it, as she hoped it meant she wouldn't have to see or speak to him again for a while.

She thought she'd rather die in that moment.

"Do you want to stay or leave?" he asked, despite not actually being here.

"Leave," she whimpered.

She was gone within her next *false* breath.

THIRTY

A time unknown, but one of unhappy departures

With his toes pointing downwards and his realm keeping him afloat and weightless – not that it mattered – Weldir folded his arms as he watched the viewing disc. Night had long descended upon the world, and the crescent moon above offered minimal light for Lindiwe to see. Light gusts of wind rustled the trees and shrubs nearby, and their sounds were something he committed to memory for later – to insert into his own realm.

The Veil's forest lay just behind her, while the waterfall Lindiwe had spent many days at was just before her.

Between her and that cascade of frothing water was an impertinent half-Demon, who was grinning amicably at Weldir's mate.

Jabez, as he preferred to be called, had his hands behind his back with his shoulders loose and lacking tension, but his pointed ears were perked upright to listen carefully. His short white hair stuck up around his head haphazardly, messy from traversing through the forest but lacking any tangles, as if it was cleaned recently.

His clothing was the same, a cream tunic and well-fitted black breeches, and he wore his cloak.

Jabez's red eyes drifted over Lindiwe's form, darting side to side, before slowly coming back. His right eyebrow twitched slightly as it raised, and his grin fell as the long wait revealed the absence of Weldir.

"I thought he was going to speak with me himself," Jabez commented, his head tipping to the side. "This wasn't what I expected. Why are you here alone?"

Lindiwe folded her arms and grumbled, "He said he doesn't want to talk to you directly, unless I'm not here."

"Then wouldn't it have been better that way?" Jabez asked, and Weldir immediately noted the way her brows pinched in puzzlement. Jabez then raised a hand and shrugged. "Don't get me wrong, I like you, Lindiwe, but this is more of a business conversation. Much hangs in the balance, and that goes beyond you and I."

Such a cold answer, one that Weldir somewhat expected.

"What is it you seek from me?" Weldir asked, mediating the possibility of them having an in-depth conversation around this.

Lindiwe was likely to argue with Jabez just as much as Weldir, and he wanted to get this over with. He already lacked the desire to be here or even have this conversation.

Her arms tightened. "He asks what you want from him."

"I would prefer that you state it in the way I did," Weldir commanded, firmer than he intended.

Lindiwe flinched and lowered her head. "My apologies. He said, 'What is it you seek from me?'"

Jabez's red eyes trailed down her, likely noting the change in her body language, before darting them back to her face. Jabez probably thought she was being soft and submissive, but Weldir knew better.

She was biting back her anger in order to not bite at Weldir.

"I would like to relieve you of your torment," Jabez answered, so confidently, so brazenly, that Weldir thought him foolish.

"One must be tormented in order to be relieved of it," he stated, which she repeated word for word.

White brows furrowing, the halfling was obviously perplexed. "Are you not trapped in your realm?"

Weldir saw no point in lying, nor hiding the truth.

"Trapped is one way to put it. Yes, I am forced to remain within my realm; however, it's not only for everyone else's safety, but my own. My soul should not leave it, as it has no true body to house it. If it were to escape, I would be unable to control how far it spread, and the flames would consume every living thing in their path. I am a danger to all."

"Is that how you killed the other deities?"

Weldir snapped his fangs with a quiet growl, which only she heard. Once more, she flinched, but in surprise.

I should not react. It affects only her.

"How the others died is not my fault, but the product of Demons and their vileness of spirit. When your kind have not fully evolved, there is nothing but darkness containing you. A sickness that eats away at everything it touches if it has nothing to house. *That* is what destroyed the others. My birthing was merely a catalyst that could have been prevented."

Jabez rolled his eyes and lifted his right hand, waving it side to side. "Whatever. What if we managed to obtain you a physical form? Then you could do as you want, go wherever you please."

Weldir couldn't help scoffing at that. "You have no such abilities."

He lifted a finger. "True, but that's from a lack of trying. There must be some way we can give you that, and I'd be willing to dedicate myself to it. There are many hidden libraries within Nyl'theria ready to be unearthed and rediscovered. An answer may be there."

"And it may not," Weldir retorted.

"No, but there could be a path to that answer. I have no moral compass to abide by, and I would be willing to shed the blood from my own veins if it meant your release. I would leave no option unturned, no matter how depraved it may seem to others."

What Jabez offered seemed rather promising.

No matter how many souls Lindiwe found him, or servants they produced to assist her, there was nothing Weldir could personally do to alter his predicament. He was what he was, how he was. He could grow his power indefinitely, but it would never give him a true physical form.

He'd never be able to smell the world, interact with it, or merely touch the satin petals of a flower and know what that felt like. *This*, what he was doing now, was all he could do.

He was unsure if his mother, the Gilded Maiden, could ever help him achieve a physical change. Or if she ever would.

Yet he was starkly aware that no such gift came without a

price.

"What do you want in exchange?" Weldir asked, his tone dull to hide his potential interest even from her.

"Remove your wards from the portals you have over the world," Jabez stated. "The Demons and I want to use them to move between the two worlds freely."

Lindiwe told him of the other portals.

Weldir didn't mind, as it mattered little. Jabez could go back and forth through any portals for all he cared. If Weldir were to block the Elven side of this male from passing through, he'd have to stop *all* Elves. And, considering communication was all but null, they wouldn't be able to ask him to lower it. He could control what *kind* of spirit was permitted to pass or not.

Then again, Weldir liked the idea of torturing Jabez a little. The other world was in reach, but only for him.

The Elysians also, in their own way, wanted him to be able to return to their city one day.

"Is that all?" Weldir asked, surprised he asked for so little.

It took Weldir a while to notice that Jabez's legs were wide and that his stance was firm. The youth in his features was hardened by someone who was learning to take up the mantle of command. It was only now that he saw it.

Which meant he was becoming dangerous.

"No," he declared. "I've gathered through different kinds of intelligence that, due to your lack of physical form, you are incapable of touching any world but your own metaphysical one. If I help you break free of that constraint, you would offer me your assistance in destroying Lezekos. You'd lower your wards to show good faith, as well as reveal your alliance to us."

"So you believe you need the power of a god in order to succeed?"

"Demi-god," Jabez rudely pointed out, with a sly grin pulling the edges of his mouth upwards. "I don't *need* anything, but it would surely make things much faster."

Floating, his body subtly moved up and down as his mist coiled tighter, only to release, and Weldir let a pause hang over them.

But he already knew the answer.

"I have no desire to destroy the Elysians, nor the humans.

Death and slaughter is for those living. I am merely what comes after life has been stolen."

Jabez's grin soured, and he tipped his head forward with a dangerous gaze. "You are currently in the way, Weldir. Whether you assist or not, if you continue to keep up your ward, then there will always be a bone of contention between us. We will always war."

Weldir laughed at that, which made Lindiwe's blank expression narrow. "You wish to fight an untouchable being?"

"But you're not untouchable anymore, are you? You've given yourself a vulnerability." Jabez placed his hands behind his back once more and straightened. Then his features turned cold and expressionless. "She even stands right before me."

Lindiwe's lips parted as she took half a step back in surprise, as well as defensively, and turned incorporeal to make sure she and their unborn child growing within her were out of harm's reach. She shook her head, as if she didn't understand exactly what he'd known all along.

Weldir didn't even need to retort; the male continued on without care that she was right before him as he spoke mercilessly.

"I like her, I really do. I see no reason why she should need to be dragged into a battle that has nothing to do with her."

Lindiwe was slow to respond on his behalf, her mouth opening and closing as she fisted her hands. "Weldir said it has nothing to do with him either. He's doing what is asked of him, that is all."

With no reward in sight, either.

Weldir didn't mind. Maybe his lack of physical heart meant he didn't feel such pestering desires and needs. He wasn't content with his situation, but he also felt no reason to be discontent.

"This is what has been gifted me, instead of my destruction. A way to live beyond my prism," Weldir continued. "I aid to repay that kindness."

Jabez's face twisted into a mild snarl. "Then don't join in our fight, but remain out of it. Be truly neutral and remove your wards preventing the Demons from going through the portals."

"I cannot." When Jabez gave a menacing snarl, Weldir tipped

his head in the direction he rolled his eyes. Looking at him was becoming an eyesore, and he was growing tired of this conversation. "This is why I felt there was no need to speak with you. I cannot – *will* not – give you what you seek."

"Then you put Lindiwe in the path of bloodshed."

"I have nothing to do with this!" she exclaimed, finally speaking for herself.

"It doesn't matter. You are his mate; therefore you are as much in the way as him. He puts you in danger, not me."

Her eyes narrowed rather hatefully at Jabez, but she did relay for Weldir: "He said, 'Then that is how it will be. I'm not the one who has instigated this. You selfishly seek something I cannot give.'"

A laugh fell from Jabez, one that was resentful and cruel. "You really don't care for your own mate, do you? No wonder she dislikes you so much."

Weldir's form floated downwards, deflated by his words and how true the latter may be. He may not show it, but he did care for Lindiwe. Yet it was true that she was unhappy with their bond. Especially after recent failed activities.

He'd tried to give her what she sought, and it had been a horrible experience for her, and a rather embarrassing one for himself. He wasn't upset that she'd wanted to stop, but him being the reason for it, how he kept hurting her, did make guilt and regret fester within his consciousness.

He was a god who couldn't even 'do it' right.

There were many things he failed at.

Once more reminded of his shameful floundering, Weldir let out a sigh. Now, more than ever, guilt plagued him, but it was only strengthened by his next words.

"Lindiwe is strong and resilient. She is also deathless. You court your own failures going toe to toe with her. You may end up finding your demise at her hands, just like many others."

Many Demons and human occultists had died due to her. And with Weldir's magic aiding her, and all that she'd learned from the Anzúli so far, she was rather formidable.

Perhaps he'd never told her how much he admired her strength, because she was rather slow to relay his words. Her eyes also widened with surprise, as if she hadn't expected him to state them.

"So you'd rather see her suffer than remove your wards?"

"It's how it must be."

And there was nothing Weldir could do about it.

He could fold to Jabez and give him what he sought, and doom the very last of the Elysian Elves. The loss of their worship would no doubt destroy his mother, as she needed it in order to live. Weldir, on the other hand, had no such ties.

He didn't need anyone to believe in him.

But what Jabez asked from him was too much.

And even if it wasn't, Weldir had no desire to be part of a mass destruction. He didn't want to be the cause of bloodshed, as he found war to be a pointless endeavour. Nyl'theria was large enough to house both the Demons and the Elysians, but only if the Demons ceased their hunts and put their efforts into building a civilised life without bloodshed.

Then again, that would require them to self-destruct enough until the non-evolved Demons were consumed and whatever Elves had been eaten in the past were absorbed by others. It was a vicious cycle that could only end internally.

They were currently too feral to be led.

Jabez, in that regard, had been born too soon. All he could do was lead the few that were in Austrális, rather than the hundreds of thousands that needed controlling in Nyl'theria.

"If that is how you must be, then I see no need to continue this conversation. There are other avenues I can put my energy into." Jabez strutted forward, causing Lindiwe to back up a step before she held her ground and looked up at him in her incorporeal form. She held no fear, but her gaze was angered. "But you will come to regret this decision, Weldir."

Just as he reached her, he stopped and towered over her with a sneer.

"You let me believe I was making a friend in you," Lindiwe yelled up at him, her ire a hot blade that was often quickly unsheathed and wielded.

It was nice that it wasn't aimed at Weldir for once.

"And you would have found one, if not for his choice today. If not for your tie to him. You've *both* made an enemy today," Jabez bit out, before walking through Lindiwe's transparent form like a rude and impertinent child. He lifted a hand to wave at them dismissively without turning around. "Her pain is entirely yours and the Elves' fault. I'll wear you all down by a war of attrition."

The only fault will be yours, halfling. It would be his decision.

Weldir tsked as Jabez walked into the tree line of the Veil.

"I should have struck him," Lindiwe muttered, slamming the bottom of her fist into the other awaiting palm. "What a conniving bastard! I can't believe he could turn on someone so quickly. None of this has ever been my fault."

Weldir offered no words of sentiment or comfort, as he had no idea how to do so elegantly. He'd likely just make a mess of it, upsetting her even worse, as per usual.

He was just glad she hadn't turned on him in her rage, and he hoped she wouldn't.

At least he'd gained a barrier between Lindiwe and Jabez, although at the cost of her safety. *Then again, this was sure to come eventually.* If Jabez sought the lowering of Weldir's ward, he would have eventually turned on her even if they'd never spoken.

I have put my offspring in danger as well. The fact that Nathair and Orson were friendly with each other made him want to create more for this continent. *They will need a larger number if it's discovered they belong to me.* Jabez and his army would no doubt target them at some point otherwise.

What an annoyance, he solemnly thought as he watched her through his viewing disc, noting the way a gust of wind swept through her clothing. *I wanted nothing to do with this.*

THIRTY-ONE

February 7th, 1738

One of the first things Lindi liked to do when placed in a new part of the world was to see what life was like for other humans.

Everywhere she went, people and societies were incredibly varied, and the continent of Zafrikaan was no different. However, unlike most of the places she'd been to, the ways humankind lived here were completely contrasting.

One part of the continent held tribal people who lived in small wooden huts and predominantly hunted and gathered to survive. In another part, not very far away, was an entire society of those who had houses made from clay with straw-thatched roofs. In another, they lived among the trees, their homes so different from those who lived in the drier plains of the desert in the north.

But there was always a constant that Lindi was used to: destruction.

Just like the rest of the world, people were struggling to survive against the chaos of Demons.

This continent was apparently one of the largest in the world, and the Anzúli were spread thin in order to protect as many people as possible. Those who had ventured into the forest did not return to any of the temples, but Lindi had seen that out of the handful that had gone there, only three had survived the journey. They used all their means, with the aid of the humans, to push back the nightmarish beings of fang and claw.

But there seemed to be a solution the entire world had

constructed without ever speaking to each other: walls.

The grand and beautiful people to the east, between the northern desert and the southern rainforest, had erected such barricades to protect themselves. They'd held back the Demons with spears and arrows, and built something impactful.

Wooden walls stood tall with jutting spears that had been wisely nestled between logs and pressed clay that sealed them in. It was almost like an echidna in the shape of a snake had been jammed into the bottom, ensuring that any Demon that did attack struggled to even reach the top of the wall. The ingenuity of it was something to be admired.

This was the first continent she'd been to, other than Austrális, that had such a large desert.

Upon realising that the trees were filled with monsters, and that the sun brought peace and protection, those who hadn't erected walls fled to the north and into the desert. There, as a large community, they kept the monsters at bay, working together to ensure everyone's safety.

The way they allowed everyone into the fold showed Lindi that humankind, when in dire peril, was a unit of people. She'd seen that same open-heartedness all over the world.

She'd also seen much cruelty, but she often tried to ignore that. Or sometimes she didn't, and she intervened to offer up quiet justice where she could.

Many of the animals had felt a similar instinct and fled to the grassy desert plains, finding relief in the tall, shading trees when they could. Upon seeing quite a few familiar animals, Lindi realised this was a location from which Weldir had stolen some creatures and placed them in Austrális. She had yet to learn where he'd taken the wolves and bears from, but she was sure one day she'd be sent there.

There were still many places and lands she hadn't visited, but she thought fondly of the *city* she'd recently been to.

Houses there were strong, tall, and sturdy. The bottoms of them were a clay brown with swirling designs, and then white to the roofing. The roofs themselves were all made of a similar thatching and often needed replacing.

The city, a part of the Shanti Empire, was grand, vibrant, and full of life despite the occasional Demon that sniffed outside their walls. They'd managed to expand an already erected wall outside of its original foundations to include basic farms, as well as giving homes to many refugees who sought sanctuary.

The darkness of her clothing had looked out of place compared to the bright and colourful loose clothing the other humans wore, but she'd done well to remain hidden. She'd perfected the craft of stealth over her many years.

From a distance, she'd seen a woman with swarthy-brown skin who wore a yellow wrap around her short, tightly coily black hair. Her dress had been a bright blue, and similar to the colour of the flowers she'd seen blooming between farming sections. Many beads made up bracelets and even a heavy necklace, each one clacking as she stepped with a grain winnower on her hip filled with an array of food. Her male companion had dressed similarly in beads but also wore chunks of gold. He'd worn a patterned yellow shirt with long, wide sleeves over a matching knee-length waist wrap.

Both had worn sandals to protect their feet from the impacted dirt and sand.

She'd liked the vibrancy of their attire, the draped clothing perfect to shade against the dry sun, but loose enough to allow a draft.

At night, the city men had patrolled the outside of the city with spears and fended off Demons with practised swiftness, minimising casualties to the occasional death.

They were strong, hearty people – survivors – just like the rest of the world she'd seen thus far. Only the bravest, the intuitive, and the quickest thinkers as a unified group had managed to survive the first unexpected waves of Demons.

Lindiwe liked to see that in humankind. Liked seeing they were capable of survival even amidst the carnage. She adored that this was a trait she'd seen everywhere she'd gone.

They were thoughts for a later time, but it allowed hope to swell in her chest as she completed her *very important* task.

Lindi was doing what she liked to call 'nesting.'

Her stomach was rounded, swollen, and already the aches and pains that came before birthing were riddling her back, ankles, and sometimes came in the form of headaches. She was lethargic, but despite that, she'd been collecting and cleaning cloth to make herself soft bedding, among other things, like for cleaning any messes. Flying while this heavily pregnant came with its battles, and she could only do small jaunts. She often went to a nearby watering hole, returned to boil the water, and then was almost tapped out of energy for a few hours.

Thankfully, she'd been wise enough to find this collection of clay huts that had been abandoned and mostly lay in ruin due to the Demons. She'd evicted all those that huddled in the other buildings through the day and then erected a magical barrier around the small village.

Weldir had been silent, likely slumbering. Or maybe he was just avoiding her as much as she was him.

I hope he just remains asleep forever except for when he wants more kids, she thought with a grumble as she pushed her bedding around into a comfortable bundle, refusing to speak out loud in case he somehow heard her. *I'm still so embarrassed. Maybe even a little traumatised.*

Lindi hadn't gotten over their terrible sex experiment. She'd been so excited to try it and was now completely disinterested in the idea.

Not with him, and not with anyone, for that matter.

In some ways, there was a relief in that.

It was something she no longer wanted, so she no longer thought about it. She found solace that she didn't feel so alone because she was no longer attracted to the idea of a physical connection.

And then there was the whole Jabez issue that she was still furious over – although her hormones might be making her angrier than necessary. She was a little angry at Weldir, too, and at herself for not listening to him, but she was tired of feeling so utterly out of place and alone in the world she was born into.

So she was trying to let go. To get over all the things that constantly nagged and bothered her.

She'd just focus more on herself and their children, doing what she could for them all. She'd already been considering what kind of horn variations she'd like for the one currently in her belly, and what other characteristics she could give them, like Nathair's fins or Orson's spikes.

I don't think it's wise to make them aquatic on this continent.

There was plenty of water, but there were also a lot of Demons that filled it. They found shade in the thick reeds or buried themselves in the sediment during the day. *There are a lot of big cats.*

She smiled at the idea of a spotty Duskwalker, and hoped such fur patterns like a cheetah were possible. The options seemed endless.

Once she was happy with her bedding on her recently swept flooring, she sat down and leaned against the intricately threaded stick wall. The outside was coated in clay, leaving it watertight – it also helped to keep out the worst of the day's heat and the cooler night. Then she pulled out her journal, one where she detailed the lives of humans and all the different animals she'd seen.

As she was staring at a drawing she'd made of a large and imposing tusked creature, one with big, flapping ears and thick, wrinkled skin, she thought, *I really do need to make a proper home.*

Austrális would always be the place she returned to, like her heart belonged there. She needed to find or build a place where she could store her precious items.

She turned a page, seeing she was close to the end of the thickly bound leather book. She'd stopped using a quill and ink a long time ago, preferring to use the ink stick she'd found in her travels. Her fingertips were often stained, but she didn't mind – except for when it went under her fingernails.

She brushed the pads of her fingers over the description and drawing she'd done of a crocodile, wondering if such a skull would be too heavy for one of her children.

It's so strange to think that there are so many varying animals in the world. Some of them she'd learned the names of by the encyclopedia she'd stolen from the great library in Turkane and used a translation spell to read, but there were many others she didn't know in English. She just adopted the name they said from where they belonged.

She cupped her chin and incidentally smudged ink down her jaw. *I like the horns of the impala.* They were knobby and thin, with a subtle spiral, and she thought they would look like a wonderful crown on top of a predatory skull.

Lindi gave a small wince before rubbing where her unborn child kicked. It was like she was trying to soothe herself as well as them.

"I'm trying to figure it out. You're not here yet and already you're so demanding." And even if they were, she had all the time in the world to figure out how she wanted them to form. "Just give me a while."

With night beginning to creep in, Lindi watched the mesmerising play of colours splash across the dusking sky. Out of all the buildings on this crest, shielded underneath a large umbrella thorn acacia, she liked this one best. It overlooked the edge of a ridge and gave her a wonderful view of the grassy plains below.

For as far as the eye could see, there was life – flora and fauna. Yet, it was so quiet that she could hear even the smallest insect not far away.

I guess there are things I'm thankful for since giving away my soul. She'd seen much beauty, none of it possible without Weldir. Her new length of life, the ability to travel into the horizon, and the safety his magic provided offered her incomparable freedom. No other human, past or future, would ever experience such wonder and awe.

Feeling the Earth on a spiritual level, investigating its life and flourishing colours, its smells, and even textures, was a blessing. It often left her spirit enlightened, as if she'd touched the mesmerising veils of life and saw beyond them in a way no other could.

Just this scene – how the plains below swam with golden sunlight, as if the sky touched the ground and created an ocean of unfathomable, intangible glory – was enthralling.

With the gentle warmth of the ending summer billowing in a refreshing breeze, Lindi let her tired eyes droop. When night finally won against the light, and she had Weldir's magic to keep her safe and snug, Lindi shut her eyes to rest.

I'm starting to rather like the quiet.

These long lulls brought on a sense of calm, and Lindi was in control of every minute. *Well, when I don't have a ghastly shadow speaking to me from beyond the void, that is.*

Lindi stirred when she heard a shout, only to snap her eyes open with a sharp gasp and sit up in shock. Except her body couldn't bend like that with a giant ball attached to her middle and she kind of flailed for a moment. Pitch night greeted her, and she squinted in the darkness, to no avail.

"Lindiwe," Weldir called, louder than usual.

Lindi searched for him, but she knew – even though she couldn't see – that he wasn't actually there.

With a groan, she rubbed the heels of her palms into her sleep-dusted eyes while shutting them. They ached like never before, and her fatigue was just as bad as ever. She'd probably only had a few hours' sleep – then again, she couldn't quite tell.

"Why did you wake me?" she whined, rolling to her side before getting on her hands and knees so she could toss her stomach forward while rearing back to sit. She straightened her legs out before her but with enough of a gap that her belly had a place to nestle. Then she lowered a hand to the ground behind her for support. "And what's with your tone?"

It almost sounded... panicked, and that didn't seem like him.

"I'm doing all the hard work here, so the least you could do is let me sleep," she continued, waving at her pregnant belly. "I don't get to slumber forever like you do."

Right now, she'd love that more than anything. To just sleep and sleep until her body didn't feel like it was straining.

Silence greeted her, and for a second, she thought she may have imagined him calling out to her. It wouldn't be the first time she'd dreamt of him saying her name – although this had less of a naughty element to it.

When too long passed, she peeked around at the nothingness. "Weldir?"

"I don't know how to tell you this without upsetting you. I... don't know how to share this delicately."

That instantly sobered Lindi from her sleepy daze. Alertness clutched her, and she fumbled in the dark for her lantern and tinder box. She needed to know where everything was in case she needed to move quickly.

She doubted she was in danger, as she could still sense the

barrier dome was in place.

"What's wrong?" she asked, striking her tinder box and setting the oil alight so she could see. Her items were mostly put away in her satchel, except for her journal and food. "Sometimes it's best to just spit it out."

"Nathair is... dead."

Leaning awkwardly to the side on her bundle of multicoloured bedding, Lindi paused just after she tucked her journal into her satchel. Her ears twitched in a pulling back motion, like she was checking they were working and she'd heard him correctly.

This horrible, sickening feeling clutched her stomach and hardened around her swollen belly in a contraction. Within a single heartbeat, her pulse was pounding in her eardrums, her throat, and in her chest. Coldness bled through her veins.

"What do you mean... he's dead?" she whispered, like the words couldn't be true. "You're a god. They're... yours. You said they can't... *die*."

"I was wrong."

Tears didn't have time to well in her eyes; they were so heavy and profuse that they quickly flowed. Her bottom lip trembled, as she knew Weldir wouldn't joke or lie about this.

"What do you mean you were wrong?!" she screamed, rolling back firmly onto her backside to cover her face. She clawed at her forehead when an agony she didn't know existed lanced her entire being. "How could this happen?! Y-you promised!"

Well, he'd never truly said he knew for certain, but she'd taken his words as a guarantee. And now it felt like her heart was about to give out.

She didn't care that her children were... were *monsters*. They were hers! They were beautiful, strong creatures, and they weren't allowed to die!

They are meant to be deathless, just like me!

"You know I am not omniscient," Weldir stated quietly.

"I know," she sobbed out through hiccupping tears shuddering her chest. Her mouth was sticky, and her saliva thick and clinging from the roof and bottom of it. "I know that, but *still*!"

Why hadn't she felt this horrible change in the world? How

could she have slept peacefully through such a terrible thing? How could that make her feel undoubtedly *worse*?

Within mere moments, her eyes and lips swelled from the onslaught of her tears, yet nothing could compare to the twisting ache coiling tighter and tighter in her chest. Her lungs shuddered as her hands shook against her face.

Lindi didn't know how to process this. Something she'd never been afraid of, had never been prepared for, because... how could a *god's* child die?

"Grab your artefacts. I think it's best if I bring you to my realm."

With a watery cry, Lindi just sightlessly fisted the strapping of her satchel and nodded. She turned into a Phantom to ease the transition, as she always found it easier when she was in the form he could touch. It didn't pull on her stomach so hard, like she'd been thrown off a cliff.

Other than the glow of her lantern being lost, his realm didn't look all that different than night. Weightlessness lifted her, yet it was like she was sinking with a lead ball resting over her sternum and she was drowning. She knew that wasn't true, but the waves of her grieving emotions were crashing over her, and she couldn't make it to the surface to breathe through her heaving chest.

She finally peeked open her swollen eyes to look at him.

He wasn't curled up in pain like she was. He wasn't crying, wasn't shuddering with the loss. He looked the fucking same, just *floating* there half visible, like nothing was the matter.

She wanted him to hurt too – to know it all meant something to him. She didn't even want strange, monstrous children to begin with, so why was she the one dying on the inside instead of him?

"*How?* How did it happen?" she croaked, covering her face in her hands once more to cry into them.

She almost considered turning physical, like turning into a Phantom in the 'real' world, so she could escape her tears. She wanted to shed the fear and grief that clung to her body and rattled her very bones.

"I believe Orson crushed his skull, but I'm not certain. I was not watching at the time." Weldir folded his arms and turned his head to the side. "He waits by Nathair's skull."

Lindi hated the way a nasty creature crawled inside her, full of disappointment and blame. A Demon was one thing, but his own brother? And worse still, she hated coming to the realisation that she may have had a favourite child.

Simply because he was her... first.

The first to be born, the first to hold, the first who ever spoke to her. Nathair was where she'd been setting all her hopes and dreams, knowing one day he may have allowed her to walk beside his slithering form. He was patient with her, unlike her other children, and he may have joined her across the world to teach the others.

And it didn't help that, out of all her children, Orson was the most... aggressive. He snapped and snarled and warded her away, even despite Nathair's promises of safety.

She didn't want to feel hate towards Orson, didn't want to cast the blame at him when he didn't know, but... it was there. It bubbled beneath the surface, and she tried everything in her might to keep it down, to keep it in. To shift the blame elsewhere, but there was no one else except her and Weldir.

With all her heart, she blamed him for not knowing, for not somehow stopping it, but she felt she was somehow at fault too.

I should have been here. I should have been watching!

Yet her children were adults who did not want her around. Most didn't trust her, *except* Nathair. And they were hundreds of thousands of miles apart.

How am I supposed to protect them when they are all so far away?!

Why did Weldir have to ask this of her? She'd been okay with it when she thought they were deathless, formidable, indestructible beings.

To know that wasn't true... was utterly terrifying. They were so far apart, out of her reach when she tended to another, and incapable of protecting each other... or themselves.

Did that mean she had to keep them apart? To stop them from creating any meaningful bonds?

But that sounds so lonely.

"I need you to collect his skull for me, Lindiwe," Weldir stated.

Lindiwe lowered her hands fully from her face. "Is that all you have to say to me?" she asked with a shake in her voice, before she inhaled. All the building rage and sorrow mingled into one, and she threw her hands out to the side and clenched them into tight fists. "It's like you don't even care! One of our children just died and all you want to talk about is his skull?! I don't want to see it!"

She didn't want to see the broken pieces of him.

She didn't want to be anywhere near it, let alone Orson right now.

Lindi just wanted a damn *moment* to digest this! It was like she'd taken a bite out of something and tried to swallow it without chewing. She was suffocating, choking on it, and the only person before her didn't have the heart to *help*.

"Of course I care!" Weldir roared, eliciting a gasp from her when he shunted forward to be less than a foot from her face. The bridge of his nose was scrunched up tightly, and his lips – the half of his mouth she could see – were pulled back to reveal large fangs. "Do not think this does not burden me as it does you."

She wanted to believe that, she really did, but she had all this rage and doubt in her and she just couldn't. He couldn't understand, not to the level Lindi did.

"What?" she snipped out, closing the distance between them to snarl into his face as much as he did hers. "Because you lost a *servant*?"

Through his chalky outline, his left eye formed like the right one, and they both narrowed. "That is vindictive," he bit, the scrunch of his nose deepening until pieces of it flaked off to join his pointed left ear.

"I am their mother!" She patted her chest as her tears bubbled faster, harder, and somehow wetter. "I carry them! I hold them, take care of them, give them their identities while you sit here doing *nothing*. You can't know what this feels like. I... *love* them!"

"They are mine, just as much as yours! Do you not think it does not weigh on me that I am incapable of being there? I *watch*, Lindiwe, as there is nothing more I can do." His head jerked as he tsked, and he reared it back with a shake. "Do you really think me this cold? This... callous? Lindiwe, I care for them just as much, but I lack the ability to cry, the ability to *feel* heartache. I cannot show you, but that does not mean this does not pain me. At least *you* have that release."

"Then *you* collect his skull like a damn trophy!" she screamed, before letting out a squeal when the child inside her punted her so hard that it felt like her ribcage was about to snap.

She covered it with her hand and released a deep sob, her lips parting as she let out all the agony plaguing her. She felt awful that she was probably stressing her unborn baby with her insanely rapid heartbeat and shallow breaths.

A shuddered exhale fell from her trembling lips before she bit down on the bottom one so hard she feared she'd draw blood. "It's not fair. I shouldn't have to go through this."

Then Weldir did something he should have from the very start.

He came forward and placed whatever physical parts of him he did have around her in the form of a hug. Lindi fought him at first, shoving her hands forward only to pass through air or nick the many edges of him. But the longer and harder he squeezed, the more she realised she needed to be embraced.

She lifted her hands to claw at his back to bring him closer, and whimpered when she lacked purchase. Then, suddenly, invisible solidness formed, and she knew he'd placed a barrier around his torso to give her something. Lindi buried her tear-stained face into the crook of his neck and wept.

A hand stroked her hair delicately, as if he'd been practising how to be gentle. The motion was soothing, even if nothing could temper the maelstrom of emotions bleeding from her heart. Their child continued to kick between them, but even that felt lighter than it had seconds before.

"I do not want Nathair's skull for such a reason, Lindiwe," he murmured quietly near her ear. "I want to keep it so I can protect it, keep it safe here, in my realm. We don't know what could happen in the years to come. I would like to keep all our avenues available."

"What does that even *mean*?" she croaked, her voice cracking.

"It means I cannot promise anything, but I will try. That's all

I can say. I can see this will pain you, but I cannot touch that world. You must do it and then make those pieces intangible for me."

Lindi nodded to say she understood, but refused to let go of him. It was the closest she'd ever felt to him, even if her chest felt hollower than ever.

I wish he was warm.

More than ever, she wished he felt... real. Human, even.

Not the semi-solid spirit that haunted her every moment.

Then he said something that touched her all the way down to the pit of her despair. "I will always be here for you, Lindiwe. Even if it doesn't seem like it."

THIRTY-TWO

February 9th, 1738

Only when Lindi thought she could brave facing Orson and retrieving Nathair's skull, did she leave the comfort of Weldir's weightless realm. He'd thankfully stayed with her the entire time as she wept, although she did release him from holding her at some point.

She didn't know how long she'd stayed there – hours, days, weeks, possibly years – but the passage of time had felt gruelling and endless.

And despite it all, she did not feel any better.

She'd just managed to suck in her emotions long enough to do this. Then she could go back to grieving in peace.

Lindi wanted to protect Nathair's skull, too, now that Weldir had shared *why* he truly wanted it. It was... theirs, and they needed to be responsible for it. Whatever his unspoken promise was, she hoped it would one day come to fruition.

Even if it didn't, knowing a piece of him still existed was all she wanted.

Oddly enough, Weldir offered to come with her to take this emotional journey. For the first time, she witnessed him consuming a soul beyond his normal means.

It was actually kind of disgusting.

He reached into his own mouth almost elbow deep and somehow pulled a soul from within his stomach. The strangest part was these gooey, inky black strings that were attached between him and the white, deadened soul.

He then shoved the white flaming spirit into his chest, and it crackled and sparked as the dusty ribbons of his body, like multi-layered see-through veils, scattered through it. They mingled together, as if his self was attaching to it and all around it.

Within his darkness, he became fully formed for the very first time – that she had seen. But she'd already witnessed all the pieces of him individually, and she'd been able to puzzle out what he looked like in completeness.

A chiselled face; short, wisping hair; and a lean, muscular body. His horns looked hard and somewhat glossy in comparison to the rest of him, and his pointed ears flicked.

"Are you ready?" he asked, offering out his clawed hand.

The tears she'd managed to hold back renewed and bubbled along her waterline and dotted her eyelashes. She took it because, right then, she needed someone, *him*, more than ever.

He dematerialised them from his realm and to Earth, within his mist that extended along the Veil. All of a sudden, her perception of him shifted even in her Phantom form. All she felt was pressure, as if the reality of this world and his did not match.

He also became half-formed once more, only visible enough that he appeared like what she usually saw. It didn't help that the sun seemed to dismiss him even further, as if Weldir was best seen in the shadows – like his pitch-black world.

She let out a whimper when she saw Orson not even a few metres from them.

He was seated on the ground, his hind legs bent like that of a dog, and his hands held up his bowed torso. He stared down at the broken white pieces of Nathair's skull, with his tail tapping and his orbs bright fucking *yellow*, as if he was delighted at winning whatever game they'd played.

She realised then that he had no idea what he'd done, but it did nothing to lessen the ghastly sting.

Knowing what was to come next, Lindi turned physical. Her hand went through Weldir's, and it reminded her of how she could hold her children in her Phantom form, and how they turned ghostly with her. Weldir was always on that side, untouchable to her when she was corporeal. And her children's skulls never turned incorporeal, no matter how much she tried to will it for their safety.

The moment she was physical, and her scent fluttered across the wind, Orson turned to them. On all fours, he lowered himself protectively around Nathair's skull with joyful yellow orbs turning bright red. A growl rumbled from his chest, warning them of his deadly intent should they approach.

As Lindi had expected, words and emotion clogged in her throat, and she tried everything within her might to keep them at bay. Weldir floated forward, being her voice when she told him she doubted she could remain impartial and calm.

In her heart, regret and guilt simmered because, as she looked over Orson – who had just murdered his own brother – she felt... hate. She didn't want to, and she knew none of this was truly his fault, but it was his meaty, large, dangerous hand that had dealt the death blow. That had rent its claws through her heart, and she didn't know if it would ever stop bleeding.

The child safely stowed away within her womb wriggled at her increased heart rate and breaths, fretting from the power and sound of her panic. For their sake, she wished she could calm herself, but it was not within the realm of possibility right then.

She held the side of her rounded, firm stomach, pressing on it as a way to soothe them and herself.

"Stay away," Orson growled in a guttural voice, monstrous and hard to decipher.

"We must collect Nathair's skull," Weldir stated firmly, inching his way closer. "Step aside so we can."

Lindi winced when Orson cupped his hand around the broken pieces and swept them across the ground, closer to his chest protectively.

"Mine," he warned.

Weldir shook his head, just as Lindi braved finally taking a step closer. It was one of the hardest ones she'd ever taken, and her hands shook as her bottom lip trembled. She licked at it, and all she tasted was the salt of her fresh tears. She wiped her face to remove the evidence of them, but they were easily replaced.

"You have broken his skull," Weldir informed him, which only caused the twist in her heart to deepen. He placed himself between Orson and Lindi's line of sight of each other when their offspring snapped his fangs at her.

"Yes. I win," Orson grated, only to stomp a front hand forward – precariously close to the broken pieces. ***"Stay back!"***

"You have won your little game, but you have destroyed him in the process."

Orson's orbs shifted from red to dark yellow, and he tilted his head. *"No. He returns."*

Once more, Weldir shook his head. "Nathair will not return." Those words broke Lindi a little more, and she choked back her whimper. "You have... killed him. You did this by breaking his skull. I have already collected his soul."

Lindi's brows drew together at that. *He collected his soul?*

Orson's head reared back as blue flickered in his orbs for just a moment. *"No... he returns. Always returns."*

"It has been longer than a day, Orson." Weldir waved his hand to the side, in the opposite direction from where Lindi cautiously approached, to distract him. "He will not return. You must sense this."

"No!" Orson roared, as the bottoms of his orbs, flicking between red and blue, wavered and broke. Floating drops leaked from them, and he stamped a hand forward again, smashing it against the ground. ***"Wrong. You lie!"***

"Stop!" Lindi pleaded with a scream, reaching her hand forward as a shuddering sob ripped out of her. "You're breaking it further!"

Orson let out a gasping whine when he lifted his hand off of the part of Nathair's skull he'd snapped – one of his thin and delicate jaw bones. He started brushing it all into a pile, as if that would help to put it back together, and his orbs finally held blue.

"Stop touching it! Stop... *ruining* it!" Lindi dared to come even closer when her heart yearned to collect it, to prevent Orson's heavy and destructive hands from doing any more damage.

Orson roared at her, his echidna spines lifting to their highest points. His clawed hands shook as he attempted to tread carefully to ward her back and stand over the pieces, then he brushed them together once more.

"N-no. He is mine," Orson whined, his claws clacking against the pile of bones. *"He come back."*

His behaviour was utterly heartbreaking. As much as she

recognised his pain, and felt it all the way to the depths of her soul, her loss was just too great. He was too inhumane and unintelligent to understand what he was doing. He couldn't be reasoned with.

As cruel as it was, Lindi pushed her hands forward and made black tentacles of magic form. They wrapped around Orson's body, but the moment she tried to yank him back, his spines tore them apart.

She gasped when the forceful release of magic made her stumble back. That had never happened before.

"Orson," Weldir warned, his voice deepening to a frightening degree. It was still calm, but rumbled like the beginnings of a storm that had not yet reached the crashing shore. "Let her collect Nathair's skull."

"No!" Orson's orbs, leaking floating tears, flared bright crimson. *"He is mine! My Nathair."*

"Move aside, you big silly oaf!" Lindi shouted, shoving her hands forward once more to create more tentacles. "You've done enough damage!"

I just need a moment. She wanted this horrible tableau to end.

She enclosed her fists and yanked at the same time, ripping him back just before his spines could tear her magic to shreds. She gave herself the slimmest opening. Pregnant, with her back and ankles sore, she ran as hard as her heavy and uncomfortable body could manage.

But Orson was faster. He rolled across the ground, leapt to his hulking bear legs and humanoid hands, and sprinted forward. Just as she managed to grab a piece, and before she could turn transparent to save herself, he ripped his claws into her.

Lindi choked out a gasp of pain, just as her face, chest, and the side of her rounded belly were gouged into. Her entire body locked up, and her stomach contracted *hard*. Just as he went to strike her again, she managed to turn incorporeal, and his paw went through her.

But the agony was too great, and she flickered between human and Phantom as she wobbled back. She held her belly as the contraction gripped her, and her legs tried to give out. She choked out another gasp as her knees locked together, and wetness pooled between her thighs – warm and entirely uncomfortable.

"Weldir," she whispered, her shock snapping through her grief when she thought nothing could. The flared wounds on her face and chest stung so bad, and the blood leaking from them tickled her, but she barely registered them against the pain from her groin. "Weldir, I think I'm going into labour."

He was by her side in an instant.

She still had a few days left of her pregnancy, but her body and the child couldn't handle everything – especially with the damage Orson had just done.

Damage she knew Nathair, who was exceptionally gentle with her whenever she'd been pregnant near him, would never have done. Nathair was different – he'd always been different. Kind, despite being monstrous. Playful, despite his wariness with her. Patient and understanding on an instinctual level.

He never would have hurt her like this, not unless he was in a bloodlust or truly enraged – and Orson, despite his red orbs and tears, was not there yet.

"I cannot do anything to help, Lindiwe," Weldir stated, and she wanted nothing more than to shriek.

She had time before this child came, but she would not leave the other one here – the broken pieces of him – amidst Orson's chaos.

When she summoned tentacles up through the ground once more, Orson snarled and evaded them. She put up a shield of magic, drew her hands back, and then shoved them forward to smash it into him. She hitched in a sharp breath when her body contracted once more, and her vision flashed a blinding white. The pressure on her cervix was intense, and her legs grew cold, like the strength in them was momentarily suspended. More liquid surged from her, and it was unpleasantly warm down her legs.

She'd already had a scent-cloaking spell in place, but she strengthened it just in case the bloody liquid set him off even more.

"Get him further from Nathair and then put a ward over it," Weldir offered as advice.

"What do you think I'm doing?!" she screamed, shoving against some of her curls that had stuck to her face and chest wounds before bringing up another ward as a divider between Orson and Nathair's skull.

Too antagonised now, Orson gave up protecting it and leapt for her. Lindi stumbled to the side to avoid his daunting speed, flickering between physical and ghostly – unable to hold the latter properly in such pain or in the middle of labour.

She narrowly escaped him, throwing her palms towards the ground when he went behind her. A big dome formed around the area, blocking Orson out while allowing her and Weldir to move freely within it. Collapsing to her knees, she blindly fumbled around the ground to feel for the fragments of Nathair's skull, her stomach impacting her view.

"You're missing the front of his left bottom jaw."

Lindi barely felt her tears, too shocked and in pain to truly register anything but one thought: grab Nathair before this child came. Each contraction was unbelievably hard, putting pressure everywhere and shoving downward into her pelvis and lower limbs. Each one didn't just knock the breath out of her, it strangled her.

When she finally had them, Weldir stated the dreaded words she feared. "I need to you to turn incorporeal so we know you've brought them to my realm."

"I *can't*," she cried, wincing each time Orson shoved against the black glittering dome with a roar, his hulking body making it tremble.

Thump. Thump. Thump, his hard shoulder bashed.

Weldir knelt beside her on one knee and, even though she couldn't feel it, hovered his hand over the top of her head as if he wanted to encourage her. "You must try."

With all that remained of Nathair, her large serpent Duskwalker, able to be held in one crooked arm, she held her belly with the other. She took in a few sharp, shallow breaths while on her weak knees, trying to steel herself against all the agony. Then in between contractions, she clenched, and her body shifted. The fragments of his skull turned intangible with her, and knowing they did – when it had never been possible before – broke her heart that much further.

Yet it was enough for Weldir to take her and himself back to his realm. The shift held, and her contractions stopped midway

– a terrible sign of being stuck in a liminal state.

"H-heal me. Heal me so I can finish," she pleaded.

"I'm sorry... but I can't," he said, taking the pieces from her before they could float out of her weakening hold and before he could no longer touch them. "I may reverse your labour. It could harm them, or you."

The sob that broke from her was tormented.

With her own blood staining her lips, her eyes bowed deeply as she whimpered, "Oh gods."

THIRTY-THREE

April 26th, 1738

Sitting on the damp grass situated next to what used to be Nathair's lake, Lindi stared at the sparkling water with a sense of gloom. Not even the bright sunshine sharing its warmth over her or the tranquil rush of the waterfall's cascade playing in her ears could soothe the worst of the ache inside. She'd managed to quell the majority of her tears, worried she'd somehow flood the lake, but they often sprang back, pooling and making her sight waver.

When they did fall, like now, she looked down to the little Duskwalker sitting in her lap. With her legs crossed and supporting their backside with a blanket, she ran her thumbs over their tiny, soft hands.

They whimpered – they made that heartbreaking noise more than anything else – but they curled their gooey hands around her long nails. More than ever, her child felt so small, so fragile, so... *breakable*.

Well, not yet, as they were truly indestructible, but once they gained their skull, that would change

They would be vulnerable. They'd have a weakness. She could... lose them. She didn't want to lose them. They were hers. They were meant to be immortal, and live just as long as she did – forever.

Maybe that's why she'd been sitting in Nathair's territory for months, stagnant. She didn't want to leave it, wishing he'd breach the surface and come talk to her like he had in the past. She didn't want to go out into the world where there were skulls and horns that this child – this sooky, whimpering baby – could accidentally obtain.

"Please stay small," she whispered, sniffling before wiping her wet cheek with the back of her wrist so she could continue to hold their tiny hands. "Just stay with me forever."

That wasn't possible, and she knew that, yet she wanted to prolong this state for as long as it took for the worst of the wounds on her heart to heal. Three months had passed, and it truly felt like an endless space of grieving, one that had no resolution. She didn't know how to fix the horrible, burning hole in her chest, nor how to make her bottom lip stop quivering, or her hands, or the very foundation of her mind.

Worse still, guilt assaulted her whenever Orson returned in search of Nathair and she made him leave. She knew it was wrong. That somewhere in the back of his clueless mind, he was grieving as well, but he was never kind to her. He was more volatile than ever. He was hateful, vengeful, and... invidious.

The moment he saw her, he'd charge her with swiping claws – until he bashed into the barrier she'd permanently placed around the area.

She thought he blamed *her* for Nathair's disappearance because she was the one to take his skull away. He just... didn't seem to understand, and she never managed to reason with him, no matter how much she tried.

No matter how much she warded him away... from his very home.

The cave she had her back to belonged to Orson. She knew this, but she just couldn't find the will to leave and let him have it back. It was too close to Nathair's lake, literally right across from it, and she needed a safe place for her and this child. A place to lay her hurt, regret, and anger. Her blame. Because out of everyone, she was truly the most blameless.

She was nothing but an ill-informed human. She didn't deliver the strike that killed her most beloved child, nor was she the one who could know that such a death was possible. She was their life giver, and had she known such a vulnerability existed, she would have done more to prevent it.

So, even if it was selfish, Orson could wait until she was ready. He could scour the forest, eat Demons, and do whatever violent things he wanted, and she would stay here to preserve Nathair's memory just a little longer. He could snarl and snap at her black magical dome as much as he liked. He could head-butt it with his bull horns and roar at her from a distance all he wanted. But she would not relent.

Not until she was ready to give this child their identity.

The original plan was to give birth in Zafrikaan, but Lindi had asked to be brought back here to Austrális instead.

Because as much as she guiltily hated Orson right now, she hoped such resentment would pass. She didn't want to leave him here on this continent by himself. Not with Jabez, who had made himself known to be an enemy of her and Weldir – and likely their children. But also wanted to protect him from the Demons. From humans. Even from himself.

She didn't want Orson to be alone.

He now knew that their skulls were precious and vulnerable. She doubted he would make the same mistake twice – she hoped.

Maybe he would cling to this sibling just as much as his older brother, and they could both learn to heal through the newest child.

But the fact that he tried to attack her repeatedly, despite her holding them, brought ill omens. Orson wasn't like Nathair, who was gentle around her while she was pregnant or had a baby on her. He was aggressive, like a wild bear protecting their territory, and she was the trespasser.

He was scary. And perhaps even more frightening than the Demons he hunted. A ruthless killer that couldn't be touched, couldn't be soothed, unless the other person wished to die.

He was her most frightening child.

Even when he'd been a baby, he'd been a biter. He'd also been the most protective of her compared to the others; she should have known then that he was antagonistic.

In some ways, their personalities showed a little when they were not fully formed. Her sleepiest children seemed to be the laziest. Her biters the most aggressive. And her active children were the wild ones who could be full of energy.

So what are you? Lindi thought, as she made them knock

their little enclosed fists together to play with them as they held her thumbs. *All you do is whimper and cuddle.*

Once more, resentment climbed its way inside her chest, and she brought them into her arms to hug them. *Please tell me your early birthing didn't hurt you.* She blamed Orson for that, for clawing into her stomach and causing such devastation when they were at their most vulnerable and precious.

When she was supposed to protect them the very most with her entire body.

She blamed Weldir for twisting her arm and making her face him just to preserve what remained of Nathair.

She blamed herself.

There must have been another way. She could have acted faster. She could have cleared her mind and heart of the hurt and been more insightful. Surely there was a reason she was to blame.

Or maybe she just wanted to bear that burden more than anything. To find a reason to condemn herself and absolve her resentment of everyone else. To forgive at a time when that felt impossible.

She longed to cease crying and love Orson like she had before, but it was so hard.

"I just want the hurting to stop," she sobbed out as she hugged them tighter, and they nuzzled back with a sooky purr. "And for you to grow big and strong."

Strong enough to take on anyone or any*thing.* Whether it be a Demon, a human, or Orson.

"I want you to be like Nathair."

Her sweet, patient, and calm little – but big in size – serpent.

She'd been feeding them boneless fish because she felt awful about being inert, but she also wanted them to carry a piece of Nathair with them. They had similar fish fins going down their arms, legs, and back, and she thought it looked just as cute as the first time she'd seen it on one of her children.

But Lindiwe already knew what she'd name them, what skull they'd have, and even what horns she'd give them.

All of them could be found on Austrális, although they once didn't belong here. She wanted them to be other, to be different.

She longed for them to be strong and cunning, ferocious and

agile. A wolf skull seemed like a wonderful fit with their large fangs, good nose, and hunting skills. She'd always liked the look of impala antelope horns from the moment she'd first seen them, and the fact that their numbers were dwindling already in this part of the world made her want to preserve them too.

Their name... she'd decided upon something that gave strength in its meaning. The mythological killer of a god, and a force of chaos in a world filled with more evil than they could possibly deliver.

A name that reminded her of her very good friend, who had likely passed away in the many years she kept endlessly living.

Fenrir, the wolf-skulled, impala antelope Duskwalker.

A giant, monstrous wolf. The child of a demi-god and a puny human, who would be able to do nothing to control them once she gave them those gifts.

Please be strong for me.

Her heart longed for that more than anything as she cupped the right side of their featureless face and kissed the other side with her heart breaking all over again.

THIRTY-FOUR

A time unknown, but one of companionship

The moment Weldir's mind opened, the darkness within his sight receded. Floating amidst the nothingness, the highlighting shadows revealed the fragments of his offspring's skull. The pieces were still, but slightly spread apart, seeming to glitter from the unknown and unreachable light.

He'd chosen to rest nearby it, like a part of Weldir wanted to be close to it for safekeeping. It resided in the same place Lindiwe's mesmerising orange soul lived: the section of him that was his heart.

He often found himself sleeping near her soul, keeping her close, even when he was as far from her as possible. He'd been doing this for a long time, although he couldn't quite place when he'd started. Now, with Nathair's skull joining Weldir's mate's flame, he knew he'd likely rest here always.

The reminder of his offspring's death was unpleasant, but beyond the sadness and cruelty of it all, he enjoyed having him near. He reached out to touch Nathair's skull for the very second time in either of their lives. It was just unfortunate it had to be in the afterlife.

He waits for me, though.

Inside his consciousness, Nathair and many others waited for Weldir. Then again, that was always the case for those who were stuck in the limbo of Weldir's realms.

Taken by the cloud of his mana, but not eaten and brought to

Tenebris.

They had yet to greet the afterworld he'd created for them.

Instead of doing this task, Weldir had chosen to rest after destroying a human soul and using its energy to place himself at Lindiwe's side in a time he thought she needed him most. He also let it consume him by shoving more energy in it just so he could remain with her longer than he should have.

It sapped much from him, leaving him with barely a tether of life – the current continuous dome she had placed around her didn't help. Then, rather than resting despite the fatigue, he'd kept himself awake to remain with her while she sobbed, wept, and grieved in his realm. He placed rigid barriers around his body to hold her when his oily physical self depleted and disappeared, just so she didn't have to be alone.

It was the most he could do, all things considered.

Like before, he'd found her pain unpleasant and saddening, but he revelled in the fact that she'd voluntarily leaned upon him.

It shouldn't have come at such a cost, but he'd take the only good he could find in an otherwise horrible situation.

But I cannot think of such things now.

He formed a viewing disc to check on her, finding she was asleep under the side of a short cliff, the rocks jagged enough below that it created a shelter. Their newest offspring had climbed their way into her hair like an added blanket and was curled up in the recently combed strands.

He watched for a little longer than he should have, taking in the sight of his own female greedily. Until the sun rose and began to caress her bent elbow with dappled light. A cloud quickly shaded it before once more drifting away, and he turned the disc's view to see the sky was not clear, the threat of rain prevalent.

Seeing all was well with his mate, he blinked himself into one of his alternate existences and materialised with hundreds of tainted souls around him. He pushed them away with nothing but the force of his mind to create a spacious path.

In the middle lay a large, folded orange soul. It didn't appear like a flame, other than the little sputters that puffed from its lengthy body. It looked more ghostly, like a spectre, and was the same size as his alive self.

Weldir looked upon his *son's* strange soul, fully intact, asleep like all the others, and tangible to him. It was divinely magnificent.

It looks just like him, minus the physical, living aspects.

It was far too large for him to consume at the size he kept himself for Lindiwe's comfort.

Weldir expanded himself until Nathair's spirit was barely the size of his palm. He grabbed it by the bend of its tail, lifted it until it folded in half and was hovering above his head, and opened his mouth. Then he gently placed him on his tongue until he was safely within the cavern of his mouth, and swallowed.

The moment he felt Nathair's spirit enter through his throat and out into his stomach, he vanished from his current location.

The giddiness he felt was foreign, and by all rights wrong, but he was excited to meet him properly. He'd never spoken to any of his offspring, and the chance to interact with one personally provoked a sense of relief.

Here, in this friendless realm, he may no longer have to be alone.

They could both be cursed here, yet together.

He followed the tether that fated them together, sire and offspring, the string black and orange like a twisting twine. At the other end, Nathair, who no longer looked like a spectre but his normal, alive self, lay sleeping in the middle of a vast meadow Weldir had made.

Pushing down long stalks of grass and lying in the false sunlight Weldir provided, Nathair's long body was folded on itself like most snakes when they rested. His head and torso were somewhere within there, as he could see a meaty arm wedged halfway out of it.

Then Nathair shifted, and he swallowed that arm into the coils of his tail to rest more comfortably.

"Nathair," Weldir called, not surprised by the thickness in his voice, as though it was laden with emotion.

The slithering slide of his tail stopped, as if startled.

Nathair popped his head out from the very top, and black orbs flared into bright orange. They shifted to dark yellow as he tilted his white serpent skull and peered at Weldir for the very first time.

Weldir lifted his arms so that his offspring could see his black, glittery, and oily body better, trying his hardest to suck in his mist to give better dimension to who he was.

Nathair yanked an arm from his coils and pointed a black glossy claw at him. "What?"

"What am I?" Weldir asked, guessing his question. Nathair nodded. "I am Weldir, the creator of this world. I'm also your creator and father. I am made of mist and shadow. Of nothing and much."

Nathair nodded as if he understood, only to shake his head when it was obvious he actually didn't. He looked around.

"Where is... bear skull? *Or...son.* Where am I?"

He no doubt was searching for his brother, who likely would have normally been there had he not been killed.

Weldir lowered his arms and sighed for his benefit. "You are dead, Nathair." Then he held his hands out and made his broken skull form in his hands. "Your skull was broken by Orson in your skirmish, and I brought you here. To Tenebris. To my realm."

"Tenebris? What is... dead? Where is *Orson*?" Nathair asked, before finally slipping his humanoid torso from the coil of his black tail, the sun casting a gleam of rainbows across his scales. "I find bear skull before he worries. We go home."

He slithered off without any direction in mind, lifting his pointed snout to the air to smell for Orson. He scratched at his nose and sneezed, as if he didn't like the scents in the air. He did it repeatedly, and Weldir made a mental note to ask him if the smells needed tweaking, as he himself couldn't smell them whatsoever.

He just guessed from the human memories he'd dived into.

Weldir followed Nathair, concerned that his lack of humanity could make this transition more difficult. He had no idea how to explain the concept of death to a being that didn't understand, despite being a part of its cycle.

When no idea of how to do so came to mind, Weldir grumbled. *No wonder Lindiwe struggles with this.*

It seemed like a difficult task. It was also disheartening that Weldir wouldn't be able to relate to an entity that struggled to connect the dots within his own mind.

Luckily, Weldir was dauntless, and had plenty of time to

assist in this endeavour.

He threw a viewing disc beside him. Lindiwe and their offspring, who bore a wolf skull but no horns or antlers, formed. *I must have missed that she'd given them their skull when I checked earlier.* She was hiding from the rain underneath the frond of a wide-leafed plant, cuddling them as she waited.

"I shouldn't have left the cave," she muttered angrily to herself. "If the rain doesn't die down, we'll head back."

A glittering barrier of his own magic, as if he himself shielded her, sheltered her from what could be lurking in the shade of clouds and forest. She lay against the trunk of a tree, the shrubs and the branches above keeping her dry. Their offspring was in her folded arms, partially hidden within her feathery cloak to keep them warm and safe.

He often worried for Lindiwe when he slumbered, as he wasn't there for her when she may need him. He had no idea if her voice calling out his name would ever stir him while he was unconscious, as he didn't think she'd ever done so. It was always a relief that she was well, even if she looked a little worse for wear.

Like now, she bore nasty cuts across her jaw, as if a Demon had struck her in the past few days. *I wonder if she got into another skirmish with one while obtaining this offspring's skull.* Demons chased after the blood scent once she made her kill, or sometimes, although rarely, she stole their prey to give it to their offspring.

Next time I bring her to my realm, I will heal her of those cuts and any other scars. He did so every time she was here.

Still, she did not require his assistance just yet, although he would make a proper confirmation of that soon enough. So, he focused all his determination on the creature who needed him just as much. Perhaps even more.

He reached out and... *touched* Nathair's tail.

With pressure pulling at his face, likely revealing a grin, Weldir didn't care that he spooked him, and made him turn with a fang-filled hiss. Nor when he unsolidified himself to escape the swipe of sharp claws so they passed through the ribbons of his body. No, instead, he peered down at his senseless hand with awe.

He's tangible to me, just like the other deceased. And he could sense he didn't need to awaken Nathair from a stupor to interact with him, as if he... *belonged* here.

He's like me. Here, alive within Tenebris.

He curled his hand into a fist, when the desire to reach out again struck him.

He couldn't wait to teach Nathair all about this world, and the one he'd just left. To *converse* with another trapped here just as much as he was. To finally share life with another.

To finally have a son, in a real sense, even if it meant in his death.

THIRTY-FIVE

A time unknown, but one of mischief

Crossing his legs into a seated position, Weldir opened his right hand and called a tainted soul to float above it. He inspected the damage to it.

It was missing its limbs with its torso split in half, but the sickness within it was much worse than many others. Cracks of red, like burning lava, streaked across its body like it had not only been struck by lightning, but was almost entirely consumed by it.

Weldir tsked, enclosed his hands around it, and concentrated.

Cracks of red lava forked over his hands and made it to his wrists before he was done healing it and putting it back together – while offering part of his own essence. He felt no pain, but the fatigue of his mana being used in a such a way drained him as it always did. He opened his hands to reveal a fully intact male, colourless like a normal, untainted soul, except for the spots of depression plaguing its head.

But Weldir could not heal the wounds of life, only what came from death.

Let's give you a new home. He opened his mouth, slipped it into the cavern of darkness, and swallowed. *Perhaps you have memories to share with another.*

Otherwise he would live within the canyon of sleeping and lonely souls. Those that did not have a strong enough connection to another within Tenebris to share memories with, instead losing themselves in their own.

Weldir found it easier to keep those within Tenebris in a form of sleeplessness. To let them dance with the souls they were entangled with in life, or drift in the swarm of those that lived by themselves in a dreary valley. It kept them quiet, and at peace, and it was the kindest afterlife he could think of giving them.

If he wanted to, he *could* have just kept all the souls asleep permanently, but then his realm would have been sad and lacklustre. He wanted there to be joyful life, even if it wasn't something he could partake in.

Well, it wasn't something he could share in the past. That was no longer true.

Many months had passed since Nathair's arrival, and their conversations, although strained and mostly unintelligent, were a welcome change.

Fenrir has recently gained their horns too.

Lindiwe tried to keep them by her side regardless of their newfound mindless desire to wander, even when they warded her back. She stayed close and protected them from Demons a little more viciously than usual.

The wounds of Nathair's loss plagued her, and it was evident in her desire to stay by Fenrir's side. Even if, at times, it was merely as a raven perched nearby.

Weldir watched over her, Fenrir, and all their offspring like he usually did. Even Orson, who had returned to his cave, was under his caring observation.

He often had the images of them in viewing discs floating around him. Just as he did now.

Right as he reached out for a new soul to deplete his mana, and re-energise it later, the creature that brought him both joy and vexation decided then to inflict a nasty wound. Weldir flinched as he felt his cloud evaporate, like someone had rudely stolen his very essence.

More than usual, the strength of his mana was depleted, and he felt himself waning. Even the ribbons of his oily, physical self thinned.

With an annoyed growl, Weldir dematerialised from where the unconsumed souls were held, and relocated himself to within his stomach – within Tenebris itself.

Nathair, as if sensing the hostility likely misting from Weldir, spun around... with part of a human limp in his arms. Two fang puncture wounds bled from the back of her shoulders, with most of her limbs gone – he'd already gotten to most of her before Weldir had arrived.

Red brightened in Nathair's usually orange orbs, and he yanked it to the side protectively, stating with his body language, *My prey*.

The sparks of sputtering little white flames twinkled around his lengthy body, and before his eyes, Nathair's flesh grew plumper.

He'd already eaten an unfortunate soul before this one, the remnants of it still evident in the air, and had been intending on eating a second one.

Weldir pointed his index finger towards the ground. "Put it down," he demanded in a strong, stern tone.

Nathair roared in his direction and then tried to slither off with her! He knew better than to go toe to toe with Weldir, who would always win their arguments.

This is the second damn time! Weldir's mind roared, causing the entirety of Tenebris to shudder from his fury. *He needs to stop eating them!*

Watching Nathair trying to disappear into the distance, Weldir stepped forward and increased his size at the same time. In one single step, he'd grown over fifty metres tall and landed just behind his naughty slithering offspring. He made sure his feet were intangible to the world, passing through the flora, fauna, and people who could have been crushed.

He reached down, causing Nathair to yelp in surprise, discard what was left of his paralysed victim – which was very little – and bolt away. It was then that Weldir felt the crush of more of his mana draining from him, weakening him further than he already was.

Weldir had been practising how to touch another being by petting Nathair's scales, grabbing his tail, and even patting him on the shoulder or back. His serpent Duskwalker offspring was quick to react, teaching him what was too firm and what was too light when he didn't notice Weldir reaching out.

It meant, while he was able, he ignored the urge to be pulled under into sleep, and pinched midway down Nathair's tail without harming him. Then he lifted him off the ground, to his naughty offspring's horror. Nathair snarled and wriggled before lifting his torso to scratch at the air.

"Down! Put down!" Nathair yelled, baring his big serpent fangs to hiss.

He managed to twist himself and bite into the side of Weldir's thumb, but no venom could penetrate his essence – or, rather, it wouldn't have any effect on him.

Lifting until Nathair was at his head height, Weldir shook him. He was barely thicker than his wrist, so he wobbled around as he screamed and clawed at the air, desperate to find purchase.

Weldir pointed a claw at Nathair's serpent skull and shook it once. "Stop it. Stop eating my precious souls."

Nathair grasped the sharp tip to get purchase and lifted his head until his skull was visible above Weldir's admonishing digit. Then he proceeded to stick his forked tongue out at him and blow a raspberry with it.

"Why you insolent little pest!" Weldir exclaimed. He shook the foul creature again, making Nathair squeal. "I cannot wait to find a way to revive you. I'll send you back to your mother and she can put up with you."

It was a tender-hearted threat, as he was sure Lindiwe would welcome this pesky creature back with open arms, and... Weldir would actually miss him dearly. Nathair's antics were rather immature and playful in nature, and he enjoyed being chased throughout Weldir's realm.

He also liked to chase and hunt, which meant a few of Weldir's souls had now been consumed. Last time, Nathair had gotten to three of them before he realised what was happening, and why he could feel life sapping from the very cloud of his form. This time, he'd managed to stop him at only two, but it had consequences for both of them.

Lethargy had set in, and what he'd gained was robbed from him.

Nathair whimpered and clutched the sides of his skull when his orbs began to shift through colours, blasting red, pink, green, and often white. He shuddered, and the coil of his lengthy tail tightened and zig-zagged in tension.

Weldir sighed and lifted his left hand to place his wounded offspring into his palm.

Nathair squirmed into a knotted ball, his fangs parting as he gave a whimpering roar. Weldir circled his hand around him and drew out the memories of the two humans he'd eaten, removing them entirely so they didn't plague him. Fragments, like glass with moving images inside them, glittered as they were pulled away from his black scales.

Only when Nathair stopped shuddering and gave a relieved expire, did Weldir cease pulling.

"You need to stop doing this," Weldir stated wearily. "If I'm asleep, I won't be able to remove their memories from you immediately."

When Weldir tipped his head to the side to inspect him, and Nathair looked up to him with a thankful huff, he sighed once more.

"I won't do it again," Nathair promised, his orange orbs flaring brighter in guilt.

It was a lie; Weldir knew it.

It was in his nature to hunt prey. When he accidentally touched the humans, they often woke from their stupor. They fled, stirring the excitement and bloodlust of the hunt in him, and Nathair chased until he consumed. Their movements often caused a wave of havoc as Nathair touched more souls while caught in the thrill of the chase, causing more to run, and more for him to frighten.

More for him to hunt.

At least his humanity is growing with each one.

He looked thicker, longer, and... healthier. The souls were often encased by a deathless body that could be eaten and then regrew so long as the soul itself wasn't harmed. It was an unlimited food source.

But it was the spirit itself that sat in the centre of their torsos that Nathair needed to eat in order to increase his intelligence. Thus far, he'd eaten five. With each one, he'd grown smarter, his communication skills benefiting from the chaos, and his personality was beginning to shine.

Nathair was mischievous, playful, and lazy. He often felt guilt for eating the souls Weldir protected. He didn't *mean* to do this.

Often, when he was snapped out of his bloodlust, he could be rather sweet with Weldir. Just like now, as he wrapped himself around the palm of Weldir's hand to rub against the physical part of him and lie down.

He didn't seem to mind what size Weldir was.

"Down you go. I'm still annoyed with you," Weldir stated, decreasing his size until he was about eight feet tall, which felt the most natural.

Nathair untwisted his body and pressed a loop of his tail to the ground to find purchase to rise to the height he preferred when leaning his torso back. He was taller than before, coming to Weldir's sternum when he'd barely come to the bottom of his ribcage before. At this rate, his offspring was going to stand as tall as him. Even his torso appeared to be a little longer and bulkier than before.

"I *was* going to make you that lake and rock you wanted soon, but I don't have the spare energy now," Weldir told him.

"Blergh," Nathair grumbled, tipping his entire body to the side until even his arms swung to the left. "But I want rock now. And sun is not warm."

The sun would never be warm, as Weldir had no idea what hot and cold felt like and struggled to emulate it.

Weldir raised his hands up with a shrug. "Well, that's what you get for eating them."

Weldir was just lucky that when Nathair consumed a soul, although it had a deep impact on his mana, it didn't destroy him like when Weldir inserted it into his own chest. Nathair didn't seem to be burned by them, like the flames only ate away at Weldir's mana and soul.

He figured it was his penance to pay for doing so, whereas his offspring was just doing what was natural to him. Or perhaps the plague of memories that tried to attach themselves to Nathair's very soul were his punishment.

Hopefully he doesn't do it again in the future. I don't want there to be any lasting effects.

For now, though, they had nothing to worry about, as Weldir knew he'd removed the fragments entirely since they were fresh. He patted Nathair on the shoulder and then pulled him forward so they could travel together.

"Let's see how much humanity those two souls gave you."
Then I must sleep to replenish what he has stolen.

It looked like more lessons were in their future.

In his own way, despite the drain, Weldir was actually pleased about this. The more Nathair understood, the easier their relationship might become.

He threw a disc to the side, letting the moving image appear of Lindiwe flying in her raven form after what looked like Odie, their otter-skulled offspring.

She's still visiting them all. With Weldir's aid, she'd been doing that for quite a few years now, greeting her children and seeing what she could teach them in the small amounts of time she allotted to them all. He couldn't tell how many years it'd been, but he knew the Earth had rotated quite a number of times.

Each time she greeted their offspring again, they seemed to both be more wary of her, but also more receptive. She'd learned all the languages of the places they'd been placed so she could teach them what was relevant to their continent. Eyropea was difficult, as there were many complex languages for her to contend with and teach.

Thankfully, she had all the time in the world to learn them, with a little help from the translation spell she'd acquired from the Anzúli.

Nathair paused to look at the disc, tilting his head at it every time he made one appear – Weldir was always watchful of his mate, even though she never knew it.

"She flies again," he stated, his voice not as deep or gruff as before, while pointing to his mother, without understanding that was what she was.

The complexity of parenthood was too much for Nathair to understand just yet. In due time, that would likely change.

Pressure spread across Weldir's face, and he wondered if he'd smiled. "Yes. She's in her raven form."

His pretty female, and her feathery form.

My little raven mate.

THIRTY-SIX

December 26th, 1755

Despite how many years had passed, Lindi struggled with the loss she felt. It was still there, ever present to this day. It lingered in the back of her mind, in a broken part of her heart, in the memories and wishes she held onto.

At least knowing Nathair was alive in some way lessened that burden. He was somewhere else, living, and she'd take that blessing even if it meant she'd never be able to see, touch, or hear him again.

It was the only hope she had.

"Pryssia is beautiful this time of year," she stated, leaning back on straightened arms to stare up at the thick canopy of branches above. White snowfall blanketed every surface available, bringing a startling yet mystical contrast to the otherwise evergreen conifers.

Most larch trees, although with similar needles to conifers, had lost their autumn orange foliage once winter truly gripped the world. But, unlike the birch trees, they had no meaning.

Ward off evil, huh? Their spindly branches did little more than hold up snow. *Then again, no leaves means no place for Demons to hide from the sunlight.*

"What is so beautiful about this place?" Weldir asked, his voice distant and revealing he wasn't next to her, but somewhere far away. As always.

She pretended he was right next to her. "I guess I like the

snow." Her voice made another companion nearby turn their head one-hundred and eight degrees, so that their big yellow eyes could lazily blink at her. "I also like how quiet it is."

The snow owl, who had made its home for the day, gave a low and raspy hoot. It lifted its wings to shake off a small amount of white flakes that had drifted onto its feathers, further concealing the large bird's presence. She thought it would fly off, but it merely watched her with a wise and calm interest, keeping her in its sights, observing her.

She was used to being watched.

"I like that owl's feathers," Lindi admitted, eyeing their mostly white downiness.

"Then why don't you take them and I'll make you a new cape?" His tone was aloft, lacking in any emotion as per usual. She'd learned to just accept it.

Lindi shrugged. "I've thought about it, but I like the darkness of my raven feathers."

"You look like a Demon," Weldir pointed out.

Lindi sighed and closed her eyes while lifting her face to the weak, wintry sun. "You have a point," she grumbled, trying to keep her annoyed disappointment from her tone. "I think maybe that's why our children don't like it when I greet them as a raven."

They were always immediately on the defensive, likely thinking she was coming to attack them like any other Demon. Over the last few years, she'd learned it was best to approach them as a human. But even then, they remained wary, although *some* were beginning to converse with her.

It was a slow and arduous process.

She had many children to meet, many languages to perfect, and it was... difficult. Not impossible or pointless, just time consuming when she wanted to move on to greet another child. To make sure they were well and living somewhere safe.

The fact that they'd needed to eat many humans was a blight on her conscience, but she tried to ignore it.

They were what they were, and she'd long ago accepted that, among other things.

Watching the owl turn its head once more to bury its dark beak into the back of its neck, hunkering down for more sleep, she listened for any danger as per usual. One of her children had made a home in the mountains nearby, and while they rested in their cave, she came here to spend her day. They preferred to be alone when they slept, disliking her nearby when they were otherwise vulnerable.

Not that her children were vulnerable creatures. Not even with their hard, although breakable, skulls.

The cold continued to swirl around her as snowflakes gently followed the flowing breeze, but the talisman gifted to her from an Anzúli of Eyropea kept her warm. She had many things hidden beneath the black feathers, but the blanket of her cloak kept her nice and snug as she sat on the ground. The thick icy powder creaked whenever she shifted her weight.

A small, sad smile minutely curled the corners of her lips. *Nathair would hate it here.* He liked everywhere hot. She'd often greeted him when he was sleeping in a knotted ball in the sun, soaking up its heat in the middle of the day. He tended to hibernate in the water when it was winter and often refused to leave it. She had a feeling the cold didn't bother him when he was aquatic.

Thinking of him had her eyes wandering the desolate, empty forest. No tears came, as she'd long ago ceased shedding them.

"How's Nathair today?" she asked quietly, trying not to disturb the peace of the area too badly.

"He's fine, Lindiwe. Just as he always is in Tenebris. Just as you always ask." There was no sigh of irritation at the question she asked frequently, without shame, nor was his tone curt. It was informative, and in some ways, she thought Weldir appreciated her asking.

Sometimes he shared what they'd done together in Tenebris, or if they'd spoken of anything notable. She knew all about Nathair's life in the afterworld, and he was as happy as he'd been on Earth.

It didn't seem to matter to him that he'd died. There was relief in that.

Then again, he'd done little other than occasionally hunt and sunbake. Perhaps it was beneficial that her laziest son happened to be the most suited for such a drastic transition.

But there was a well of guilt that constantly dripped along the waves of her conscience. Especially since the more humanity Nathair gained, the more it *did* bother him. He was beginning to understand, and she and Weldir were both waiting for the day he felt trapped.

Felt anger and betrayal that he'd been the one to die.

Or maybe he'd already begun to show those emotions and Weldir was hiding them just to save her. Whatever trials Weldir dealt with when it came to Nathair, she was privy to as much as he cared to share. Which, knowing Weldir, was not the whole story.

But Lindi had already begun to face that regret and guilt, even if he tried to protect her from it. She was growing strong enough to acknowledge it.

"Where will you go next?" Weldir asked, obviously desiring to keep their conversation going.

"I'm not sure yet." She shrugged her right shoulder, which dipped that side of her body forward while she was reclined on her arms. "Maybe Austrális again? It's been a while since I visited Fenrir. I'd like to see where he is with his humanity now."

Over the last few years, they'd grown into an ebb and flow. She'd come to accept Weldir's presence entirely and often filled the quiet void between them. It was due to the lack of any shared tenderness.

They were... friends. If friends lacked any common ground except the proximity of their minds. She had their children to contend with, but they weren't great companions, and he had Nathair. Other than that, all they had was each other.

She'd found solace in that.

"As you wish, Lindiwe. Do you wish to fly this time, or would you like my assistance?"

He always says my name, Lindi thought, once more lifting her eyes to the owl, only to blink rapidly when she realised it was gone. A silent predator so skilful she hadn't even heard it depart.

She kind of liked that aspect of it.

Lindi... Lindiwe... She looked up to the blue sky between the stark and needleless branches above her instead. *I... don't remember the last time someone called me by my nickname.*

It'd long ago felt foreign. Like a part of her that she'd been holding onto – a sickness, a disease even, that continuously festered. A wound she could heal but refused to bandage.

It's been so long since I saw my parents' faces. I don't even remember them anymore. How many years had it been? seventy-three years, perhaps. *I can't believe I'm ninety-four and I still look the same as the day I died.*

Why was she holding onto the nickname? Why was she holding onto people who only mattered in her memories from so long ago? They'd always be cherished and valued, but why linger on them when they only brought her pain?

I keep losing those I hold dear to my heart. Her parents, Furir, Nathair... the countless other humans and Anzúli she'd befriended, only to part ways with them and return to find they'd died or aged beyond recognition.

Her heart shifted. With snowflakes collecting on her lashes and causing her eyelids to twitch, she thought, *I think Lindi is gone.*

The child she'd been. The inexperienced and unjaded woman. A daughter to parents who were gone. A friend to people who were long dead.

Lindi hadn't been used to being an original thinker.

She'd done what she was told, because what she was told to do was best for the family. She'd been allowed to make choices that would impact her future, but until she married, she was under her father's rule.

Of course, Lindi once had fantastical thoughts.

She'd wondered about the world, the stars, and what it all truly meant. She could be stubborn and headstrong, and determined in all the best ways, but she'd done as she was told, because that's what made her parents happy.

It was all different now. Other than Weldir, who was a soft voice in her ear, there was no one to tell her what to do, and no one she needed to make happy.

Other than doing her duty for Weldir, she was free, but that freedom came with longing and loneliness. Isolation. She was given freedom to explore and learn as she once dreamt, but she'd lost the heart for it once it was in her grasp. She never realised how much she needed and relied on those restrictions to keep her rigid and determined until they were taken from her. They'd kept her complacent. She'd had her dreams and loved the idea of them until the rains of reality were different to what she'd imagined once she experienced them.

They weren't refreshing, inviting, and serene; they were cold, barren, and tiresome. Her life was different, and she'd come to shoulder all those burdens in a way she'd never thought possible.

She, *Lindiwe,* had explored much of the world and had borne witness to much wonder. She'd learned far more than an average farm girl could have.

She'd birthed monsters, and had come to adore them and all their strangeness. She'd murdered vile occultists and had long shaken away any guilt regarding those actions. She'd died far too many times than she cared to admit or remember. She'd learned new languages, experienced different cultures, and had even travelled to an Elven realm.

Lindi, the commoner, the farmer, the young woman naïvely seeking love in a world about to be overrun by Demons, could never have done those things.

No, it was Lindiwe. The raven, and the one who a demi-god made of black cloud and mist called out to. *She* could do those things, had done those things, and still managed to hold onto what remained of her humanity. Could still smile and find the light and contentment in an otherwise dreary existence.

She found the precious things that made her grip on life unyielding and strong.

"Weldir," *Lindiwe* called out.

"Yes, little human?"

"I think I'm ready now," she answered softly, bringing her legs in so she could fold them. At the same time, she scooped up a handful of snow and compacted it so she could begin to make a sculpture of ice. "And I want to finish what we started in Zafrikaan and then go to Austrális. I don't want Fenrir alone with Orson for much longer."

"Are you sure?" There was a frown in his voice. *"I don't mind waiting a little longer, if it helps you heal."*

The offer allowed the very rare tenderness for him to spark in her chest. She didn't often feel anything for Weldir, but he was good to her in his own way. Patient. And he'd somehow learned how to be understanding. He'd changed much, had become more relatable, as if he'd been watching humans to emulate how to be or act like one.

She wondered if he had done that... for her.

"Yes, I'm sure," she muttered, slipping her hands around compacted white powder to make it smooth and hard before grabbing a little more. "You said it could be my choice this time."

"Why now?" he asked, and his voice hinted at curiosity.

Because it's been seventeen years. Because she had to move on eventually, even if her will sometimes crumbled at the thought.

Lindiwe was also done with this part of the world now, and she'd made a promise to Weldir she would place a child on Zafrikaan when she was ready. He'd been waiting for that for many years, and she wanted to keep that promise now, after all the support he'd offered through his company. He'd been there for her, even if it was distantly.

He'd let her weep while offering her words about Nathair's life in Tenebris. He'd filled the void when she no longer wanted to feel alone. He'd even occasionally brought her to his realm at her request and held her when she sought some kind of physical touch.

It was more than she'd ever expected from him, and it allowed her to have a deeper appreciation of him.

But more than that, Lindiwe wanted to go to her homeland. The quicker she finished up her task and kept her promise, the faster she could go back to Austrális.

She wanted to see Fenrir, but she also longed to see Orson.

Her relationship with Orson was impossible. He seemed to hate the very sight of her. She couldn't get within sniffing distance of him, otherwise he'd either hunt her to destroy her, or flee to avoid her entirely – like he didn't wish to look upon her.

It hurt her terribly, but she knew she had no one else to blame but herself. They shared wounds that she didn't know how to heal, not when his humanity was so low, as was his ability to speak. Not when looking upon him still brought on an overwhelming amount of sadness, regret, and pain.

Not when the opposite was obviously true for him.

Maybe in the future that would change, and she'd keep trying to nurture any possibility of them having a harmonious relationship. She'd need to put in the effort and be the one to reach out, even if he never came around to forgiving her.

But she'd keep trying – forever if she needed to.

She could blame her grief and pregnancy hormones forever for how she'd treated him, but she'd also found a way to absolve those same feelings for those very same reasons. She was to blame, even if the situation made her blameless.

Being a mother is... hard.

"I just want another child," she finally answered, once she'd made her sculpture.

Lindiwe knew if she was patient, maybe one day, one of her children might come to love her, or even just appreciate her. The more she had, the more likely there would be one.

She'd take just one, if that was all the world had to offer.

Just one child who might, someday, like her company. Might even hug her, sleep next to her, feel fondness for her. One who might actually let her feel like a mother, rather than an entity to be fearful of or disdain.

She'd like that, even if it took forever. Even if it took birthing a dozen more Duskwalkers.

With that thought and longing in mind, Lindiwe placed her sculpture on the grey, mostly flat rock just peeking out from the white powder beside her. Then she stood and brushed the snow from her men's trousers and readied herself to be transported away from the real world.

She left behind the icy version of a baby Duskwalker – who was in the midst of a cute, scampering stride with their right paw out – to melt when the summer came. As Weldir whisked her away, a cold ray of sunshine made the ice glitter off its blobby paw and pointed snout.

THIRTY-SEVEN

December 26ᵗʰ, 1755

Lindiwe was so used to the way Weldir summoned her to his realm that she just closed her eyes and accepted it. She fell, like the world had opened up below her feet and swallowed her whole into the abyss of the void. She was caught by comforting weightlessness, as though she was thrown into water but couldn't feel its chill or wetness.

When she blinked her eyelids open, swallowing darkness invaded her sight. It was such a stark contrast to the blinding white she'd been surrounded by.

At least it wasn't cold, and the talisman tied to her belt ceased pulsating with magic.

Her arms, clothing, and hair floated. She stiffened her muscles, flexed her fingers, and righted herself so she could find Weldir. And there he was, waiting like he always was when she arrived. He hovered, his posture relaxed, his toes tilted downwards, with his hands limply raised to show the lack of gravity didn't make them droop rigidly.

There's a little more of him than usual, she thought, noting the way his mist fluttered around him.

Sometimes the way it sat changed. Often he was misty with streaks of chalkiness making up his body, and other times he looked like black rain against glass. This time, ribbons of sheer black material, so see-through it took layers of mesh to show a hint of colour, made up his form.

"Hello, Lindiwe," he greeted, his face as stoic as ever. Expressionless, blank, and not forthcoming.

Before he even needed to ask, Lindiwe turned into her Phantom form to be tangible to him. Only then did his expression shift. It softened somehow, and one side of his mouth raised ever so slightly like a barely formed half smile.

Avoiding his piercing, pupilless gaze, she opened her side satchel and rummaged through her bag.

"I have some new items I'd like for you to hold onto for me," she stated, pulling out a small burlap bag no bigger than her palm. Inside it, lemon seeds were safely nestled.

Lindiwe pulled out a few more items and seamlessly handed them to Weldir's tendrils when he presented them to her. One caught a small bag filled with apricot seeds, another a pretty stone she'd found along a riverbank in Francia. They even collected a pretty porcelain doll she'd found within the wreckage of a doomed town that hadn't survived a Demon infestation.

"You have a lot more than usual," Weldir noted. His voice, rough and deep as always, lacked any judgement.

It didn't have the same impact as it used to, now that she no longer truly felt desire. She found it pleasant, but more like a sweet, handsome lullaby rather than something that tingled her between her thighs.

When she saw in her periphery that he brought the doll to his face to twist it this way and that as he closely inspected it, she knew he was curious about her *artefacts*, as he called them.

Although Lindiwe mainly obtained these items for herself, she also found herself wanting to bring him things. They were little gifts for the inquisitive demi-god, although she brought them here under the guise of safekeeping.

She didn't have a permanent home yet; she didn't see the point. She never stayed in one place for long, and often just set up camp in whatever haven she could find, whether that be a nice – although abandoned – home, a cave, or even under a shelter of leaves. Whatever was dry and comfortable, that's all that mattered to her.

Lindiwe shrugged, giving a black, wormy tendril a pretty diadem she'd found in an overrun castle – she'd lived like a princess for a little while. She'd even taken to wearing an elaborate blue gown and gem-encrusted heels during her residence there.

"Well, it's been a while since I was here."

The likelihood of Lindiwe dying was exceptionally low, if ever these days. Using Weldir's magic was like second nature to her now, and her senses were keener than ever. Sometimes it felt like she could hear or smell a Demon or animal from a kilometre away.

Even her children kept her on her toes, and they found it difficult to touch her when she didn't want them to. Being able to turn intangible helped, as did her protective barriers. Sometimes she got hurt, but that was often a risk she took if she wanted something bad enough and had no other option but to leave herself open to a stray claw strike.

Once she was done offering gifts to his tendrils, she flipped closed the flap of her satchel and then buttoned it closed. Then she stared at him, resisting the urge to place her arms behind her back, rock on her heels as if she was on solid land, and avert her gaze. Maybe even start whistling, especially when he did little more than stare at her as her items disappeared from around him.

It never ceased to amaze her how fucking *awkward* their relationship was.

This was the best it'd ever been. Lindiwe had no expectations of love, lust, or true companionship. He was a distant and infrequent friend. A person she knew, and someone she'd begun to think of as just her... boss.

She worked for him and thought of their deal as a contract. Everything was impersonal; she'd long ago not only accepted it, but came to welcome it.

She didn't need nor want anything more than what they had now. It was comfortable. It was safe. And, most of all, it was consistent and lacked any confusion.

Which was why she felt no embarrassment when she loosened the tie of her feathered cloak to let it slip off her shoulders and removed her satchel. There was nothing in her heart when she then reached for the ties of her breeches.

If anything, she was mostly embarrassed by the state of them. They were clean, but the dirt and grass stains were impossible to remove no matter how much she scrubbed them with a pressed bar of soap. The inner seams, right where her thighs chafed together, had, over time, become so thin they were threatening to disintegrate, with the tiniest pinholes visible.

Maybe I should just give up on pants.

She'd given up on shoes a long time ago since she always had to replace them, and she went through twice as many trousers. No matter the quality of the item, it just couldn't last against the test of never-ending time.

Oh well. I doubt he cares, she thought, just as she pulled on the drawstring. *Let's get this over with.*

The sooner he did his gross, wormy, tendril thing inside her, the quicker she could leave. And hopefully she'd be pregnant, so she didn't have to repeat such an offensive feeling for quite some time.

A black tendril wrapped around her wrist, halting her. Weldir came closer, albeit slowly, to breach the constant distance between them like it was a living, breathing barrier.

She tilted her head at the tendril around her wrist before doing it at him.

"Things did not go well last time, and I would like to try to rectify that," he stated, his voice caressing over her senses since he spoke lowly.

Memories of a time she'd much rather forget pulled at the fringes of her mind. Raising her knees to hide the apex of her thighs, while squeezing them tight in a resistant defence, Lindiwe pulled out of his tendril's hold. She brought her wrist to her chest so she could soothe it with a rub while looking away.

"No, it's fine," she muttered, giving him her shoulder. "We don't have to do it again."

She'd much rather not go through that mess again.

When he didn't say or do anything in response, she eventually peeked at him from behind a curl. Only when their gazes met, as if he'd been waiting for her to look at him, did he let out a sigh.

He turned his face away, and oddly enough, ran his clawed fingers through his hair. She'd never seen him do that before. Actually, in the past, Weldir could be quite unmoving. It was as though he'd started forcing actions so he'd be perceived as more personable. Human, even.

"I know I hurt you, but I'm asking you to trust me." He covered his mouth and purposefully tapped his forefinger against his cheek. "I have been... researching into how to do this better."

"Researching?" she asked with a gawk, her eyes widening in disbelief.

"I know I've told you before, but I'm able to access the memories of the human souls I keep. I've been watching how to perform this act properly, from both the perspective of the woman and man."

The *how* wasn't why she was surprised or confused, but the reason!

Lindiwe's bottom lip fell while the top twisted up on one side. She'd always found it a little creepy that he was just gallivanting his way through private moments that should be kept secret. She doubted any one of those humans would have consented to the violation of their privacy had they been aware of it.

At the same time, in a dark corner of her heart, she found it oddly... sweet? Weird. She couldn't imagine what he'd learned, but the effort shouldn't go unappreciated.

Still, Lindiwe shook her head with her thighs tightening further. She trusted him, but not at all with her body. She wasn't someone to experiment on, especially if it came with pain.

"It's okay, Weldir. Truly. I don't mind if we don't do *that* anymore."

His brows narrowed in her direction. "But you should mind. This is a normal act for mates, yes? A way to bond."

"We bond plenty," she tried to say with a joyful exclamation. It came out panicked.

Weldir shunted his form forward until there was barely any space separating them, causing her to gasp in surprise.

"Why must you fight everything?" he asked with a deep expire, as if she was being tiresome.

She probably was, but she was quite fine with that.

"I don't know," she grumbled with her bottom lip sticking forward with a pout. "I've always been that way."

He tilted his head, inspecting her closely, just as something thin and long wrapped around her ankle. Lindiwe went to pull her leg up and away, but with the way her knees were folded, there was no way to get them further from his reach.

"Why don't you just accept my offer for once?" he asked, his voice soft and coy, as if he was trying his absolute best to be convincing.

"Because you make me nervous."

Because even though Lindiwe had changed over the years, had become hardened, resilient, and no longer the naïve woman she used to be, *he* somehow always brought out a strange side to her. The one that was shy, unsure, and nervous.

Even now her heart sped up at the idea, like it wanted her pussy to flutter alongside it, but that sense of wary dread cycloned through her. Her cheeks warmed, and she found her gaze turning meek when with the rest of the world it was sharp, focused, and unyielding.

"I thought after so many years you would be used to me by now," he stated with the tiniest hint of humour, even if it didn't show on his face.

She waved her hands beside her hips to swim backwards to escape his daunting presence. The tendril around her ankle tightened, yanked her back, and then *grew* up and under her pants until it had spiralled around her leg. It tickled as it went, the lightness of it making her foot arch.

"I actually think time has made it worse," she admitted with a rasp, trying to ignore how fast her body responded to something that usually had her lashing out. "Everything about us is stilted. Like two puzzle pieces that don't quite fit."

The tendril lengthened until it wrapped around her knee and then slipped higher still. "Then we can reshape our own pieces until they do."

Lindiwe's back nearly arched when it tickled its way over the bundles of nerves that trailed up the inside of her thigh. Not only her pussy, but even her womb seemed to quiver in reaction – a feeling she'd never ever experienced before in her life. And that fact alone made her want nothing more than to run away.

I'm afraid of sex. With you. Because he was a fumbling god who wielded too much power and strength for a being who was half-formed.

When she didn't say anything, her hands still bundled near her chest and unsure, he inched his way just that bit closer. He placed his right hand on her knees and pushed them down like he wanted her to relax.

"I'm asking you to trust me, Lindiwe."

I don't know if I should trust you, though, she thought, never daring to say that to him. Yet despite her trepidation, her body betrayed her by growing warm for him.

Okay, so maybe her *body* wasn't as disinterested in sex as her mind was, but she didn't know if that was a good enough reason to do this.

But... Lindiwe licked at the seam of her lips. *What if he doesn't hurt me this time?* What if it actually felt... nice?

A time unknown, but one of sensuality

Weldir enjoyed gravitating into this little female's space. Whenever he did, she let down her guard with him, as if the distance allowed her to put up an invisible barrier between them.

It also allowed him to better see the changes in her.

Like how her pulse, although constantly thrumming from her in waves that pumped through the air around her for him to perceive, fluttered a little faster in the delicate column of her throat. How she nibbled the inside of her lip, so subtly that had he not been closer, he doubted he would have noticed.

Or how her eyes, which were either sharply narrowed or dull, widened ever so slightly and made her appear more doe-like. Shy, ready to flee, and reserved.

Oddly enough, that seemed to be the only time she was ever receptive to him.

"We don't have to have sex, if you prefer," he stated, manifesting part of his physical self to coat his right hand in its entirety. He gently placed the tips of his fingers against the top of her thigh so he could slip it under her tunic and to the waistline of her pants. "I have learned there are other things we can do."

Things that would have her pleasure in mind.

It'd taken him a while to realise *that* was what she desired. Pleasure, touch, a connection. He'd given their coitus much thought to begin with, but not enough. He'd regarded them, and it, but had lacked appreciation for the things she likely actually wanted.

They could start small and maybe from there grow confidence together.

"You absolutely swear you won't hurt me this time?" she asked in a small voice, her bundled hands against her chest gripping each other tighter.

A sense of triumph radiated through his mist at her faltering. *Seems I haven't completely ruined this.* Lindiwe didn't ask for much, or really anything at all, since they'd created their bond. He'd been disappointed in himself that he'd failed the one thing she'd openly requested from the heart.

"I won't," he vowed, slipping his hand higher under her tunic until he went past the bumps around her waist from her trousers, and perceived smoothness where her skin must be. "I will go slower and be gentler."

Lindiwe then nibbled her fuller bottom lip blatantly before lightly nodding. Weldir was pleased that she was choosing this rather than wanting to scamper off like frightened prey. Such a creature didn't suit this often bold and lionhearted human – whom he'd seen battle the world with tenacity and determination.

Now that he had her consent, he raised his wrist so her tunic would lift up as he brushed his fingertips higher. Her stomach concaved under his careful touch before expanding, her breaths growing more rapid at an increasing rate.

Then Weldir separated his sight from his physical body, allowing himself to see what he was doing at a better angle. Close enough to view her tiny tells, but far enough he could observe an overall image of her, and himself.

Weldir also used the change of pressure to know when he reached the underside of her breast, and how his hand made a noticeable imprint under her clothing. He neared his body a little more and lightly grasped her hip to run his hand up her side, trying to give her more touch.

She let out a sharp breath and her body bent to the side to escape his hand. "T-that tickles!"

Holding her waist with the underside of her breast between his thumb and forefinger, he paused. "Sorry. Should I go firmer?"

"I think some tickles are okay," she answered, then licked at the seam of her lips nervously. "Like when your tendril caressed my thigh, it made me feel good, but I think my side was a little too intense."

Weldir appreciated her honesty, as he needed her guidance more than she knew. He made sure he'd remember that information for later, and continued his path upwards, the hand on her side pulling her tunic further up so he could see better.

He revealed her sizeable breasts, both peaked with dark-brown nipples and bumpy areolas. His fingers sunk around the softness of the right one as he gave it a squeeze, not daring to touch those points that were hardening before his eyes just yet.

All the practise with Nathair has been helping, he thought, when she didn't shy from his knead but appeared to push into his hold for more. He was strong and could destroy just as easily as he could caress. Learning not to harm his own offspring had been a challenge. One that now benefited him by being able to touch something far more precious and fragile.

With her tunic bundled above her breasts, Weldir lifted his left hand to cup the side of her neck, brushing his clawed thumb underneath her jaw. With the other hand, he rubbed his thumb over her nipple. It moved under his touch, as did she when she gave a raspy gasp with a breath that concaved her stomach.

"Is this okay?" he asked, rubbing back and forth over the peak.

With her gaze fixated on his hand and her breast, she nodded. He circled around her nipple, trying to see how she best liked being teased – he'd seen many options, and knew there were dozens of ways to do this.

These can be very sensitive for a female. And even just brushing them against a male's chest could be pleasurable for some. As could be hands, mouths, tongues, and even genitals.

The thumb underneath her jaw slipped higher, and Weldir petted her bottom lip, which was much fuller and poutier than the top. He did this more for himself, rather than her, as he'd grown increasingly more curious about her lips since their first kiss.

He'd been surprised by how much a kiss could spark desire

in her to the point she'd somewhat clung to him. She'd even reached for him, and he often wondered if he tried again, would she react the same way?

As much as he wanted to lean in just to see, he didn't.

He'd rather see how she reacted to his touch. Especially when he gave her nipple a light pinch between his thumb and forefinger while he kneaded the yielding mound of her breast.

Her lips parted under his thumb, and a soft, barely noticeable moan slipped from her.

Her eyes then widened a little and she covered her mouth with her hand as if she hadn't expected herself to moan. He could see a hint of pinkness in her cheeks, a flush of arousal causing her brown complexion to glow. Even her relaxed face, her beseeching eyes, and the way her appearance shied told him she was blushing.

She even nibbled on her bottom lip a little, like she wanted something to do. "You're being very gentle," she stated, her voice barely reaching a whisper.

"I've learned there is a journey to take, one which is to be sensual."

After brushing her cheek, he finally lowered his hand from her face so he could remove her tunic. Whatever shyness she held had been eaten up by her desire, since she not only didn't resist, but also aided him by wriggling her arms from it.

He then cupped both her breasts and swirled them around with a firmer pressure, massaging them.

Lindiwe reached out to hold his biceps, but her hands merely passed through him as he was focusing the physical parts of himself on his face, so she could see him, and his hands, so she could feel him. She moaned again when he pinched both her nipples like he had before.

"Why do you feel like nothing?"

Weldir paused. "You don't feel anything?" he asked, surprised since she'd been moaning for him. He could also see her tender skin dipping beneath his restrained strength.

"I do. You just don't feel hot or cold. Like you're not really real."

Weldir was quite proud of himself when he had what he thought might be a witty and playful retort to offer. "Maybe I'm just waiting for you to warm me up."

When his joke was met with a dull look, he laughed. He'd never teased her before and found it quite thrilling. *Why have I never tried to do that?* Teasing, flirting, anything sensual really, had been quite out of the realm of his wants. He was finding it, and this, remarkably enjoyable.

Keeping his left hand on her breast to play with it, since she seemed to like it by the indication of her breathiness and the way she pushed into his palm, he lowered his right hand. Weldir steered clear of her side and instead *tickled* the backs of his claws down her abdomen to see how he fared.

His mist collected tighter in reaction to her shuddering moan, the way the muscles beneath his stroke tightened and spasmed, and how she arched. Then she bowed inwards when he did it down the line of one hip, and her thighs parted slightly when he skimmed his fingers across her waistline.

He dipped his claws underneath them, hooked his fingers, and slowly brought her trousers down her strong legs. Lindiwe aided him by lifting one leg at a time until the pants were gone from the long limbs.

Then, she was finally bared to him – fully – for the first time in his realm.

I've seen her naked plenty of times. But somehow it felt different when her skin was surrounded by the depths of his darkness. She seemed fuller, more beautiful, more... tantalising under his direct gaze, rather than through a viewing disc.

She even offered him a raspy breath when he palmed the inside of her thigh, intending to part them himself, but she willingly split them. When he looked up, trying to gauge if he was going too slow and she wanted him to quicken the pace, he paused once more.

Her doe-brown eyes were locked on his hand close to the junction of her legs. She appeared enthralled, as if all these minor touches were exactly what she wanted. Even her skin flared with little prickles, like waves of goosebumps were assaulting her with every small gesture he made as she gave a little shiver.

I never knew my touch could have such power. Especially not over her.

Weldir inspected himself from afar, wondering what it was like for her. What it was like to be touched in the same way he was gifting to her. Would he like it just as much? Did she even want to reciprocate, and would he allow it?

These were questions he'd fixate on another time.

Lindiwe parted her thighs just a little more and bucked her hips, her eyes flicking up to his face. He could almost read her impatient expression.

He'd stopped, and she wanted more.

I have to be careful, he thought, as he finally continued his path higher.

He'd learned that some women don't like their clit being stroked from underneath, so he intended to avoid that motion for now. They could experiment more another time, as he wanted to do what he thought would be safe after the last time he'd ruined this.

Instead, he brushed through her curls and the outside of her pussy lips, noting how the folds of her clit were deeper brown than the rest of her skin, and the inside was a dark pink. She looked feminine, soft, and lovely. He liked that the pinkness of her pussy indicated where he needed to eventually go, her slit already glistening and pooling. It would be more delicate.

He brushed through the curls covering her pubic mound, and her thighs twitched. Yet before he could go lower, she grabbed his hand, her fingers curling behind what was physical.

"Y-your nails... claws?" she sputtered hoarsely, her voice airy and sweeter than usual.

Weldir had already thought about that and showed her by turning his hand over and scratching down the inside of her wrist. His middle and fourth finger lacked any sharpness, as he'd evaporated the claws from them for her.

Females didn't like sharp things inside them, and their bodies were made to give around girth and not be rammed into too hard – a mistake he'd made last time.

They had limits. Limits he'd taught himself about.

Seeing she was safe, she nodded and removed her hold on his hand. Weldir dived down and into her wet slit to pet the nub of her clit with two fingers. Quick to moan, she easily shared more with him when he applied just enough pressure while he went in a circle over it. At the same time, he thumbed her nipple with his other hand still on her breast, occasionally giving it a knead.

The thrum of her heartbeat quickened, as did her breaths that grew shallower with each foray. More liquid pooled at the entrance of her pussy, and it split open slightly when she parted her thighs for more. Her eyes grew glassy and never left where he touched her pussy. She bucked it against his fingers when he must have petted her just right, and her hips never ceased waving, even when he went side to side over it.

"Please," she whispered, her voice holding a strange ache to it that even reached his inexperienced ears. "Inside me."

One thing Weldir knew he'd struggle with was when to move on. Thankful she'd told him, he slipped his fingers through her swelling folds and dabbed at her entrance. He was about to push both inside, then thought better of it. He wrapped a tendril around his middle finger in preparation for later and penetrated her.

"Oh *god*," Lindiwe moaned, tilting her head back as she went to grip his forearm.

Weldir grunted just as he moved part of his face away so he could give her something to hold onto. She rode his finger herself, and he didn't even need to do anything but watch.

She gave a deeper moan, her hips waving back and forth, as her expression softened and her lips parted to let out quick pants. Then she appeared to grind hard, and her knees buckled inwards a little.

Look how needy she is being... With just one of his fingers.

He considered making his body bigger to give her something girthier to ride on, but she suddenly paused.

With eyes wide, she looked down at him in what he thought might be horror at her own lustful actions. But Weldir had thoroughly savoured her doing so. And seeing she'd stretched herself enough, he shoved a second finger inside her to see if she'd do it again.

"Nnh." She arched again, and her grip on his forearm tightened as she gyrated on both his fingers.

Her breasts quivered as she released a cry. Weldir released his hold on the left mound so he could see the way it trembled, how her nipples seemed to grow harder when goosebumps trailed over her chest.

I'm... actually enjoying this much more than I thought I would. He placed his arm around her back and squeezed one of her arse cheeks instead, kneading it to see if she liked it, and her hips visibly dipped into his palm's hold.

Wanting to aid her in some way, he hooked his fingers forward to press against some kind of special place inside females that seemed to make them turn into the most lecherous creatures. Her lips parted more, and her nails dug into the solidness of his form around his forearm, causing pieces to flake off.

"Weldir," she softly, gently, lustfully *moaned*, and he'd never heard his name being uttered in such a mesmerising way before.

He didn't even know it could be.

The strangest growl radiated from him. *I like that. A lot.*

With his hand gripping her arse tightly, he halted her and thrust his fingers. He made sure he didn't do it too hard, and when he did it again and she only moaned for him, he repeated the motion again and again. Each time he increased the pace until she was forced to let his arm go.

He moved the tangible part of him to his shoulders so she could hold onto them, filling out what he couldn't with a barrier. He watched as her little nails tried to bite in deep as she dipped her head back with her lips parted wide. Then her noises ceased their volume, as a squelch came from where his fingers and the tendril wrapped around them pistoned rapidly inside her. Her breaths panted out of her, each one simmering with a cry, while her knees drew up and spread.

It took him a moment to realise she was climaxing. Her body spasmed and trembled all over, her thigh muscles, abdomen, and even biceps clenching. Her toes curled while her feet arched and her brown skin, coated in a thin layer of dewy sweat, erupted with goosebumps.

She managed to suck in a strangled breath, but with Weldir refusing to relent, his fingers still pumping, she only managed to choke out a sweet, lost little whimper.

Just when he thought she might start to finish, he whisked away his thumb claw and placed the pad of it against her clit. He also formed a new tendril, this one misty and mostly clear from the overuse of his mana, and wrapped it around her right breast. He made it coil around the soft mound, clamping the tendril around the base of it until it was perkier than before, and circled her nipple in a tight pinch.

With her body still tremendously shaking, she shunted her head forward. She darted her gaze between his tendril and his hand, her dark brows so furrowed he would have thought she was in agony.

Eventually her legs started to kick as she squirmed against his tempo, Weldir going faster and faster until he found a rhythm he liked. One that he didn't feel any adverse effects from, like mortal tiredness or strain, and was probably far too much for her human body. But he relished the way she twisted and squirmed, and how her hair waved in all directions as she threw her head around.

Little bubbles of creamy-white liquid floated around them, the evidence of her ongoing climaxes. Her release coated her pussy, her clit, and even trailed down her backside before dripping off to join the others hovering away from his pumping hand.

He rather liked that too. It was adding to his realm in a way he never thought possible, one of pleasure and need.

Her features pinched, and she let go of his shoulders to grab his hand.

"Please. Stop." Her nails tried to dig into the darkness of his body, but she couldn't find purchase when he didn't want to give it. "I can't take anymore. It's too much."

Weldir let out an annoyed, growly huff, not wanting to stop playing with her when he was rather enamoured with the moment. He'd never had this female soft for him before, this pliable, or this close, without her having a wary gaze.

Yet despite the longing to continue, he did as he was asked. Only then did her body, which had entirely locked up, relax. Just as he went to pull his fingers from her, he realised he'd almost forgotten the point of her coming to his realm.

With the tendril wrapped around his fingers so she wouldn't be bothered by it, he released his essence within her pussy. He waited a moment to make sure it was deep and then removed everything. He was slow about it when her breath hitched with each inch he withdrew, her little *cunt* quite swollen.

He'd learned all manner of words he could use.

When he was gone from her, he noted her slack-jawed gaze. There was surprise in it that he'd pleasured her well, perhaps even a little bit of awe, and both left him and his mist vibrating with contented satisfaction.

Liquid dripped and floated off his hand and bubbled through the air in his weightless realm. He looked down, inspecting the sheen of light grey from his essence on the tips of his fingers, while the rest of their lengths and much of his palm was covered in a wetness that was solely hers.

Seeing the contrast of its shine against his hand, he realised he wasn't as oily in appearance as he'd thought and was actually quite matte. He'd never had anything to compare himself to before.

"Interesting," he muttered, brushing the pad of his thumb through the evidence of her climaxes clinging to his fingers.

He was disappointed when he eventually had to let go of the mana-fatiguing control he had on his physical manifestation, and let it disappear into the nether of his realm as parts of him dispersed. He knew he disappeared from her sight entirely, even if he never left her side.

It took her a long time to stop shuddering and quivering. To grasp some control of her unsteady breaths and thundering heart.

When she did, she looked around at the emptiness, with her eyes wide and her lips wordlessly muttering.

He thought it might be, "What the fuck did he just do to me?"

He was rather pleased and triumphant about that too.

THIRTY-EIGHT

January 3rd, 1756

As the summer midafternoon sun slowly warmed her raven feathers, creating a warm blanket across her back and shoulders, Lindiwe sat on the very edge of one of the most exquisite and majestic places she'd found thus far in her travels.

Discovering it the first time she'd touched her feet down in Zafrikaan had been an accident. She'd merely followed a daunting and expansive river as it snaked its way across the lower end of the massive continent. With wings unfurled and flapping as she flew, it'd taken hours as she strived to discover where it ended – without taking a smaller, thinner path that branched off it.

The moment she came to this location, it was like her very soul had returned to her chest and doubled in its size and heat. This overwhelming sense of awe had struck her, and she'd been stuck in the air, doing enough to keep herself from falling but unable to tear her eyes away. It radiated immense beauty and power.

For as far as the eye could see, the world dropped off into a great gorge. Nothing like the Veil, as it was much thinner and definitely not as long, but it was surprising that something like it could be naturally made.

The impressive river she'd been following, that was so large it had lush green islands scattered all throughout it, ended in that gorge. Water cascaded off the edge for what had to be thousands of kilometres. Thunderous mist sprayed into the air, the falls loud and ravenous as they fell to the bottom of the gorge. Rainbows glittered constantly, refracting the sun above and creating an almost heavenly aura.

Upon viewing it, if it wasn't for her attachment to Weldir, the old Lindiwe may have thought the Heavenly Father truly existed by the mere design of it.

On the other side of the river that disappeared into the depths lay forests and meadows teeming with wildlife. Of course, Lindiwe had also spotted the telltale signs of a few Demons, yet the area had been mostly untouched.

But this place was a testament to the power of nature.

She'd appreciated it back then, and even more a second time.

Which was why she'd chosen to take a seat on a tall yet narrow island of wet stone between two cascades and soak it in as she had before. Not even the early summer heat bothered her, although she did have her tunic sleeves rolled up and her hair twisted into a thick bun.

Being here, she felt a sense of change in her, a sense of renewal. Like the waters here were divine enough to wash away her worries, fears, and regrets under their harsh drops and scour her clean.

She needed that, as the last time she came to this continent, she'd received the most heartbreaking news and loss. But it had been seventeen years since then, and in her womb, she was growing a new child.

This time, she had every intention of finishing her duty by leaving them here.

With one leg lying down along the rough slope of rock and the other bent, she rubbed the barely noticeable bump of her belly. They were still small, and she had a few weeks to go. They grew so fast, yet when they were just starting out, they seemed even more precious and vulnerable than usual.

I hope you adore this place as much as I do, Lindiwe thought, keeping one hand there as she placed her elbow on her bent knee and then rested her chin on the top of her forearm. She winced a little, her firm stomach repelling the tightness, but it was bearable for now. Soon, she wouldn't be so flexible.

It'd only been a week since she left Weldir's realm, and she'd been trying everything in her power to not linger on what had happened there. Yet, no matter how she tried, her mind kept drifting back to it, which often made her sensitive and hormonal nipples harden and her clit tingle.

She had much to reflect on.

The last time she'd sat at this beautiful gorge of disappearing water, she'd had this horrible sense of disappointment. She'd been despondent, and the idea of performing any kind of intimacy had been terrifying. She'd lost her will for sex, for pleasure, for anything really.

This time? Well, it was like Weldir had cruelly snuffed out the original flame, only to spark it much wilder. He'd rummaged through her untended garden of desire, unearthed it, and then replanted it with vibrancy.

Lindiwe groaned and buried her face against the soft crook of her elbow. *Whyyyy? Why did he have to be so good at that?* She'd been fine with giving it up!

She'd accepted it, and once she did, she found she was content. She'd felt sturdy within herself. Everything had been easy to read, easy to understand, and the future of her emotions was easy to predict. She never got upset with him, as she had no expectations. She'd begun to find his infrequent company agreeable and sometimes relied on it to ease any pestering loneliness.

Now? Well now she was fucking confused all over again!

Lindiwe threw her hands up into the air and screamed. Nothing reacted to her noise of frustration, the thunderous gorge much louder than she could ever be. She slammed her face into the crook of her elbow again before sighing and tilting her head to the side to watch the view.

I can't believe he made me come. She couldn't even count

how many times! It was like her touch-starved body had released a dam that had been overfull. Over and over she'd climaxed until it'd become so painful that the pleasure was all too much. Until her nipple had strained under his *tendril*, and her clit had throbbed so hard her groin thrummed and her legs shook.

The fact that *Weldir*, of all beings, could do that made her want to tear her hair out. He was meant to be this inexperienced, emotionally lacklustre entity. She'd been hoping for at least one orgasm but thought there'd be a lot more fumbling for it, and for it not to be so powerful that she thought she was going to disintegrate under the waves of bliss.

I guess I did kind of explode. At that thought, remembering how her eyes nearly fell from her skull at his *drenched* fingers, her face grew so flushed she thought she'd fucking faint from the heat.

She didn't even know why she was so angry over it.

Maybe because they could have been doing *that* the entire time they'd been married. Lindiwe didn't actually mind a life filled with endless pleasure between them, considering her time on Earth was mostly filled with pain and loneliness.

Maybe it was because she was embarrassed that she'd come so quickly and so much. She remembered grinding on his damn hand like a wanton, lusty woman! It was only her second time doing anything sexual and yet her body, singing from the affectionate caresses, had just taken her by the throat.

Maybe it was because things shouldn't need to be this hard between them. Why did he have to be so... distant? So obtuse and reserved. *He makes it so hard to connect with him.*

And now that he'd given her pleasure, she wanted that stupid demi-god to connect with her pussy constantly.

Her body *hungered* for it.

It had been starved for too long, and it was now a ravenous beast that wanted its deserved treats. It craved more touch, more lust, more gentle tickles and rough squeezes. It even wanted the tendrils that used to sicken her stomach to wrap around her limbs and breasts again.

It wanted to feel... alive. Like it wasn't the ghostly creature she could become.

Please tell me it's just pregnancy hormones, she pleaded, as she groaned again. *If my pussy is going to throb like this for the rest of my life, I think I'd rather it end.*

Especially as she had no intention of ever admitting to Weldir just how much she'd liked it. Or that she wanted to do it again so desperately that she might be willing to have many more of his kids if she got to experience that each time.

Lindiwe covered her face with both hands, ashamed of herself when she thought, *A part of me wishes I didn't fall pregnant straight away.* How pitiful!

She'd gone through a personality shift! She'd told herself she would no longer be that naïve or shy woman she'd been. That the *Lindi* part of her was gone – just like her parents, her village, her very home.

And yet, here she was, about to have an aneurysm because she was horny for a shadowy cloud of weirdness.

"Lindiwe, what are you doing?" Weldir asked through their bond, and she screamed in fright – which was unusual for her.

Mortified that he'd been watching her have what she thought was a private moment, Lindiwe's heart nearly burst out of her chest. Even the child within her stomach seemed to bounce around and flutter from the shock.

"Nothing!" she yelled, so glad her flushing ears were obscured by the loose bangs of her hair so he couldn't see their heated tips.

"It doesn't look like nothing," he said, and his rough, decadent voice had her insides twisting into desirous knots.

The man's vocal cords were a sin, especially as she doubted he lacked any!

"H-how's Nathair?" she asked, reaching for something, anything, other than the conversation revolving around her.

He gave a hum of thought, likely wanting to press the issue. He must have decided against it, since he said absently, *"He's good. Trying to hide from me."*

Her brows twitched before furrowing. "Is that even possible?"

Weldir laughed, all deep and masculine and right in her damn ear, and she almost wanted to moan like a horny idiot. *"No, but I let him believe it is."*

"You must have a lot of souls there now. How do you find him if he slithers off? Or can you just sense him no matter what?" she asked, actually curious about this.

I've always wanted to visit Tenebris. Considering that was where Nathair was, and that Weldir spoke of it often, it was the one place she wanted to visit. But the idea of being swallowed whole kind of gave her the heebie-jeebies, so she hadn't asked.

She didn't know if she ever would.

"I follow our fate strings, just like how I'm able to determine how far you are from our living offspring."

Oh. I forgot about those. Actually, she hadn't, but her mind was too fixated on getting caught freaking out about sex with him, the past, and the potential future, that she was too scrambled to think properly.

Lindiwe tucked a thick clump of her wayward curls tickling her temple behind her ear. "What do they look like?"

"My side is always black, just like the rest of me. Everyone else's varies, but it often matches their orb colours. Nathair's end is orange, and our strings tangle and twist together."

"What's mine?"

"It's multicoloured, with a more reddish-orange hue like your soul flame. The other end reflects the colour of my mana, of me."

"So we're literally intertwined?" she asked sweetly, bending her other leg so she could lay her chin across her raised knees. "I always thought so figuratively, but never literally."

"Yes. I'm also intertwined with all the consumed human souls here in Tenebris, although their strings are all white on the other end."

The muscled knot in her jaw popped as her lips tightened. *What a way to make what could have been special, common.* Then again, that was Weldir. He had no sense of coyness, and he didn't even catch that Lindiwe may have tried to flirt with him. *Blergh.*

"How do you find a particular soul you are looking for? Or are there too many for you to wade through now?"

"Hmm. That is a rather peculiar question. I do remember many of the humans here by their memories, but that is only if I've looked into them. I use those memories to call their string to me. As for those I haven't... I'm unsure as to why I would ever need to call upon them. I have no care for them beyond making them content here."

Lindiwe snorted an expressionless, near soundless huff of humour. *Such a Weldir answer to give.* He cared, but also *didn't*, for the souls he had trapped in his realm.

Finding that his voice was oddly soothing her, Lindiwe asked him an array of questions surrounding fate strings, the souls of Tenebris, and his realm. Much of it she'd already heard before.

With the late sun beating on her back and the harsh sound of water falling, she just wanted to hear him talk.

She allowed him to fill in the empty space beside her, and for once, she truly enjoyed it.

A time unknown, but within a cave of wonders

Walking through his realm didn't give Weldir the same sense of satisfaction and relief as it used to. Not when he'd begun itching to explore outside of it more than ever.

With a certain female.

She doesn't know how much of her world she has shown me, Weldir thought, as he looked over the shelf of water falling into a large ravine below.

In some ways, he thought it looked like wet smoke. Like a whitened version of how he could appear at times. A mist, a cloud, colourless and yet holding every colour utterly possible.

It shone with a multitude of rainbows which he wished his

shadows could swallow for him to keep.

However, that wasn't the exact view which had him wanting to leave his realm, but the other one he was gifted with. Lindiwe appeared at peace as she sunbaked, her feathers ruffling around her shoulders from the lightest gust. Her loosened bangs bounced and swayed around her high cheekbones and jaw, and he wondered if that was why she tucked them behind her ear – to control those windswept tresses.

I like her hair this way. Weldir had seen Lindiwe style her hair in dozens of different ways, but she seemed to prefer having it loose most of the time. Seeing it in a bun was common, but each one was a new facet of her, a new way for him to appreciate her.

"I have grown more fascinated with watching her," Weldir stated to no one in particular, sitting on the edge of his own cliff as he stared out at his realm.

The water below him wasn't as grand, but it did shelter his water-seeking offspring. Nathair had hidden himself away in a nook deep below the surface, likely thinking Weldir couldn't see him.

He could, especially from this angle.

Weldir considered dropping a stone into it to spook the big serpent, but decided against it. If he really wanted to, he could just rumble the water from afar until Nathair slithered out of it with fear or uncertainty.

He'd rather sit here with Lindiwe... when usually he'd find a task to do while he had his viewing disc of her, or their other offspring, floating around him. No, instead, he just sat with her, watching her every movement, every muscle tick, every single hair strand sway, and even the way her pulse fluttered.

What had turned into mere intrigue had started to twist into obsession. If he wasn't watching her, he was trying to half-heartedly complete a task to stop himself from doing so. He'd even rifled through the souls waiting for him to consume and only picked those either she or their offspring had delivered. Those that had no Demon taint and missing pieces to them, so he could just receive power and resist the urge to rest as he often did.

The constant use of my own mana is mind-numbing.

Yet, as his conversation with Lindiwe died, and they sat there in silence, he considered using more – for an entirely selfish reason. Especially when she stood and brushed off her round backside to clear it of any muck.

"If you're still there, the sun is going down," she told him, her tone mellow and... gentler than usual. Her voice lacked the cutthroat depth it usually held when she spoke to him.

Weldir didn't know why he was compelled to stand when she did, but he found it remarkably asinine of him, considering she couldn't see him. But that was the polite thing humans did, yes?

He silently sighed at himself as he covered his eyes in the way they did when they were annoyed at themselves. He thought even his pointed ears may have flicked for punctuation.

Without removing his hand, his words were clear. "Enjoy your flight, Lindiwe."

"You don't always have to say my name, you know," she commented as she flicked her feathery hood over her head, obscuring her pretty face.

I say it because I once lacked the compassion to do so.

It was a reminder to him of his failings, and his way of showing that he would always try, even when he didn't know how. It was also a way for him to hopefully provoke her into telling him what he was doing wrong – offering just that touch of guidance.

Lindiwe then shifted into her raven form. He watched as black feathers sprouted across her brows, up her forehead, and into her hair, before scattering all over her body.

She looks like a Demon, but I like that she is also like me.

Weldir was quite proud of his darkness, his shadows, and the way they could swallow up anything that came into them. He chose not to have dense fog, but he could obscure one's sight if he so desired – even in the mortal realm.

He didn't, as that cost him quite a lot of mana to do so.

Through the viewing disc, Lindiwe unfurled her arms that had morphed into great wings and flapped them. She lifted off, causing mist to spray forward under her power, and then glided into the ravine before quickly banking right.

Even though he remained stuck within his realm, he flew with her for quite some time. He doubted she knew he continued to follow along, but he was completely unashamed by his new obsession with her.

She was his mate, after all.

He could do what he wanted, and stare all he wanted.

He also gave into the nagging desire to use more of his mana from just the mere sight of her.

Like usual, he kept that disc, with a black, smoky edge to it, hovering around him as he began to float up the mountain. He went back to his task before she'd captured his attention with all her squirming and shouts – unaware she had a spectator.

A little further down, coming away from Nathair's 'claimed' territory within all of Weldir's realm, he found the concave he'd already begun mentally carving. The edges were jagged and messy, which he hoped gave the appearance that it was naturally formed.

I doubt Nathair will come here, he thought, since it was rather close. *He's already searched this mountain and knows nothing of interest is here.*

Weldir doubted he'd climb the cliffs again. But if he were to create a new mountain that wasn't so close, Nathair would no doubt go in search of it and might stumble upon the private spot he was making.

With a sense of confidence, he pushed forward, and fake stone made way like someone bashing into a metal bowl. It disappeared under his will as he created an extensive tunnel. He was slow about it, needing to imagine in perfect detail each part of the surface from the memory of humans who had been inside mines or natural cave formations.

During this lengthy time, day and night had rotated multiple times for Lindiwe. She often asked if he was there, and he always answered in the affirmative before they shared a light, meaningless conversation. He occasionally paused, letting himself be immersed in the image of her, the sounds of her lovely, contralto voice, and her little emotional tells he was learning to unravel. The bigger her stomach grew, the more her hand would absentmindedly rest against it, and it had become so natural to her that he doubted she knew when she was doing it.

Every pregnancy was different and special in its own way, each having unique ebbs and flows of struggles, nurturing, and adoration.

Even just witnessing them – although he had unfortunately missed a few in slumber – could be rather enthralling. They were his, as much as hers, after all.

He captured a certain scene of her sitting inside the simple hut she'd called home for now – since it was isolated and vacated from humans. He figured she'd discovered it to likely give birth in the near future. Experiencing that moment with her while she lazily peered out at dusk, where she looked at peace, he eventually continued on with his task.

These were simple moments, simple pauses he shared with her, but he committed them to memory.

By the time her stomach was large and rounded, and darkness completely shrouded the tunnel he made, he lit up little orbs of white light.

He hummed a small chuckle as they floated around him, brightening the walls. *I doubt Lindiwe has realised yet that I can utilise both dark and light magic.* Although he wasn't overly confident with the latter.

It was also weaker, and not his preference.

He liked his mana to emulate himself. Light was not his companion, and the pitch-black was comforting in its embrace.

It'd been his friend for eons.

When Weldir thought he was deep enough, he stood still and then imagined the walls and ceiling pushing out from around him. He created a large dome-like cavern, one which he could expand later should he choose. He made sure the ground was utterly flat, and only the walls were bulky and misshapen.

Then with his hands behind his back in thought, he slowly skimmed along the edges. His mist whisked around him as his gaze kept flicking to the middle.

He told himself it was because he wanted to inspect the stone and jagged walls to make sure they were suitable and looked natural, whereas in reality, it was nervousness that skittered throughout his cloud.

He had no issue unashamedly watching her. Whether it be while she was awake, asleep, or even bathing, he never felt guilt. Yet... perhaps a little bit of embarrassment tremored through him for what he was about to do.

For a creature who lived endlessly, memories could often become murky. Like crystal-clear water that was sullied with a cup of mud at each new memory, the clarity could often be lost without deeper wading.

After living for almost two human millennia, and at least three lifetimes for an Elf, he... had forgotten much. He remembered in clarity the important things, but much was lost to the weathering of time.

And what he currently longed to remember, he didn't want to lose in the foreverness.

I don't think she'd appreciate me doing this. Then again, as he raised his hand out to the centre of the cavern, he thought, *It's not like I am making this anywhere except in the corner of my stomach.*

It wasn't *technically* real. It was as imaginary as if he'd created it in the back of his mind, except he already had the materials here to mould. He was just giving it a visual for his ultimate clarity.

It's not like she'll ever know, he added, to assuage any guilt. *Or anyone else, for that matter.* Only Weldir would ever come here.

A place just for him.

Where the echo of her lingered.

With that thought, and determination in mind, he began to

construct a sculpture of Lindiwe. To form her image in stone that was flecked with different browns, ranging from a matte sandy hue all the way to brown glittering topaz. He made the hair on top of her head darker, matching it to her brows and the thatch between her thighs. The last variation was her dark nipples and clit, which were a brownish pink.

The only colour that was added was the pinkness inside the seam of her lips and deeper within her mouth, and the slit between her thighs.

The sculpture was entirely naked, although he could have clothed it had that been his intention.

Perhaps I will make another of her in the future. One he didn't intend to be salacious.

Instead, this image of her, he repositioned until it was one he wanted to remember perfectly.

Lindiwe, with her back arched, legs spread, and her hands gripping nothingness – unless he was to place his arm in their hold, and his fingers deep inside her pussy. He neared the statue and positioned his hand between her thighs just so – to replay that moment of her climax, his body frozen and finding no reason to thrust his fingers.

Now that he was closer, he reshaped her slightly to perfect every line of her body in that moment, every concave, every dip of muscle. He tracked every detail from head to toe, all the way down to the little prominent veins across the backs of her hands and the one that pulsed in her forehead when she was truly vexed – or, apparently, coming.

Two such powerful physical reactions, both polar opposites of each other.

Not only had Weldir been fixated on watching her, as he did now in his periphery through the hovering disc that followed him everywhere, but also on these memories.

Even now, he could make it move. He could make it shudder like she did, could spread its lips to create a silent moan – but he would remember that cry with a vividness.

His mist vibrated as it sung through his mind, and even more so when it had been his name on her lips.

He'd never known that he could have a physical reaction to such a moment, could derive pleasure in his own way from it. But he'd found it, and it'd been choking a throatless male ever since.

Now... he found he was rather electrified to create another offspring, but for an entirely different reason. It was an excuse to pleasure her, to experience all this again and hope they could do more. He wondered what she'd be like if he did so through sex, or even if he used his mouth along every inch of her body.

He had no idea if she was needy for more, but at least she had softened to him. Enough to have a lengthy conversation with him, enough to check often if he was there. To reach out for his presence, rather than avoid him with disdain.

He didn't know her, or humans, well enough to know if she thought about this memory as deeply and fervently as he did. Perhaps she did, but if she didn't, could he train her body to hunger for it... for him?

I would like to inculcate her with feelings of arousal for me. He'd take that task rather fervently by the devilish horns, should he need to. *I would like to see her come undone by me repeatedly, so long as it continues to soften her dispirited personality towards me.*

The more he thought on it, the more he'd like this female to be yearning for him and what his uniquely formed body and mana could do for her. He wanted her clawing and biting at his mist for more in the throes of pleasurable overstimulation, rather than offering him shy gazes of nervousness and oppression.

Once the sculpture was complete and his memory of this moment solidified permanently, unable to fade away to time within his mind, he stepped back.

He made it shift, and it played out a few seconds of his memory... and then a few minutes to when she'd unabashedly ridden his finger. He wasn't there currently to join it, but seeing her body wave and move as it once did was enthralling nonetheless.

Especially as it *had* involved him once.

It stopped and then became as still as the stone it was made of.

Weldir looked down the tunnel he'd originally created and tilted his head in thought. *This mountain is large, and mine to shape.*

Now that he'd made one memory, one sculpture, he had the desire to make many others. Not just of her, but also the pieces within his heart he didn't know how to fully manifest.

He began to make other tunnels and rooms shooting off from this central one of her, carefully shaping them like the original he'd made. He left a few empty, as he had no need for them just yet, but he hoped and intended to fill them in the future.

He ignored all his other tasks to do this, from eating souls to growing the buildings in their memories. He only paused to support Lindiwe during the birth of their offspring, as he often tried to do despite the distance between them.

She'd long ago grown comfortable, and perhaps even appreciative, of his presence during these times. It was the most he could offer.

He left this space, with her stone form and nothing else but undefinable blobs of rock, so he could call her back to his darkness – the entry point to his realm. Blackness, his darkness, surrounded them both as her tired, sweat-slicked body floated limply except for the handle of her satchel in her closed fist.

He healed her of the strenuous and painful blessing of a healthy birth, checked their offspring and held them like he did each time. Only once she'd slept – like she always did afterwards, and he remained by her side while he spent the only time with his offspring that he'd ever be allowed – did he then send her and them back to Earth when she was ready.

Then he returned and continued to sculpt his cave of memories.

Once seven tunnels were made, with six caverns at the end, he ventured down the original path. Halfway down the dark tunnel, his floating orbs of light following him, he made one final cavern.

Each alcove represented the continents of Earth, and the fourteen portals, including Jabez's that covered them. Each land was different, and he was sure Lindiwe, in the future, would dress differently to match them.

He'd later create statues reflecting those times, those outfits, and maybe even create the one in which they'd originally struck their deal. But, at the moment, in this first cavern, he formed his first born.

Nathair, with his exceptionally magnificent length and size, took quite some time to perfect. Weldir had stared at him so often that he knew every scale with clarity.

Orson was a touch more difficult, as he was constantly changing and not before him. He created a viewing disc of him so he could perfect his carving, down to each echidna spine jutting from him like a menacing shield of armour.

Weldir halted when he noted where Orson was. *He's very close to the centre of the Veil.* In the distance, he could see the recently erected castle belonging to who he assumed was Jabez.

He didn't like that at all, as he preferred his offspring had little to do with that half-Elven menace. He didn't want them harmed or used as a potential tool for whatever war he was conjuring up.

But all he could do was wait and see what happened, and tell Lindiwe if there was any reason for them to worry.

He continued onto Fenrir, who was innocently sitting in some snow... with blood slashed across his white, bony snout. He was thin and gaunt, with arms longer than they should be, but he did look strong and mostly content. Especially when he lifted a big, meaty hand to lick the blood off the back of his claws.

Whatever he'd eaten had been consumed in its entirety.

Now that he'd completed those that lived within Austrális, Weldir moved onto another alcove, one that was deeper within this cave of cherished people and memories.

He began to sculpt Dymphna, the fanged, deer-skulled Duskwalker...

THIRTY-NINE

A groan of frustration slipped through clenched teeth, as Lindiwe placed a wave of black glittering magic between her and her own child. Or, rather, between her and the damn village they were trying to attack!

In less than four years, not only had she obtained their skull and horns, but they'd managed to wander into the savanna desert and kill a number of poor humans. Male, large, and very powerful, she was finding Ari to be the most rambunctious and bravehearted of her children.

He also seemed to be enthralled with the hunt from the moment he'd been born.

She'd wanted to take her time with finding his skull, but his constant manoeuvring and scampering away revealed he desired independence. The moment she'd given up and obtained his lion skull, she regretted it when he became nippy with his newly acquired beastly fangs. Her forearms had been playfully gnawed on to the point of scarring, and it was likely only the scent-cloaking spell that had stopped them from attempting to eat her. Although... she did have a few close calls after being chased by her baby in a state of rage from the mere droplet of her blood on their purple tongue.

Like Fenrir, she'd given him a set of impala horns simply

because they were one of her favourites.

The moment he obtained them, crimson orbs flared to life, and he immediately began to hunt – her, Demons, other creatures. Humans.

She thought he may have been the quickest to obtain his gender, and it'd been by a hair that he had not been a female, since he'd tried to decimate an entire small village before she intervened. She hated the idea of witnessing human death and only turned a blind eye when she was not with them.

She'd managed to get him to back off, but only due to her picking him up by her raven talons and flying off with his impossibly heavy body. That had been when he was thin and gangly. Already he'd begun to fill his furry body out with taut muscle, and she doubted she'd be successful with such a feat a second time.

Since then, on his large rear paws and human hands, he wandered the savannah incessantly, like he was always on the prowl. The lions immediately sensed danger and spooked, quick to hide, and not even the spotty jaguars were willing to take him on. The Demons were wary, especially when alone, but they were brave, and *stupid* enough to try to take him on.

Only to die quickly by his deadly claws and fangs.

"Go away!" Lindiwe yelled, throwing her arms up to put strength behind the wave of her magical barrier.

Ari's red orbs flared brighter, and he let out a raspy roar as he shoved his shoulder against it with all his might. His fluffy black lion's mane glistened with blue highlights under the sun's heat, showing just how soft and glossy it was. He could be rather handsome when he didn't have his maw parted and his fangs on show just to look menacing.

"I said no!" she yelled, before whipping a tentacle forward to block his path. He gave a yelp in surprise at the sudden cracking sound, his hips ducking forward with his thick lion's tail flicking to the side, and he scrambled back on all fours. "You can't attack these people. Leave them alone."

Lindiwe didn't know them well, but she did know they were

already suffering. The small city currently had a sickness going through it, like many villages and towns across the world that were overpopulated and lacked the tools for medicine. Normally this wouldn't be an issue, but one of the two Anzúli recently protecting it died from that same sickness, thinking it was nothing but a harsh bout of hay fever before she grew ill during her sleep.

The other had sent a message through their communication scrying tools, but it took time for people to traverse across this giant continent. And they needed to sleep for some time after spending all their magic on protecting the city and helping them heal their sickness.

They were one person. They could only do so much. *She* could only do so much, but she hadn't yet learned how to heal another, although this was something she'd been researching for a long time.

The least she could do was protect them throughout the day from her own violent nuisance of a child!

But Ari wouldn't relent, no matter how much she drove him back.

"Lindiwe," Weldir called.

"A little busy here!" she shouted, whipping the ground just before Ari's paws to halt him once more. She was careful, as she refused to harm him.

He scattered, only to try to run around her.

The Duskwalker was faster than lightning, and she had to half shift her cloak to give her wings so she could quicken her speed. She managed to curl a black void tentacle around his back ankle and pull until he fell on his front. Then she dragged him back just enough so she could get between him and the shortening distance of the village. She made a square of magic and used it to bash at him repeatedly until he retreated backwards with low grunts and high-pitched growls.

"You have been at this for quite some time. I don't think he is going to give up," Weldir noted blandly, stating the damn obvious, and tired irritation pinched the back of her neck,

causing her right eye to twitch. *"Would you like me to try and assist?"*

"How?" she yelled, ignoring the bead of sweat that trickled into her eye. She was hot and tired, her insides tight from the exertion while her muscles *screamed* in protest.

It didn't help that thick dust had gotten into every nook and cranny on her person, due to Ari's and her movements, and the harsh, biting wind. She coughed, and her left eyelid flickered in pain when some grit blew into it.

She placed a protective dome around herself when Ari attacked her instead. Just as he dived for her and was barely an inch away, she expanded the dome with a slam, and he went flying back across the dry grass and dirt.

For a short while, nothing happened as she stayed on the defensive with Ari, who prowled back and forth with snarls. She'd never do anything to actually hurt him, but a part of her *was* considering cutting off his head. It was the easy way out. To decapitate him and then fly his light skull as far as she could from humans before his body healed and rematerialised in twenty-four hours.

But Lindiwe had never needed to do that before and would only ever use it as a last resort.

"I cannot call Ari to me like I can you. Our fate tether is not as rigid."

"But you already knew that," she stated while huffing, Ari giving her a moment of reprieve as he paced before her. He was trying to figure out a new avenue to get past her, *thinking,* rather than just being purely mindless, like most of her other children.

It revealed just how many humans he'd eaten already.

Unfortunately, he was a terrible conversationalist.

"Let... me try something else," Weldir said with a sense of hesitancy in his tone. *"Don't move from your location."*

She nodded and remained where she was while keeping Ari near her. Then he backed up and leapt, just as a white flame appeared so close to her face her eyes crossed.

Is that a soul of a deceased human? Distracted, she'd almost forgotten about Ari as she backed up... right where he was about to land.

The soul split in two before her very face, and then a sucking sensation whirled around her as a bright-white light flashed. The ends of her elaborate thin braids swayed towards that suction. An oval disc opened up and, just as Ari was about to land on top of her, he disappeared right into it.

It closed quickly behind him, and if it wasn't for Ari's disappearance, she may have thought she'd imagined it.

The area grew so quiet that only the rustling of tall grass and the whistle of wind could be heard. If anything, the sound of her pounding heart, desperate to give up from all the exercise, was the loudest thing to her ears.

Her torso heaved as she looked around just to make sure all was safe, her eyes catching on the wall of spears in the close distance protecting this village.

"Now may I have your attention, little human?" The proudness in his tone was unmistakable.

"What did you do?" she asked, brushing back her heavy, sweat-saturated braids from her forehead.

"Opened a portal to my realm and then sent him back to my mist within the forests quite some distance from you."

Lindiwe nodded absentmindedly. "A portal..." Then what he said truly registered with her. "A portal?! Since when can you create portals?!"

"I may *have inspected the runic code of one of Rökul's portals and imitated it while using a soul. Ingenious, right? He'd be quite angry with me for doing so."*

Lindiwe grumbled incoherently under her breath, but she was very thankful for his quick thinking. *He couldn't have done that sooner?*

"What is it you need?" she asked, dusting off her sweaty palms on her orange skirt, having adopted the looser clothing these people wore. They'd also been the ones to braid her hair, as they'd accepted her into their small village, like many others across the world did, with open arms.

Most of them did so selfishly for her protection and aid, but these people were just warm hearted and doted on her because they wished to. They'd also taught her their dialect of language, as Zafrikaan had many.

"I wanted to enquire if you were ready for another offspring?"

How did I know he was going to ask that? she thought with a mean grumble. *He's asked me thrice since Ari was born.*

"But it's still only been four years. And Ari is currently giving me hell."

And Lindiwe wasn't quite ready to face him after their last intimacy. She was more nervous than ever, as she suspected he wanted to make it pleasurable for her. She'd been giddy about the prospect years ago, but now that it was a possibility, this awkwardly shy fuzzy creature had nestled its way beneath her flesh. It had a way of thumping around inside her chest cavity like a ball bouncing without rhythm, like it wanted to battle her heart and lungs at the same time.

It constantly made her stomach flutter with nervousness. With want. With desire. And she wasn't quite sure how to settle it.

She was almost a hundred years old now, for pity's sake. *By this age, I should be well versed in sex.* Especially as someone who had been in a very committed relationship for most of it.

At the time of their *pleasurable* intimacy four years ago, she'd been ninety-five, and bonded to Weldir for seventy-three of those years. She'd been longing for sex each and every day, then her body had taken her by the reins and made her act out of character when she finally got it. Horny as it ground on his fingers, needy and bliss filled as she moaned with abandon and scratched at him for more.

She was still embarrassed he'd witnessed that, while getting nothing in return.

She was still rather eaten up by it.

She should have offered *something* for him, to return the pleasure he'd just given her, but she'd been so gobsmacked at the time she'd fled with her cheeks so hot she thought her skin would melt from her bones.

"Ari is doing what is natural for our offspring. You are interfering with their evolution. Isn't this what you wanted? One of them to develop enough humanity to converse with them? Stopping them from doing so is only opposing your goal."

I hate it when he's right, she thought, then rubbed her eyes with fatigue and to clear them of dust, which was a poor decision, as she was covered in it from head to toe. *But... I just don't want to be the reason humans die, if I can.* Did Ari really need an entire village for a meal? Surely just a few humans would suffice.

But there was no point in her staying here much longer.

"Fine," she conceded, before noticing the dirt under her nails. "Can I at least bathe first?"

Time to get these braids taken out. But she did like how they protected her hair in this environment, and the person who did them explained their meaningful significance as they braided them. *I should have learned how to do them myself.* She'd thought she had more time, which wasn't something she was used to feeling.

"Whatever you wish."

She looked up at the bright and cloudless sky with a sigh.

I guess it's time to face him. I can't run from this, no matter how much I want to.

Thought the person who literally wanted this in the first damn place. Then again, she hadn't expected it to be *that* good.

Her insides clenched in anticipation, and her cheeks heated as a groan fell from her. *A bath first.*

To cleanse her body and her naughty mind.

FORTY

May 22nd, 1760

Clean from head to toe, her hair combed with a lustrous shine from silkening oil, and loose, and her body groomed and nails trimmed, Lindiwe had finally run out of excuses to delay any longer. Still, despite her trepidation and the nervousness skittering along the edges of her consciousness, she found comfort in escaping the summer heat by being pulled to the never-ending darkness. As usual, it wasn't hot, wasn't cold, and held her in the perfect temperature.

If only her body would react the same and didn't immediately flush with warmth. Giddiness also simmered beneath the surface, stimulating her muscles until they were twitchy and leaping with anticipation. Her fingers trembled before she came here and only seemed to intensify the moment she met Weldir's direct gaze on her.

She'd shy away from his penetrating stare, but she wasn't that insecure. Instead, she held his glossy eyes, no longer unnerved by his black sclera.

Reaching up to the tie banding across her chest, she pulled on one of the strings to remove her feathered cloak.

"Hello, Weldir," Lindiwe said, cutting in before he could greet her first, like usual.

Before she could release her hold on her cloak, and it turned physical within Weldir's nothingness, a tendril stuck to the corner of it and kept it within his touch.

"You've damaged this again," he stated, pulling it to himself so he could hold it. He pulled the material taut and thumbed the feathers, putting them in disarray, while checking the rips – results from sharp claws.

"You can blame Ari for that," she stated, as spare black feathers appeared from the abyss.

Her children were a hazard, as were their main food source: Demons.

Multiple tendrils attached a single feather at a time, Weldir's magic seemingly sparkling while the tears in it closed shut like he was a mystical seamster. For a moment, the mana stone attached to the inside of the cloak floated upwards. The stone glowed a light blue, with a paler Elvish rune carved into the centre of it. Then it disappeared once more, and Weldir released the cloak so it could turn physical and out of his reach.

Weldir drifted his body towards her, part of his cloud lagging behind before catching up to him with a swiftness. "Your clothing is much more vibrant up close."

His features were more minimal than she expected. She saw much of his face, but that was usual for him these days – ever since she first said she'd prefer to see his face over feeling his hands. The rest of him wrapped around his torso like twirling ribbon, barely making up a sixth of his large body. His right hand and left foot were visible, while the opposing biceps and thigh were.

All this talk of nothing managed to soothe the worst of her nerves, and she looked down. Both his hands patted down the patterned yellow-and-red skirt that had been rolled at her hips, while her loose bright-yellow overshirt hid most of her curves. The sleeves were loose, flapping often in the wind, but she found it agreeable underneath the heat of the sun – like permanent shade.

The thick red cloth she'd tied around her head after her bath to push back her thick curls was then loosened without her knowledge, and she flinched when it pulled away. Her tresses waved forward and framed around her face, tickling the tops of her ears and her cheeks.

"You seem more uneasy than usual," Weldir stated, tilting his head sideways less than a hand's width from her nose. The rest of his body seemed to lift upwards, dissipating for a moment before settling back down. "Is it because of what happened last time?"

His lips pulled apart and widened into a grin, and she tried to remember if she'd ever seen him this way before. Her stomach flipped as it filled his expression, somehow making a creature of the void more mischievous, sinful, and devilish – *especially* with his horns, pointed ears, and canine fangs.

Dear heavens, why did he have to say that? Voicing what they were about to do only made it seem naughtier.

Lindiwe tried not to shy away from his intensity, despite finding him more hauntingly beautiful than usual. His wispiness, his overall cloud, just had a dark aura to it – that had nothing to do with the colour of it but the tingle of desire *she* felt.

His nearness had her pulse racing. He was too close when, for so long, he'd mostly been out of her reach.

"No, I'm not," she blatantly lied.

How can he tell? She'd gotten pretty good at playing pretend with her emotions – at least with her face. She often hid her fidgeting hands behind her back or in the layers of her new skirt.

"Your heart is accelerated." He reached out with a partially visible hand, the ribbons of it messy and thin, and touched the hard bone of her sternum. The traitorous organ below beat faster under his touch, especially when he caressed right above her left breast and parted the vee of her shirt. "It's so fast and loud that it echoes in my realm. You can't lie to me when your very body gives you away. It's not often I can surmise that about you."

Lindiwe couldn't hear anything other than the pounding in her ears. Her cheeks grew warm in self-consciousness. *I didn't know he could sense me like that.* And here she was, thinking she had been fooling him for all these years when before him like this.

His fingertips inched their way down her body, against her very flesh when there should have been clothing, and Lindiwe didn't stop him. Instead, she waited for what would come next with thundering suspense.

This... doesn't seem as awkward as usual.

There was no negativity from her, no unfeeling mask from him. It felt... natural, for once, and that alone had a greedy pool of wetness gathering at her core. Even when his face ceased offering an expression, it didn't diminish this, or him.

There was no circulating air to inform her hardening nipples when they had been exposed, only the shift of material across them floating off her.

Lindiwe looked down when he tickled around her naked navel, causing goosebumps to prickle her. She produced a tiny, hidden groan of anticipation and surprise when she saw that he'd unthreaded the seams of her shirt with his very will without her knowing.

I've seen him fix my cloak with such magic, but never the opposite. Then again, Weldir had never undressed her before.

"Your heart is even faster now," he commented, his tone laced with curiosity and... mirth? His face, often stone-like in expression, didn't change. "I did tell you why I brought you here."

Fabricating the confidence that she usually wielded, Lindiwe pulled her arms back and let her shirt slip off when a tendril yanked at the back of her collar.

"I think it's normal to feel a little nervous when you're about to be intimate," Lindiwe quipped, actually having no idea if that were true or not.

"Is it? I'm not nervous," he stated, his head cocking before a rather wide grin spread across his lips and revealed his large fangs once more. Even his eyes crinkled this time, making them slitted and hiding away those glossy pools of ink a little. "And here I thought it was because you found me alarming."

No. Just this, she thought, trying her hardest not to worry her bottom lip when his hand skated up her torso. Her abdomen muscles leapt at the featherlight touch.

Perhaps it was because of his obvious intended path, but her naked breasts felt... heavier than usual. Like they wanted to drop into his approaching palms for affection.

The suddenness of this, the fact that Weldir hadn't *asked* like usual, made his conflicting slowness all the more confusing to her senses. Her mind hadn't had time to prepare, and it had her pulse racing, while her body warmed and tingled before his hand even cupped around her left breast.

At the same time, a hand found its way under her long skirt, without even lifting it! Lindiwe shivered and looked down to see the coy man had materialised his hand under there, while his wrist and forearm lacked any physical aspects to them. He'd crept under there like a ghostly entity moving through solid objects.

Her thighs pressed together as more liquid pooled at her entrance, especially when his thumb brushed between them, uncaring of her squeeze. He flicked her hardened nipple with the other hand before giving her breast a nice firm knead which she pushed into.

"It's time for this to go," Weldir said, his voice softer in volume, and yet deeper... with a huskiness to it she'd never heard before.

Her skirt ripped down the front and she gasped when it was harshly yanked from her body to leave her bare. The threads sewed back together, and when whatever he was using to touch it removed itself from her skirt, it turned transparent, showing that it'd stopped being intangible and once more solid. It was completely out of his reach, and hers – unless she shifted out of her Phantom form.

"Am I going too fast?" he asked, when he tugged her thigh to the side, but wasn't able to budge it due to her resistance.

He could have forced it if he wanted to, but she appreciated that he didn't.

Yes. No. Both? She didn't know how to answer that, and why this awkwardness she had about him, and this, returned to coil uncomfortably in her belly. Now that she was fully exposed, her nervousness rebounded twofold.

She'd always wanted to be an active participant, rather than a doll to be played with.

"Can I touch you?" she asked, reaching out, only for her hands to pass through what should have been his chest. She fisted them in annoyance and brought them back to her sides.

"No." His face tilted down, as if to avoid her gaze while he flicked her nipple side to side. "There is not enough of me right now to maintain what I currently am. The soul I destroyed in order to remove Ari and relocate him for you took much from me."

"Oh." She tried not to feel disheartened, but she wanted to reciprocate in some way. To offer him pleasure like he had for her, and was doing so now.

"I could cast barriers to give you something to hold onto, but I doubt that would be the same to you."

She shook her head to show she agreed and followed his gaze to her breast. Only then did she notice that the parts of him she could see were limited to his hands and the front of his face – the back of his skull was missing and waving like water lapping at the shores of a beach.

Weldir then removed his hand from her chest and delicately placed his palm against the side of her face. He thumbed both her lips before pulling the bottom one down. "But I could kiss you."

Her lips pursed and her eyes narrowed into suspicious slits. "Do you promise not to punch me in the mouth again?"

His nose crinkled, causing flakes to flick off and collect upon the side of his cheek. "I did not punch you," he snapped out in protest. "I tried to kiss you. I was better the second time, correct?"

She had to bite her lips shut to stop herself from laughing. Lindiwe waved her hands backwards, so she'd swim forward, crossing the distance between them herself – for once.

"I guess a kiss might be nice." The very idea had her stomach fluttering.

Whatever had gotten into Weldir and made him actually sensual and arousing, she liked it. She liked this difference, and how much he was obviously trying. She didn't dare question it or ruin this by being rigid and stubborn.

He was slow to close the last inch. When he did, his lips were soft against hers, yielding even. His mouth was a little big, his form always a little larger than hers, but she didn't mind. Not when she instantly wanted to melt at the pressure. The kiss was light, gentle, and the movement of their lips just perfect enough that her moan muffled into it.

When she tilted her head to deepen it, the tension in her muscles finally unlocked. Her legs willingly parted, and she almost moaned again when his hand inclined up her right thigh as he cupped her breast again with the other one.

She wanted to wrap her arms around his neck, but there was no point, as there was nothing there to hold onto. Instead, she carefully pressed her fingertips to his cheeks and the side of his jaw that was solid. Her eyes closed of their own accord, as heat and want and arousal flooded her.

A heavy breath left her when his palm cupped her pussy, and she ground her clit against it in welcome. Only once, holding back unlike last time, so she didn't feel as though she was so desperate. Yet she was, her entire body – from head to toe and breast to pussy – throbbing with need, vibrating with it like an earthquake. Desperate for sensation, for affection, to be stroked and played with until she broke apart again.

Nearly a hundred years had been too long for this. To be given pleasure and *share* her body with the only person she could, or would, give it to.

She wanted to be resentful about that, remembering all the loneliness she'd suffered because of his negligence, but the moment two of his fingers found her clit, she completely forgot. Or stopped caring. Not when he pressed against it so perfectly that her tongue darted out to lick between his parted lips with a soft cry.

Her right hand darted away from his face and down to clasp the back of his. *Oh, heavens,* her mind called, as she ground against it hard. Her features pinched as her inner walls clamped down on nothing, and she had the overwhelming urge to shove his fingers inside her.

"Please, Weldir," she whispered. "Faster."

This slowness was an agonising pace, her starved body greedy and hungry for more *now*. She'd been thinking about this for the past few years, putting Ari first before any of her own needs.

"Is this better?" Weldir rumbled as he speared her pussy with both fingers.

Her body lifted and arched as she threw her head back with a choking gasp. The fit was so snug that the stretch had been just painful enough to burn, but her wetness eased the sudden glide. The filling sensation was so welcome that her inner walls happily clamped and fluttered around his fingers, and she lifted her knees and spread her thighs more to give him better, deeper, access.

Her brows furrowed and her lips parted when she felt his mouth trailing down the arch over her throat. She could almost perceive her pulse dancing beneath his firm lips, and a shiver tore through her, causing her skin to prickle. Only for her entire being to melt for him when he pulled his fingers back and thrust them forward just right.

Lindiwe arched into his pumps, her eyelids fluttering open to gaze at the nothingness. The tips of his fingers continuously grazed against a spot inside her that made her legs feel weak, and she was utterly thankful for the weightless floating keeping her steady.

In that moment, Weldir became her anchor.

When his palm joined the foray to press against her clit, she reached to grasp something, *anything,* and met air. Seconds later, firmness formed beneath her forearms, and she pulled back to dig her nails into the pliable barrier he'd formed over his shoulders.

His lips trailed down, and she thought she felt a tongue against the hard, flat plain of her chest right above her breast. It didn't feel wet, not like it had on her throat, but she liked the way he sprinkled kisses against her skin.

His hand drifted away from the breast he'd been teasing, and she gasped and arched when it tickled her side. The sensation was stolen when he placed his hand between her waist and hip, and clasped his mouth around her nipple.

Lindiwe flinched and looked down.

She couldn't tell if his fully void eyes were peering back at her, but she thought they might be. She bit back her tiny moans as she watched him suck on the hard peak.

"That feels really odd," she admitted with a wince, wishing her cheeks didn't flare hotter.

"Odd... good?" he mumbled around the hard peak. He spoke around her nipple! Yet there was no breath to caress it like there should have been.

She wished she didn't have to shake her head. "It feels dry."

Which was the opposite of what was happening between her thighs. Her pussy was so wet that he didn't need any added lubricant, his fingers gliding through her arousal with utter ease. She was plump, swollen, and everything was just perfect – that was until he paused his thrusting.

Weldir surprised her when he closed the distance between them once more. His lips slanted over hers, and her eyes flung open wide when he shoved his tongue inside her mouth! She didn't know what to do with it, especially as there was absolutely no rhyme or rhythm to its movements as it brushed over hers, against her teeth, and even her cheeks.

When he pulled away, a string of saliva clung between them before it broke when he descended downwards. His mouth then clamped around her nipple again, and he flicked his wetted tongue covered in her saliva over it.

When he did it again, he tilted his head slightly.

Biting her bottom lip, Lindiwe could almost *see* his silent question. She nodded. *Much better.*

Just when she started to dwell on the complicated efforts they needed to put into this, his hand started to pump between her thighs again and she lost the fraying thread of her thoughts. Actually, he seemed to hook his fingers forward. He pressed hard against the special tender spot inside her while he sucked her nipple tight enough that Lindiwe's sight grew cloudy.

She reached out to grab something, but as usual, she grabbed nothing when she reached through where his hair should have been.

"What is it you seek to hold?" he asked around her breast.

She was too far gone to flush in shyness as she whispered, "Your horn."

He fucking paused, and Lindiwe wanted to smack his forehead for doing so! "I thought you'd be averse to touching them."

"I've been looking at you for a long time, Weldir," Lindiwe bit out, her needy ire making her short-tempered. "I can piece together what you look like in full." Then she shoved her hips forward. "Please don't stop."

His deep chuckle was almost her undoing. "Here."

Part of the top half of the right side of his face disappeared to give her his left horn to hold onto.

Rather than reaching out tentatively, when he nipped her nipple and shoved his hand deep to stroke against the swollen, hot, needy part of her insides, she snatched his horn. She tried to pulverise it when he started moving in and out of her at the same time, adding to her pleasure.

"Nhnn." The moan escaped her, and she stopped caring to hide them.

Instead, her lips stayed parted as she cracked out little raspy breaths, each thrust of his fingers and swirl of his tongue causing her insides to tighten.

Then, her nails tried to bite in deep against the barrier, as she cried, "Weldir..."

Her pussy clamped hard when she came, just as her lungs

seized in her chest. Her eyes rolled back as she clenched them shut, and her hips bucked as she tried to match his pace. Prickling goosebumps cascaded down her arms and legs, causing her fingers and toes to clench as her orgasm ripped through her like a cruel, yet pleasurable set of claws.

Oh gods... Finally.

When her core eventually stopped gripping onto him for dear life, he didn't stop. Instead, a small growl tingled her ears, and his thrusts sped up.

Oh! Her hips twitched, unsure if they wanted to get away from him or to selfishly have more.

"W-wait," she rasped hoarsely. She reached down to still his hand. "That's too fast. I'm too sensit–"

Before she could finish, his free hand dived into her curls and shoved her head down as he lifted up. He slammed his mouth over hers again to silence her, a little too hard, but she only moaned when his tongue dived again. She tried to playfully fight it with her own. There was a thrill that sparked across her essence when her tongue caught the sharpness of a fang, and she tried not to break apart as his palm massaged her folds and clit at the same time his hand moved.

It really was a pointless endeavour when her body was being swiftly hurdled towards her next orgasm. Just as her mouth slanted and became unresponsive, a loud moan bubbling in her chest, his hand stopped and robbed her of it.

He removed his fingers, and her brows knit together when his kisses didn't relent. Both his hands hooked behind her knees and spread them as he repositioned her, one leaving a smudge of her own wetness behind when it disappeared.

Then something hard, long, and impossibly *thick* penetrated deep and she tensed.

"Oh... *fuck*," Lindiwe moaned loudly against his tenacious mouth, as she ground her pussy onto what was deliciously inside it. Stretching it. Filling it.

She tried to push at his chest, her hands going through it, so she could put space between them to see. To know for certain that it was his cock he'd slammed inside her. She felt the tickle of fingers barely in existence, as if the smallest specks of them were physical, holding onto the back of one knee to keep her in place. His face was less visible than before, just enough to kiss her, let her see one eye, and his horn – and maybe some wisps of hair.

He pulled back and she saw a rod of darkness leaving her, and her pussy clamped down to keep it inside. It was so big that her lips were spread around it, and her breath hitched at it. It was also so wet from her that it was no longer chalky and had a glistening sheen to it.

Oh. My. God...

Watching it leave her and then push back in was ridiculously obscene, but she couldn't drag her eyes away from the erotic view. She grew wetter because of it, her face and chest so flushed with desire she wanted to combust.

When Weldir tried to wrangle her in for another kiss, she pushed at his face. So he shifted his head to move around her hand like a ghostly entity.

Fangs glided across the side of her neck, making her want to crawl out of her skin from their points as he rumbled, "Female, you are making it really hard to fuck you gently if you watch like that."

Gentle? Right now, Lindiwe wanted the opposite of that.

She lifted her gaze, but he didn't pull back to meet her eyes, and instead she released a raspy exhale to the nothingness.

"I'm trying not to hurt you again."

Oh. She'd completely forgotten about the last time in the wonderful intensity of this time.

"I don't know how deep is too hard. If I'm the right size," he stated, just as he pressed his fangs into the soft skin of her throat, "or if my bites are welcome. I need to see your face, and I can't if you look down like that. Nor do I understand why *seeing* you watch us makes me want to be feral with you."

Lindiwe nodded, just as she noticed that his horn was fully solid and perfectly together. She reached out, figuring he wanted her to hold it again like before, otherwise he would have let it disappear.

The moment she did, and leaned her head back to give his mouth more room to play, his cock shoved in to the base.

"I do not have a lot of time left before my form disappears," he said softly right beneath her ear, and she shivered in response to his husky voice *right there*. "So excuse my speed. I just wish to see you come like this."

The warning was insufficient.

Not when the usually slow and careful Weldir drove into her with such swiftness her heart stuttered. Her eyes flung open wide, her back arched deeply, and a rasping, loud cry burst from her. He used her wetness to fight against the cling of her pussy trying to clamp down tight around his cock.

He was so much stronger than her that she doubted it would have mattered, to the point that when she yanked back on his horn with all her strength from the rapture of his speed, he didn't budge a millimetre. What remained of his fingers disappeared, and something pressed against her back to keep her in place as he fucked into her with force and unbelievably fast.

Lindiwe's legs kicked just as she screamed so hard it came out soundlessly. Her features pinched tight as she started to climax within seconds, already so close that she was shoved off the edge and into the waves of bliss before she could even wrap her mind around it.

Then he disappeared entirely, what was left of his physical body crumbling in her embrace. His horn in her hand faded, as did the overwhelming pressure and blissful movement inside her. His mist was touchless as it sprayed over her.

"Fuck!" Weldir snapped out, causing the darkness around her to rumble.

His form flickered before he managed to regain a small amount of solidity again. Parts of it were missing, unlike before, and her breath hitched when the emptiness inside her was replaced with a spearing cock. Then he was faster than before, and Lindiwe could do nothing but take it as her entire body grew so tense that her limbs just clamped up.

She couldn't fathom the word stop, or wait, or even please. She couldn't even remember how to part her lips to tell him it was too much, not that her choking lungs would have let her.

She didn't know if she orgasmed again or if the pleasurable pain was just the result of bliss, but she released moan after moan. Her breasts itched to mould against something, like his chest, rather than bouncing around without control or steadiness. Her nipples strained for attention as if that was what might send her spiralling off again, or they just wanted to be soothed by grazing something.

Her nails bit into his horn, and it surprisingly crumbled under her squeeze as she held onto her anchor.

Yet he did something that shocked her system into motion again, enough to get two syllables out. "Weldir!" she yelled with her back arching, when he snarled against her neck and bit into it a little *too* hard.

He finally stopped, and Lindiwe wanted to weep with relief.

Twitching and trembling all over, her clit throbbed while her pussy quivered around him. Unable to help herself, the swiftness of suddenly stopping made her grind on him just so she could bring *herself* down gently. To ease back down to reality like a fluttering leaf rather than a crashing rock. She released shivering moans, her entire being trying to find a way to settle on its own, otherwise she might evaporate against her will.

"Nhnnn," she groaned, her knees knocking together while his cock was still deep, when a set of hips should have prevented her.

She was covered in a thin layer of sweat, like her blood had been boiling. Her breaths were so heavy and laboured, each one hurt to produce as she tried to catch up on all those she lost. With her head spinning and pounding, her vision grew dazed, only to sharpen before she lost her hold on it again.

She would have missed the trickle inside her that didn't belong to her, between her thighs already messy from her orgasms, if it wasn't thicker as it left her.

The black cloud of Weldir puffed away this time. She lost her hold on his horn, the sight of his face, and gained emptiness when his cock disappeared from within her without ever withdrawing. Her body, singing with satisfaction, disharmonised in disappointment over the loss.

When she finally managed to unlock all her muscles, her body was surprisingly heavy in the weightlessness of his world. Utter euphoria hummed within, and Lindiwe basked in it. She adored it, had adored this, and she was thankful that he'd instigated it.

Hopefully next time, he has better control of his form. She'd like to touch him properly, and reciprocate by pleasuring him. She had hands and a mouth she could use. Now that it was proven they could do this without any pain... Lindiwe had a deep-seated urge to try everything.

She wanted it to be naughty, and playful, and maybe even a little... sinful? Now that those tendrils weren't worming their way inside her, she wondered how they could be used to touch her.

Maybe if there's more than one going inside me... or if it was thicker... The possibilities now seemed endless.

"Better?" he asked, letting her know he was still there even if she couldn't see him.

Her lips curled upwards in response, making her eyes crinkle with joy, but she was still huffing too much to speak properly. She also doubted her voice would do anything more than crack incoherently from all her screaming.

Something touched her parted bottom lip, and it took her a moment to realise it was the pad of his thumb. It was flaky, and barely there, and it felt so soft that it moulded to her full lip rather than the other way around.

"You know what?" He rubbed against the middle of it, and Lindiwe had this overwhelming urge to lick it. Maybe even twirl her tongue around it. "I think this may be the first time you've ever smiled at me."

Her smile faded as her heart stuttered coldly. *Surely that's not true...*

Yet, in all the years she'd known Weldir, Lindiwe couldn't recall a single time when she had smiled because of him.

FORTY-ONE

April 23rd, 1761

Leaning her hands on the rock behind her and one leg bent so her foot was tucked under the opposing thigh, Lindiwe kicked her other leg back and forth as it dangled over the edge of a cliff. Bright, barely warm sunlight showered over her as orange-and-brown leaves fluttered around her from a light gust and swept into the canyon below.

She soaked in the crisp, cool air, taking in deep, refreshing draws, as she kept her eyes closed and tilted her face towards the sun.

The tangle of rot was present in the air, a sweet decay, but Lindiwe was so used to being in Weldir's mist that her mind was able to separate it from the rest. Most might consider it foul, but she knew the truth of it.

It was the result of healing. Of Weldir fixing the tainted souls Demons destroyed, then purging that sickness from his realm to here. It would dissipate and return in waves, depending on if he was actively healing and consuming new souls or not.

Today wasn't too bad, especially as he hadn't done it for almost a year. Then again, he had not spoken to her in that long either. He slept all that time, and had since she was last in his realm. The use of destroying a soul to save her from Ari, and the excess use of his magic during their intimacy, had taxed him exponentially.

She'd been alone, and oddly enough, it gave her space to miss his voice. His very presence, despite it never being next to her on Earth.

Her heart and mind had flipped regarding him ever since that fateful day. He'd made her body sing, and it hadn't stopped humming since – even despite the stretch of time. She often found her lips curled upwards, and her pussy throbbing in memory.

For the first time since she gave him her soul, Lindiwe felt... hope. The desolation wasn't as pressing, the loneliness not as yawning and deep. The feelings were still present, but that was because they had much left to resolve and Lindiwe doubted either of them truly knew the solutions.

We're still worlds apart.

He was there, and she belonged here. He didn't have a real form, and she did. Despite the pleasure they'd shared, she didn't know if there were any deeper emotions present from him, and she still felt empty regarding that.

A loveless marriage. An unsteady bond.

The foundations of them were rocky and as weak as his magic, coming and going in strength. Pushing and pulling, barely warm and then cold.

It was a lot to think about, and she'd been reflecting much in the quietness he'd given her.

Lowering her face from the blinding light, she opened her eyes to look down at her brightly coloured skirt, yellow and red in bold patterns. Balancing back on her left arm, she placed the right on top of a small white skull, and petted the baby Duskwalker currently nestled up in her semi-folded lap. Her skirt was like a temporary hammock for them, making sure they were truly comfortable and supported.

Leonidas wasn't as much of a lion as her dear Ari, but they bore a similar feline skull, and she believed that was enough. She couldn't quite remember who the name belonged to, but she remembered reading that it was related to some kind of warrior.

They'd need that loan of power in this violent world, and she hoped the name could give that.

Except her lips pouted as she looked down at them. "You're pretty lazy though."

They reminded her of Nathair. They wanted nothing more than to lie in her lap and cuddle, often burying their nose into some crook of her body.

They were also a rather curious creature, quick to be alert and chase after any new scent and sound with tenacity. She kind of admired that about them.

Hooking her thumbs underneath their gooey armpits, she lifted them into the air. They gave a feeble mewl of protest, their tiny hands closing and opening in her direction, as their long feline tail curled in agitation.

"I wonder what colour your eyes will be," she asked them with a laugh, unafraid that she was dangling them dangerously close to the Veil's deathly fall.

She'd never drop them. They were utterly safe in her hands and embrace at all times.

They eventually gave up protesting and just hung there. Their lower end sagged as their middle stretched, but she knew they wouldn't tear in half. It would eventually stop, and it did when their back paws just brushed against her knee.

"What horns or antlers should I give you? I want you to be different to your brothers."

They gave a yawning yip before reaching out a back paw towards her – desiring to kick and move now that they were awake.

"Maybe goat horns?" She tilted her head, eyeing their features with a thoughtful inspection. "No. That might make you look too much like Ari. What about a ram's? They could curl down the sides of your head."

A bright grin spread her lips apart, revealing her teeth as she decided.

She dropped her gaze to the lizard spikes going down their forearms and calves – the result of their curious explorations.

She still remembered finding a tail hanging from their mouth when she was unaware, and how they slurped it down like a noodle. Thankfully, they'd already consumed the mountain cougar she'd stumbled upon, a creature she hadn't known Weldir had brought to Austrális.

I guess he isn't all that bad.

He obviously cared enough about Earth and the occupants on it to move creatures around to stave off the impending doom of Demons. It'd been short-lived, as those nightmarish creatures preferred the taste of human blood, but his efforts did allow Austrális more time to prepare.

More than other countries she'd visited.

She laid Leonidas in her lap once more, and they sat with their back to her front. She grabbed their little hands and waved them up and down, playing with them, as they were so free-spirited that they let her. They never nipped, never growled, and so far, had been one of the easiest of her children to keep young.

So much so that she was extending it for as long as possible.

Lindiwe had all the time in the world to help them obtain their horns. She could spend just that little bit more time with them, especially as she knew both Orson and Fenrir were doing well.

They were safely apart from each other, Orson traversing the Veil while Fenrir explored the northlands. She'd like it to stay that way for a little while longer.

Should I wait until Weldir wakes up? He did like to witness the whole process of their children's evolutions, even if he couldn't actively participate.

He'd missed the birth of Leonidas, as well as them gaining their skull. Would he be annoyed if he missed their final growth too?

Probably not. He didn't seem to feel much emotionally.

It was another reason she didn't open her heart to him.

Apparently there was no pain greater than unrequited love, other than losing a child, and she'd already done one of those things. She'd lost much and gained very little. She had a closed and tightly locked cage around her heart.

She only ever shared a piece with her children, including Orson and Ari, who were the most harmful.

Giving away any more, especially to a shadowy being who struggled to understand basic social etiquette, might just be too much. Forever was too long, and she didn't want to suffer for all of it.

Just when her heart began to sink, and she stopped playing with Leonidas' hands, a familiar, deep, and tantalising voice reaching into the recesses of her mind.

"Hello, Lindiwe," Weldir rumbled, louder than usual, as if he was right there next to her. It didn't even have the aura of an echo to it like usual.

With her sitting among his mist, he very well could be there – just like when she'd first met him... and gave him her soul.

"Hello, Weldir," she answered, feeling her tribulation melt at finally hearing his voice. She let a weak smile curl her lips and resumed playing with her feline-skulled child's hands.

"A long time has passed."

Lindiwe paused as her brows furrowed. "How do you know that?"

Weldir didn't ever notice the length of time that passed. To him, his little nap could have been a few days or years.

"Because I can tell by our offspring that much has changed."

I guess a few have grown stronger or even gained their genders. Who knew, with Lindiwe so far from the rest of this impossibly large world.

"All good things I hope," she stated with a humourless laugh, trying to keep herself uplifted.

"Unfortunately, no."

Lindiwe sighed, suddenly wishing he'd go back to damn sleep. She'd been enjoying the day, sipping at the peace and basking in the way it made her heart fuzzy.

"You would have woken up if one of them..." She trailed off to chew her bottom lip, while wrapping her arms around her youngest and most feeble child. Then she whispered, "If one of them died. Right?"

"Yes. I believe so."

A strong gust of wind scattered autumn leaves off the cliff and punctuated her next words. "Then who?" Or were multiple of them in trouble?

Can't everything just go right for once?

"Orson," Weldir stated in a low, slow voice, like he'd been worried about stating his very name.

"But I just checked on Orson," Lindiwe replied with a groan, palming her face and rubbing at her closed eyes. "How much trouble could he have gotten up to in just a few weeks?"

"You and I both knew he was wandering the middle of the Veil. It seems he's caught the eye of our foe."

A sickly, cold trickle ran down her spine. Suddenly the warmth of the sun faded under the weight of her fear. "Jabez?"

"Yes. It appears they have found... a companionship."

Lindiwe swiped her hand up to her forehead before pushing a few tresses from her face. She blew out a deep breath. "Well, I don't know whether to be annoyed that this has happened, or relieved that he isn't being targeted as an enemy."

"I doubt it will go well if Jabez is to learn the truth."

"Then do we withhold it? Do I intervene, or do I leave it alone and hope they drift apart?" Her eyes bowed as she looked over the eery mist and the never-ending treetops of the Veil. "What do I do, Weldir?"

For once, she truly needed his advice.

"I would prefer none of our offspring to be near him, as that will only bring them danger, but..."

But... There was always a *but*.

And he didn't know either.

He was leaving the choice up to her, while putting aside his general disfavour of Jabez.

Once more, Lindiwe looked down at the small child in her lap, barely the size of a newborn human baby – yet so much more mobile and agile. So much less fragile, yet precious all the same.

"There's nothing I can do right now," she muttered, her

features tightening as her lips thinned when she pursed them. "I need to spend time with Leonidas. Gain their horns, help them navigate their new world."

Even if they pushed her away once they gained their sight. Even once they forgot their name, and who she was to them – that she was safe and welcoming. Even if they somehow came to resent her nearness.

Lindiwe would always try to be there.

Weldir rumbled out a hum of thought and apparently accepted her inactivity as a temporary solution for now. He moved onto something else she said instead. "Is that your name for them? Leonidas? Does this have deep-seated meaning like all the others?"

Of course it did, just like all her children had carefully selected names. She'd continue that endeavour, no matter what. Because despite what they were, and how dangerous they could be, they were her children and she loved them all the same.

She'd give up her life for them, her happiness, so long as they all continued to roam.

She opened her mouth to tell Weldir all that he'd missed in the year he'd been asleep, the conversation welcome.

A reminder that, even if it felt like it, she was never truly alone.

End of book one.

Thank you so much for reading **To Trap a Soul**, the first book in the **Duskwalker Beginnings** miniseries.

For those of you wondering, there will be two books.

I hope you're enjoying the beginning of Lindiwe and Weldir's story! I'm sure many were confused about why her cloak was black on the cover and now you know! She goes through multiple forms of metamorphosis during the miniseries, which makes sense for someone who has lived over three hundred years.

Ah, poor Weldir. He's so cold and calculating that he kind of just keeps messing up, and poor Lindiwe has to bear the brunt of it. I don't know who I feel worse for, to be honest. They're so unsure of each other, and when they do communicate, issues arise. Sorry about the slow burn! But sometimes things need to warm up.
I promise book two will be much spicier.

I hope you didn't mind the cliffhanger. Picking the best spot to stop was a challenge, but so much happens from here on out and I wanted to condense it all.

My betas have ensured me that the jumping around in time wasn't too disorientating, which I'm really pleased about. I can't detail every little thing because, as you've seen, the prequel starts over three hundreds before A Soul to Keep! There's a lot that's happened, and a lot more to come.

Nathair's passing was exceptionally hard for me to write. Having to write about child loss only months after I gave birth to my son was really hard on my mental health. I broke down a few times because it made me really paranoid and scared. Although it may have only been a few chapters, and therefore only an hour for you, for me, as an author... it took me days. Words are much slower to put down than they are to read.

Like I said, there is a book two. I'm hoping that comes out around August or September, so you won't have long to wait. We'll be diving into the foundations of A Soul to Keep. So that means... uh oh, Katarina comes into the picture! We'll get to see Lindiwe's perspective of this, and it will shed some light in real time of what Orpheus and Katarina's dynamic is like. We'll also get a lot of Lindiwe's point of view of things that happen within the Duskwalker Brides.

I'm most excited for the ending of the prequel. I have a surprise in store for you all.

Please stick with me and consider reading my other books in the meantime.

Also by Opal Reyne

DUSKWALKER BEGINNINGS
To Trap a Soul
(Book 2 title coming soon)

WITCH BOUND
The WitchSlayer
The ShadowHunter
(More titles coming soon)

Completed Series

DUSKWALKER BRIDES
A Soul to Keep
A Soul to Heal
A Soul to Touch
A Soul to Guide
A Soul to Revive
A Soul to Steal
A Soul to Protect
A Soul to Embrace

AN MM FAIRYTALE REIMAGINING
Chased by the Fairy

A PIRATE ROMANCE DUOLOGY
Sea of Roses
Storms of Paine

If you would like to keep up to date with all the novels I will be publishing in the future, follow me on my social media platforms.

Facebook Page:
https://www.facebook.com/OpalReyne

Facebook Group:
https://www.facebook.com/groups/opals.nawty.book.realm

Instagram:
https://www.instagram.com/opalreyne

Twitter:
https://www.twitter.com/opalreyne

Discord:
https://discord.gg/opalites

TikTok:
@OpalReyneAuthor